JASMINE CRESSWELL

SUSPECT

JASMINE CRESSWELL

SUSPECT

MIRA®

MIRA®

ISBN-13: 978-0-7394-8955-0

SUSPECT

For Diane Mott Davidson, who helps to make my summers in Colorado so wonderful.

One

Liam Raven looked at the woman sleeping in the bed next to him and tried to remember her name. He vaguely recalled that she enjoyed snowboarding. He knew for certain that she was studying to be a nurse. Her name, however, escaped him.

He stared at the light filtering through the broken slats of the miniblinds and wondered how it came about that at thirty-five years of age—pushing thirty-six—he hadn't found a better way to spend his nights than sleeping with a woman he never planned to see again and whose name he couldn't remember.

His cell phone rang—his work number—saving him from delving too deeply into the murky depths of his psyche. He was grateful for the interruption. Self-analysis was guaranteed to give him nightmares but work, thank God, usually proved a reliable anesthetic.

He eased out of bed, flipping open his phone. Out of deference to the still-sleeping No-Name, he waited until he was in the living room before he responded. "This is Liam Raven."

"Thank God I reached you. This is Chloe Hamilton." The woman on the other end of the phone drew in an audible gulp of air but her voice still didn't steady. "Do you remember me? I came to see you a few months ago. I asked for your help in filing for a divorce—"

"I remember you well, Mrs. Hamilton." Even among Liam's client roster of rich and famous Coloradans, it would be hard to forget a woman who'd won medals in four Olympic skiing events and was married to the mayor of Denver. Not to mention the fact that Chloe Hamilton had the sort of lithe, athletic body guaranteed to provoke a major case of lust in any straight guy still breathing.

"We discussed ways to keep the proceedings confidential until the decree was granted," Liam said, letting Chloe know that he genuinely recalled their past dealings. "In the end, though, you decided to stay with your husband for the sake of your daughter. How can I help you, Mrs. Hamilton?"

"Jason's dead," she blurted out, her voice catching on a suppressed sob. "He's been…murdered."

The mayor of Denver had been *murdered?* Holy shit! Liam smothered the exclamation. "I'm very sorry to hear of your loss—"

"I was the person who found him. I came downstairs and he was lying on the floor in our basement media room. There was blood everywhere. All over the wall. All over the floor. God, it was terrible." Chloe's explanation erupted in short, staccato bursts and it sounded to Liam as if her teeth were chattering.

"There was so much blood." Chloe's voice faded to a whisper. "My God, there was so much blood."

Liam spoke swiftly. "Have you notified the police? Called a doctor?" A doctor might be able to help Chloe, even if there was nothing to be done for her husband.

"The police think I killed him." The words tumbled out, harsh with fear. "I'm sure they're going to arrest me. I need a lawyer right away. I can't let them take me to jail, even for a couple of nights. Sophie's just lost...she's just lost her father. She can't lose me, too. She simply can't."

Sophie must be the name of Chloe's daughter. Liam had never seen the child and couldn't remember how old she was. A preschooler, he thought. Maybe three or four? He spoke quickly. "Are the police with you now?"

"Just a couple of uniformed officers guarding the crime scene and holding the reporters at bay. They've already taken away—" She broke off and started again. "They've already taken away Jason's body."

"Whatever you do, Mrs. Hamilton, don't say anything to the cops. Nothing, do you hear me? If they ask your name, you're obligated to identify yourself, but that's it. It doesn't matter how innocuous the police questions seem, don't answer them. In a murder case, the spouse and immediate family of the victim are often considered suspects. Unless you have a rock solid alibi—"

"I was here all night," Chloe said. "It must have happened...Jason must have been killed while I was sleeping."

She'd been sleeping—unless she'd killed him, Liam reflected cynically, but he kept any trace of skepticism out of his voice. "In the circumstances, you should assume you're currently the prime suspect, Mrs. Hamilton. It's nothing personal on the part of the authorities. Just routine police procedure in the early stages of an investigation."

"Their suspicions seem a lot more than routine to me."

Yeah, well, most likely because the evidence pointed straight to her, Liam thought. However, that was beside the point. Guilty or innocent, his advice to Chloe Hamilton would remain the same: get a competent criminal lawyer and say nothing.

He spoke briskly. "In view of the fact that we're talking about the murder of a very prominent citizen, the police department will almost certainly send one or more of their senior detectives to question you some time soon. Whatever these detectives ask—even if it's something as simple as the date or the time of day—tell them you need to consult with your lawyer before responding. Got that?"

"Yes, I understand. But I guess it's too late for that piece of advice. I already answered a ton of questions about what happened last night."

Liam shook his head, groaning inwardly. He was constantly amazed at the way even sophisticated and well educated people failed to take advantage of their right to remain silent in the wake of a crime. He attempted to reassure her anyway. Right now it wouldn't help to add to Chloe's stress level by telling her she'd screwed up, big time.

"There's probably no real harm done." For her daughter's sake, he hoped that wasn't a complete lie. If you really wanted to mess up a kid, he couldn't think of a much better way than having one parent murder the other. Growing up with your mom in prison wasn't exactly calculated to make for a picture-perfect childhood, either.

"Make sure you don't answer any more questions until you have legal counsel right there with you, okay?"

"Okay. I understand."

"Do you have a pencil and paper?"

"I must have, I guess." Her voice trailed off and he could visualize her staring vaguely around the room, still too much in shock to register her surroundings with any degree of clarity. He was surprised at how sharp his mental images of Chloe were. Apparently she'd made even more of an impression on him four months ago than he'd realized.

"There must be a pencil somewhere," she muttered.

"You definitely need to find something to write with. I'll hold while you look."

It was a full minute before Chloe picked up the phone again. "Thank you for waiting, Mr. Raven. I'm sorry. I'm not usually this disorganized. I have a pen now."

"Write down this phone number and office address. It's for a friend of mine, Bill Schuller. Bill is an outstanding criminal defense attorney and you need to call him before the police question you again."

"But I don't want Bill Schuller to be my lawyer!" Chloe protested. "I want you to represent me. That's why I called. Mr. Raven, please, you have to help me."

"I *am* helping you. Trust me on this. Bill Schuller is the best criminal trial lawyer in Denver—"

"No, you're the best. Everyone says so. You won an acquittal for Sherri Norquist when the experts all predicted you were going to lose."

Liam's stomach knotted at the mention of Sherri's name, and he was immediately angry with himself for reacting to a case—and a woman—that were now more than three years in his past. He'd been a complete idiot over Sherri Norquist. He'd allowed himself to be manipulated into falling in love with a murdering bitch. But hey, shit happens. It was time to move on. God knew, Sherri certainly had, and seemingly without the smallest trace of guilt or regret.

He spoke crisply, skilled by now at keeping a barrier between his outward demeanor and what he was really feeling. "I appreciate the compliment, Mrs. Hamilton, but it's undeserved. The bottom line is that I just happened to make a big splash with a couple of my early cases. I haven't practiced as a criminal defense attorney in several years. These days, I deal only with divorce cases." Which not only kept him away from an unsavory assortment of accused murderers, drug dealers and armed robbers, but provided him with the added pleasure of saying a mental *fuck you* to his bigamist father every time he took on a new case or signed off on a completed one. Liam understood that many worse things could happen to a kid than discovering his father had two wives, and two separate families. And he hadn't even been a kid, really, when he learned the truth about his father's second family. Still, his disdain for his father ran deep; even the fact that Ron Raven had recently been murdered hadn't put an end to his anger.

He brought his attention back to Chloe. "You need to call Bill Schuller, before the police come back to question you again, Mrs. Hamilton. And keep in mind that the cops aren't joking around when they warn you that anything and everything you say can be used as evidence against you. Here's Bill's office phone number. Call him right now, before you do anything else. It's important." He reeled off the number, repeated his condolences on Jason Hamilton's death and hung up before Chloe could protest any further.

Just as he finished the conversation with Chloe, No-

Name came out of the bedroom, wrapped in a towel. She looked sleepy-eyed, cute and appallingly young. Jesus, what had he been thinking last night? Or not thinking, more like it, Liam reflected grimly.

"Oh, you're still here," she said, smiling in relief. "I was afraid you'd left already."

"No, I'm still here, but only just. I was answering the phone and didn't want to disturb you." He returned her smile with all the warmth he could muster. No-Name couldn't be much more than twenty-one, which would make her almost fifteen years his junior. There was still an appealing hint of hopeful innocence in her expression and he felt a sharp twinge of remorse for having exploited her naiveté. He had years of experience in developing pickup lines that worked, and she'd fallen for them all. True, he'd met her in a LoDo bar notorious as Casual Sex Central. Still, even for a one-night stand, she deserved somebody a hell of a lot less cynical about relationships than he was. Three months ago he would almost certainly have dismissed her as off-limits, but since his father died at the beginning of May, it seemed as if the small store of human kindness left to him in the wake of the Sherri Norquist fiasco had vanished, rotting deep in the Atlantic Ocean alongside the bodies of his father and his father's mistress.

"I wish I could stay." Liam aimed another smile in No-Name's direction, a rueful one that suggested if only his job were not so demanding he'd be thrilled to spend the rest of the day with her. He wanted to let her down lightly. Or perhaps he wanted to convince himself that he hadn't been a total asshole to have slept with her in the first place.

He tapped his cell phone. "I'm sorry. I just answered an urgent call from my office and I have to leave right away. There's a family crisis involving one of my clients and they need me to catch the fallout."

"Now?" she asked, pouting. "So early? It's not even six-thirty!"

"I know. Wild, isn't it? I swear, lawyers get more emergency calls than doctors."

"But you're a *divorce* lawyer. I wouldn't have expected divorce lawyers to get any emergency calls."

"Oh boy, are you wrong." He chucked her under the chin, feeling a hundred years old as he coaxed a smile. "I sometimes think divorce lawyers get more emergency calls than anyone else. Especially on a Monday morning. Weekends are tough on couples who are splitting up. That's when all the custody battles erupt and sometimes they aren't just battles of words."

"Tell me about it." No-Name's eyes turned sad. "My parents divorced when I was fifteen. As far as I'm concerned, they'd have done us kids a huge favor if they'd split ten years earlier. They weren't physically violent, but the shouting was horrible."

"Failing marriages are rough on the kids, whether you stick it out or cut through the pain and file for divorce." Liam really didn't want to get into a discussion of the problems associated with couples who weren't willing to admit their marriage was over. That was a subject that cut too close to far too many bones.

He walked back into the bedroom, wondering if it was a custody battle between Jason and Chloe that had precipitated the mayor's murder. People killed their spouses over custody issues almost as often as they killed them over money, and a lot more often than they killed them because of unfaithfulness. He'd barely been fifteen minutes into his first consultation with Chloe Hamilton when he realized that her daughter was the focus of her life. She might well be capable of killing in defense of her daughter, Liam reflected, even if such an act would be impossible for her in other circumstances.

When Chloe first came to see him, his professional instincts had shouted that there was more going on than a simple desire to get divorced. Equally, there had seemed to be something more behind her decision to stay with the mayor than a straightforward decision to reconcile. Despite his efforts to persuade Chloe to confide in him, she'd insisted she was the one who'd changed her mind and now wanted to give her marriage a second chance. He wasn't sure he believed her, then or now. At the time, he'd suspected that Jason Hamilton had applied some sort of blackmail to prevent her walking away from their marriage. If the mayor had threatened to fight her for custody of their daughter, Chloe might have decided to end the emotional blackmail by getting rid of her husband.

No-Name followed Liam into the bedroom, forcing his attention back to her. She leaned against the doorjamb, her towel slipping provocatively as she watched him dress. "Don't you want to take a shower before you leave? Or at least have some coffee?"

Liam tucked his shirt into his pants, zipping his fly as an excuse to pretend he hadn't noticed No-Name's bare breasts. "Thanks for the offer but I need to go home and get some clean clothes. I'm scheduled to appear in court today and my client is paying big bucks for the privilege of having me turn up wearing a starched shirt and a silk tie."

No-Name protested some more, but not too forcefully,

as if she didn't quite believe his excuses but didn't want to push too hard in case he told her something she didn't want to hear. He managed to get out of her apartment in less than five minutes. It would have been easy to lie, to promise to be in touch, but a final flare of conscience kept him silent, so that he left her standing at her front door looking crestfallen. Truth, Liam thought wryly, was vastly overrated as an ingredient in sexual relationships.

By the time he made it to his car, his gut was twisted into a hard coil of tension. He chugged a handful of antacids—his usual breakfast—and drove with fierce concentration through the already dense traffic. Denver was a city that started early and 7:00 a.m. was well into the Monday morning rush hour.

It was a relief to enter the soothing austerity of his newly purchased condo overlooking Confluence Park. Liam had selected the white walls, slate floors and sleek contemporary furniture as a deliberate contrast to the cluttered, homey comfort of the Flying W, his parents' ranch in Wyoming.

He recognized that his almost compulsive desire for orderliness in his surroundings was a direct reflection of the chaos of his inner life. Sometimes he wondered if he was ever going to reach the point where he would be able to let down his guard without risking an emotional meltdown. Still, whatever the psychological underpinnings of his decorating choices, the immaculate neatness and careful functionality of each room offered balm to his soul.

He tossed his car keys into the wooden bowl set on the chrome and glass side table in the entrance and made his way through the master bedroom to the shower, stopping en route to check his voice mail. There were four messages, all of them work related. It looked, thank God, as if it was going to be another frantic workweek. Just the sort of heavy-duty schedule he liked, with no time to stop and reflect.

He switched on the TV as he dressed and discovered that the murder of Jason Hamilton was making headlines on virtually every channel, not just locally but nationally as well. Not surprising, he supposed, given that Jason had been the mayor of a major city and Chloe had worn the crown as America's Sweetheart for several months after the 1998 Winter Olympics. To make Jason's death even more tabloid-worthy, the mayor was also a successful multi-millionaire real estate developer, and the son of a U.S. army general who was a minor celebrity in his own right, having won the Medal of Honor for his bravery during combat service in Vietnam. Jason Hamilton's violent death represented an irresistible combination of wealth, fame and mystery for the ravenous maw of the twenty-four-hour news machines. Flipping from one breathless report to the next, Liam figured the cable news networks must all be praying that Chloe didn't get arrested too soon and spoil the potential for weeks of rabid speculation about the crime.

Facts about the murder were sparse, but it seemed that Jason's dead body had been discovered in the basement of their family home in Park Hill by his wife at approximately 3:30 a.m., Denver time. Death was apparently due to a stab wound, or possibly multiple stab wounds; the reports weren't clear. Chloe Hamilton had tried to revive her husband. The newscasters—discreetly noncommittal at this stage of a developing story—refrained from speculating as to whether Chloe might possibly have gotten there before Jason died rather than after.

News editors were making up for lack of hard data

about the crime by filling in with copious back stories. They reminded everyone that Jason Hamilton had been one of Denver's most popular mayors, with approval ratings consistently hovering in the high seventies. He'd even managed to clear snow from obscure city side streets after last year's biggest blizzard—a feat that far exceeded the abilities of most of his predecessors and had won him the heartfelt gratitude of his constituents.

Between lectures on the political and civic consequences of Jason's death, the news shows ran footage of Chloe during her record-breaking gold medal run. It was the first U.S. gold medal in that particular event and, in the wake of her win, Chloe had been the recipient of wall-to-wall media attention, so there was plenty of film footage to be trotted out. The close-up shot of Chloe on the victory podium—teary-eyed but joyful—seemed to be the special favorite of news producers this morning. Liam could understand why. She was a stunning woman and her radiant smile made for a fantastic TV visual.

Having endured two weeks in the full glare of the media spotlight when his father was murdered back in May, Liam sympathized with what Chloe Hamilton must be going through right now. His sympathies were tempered, however, by the strong likelihood that she had, in fact, killed her husband. Spouses were always the first suspect in a murder case, and Liam's experience as a criminal lawyer had given him no reason to doubt the statistics. He figured that any Olympic gold medalist who chose to stab her spouse multiple times had to be prepared to face a little negative publicity.

Whatever the facts, whether she was the murderer or an innocent bystander, Chloe would be wise to steel herself for a continuing onslaught from the media ghouls. If the cops didn't identify her husband's killer within forty-eight hours, she was going to find herself soaring into the stratosphere of national attention. A miserable place to be when the attention wasn't favorable.

Fortunately, none of the problems resulting from Jason Hamilton's murder were his to deal with. Liam shoved aside a twinge of irrational regret for his previous career as a criminal defense attorney. Yes, he'd relished the cut and thrust of courtroom battle and he savored the memory of a couple of innocent clients he'd help to set free, but his current work provided more income, more predictable hours and a lot less stress. He'd have to be crazy to consider switching back to the high pressure work of defending criminals, especially with a famous client like Chloe Hamilton as his means for reentry. That would generate the sort of public scrutiny nobody in his family needed right now.

He drove to the office, mentally reviewing his schedule for the day. His first appointment was with Heather Ladrow, whose divorce from one of Denver's most successful venture capitalists he'd helped negotiate fifteen months earlier. Heather had indicated in making this morning's appointment that there was now a problem with the financial settlements.

Heather looked older and a lot more worn than Liam remembered. Once he learned what she was going through, he wasn't surprised by her frazzled appearance. Heather's former husband, multimillionaire Pierce Ladrow, had reneged on his legal obligations and stopped paying child support.

"Don't worry," Liam reassured Heather. "We'll get a court order to compel him to pay everything he owes.

We'll ask the judge to impose penalties and interest. If he still refuses to pay up, we can garnish some of his assets."

"I wish it was that easy," Heather said, plucking angrily at the strap of her purse. "But he's left the country."

Her ex-husband had married a Frenchwoman and moved to Monaco, she explained, taking out French citizenship for good measure. He'd sold his remaining property in the States and put his entire fortune in various complicated trusts held in banks scattered around the globe. Financially speaking, as far as the U.S. authorities were concerned, Pierce had dropped off the edge of a cliff. What's more, he'd told Heather the last time they communicated that the moon would explode in the sky before he'd send her or the kids another dime.

Liam listened in grim silence, not enjoying the advice he felt obligated to give. "The unwelcome fact is that your former husband has put himself out of reach of our American civil courts, Mrs. Ladrow. We can get a court order to attach his assets anywhere in the States, but from what you've told me, it seems clear there are no assets in this country for us to go after."

"What about all the money Pierce has in Europe? And in the Cayman Islands? And the Bahamas? And Hong Kong, too!" Heather Ladrow's cheeks were scarlet with frustration. "My pig of an ex has twenty-five million dollars and I'm struggling to afford new running shoes for my son! Meanwhile, my daughter had to give up ballet lessons because we can't afford them."

"I understand how unfair it must seem, but I don't see any effective legal recourse open to you—"

"But Pierce *owes* me that money!"

"Yes, he does. Right is absolutely on your side. The law

is, too. The difficulty is that nobody is in a position to enforce the court rulings."

"Then what am I supposed to do? Let Pierce win? Dammit, I won't let that bastard win!"

Liam suppressed a sigh. The Ladrows were so angry with each other that their divorce was a bloody battle ground, not a mechanism for dealing sensibly with a failed marriage. "Fortunately, you own the house in Cherry Creek. There's no mortgage on the property and it's worth at least two million dollars." Liam had insisted, despite fierce opposition from Pierce Ladrow's lawyer, that Heather was entitled to the house, free and clear of a mortgage. Now he was doubly grateful that he hadn't accepted the attorney's offer of a divorce settlement that granted Heather extremely generous annual payments but left all the capital assets in Pierce's hands. In retrospect, it was obvious why Pierce had been so willing to pay his wife far more alimony than any court would impose. The guy had clearly planned all along to renege and then decamp abroad.

"It's outside my area of professional expertise to offer financial advice, Mrs. Ladrow. But in your situation, I would sell the house and buy something smaller and cheaper. Then I'd invest the balance in a mutual fund. That would generate more than enough income to cover dance class for your daughter and running shoes for your son."

"I thought there was a law against deadbeat dads in this state," Heather said bitterly.

"There is, and I'll certainly do the paperwork to get a warrant issued for Mr. Ladrow's arrest—"

"You can do that?" She brightened.

"Absolutely. If Mr. Ladrow comes back to Colorado, he'll face a choice between paying up and going to jail. But how do we enforce the warrant if your ex-husband remains out of the country?"

"Can't we get the police in Monaco to arrest him?"

"We can try, but there's almost no chance we'll succeed. The authorities in Monaco aren't going to arrest your husband on charges stemming from a contested divorce settlement, especially since he's now a French citizen."

"But nonpayment of child support is a criminal offense, not just a civil matter like divorce."

"True, but it's not a criminal offense that foreign countries are willing to extradite for. Bottom line, as long as your ex-husband and his money stay out of the country, he's found an effective way to thumb his nose at the American legal system."

"I hate him." Heather spoke with quiet venom. "I really hate him."

Liam let that comment slide. "Is there no chance that your ex-husband is going to decide he misses his children? After a few months, he may decide it's worth paying the money he owes in return for the chance to visit with his children."

"That's not going to happen," she said bleakly. "My children are adopted. They're wonderful young people, and the light of my life, but in fairness to Pierce—and God knows, it kills me to be fair to him—I have to admit that he always told me he'd never be able to love children who weren't his own flesh and blood." She gave a bitter smile. "That seems to have been the one thing he didn't lie about."

"I'm very sorry. The situation must be very hard for you and for your children."

She smiled sadly. "I should have listened, shouldn't I? It's amazing how easy it is when you're inside a marriage to ignore what your partner is telling you. The reality is I should have seen this coming, but I refused to accept that Pierce meant exactly what he said. He didn't want to adopt children. I insisted, he went along to the extent of signing the papers, and—here we are."

We get too soon old and too late smart. That had been one of his grandmother's favorite sayings and Liam's work provided almost daily reminders of its truth. Married couples, it seemed to him, took an especially long time to get smart about each other. His work had convinced him— if he'd needed further convincing—that marriage was a damn good way to expose yourself to the agony of hell without the extra inconvenience of dying first. He had no idea why so many otherwise sensible men and women chose to submit themselves to the torment. He realized, of course, that not every marriage degenerated into the sort of vicious endgame that Pierce Ladrow had inflicted on his wife and kids but, from Liam's perspective, far too many of them came disconcertingly close.

Jenny, the young woman who kept watch over the re-ception area, came in as soon as Heather Ladrow left. "Chloe Hamilton is waiting to see you." Jenny had clearly watched the morning news. She spoke in hushed tones, dazzled by Chloe's celebrity and the aura of criminal scandal surrounding her. "She realizes she doesn't have an appointment but she says she really needs to see you as soon as you can spare a moment."

"Tell her I have no openings in my schedule this morning." Liam was in no mood to pander to Chloe Hamilton's strange fixation for hiring him as her defense attorney.

"You have almost half an hour before your next client is due to arrive," Jenny pointed out.

"If you watched the news this morning, you know Mrs. Hamilton needs a criminal lawyer," Liam said curtly.

"You were a criminal lawyer until a couple of years ago."

Liam glanced up, startled by Jenny's comment. She'd been with him eighteen months and had never before indicated that she knew anything at all about his professional history.

"You're correct," he said coolly. "I *used* to be a criminal lawyer. Mrs. Hamilton is almost three years too late to hire me."

"Okay, you're the boss. I guess I'll tell her you're not avail—oops." Jenny stood aside as Chloe walked into Liam's office.

"Mr. Raven, I'm sorry to force my way in, but I'm desperate."

Chloe gave every appearance of speaking the truth. She looked nothing like the self-possessed, elegant woman who'd visited Liam's offices back in early April. Her hands visibly shook and her blue eyes had huge dark circles under them, all the more visible because her face was so pale beneath its golden tan. Her outfit passed beyond casual and well into ratty. She was wearing a misshapen lime-green T-shirt that didn't match the formality of her tailored beige slacks and her hair was haphazardly tied back with a black scrunchie. Oddly, Liam still found her attractive, a fact that did nothing to improve his mood. Sherri Norquist had taught him everything he needed to know about the idiocy of defense lawyers who took on clients to whom they felt sexually attracted. He didn't need Chloe to provide a brush-up course in stupidity.

"As I informed you earlier this morning, Mrs. Hamilton, you should make an appointment to see Bill Schuller. I can assure you that Bill will provide outstanding counsel."

"I tried to hire Mr. Schuller. It can't be done. He's fishing in the Alaskan wilderness. Nobody can reach him until he gets back to the base camp on the Alagnak River, and that's going to be another forty-eight hours at least. I can't wait forty-eight hours, Mr. Raven. I need a lawyer now. This minute."

"Why the urgency?"

"Because I think the police will arrest me as soon as I go back to either my home or the official mayoral residence. My sister called me a few minutes ago. The cops have even been out to her house to see if she knew where I was."

Liam looked at her assessingly. If Chloe was right, she definitely needed immediate legal help. "I can give you fifteen minutes," he said, although he wasn't sure why he made the concession. He gestured for her to take a chair.

"Do you want me to take notes?" Jenny asked hopefully.

Liam inclined his head. "Yes, thank you."

"No," Chloe said abruptly. "I prefer to speak to you alone, Mr. Raven. No notes."

Jenny looked at him inquiringly, and Liam shrugged, then nodded to indicate that she should leave. As soon as they were alone, Chloe sat down, although she perched on the edge of her seat as if she might take flight at the slightest provocation.

"Tell me why you think the police are going to arrest you," Liam said. Since he only had a narrow time window before his next client arrived, he figured they might as well cut to the chase.

Chloe's hand fluttered, then she clenched her fists and shoved both hands into her lap as if despising the helpless gesture. "They have a witness who claims to have seen me stab Jason."

"Who's the witness?"

"Sophie's nanny."

"Does the nanny dislike you?"

"I don't think so. Trudi's from Finland and came over here to improve her English. She's reliable and honest and she's never given the slightest sign of having a grudge against me. I like her and thought she liked me. Or that she used to, until this morning. Now I daresay she thinks I'm a vicious killer."

"Is she right?" Liam asked mildly. "Did you stab your husband?"

She looked straight at him. "No, Mr. Raven, I didn't stab Jason. I didn't harm him in any way. When Trudi saw me, I was trying to unbutton Jason's shirt and look at his injuries. I know it was a crazy thing to do, but when you see somebody you love lying in a pool of blood, you don't think, you just react. I thought that if I could only get the knife out and pad the wound, then maybe I could give him CPR and he'd start breathing again."

Her explanation was ridiculous coming from a woman as smart as Chloe Hamilton, especially in view of the knowledge she must have of human anatomy after her years of intensive athletic training. However, that didn't mean her account was a lie. Liam's training and professional instincts all suggested to him that Chloe was the most likely murderer, but he also knew that innocent people occasionally ended up in the wrong place at the wrong time—and not only on TV crime shows.

Jenny buzzed the intercom. He picked up the phone, so that Chloe wouldn't hear whatever Jenny had to say. "Liam, Terry Robbins has arrived."

"Thanks, Jenny. I'll be right with him."

Liam glanced at his watch. Terry Robbins was ten minutes early, but he was a man with a high regard for his own importance—not a good client to keep waiting. Terry couldn't be shunted aside for a preliminary meeting with Helen, Liam's highly competent paralegal; his self-importance meter would explode from righteous indignation at the prospect of discussing his failed marriage with a mere paralegal.

Liam started scribbling a list of names onto the notepad on his desk. "Mrs. Hamilton, I'm sorry but my next client has already arrived." He tore off the sheet and handed it to her. "These are for you. In my opinion, those are the half dozen best criminal attorneys currently practicing in the Denver area. As I mentioned earlier, Bill Schuller is the best, but any of these six would be more than competent. I've also included Robyn Johnson's name on the list. She's outstanding, but she's approaching sixty and these days she spends most of her time on pro bono work for people who've already been convicted."

Chloe ripped the list in two and tossed the crumpled pieces onto Liam's desk. "I don't want Bill Schuller or the great Robyn Johnson, who probably isn't available anyway. I don't want any of these other attorneys. I want you."

She really was beginning to sound somewhere close to obsessive. What the hell was her problem? There was something going on here that he was missing, Liam decided.

"I'm a good lawyer, Mrs. Hamilton, but I'm not *that* good and it certainly isn't to your advantage right now to have a lawyer whose courtroom skills have been rusting for almost three years. You ought to be begging Robyn Johnson to put aside her pro bono work and take you on, if you want truly brilliant representation. Why are you so determined to hire me?"

She looked at him in silence and for a moment he was sure she wouldn't answer. Then she gave a tiny shrug, as if clearing some final mental hurdle.

"Because you're Sophie's father," she said. "I thought that might give you a vested interest in keeping me out of prison."

Two

Right up until the moment she spoke, Chloe hadn't been sure she was going to tell Liam the truth. She'd imagined this scene a thousand times, but it seemed despite all the practice, she'd never envisioned Liam's reaction correctly. He didn't shout, he didn't protest, he didn't appear angry. He didn't even look surprised. Disconcertingly, his face displayed no expression at all. She'd decided back in April that he was one of the most self-controlled human beings she'd ever met, but his calm right now was unnerving. He simply fixed his gaze on her, his expression shuttered and his amazing hazel eyes bereft of emotion.

"Sophie is your daughter, isn't that right, Mrs. Hamilton?" Liam's question was polite, but distant.

"Yes."

"How old is Sophie?"

His coolness set Chloe's jangled nerves on edge. "She's three and a half. A little more. She'll be four on the first of October."

"I see. I thought she was somewhere around that age."

Liam opened a gilt-embossed, leather-bound appointment diary on his desk and flipped quickly through a few pages. Chloe was too emotionally battered even to wonder what he was doing.

He apparently found what he was looking for. Swinging the diary around on his desk, he pushed it toward her so that she could read the entries and pointed to a line in the middle of the left-hand page. Her name—*Chloe Hamilton (Mrs. Jason Hamilton)*—was written in the space for 2:00 p.m. on Wednesday, April 5 of the current year.

Liam spoke soothingly, as though to a lunatic, or an overexcited child on the verge of pre-Christmas meltdown. "As you can see, Mrs. Hamilton, we met for the first time almost exactly three months ago. In April this year, to be precise. Quite apart from the fact that there has never been any form of sexual contact between the two of us, you'll understand why I'm quite sure that you're wrong about the paternity of your daughter. Sophie can't possibly be my child. She was already three years old the first time you and I met."

Chloe wished that she had an elegant leather-bound diary in her purse with a notation showing the night when they'd really met for the first time. It would have been eminently satisfying to pull it out of her purse and shove it under Liam's patronizing nose.

She'd wondered for years if he had recognized her the night Sophie was conceived. In April, when she approached him about the divorce, she'd been *almost* sure that he had no recollection of their previous encounter. Now, unfortunately, she was convinced he didn't remember the time they'd spent together. Liam wasn't trying to evade the fact that he'd fathered a child by denying the fact that they'd been lovers; he was simply humoring a woman he believed to be mentally unbalanced. Presumably he was afraid she would start frothing at the mouth or throwing wild punches if he showed surprise or anger.

"I'm perfectly well aware of the fact that we met on April 5 to discuss the possibility of my filing for a divorce from Jason." Chloe repeated the exact date of their meeting in an effort to sound as sane and in control as possible. "But that wasn't our first encounter. We'd met before. To be precise, we met at the Grovelands' New Year's Eve party four years ago."

Liam's expression remained controlled but she saw a faint flicker of emotion in his eyes before he once again retreated behind his mask of impassivity. "You're claiming that your daughter was conceived at the Grovelands' party?"

"She was conceived in a motel on Hampden Avenue, but we met at the Grovelands' house in Cherry Creek. Do you remember the occasion? It was the year the Grovelands threw a fancy dress party."

Liam's eyes narrowed and the faintest trace of color flared along his cheekbones. The color vanished almost as soon as it appeared. "I remember the party," he admitted.

"You came as John Jay, the first Chief Justice of the United States." And he'd damn near taken her breath away in the velvet coat and ruffled cravat of an eighteenth century gentleman.

Liam said nothing.

"I came dressed as Cleopatra," she added.

His head jerked up, but his face still gave away nothing. *He remembers,* Chloe thought. *Thank God.* She was relieved that he had some recollection of their time together, even if the memory hadn't been scalded into his soul.

Given how smooth Liam's seduction techniques had been, Chloe suspected that sleeping with a woman he barely knew was his standard operating procedure. But from her perspective, their encounter had been infinitely memorable, and not just because Liam had been a fantastic lover, or even because of the epic fact that it had resulted in Sophie's conception. It had also been her single foray into adultery. No point in telling him that, though. He certainly wouldn't believe her.

"My costume explains why you didn't recognize me," she said. "I wore lots of eye makeup and a dark wig. Almost nobody recognized me that night."

"Tell me something, Mrs. Hamilton." She was sure Liam's continued use of her married name was intended as an insult, not as a mark of professional courtesy. "Did you deliberately set out to get pregnant that night, or was I just the lucky son of a bitch who happened to be hanging around when you felt in the mood to get laid?"

"I didn't plan to get pregnant. I swear I didn't." On her good days, Chloe was almost sure that was true. On her bad days, she considered that, mere hours before the party began, she'd discovered Jason was sterile. Not only that, but he'd known of his sterility for over two years and had chosen not to tell her, for fear that she would leave him. She'd gone to the Grovelands' party in a volatile state somewhere between furious anger and extreme despair.

But surely even in that dangerous mood she'd been smart enough to realize that the solution to the multiple problems of her marriage was divorce? She *couldn't* have been brainless enough to think that getting herself impregnated by a virtual stranger was a smart or correct thing to do.

"It's highly unlikely you conceived your daughter that night we were together," Liam said tersely. "I know I used a condom. I always use condoms."

"Condoms aren't fool proof. There's something like a five percent failure rate."

Liam's gaze touched hers. "Well, hell, didn't I get lucky?" He gave a short, hard laugh. "One chance in twenty and you're claiming I hit the jackpot?"

Chloe drew in a shaky breath. "I'm quite sure you're Sophie's father but we can arrange for a DNA test if you want to be one hundred percent certain. There are plenty of labs that will make the identification without needing to know the names of the people being tested."

He raised an eyebrow. "Whose identity are you trying to protect, Mrs. Hamilton? Mine or yours?"

"Everyone's," she said. "Especially Sophie's. If there's anything we can agree on, surely it's the fact that she's the one completely innocent person in all of this."

"I'm feeling pretty innocent myself," Liam said curtly. "I didn't go to the party planning to have sex with a married woman. More to the point, I came away not knowing I had."

"I didn't plan to commit adultery, either. I'm not in the habit of sleeping around."

"That's hard to believe. You were married, Mrs. Hamilton, but you told me—more than once, in more ways than one—that you were single."

She made the mistake of attempting to justify the inexcusable. "Jason and I had an argument right before we left for the Grovelands' New Year's Eve party. We both said some hurtful things and I was in a reckless mood by the time you and I met."

Liam's expression remained controlled but she realized that his anger was rapidly escalating toward the tipping point. "So I was your therapy for the night? A little bit of sex on the side to get back at your husband?"

The wretched truth was that her flirtation with Liam had started out pretty much as something that sordid and that unforgivable. She'd just never intended to let the situation progress beyond mild flirtation. "You're sounding very self-righteous," she said quietly. "But I seem to recall that you were the person who put the moves on me, not the other way around."

It was absolutely the wrong thing to have said. Liam leaned across the desk, his hands gripping the edge until his knuckles gleamed white. Probably so that he didn't give in to the temptation to bop her one, Chloe thought wryly.

"You're forgetting one minor fact," Liam said, teeth clenched. "I had every right to solicit sex with you because *I wasn't married!* I wasn't even dating seriously. You, on the other hand, had a husband."

"It was wrong of me, I know—"

"*Wrong?* A little more than that, Mrs. Hamilton. Do you happen to remember that annoying bit in the marriage vows where you promised to remain faithful and hang in there when times got tough? As I recall, there's absolutely nothing in the wedding ceremony that says adultery is okay if the spouses have had a spat before they leave for a party."

He was quite right. There was no defense for what she'd done, and Chloe felt her face burn with shame for the lies she'd told when they first met—and since. "I'm sorry. I'm really sorry. Except that I can't regret what happened that night because I have Sophie as a result."

"Unfortunately, I can and do regret what happened that night, Mrs. Hamilton, precisely because you have Sophie."

"If you'd ever met her, you'd know that she's the most wonderful person—"

"But I haven't met my own daughter, and that's the point, isn't it?" He looked at her with shriveling scorn. "Did your husband know that Sophie wasn't his child? Come to think of it, why are you so sure Jason *isn't* her father?"

There was no way to preserve Jason's privacy at this point. "My husband is…he was sterile."

"So how did you explain the fact of your pregnancy to him?"

"He was shocked when I told him, of course—"

"You have a gift for understatement, Mrs. Hamilton."

She ignored his mockery and plowed on doggedly. "Jason was shocked and upset, but once Sophie was born, he fell in love with her. She is…she became Jason's daughter in every way, except biologically. He loved her as much as I do."

"As a divorce lawyer, I find that hard to believe. My experience strongly suggests that men have a difficult time accepting living proof of their wife's infidelity."

"Hard to believe or not, it's the truth." For once, the whole truth and nothing but. Jason had adored Sophie and been grateful for her existence.

"In case this hasn't occurred to you, the cops are going to find your husband's supposedly forgiving attitude impossibly hard to believe." Liam sounded grim.

She stared at him, appalled. "Why do the police have to know Jason isn't Sophie's father? What on earth does my daughter's biological background have to do with Jason's murder?"

He shook his head, clearly impatient with her naiveté. "The cops have to know upfront. You're setting yourself up for disaster if you let them discover this information for themselves."

"Why would they find out?"

"The postmortem might easily reveal that Jason is sterile, depending on the cause of his sterility. Or the cops might subpoena his medical records and find out that way. Trust me on this, if you keep quiet and the truth comes out during the course of the investigation, the cops will interpret your silence as an admission that you consider Sophie's paternity a dirty little secret. They'll assume your husband was furious when he discovered Sophie wasn't his biological child. They'll imagine her existence caused bitter arguments between you and Jason. They'll conclude the arguments escalated over the years and, after an especially violent disagreement, Jason ended up dead on your living room floor, with you wielding the murder weapon."

His scenario sounded chillingly credible. "Is that what you think happened?" Chloe asked. "That I killed my husband because we were fighting about Sophie?"

"As a possible scenario, it matches all the known facts." The complete lack of inflection in his voice somehow transformed his statement into an accusation.

"Nobody who'd ever seen Jason with Sophie would believe something so crazy."

"But the cops haven't seen your husband with Sophie," Liam pointed out with infuriating calm. "Neither have the potential jurors if you end up being brought to trial. However, you *were* seen poised over Jason's body with the murder weapon in your bloody hands. I can only hope for your sake that nobody heard you and Jason arguing last night?"

There was a definite question in his final words. Add one more person to the list of those who were already convinced she'd murdered her husband, Chloe thought wearily. She dropped her gaze. No doubt Liam would interpret her silence as an admission that she and Jason had been arguing last night. Unfortunately, his interpretation would be correct. Their disagreement had been about Jason's political ambitions and how best to achieve them, certainly not about Sophie.

"Jason never regretted his decision to welcome Sophie as his daughter," Chloe said finally. "She was a source of joy to both of us. I have no way to convince you of that, but it's the simple truth."

"Did Jason know I was the man who'd impregnated his wife?"

"Yes."

"I don't believe you. How come he never confronted me? Why didn't he demand an explanation as to why I slept with his wife?"

Chloe met Liam's derisory gaze head on and a ripple of anger floated across the surface of her despair. "The truth is he considered the precise identity of our daughter's biological father somewhat irrelevant. As long as you didn't know the truth, he had no interest in confronting you."

Her barb found its target and Liam's mouth tightened. "As the man trapped into impregnating you, I can't say that I agree with your husband's point of view. I consider the fact that I have a child to be extremely important and I'm furious that you kept the information hidden from me."

"I couldn't tell you about Sophie," she said, realizing there was almost no hope that Liam would understand why she'd felt compelled to remain silent. "If Jason was willing to accept Sophie as his daughter, I felt I owed him the courtesy of not telling anyone how she'd been conceived."

"Not even the lucky father?" Liam's voice vibrated with irony.

She shook her head. "Not even you. Perhaps especially not you."

"I'm sure you agonized over the ethics of the situation."

"Yes, I did," she said, ignoring his sarcasm. "Especially when I decided to end the marriage and came to you for help with a divorce."

"Let's talk about that for a moment. Why did you choose—" The intercom buzzed again and Liam snatched the phone. "Yes?"

Chloe couldn't hear the receptionist's part of the conversation, but Liam responded by saying he'd be right there.

He hung up. "I have to end this conversation, Mrs. Hamilton. My client has been waiting for fifteen minutes—"

"For heaven's sake, would you stop calling me Mrs. Hamilton!" she snapped. "My name, as you very well know, is Chloe. I think our acquaintance has reached a stage of intimacy where it's okay for you to use it!"

"Nothing about our acquaintance has anything to do with intimacy," he replied angrily.

"Whatever." She lifted her shoulders, then let them fall, too exhausted to fight anymore. She stood up, struggling to regain at least a vestige of her old pride and determination. "I should leave. This has been a mistake and, as you keep reminding me, you have important clients waiting."

She turned to go, suddenly chilled by the air-conditioning. She wrapped her arms around herself to ward off the cold air and realized as she did so that she was still wearing the scruffy T-shirt that she'd grabbed first thing this morning when the police sergeant sent her upstairs to shower and change out of her blood-soaked robe. Apparently she'd been in such a state of mental turmoil when she prepared to leave the house that she'd changed into decent slacks but forgotten to put on the silk blouse that went with them. Good grief, she must look like a demented bag lady. Chloe felt a wave of embarrassment sweep over her.

With all that was going on right now, it was crazy to come unglued because her outfit was less than perfect, but somehow the knowledge that she was wearing a worn out T-shirt was the last straw. She hated the fact that she had been so overwhelmed by the police interrogation that she couldn't even dress herself properly. She was annoyed by the fact that she wanted Liam's approval, or at least his acceptance. Why did she care if he disapproved of her? He was an accidental sperm donor, nothing more. Still, if she'd looked a bit more elegant, maybe he'd have worked a bit harder to hide his contempt. Tears threatened to overflow, and she blinked them away, pride coming to her rescue when everything else failed. She wasn't going to give in to self-pity, not in front of Liam, who so clearly had no interest in joining her sob party.

He walked around from behind his desk and came to stand between her and the door. She was relieved when he gave no sign that he realized how close she was to breaking down.

"Obviously there are a lot of things we still need to talk about," he said. "I can't spend any more time with you right now and I have to be in court right after lunch. Can you be back here at four?"

She hesitated for a moment. "If the police don't arrest me, I'll be here."

"Go to the movies," he said. "Pick a theater in a nice, family-oriented suburb. Movie theaters are great places to hide from cops." He tapped briefly on a side door she hadn't noticed before and a female voice responded.

He opened the door. "Hey, Helen, I have a client coming through if you don't mind." He turned back to Chloe. "This leads to my paralegal's office. If you go out this way, you can access the main corridor directly. It's probably better if you avoid exiting through the reception area. I think you and my next client probably know each other."

"Thank you." She walked towards Helen's office, numb enough to follow his instructions without question.

"Chloe."

She stopped and swung around to look at him, grateful for his small concession of using her name. "Yes?"

"Where is…your daughter…right now?"

"My sister came and picked her up early this morning. She took Sophie back to her house in Conifer."

"How long can you leave…Sophie…there?"

"As far as my sister is concerned, forever. As far as Sophie is concerned—at least until bedtime. My sister has two preschoolers of her own, and Sophie loves to play with her cousins."

He gave a quick nod to acknowledge her answer. "Then I'll expect to see you here this afternoon at four. Try not to get arrested in the meantime, okay?"

Three

He had a child. Sophie was his daughter. Chloe Hamilton was the mother of his child. His daughter was three and a half years old.

However many ways he found to express the simple facts, Liam still couldn't wrap his mind around the crazy notion that he was a father. A father, for God's sake! If ever there was one role that he'd been determined never to take on, fatherhood would have to be it.

Among the worst of the unpleasant emotions accompanying the discovery that he had a child was the shame of knowing he'd behaved no better than his own father, the late, not-very-lamented Ron Raven. Ron had impregnated Avery Fairfax twenty-seven years ago, when his legal wife, Ellie, was already pregnant. Then Ron had solved the dilemma of two women simultaneously pregnant with his child by marrying Avery—without bothering to divorce Ellie first.

Ever since he learned about his father's bigamy, Liam had derived a morbid satisfaction from heaping scorn on his father's head for the idiocy of contracting a fake marriage. He'd harped on Ron's carelessness in causing the pregnancy that had precipitated it. Now it seemed that he had been as careless as his father. Juggle the pieces of the Liam-Chloe-Jason triangle, toss them up in the air and you could watch them fall to the ground in a pattern humiliatingly close to the Ellie-Ron-Avery triangle. *Like father, like son* wasn't a cliché he'd ever wanted to live up to, Liam reflected cynically, but it seemed he'd done just that.

Court, thank God, was over for the day, and he'd managed to focus on the Cellinis' civil war, euphemistically described as their divorce petition, long enough to avoid disaster for his client. The financial decisions had gone in favor of Mr. Cellini, more because the legal facts were overwhelmingly on his side than because Liam had presented them with any special brilliance. Still, right now he'd take his victories any way he could get them.

He parked his car in the lot at the back of his office building and sat drumming his fingers on the steering wheel. Five hours had passed since he learned he had a daughter and he still had no idea what he was going to say to Chloe Hamilton except that he wanted to see Sophie. He felt supremely ill-equipped to assume the role of father but, despite his fury at having been tricked into parenthood, he had no intention of taking out his anger on Sophie.

His child. His daughter. The unbelievable refrain started up again. Jesus, there was absolutely no way to make those words sound anything less than insane.

His cell phone rang just as he was getting out of the car and he answered automatically, his attention focused four years in the past on a sexual encounter with Chloe that—surprisingly—he could remember quite clearly.

"Liam Raven."

A woman responded, her voice tinged with laughter. "Golly gee, big brother, your bark is getting worse by the day! If you always sound this fierce, it's a wonder you have any clients left!"

"Megan! How are you doing? Sorry to sound so abrupt. I was distracted." At almost any other time, Liam would have been delighted to hear from his sister. Megan was nearly nine years his junior, so their childhoods had followed separate paths, but he'd always loved her and he was pleased that she seemed so happy in her new relationship with Adam Fairfax. The Fairfaxes weren't the family he'd have chosen for Megan to marry into, to put it mildly, but in his more rational moments, he realized Adam was no more responsible for the multiple sins of Ron Raven than anyone else caught up in the fallout from Ron's bigamy. Adam, after all, couldn't help the fact that he was Avery Fairfax's younger brother.

Liam shook his head, trying to clear away the fuzziness of shock lingering from the morning's revelations. He wanted to respond to his sister without alerting her that anything was wrong, but Chloe's news was so much at the forefront of his thoughts that he was in danger of blurting out something about Sophie if he didn't watch himself. He loved Megan and respected both her intelligence and her integrity, but he was more in the habit of protecting her than asking for her advice. Besides, he had no intention of telling anyone—friends or family—that he had a child until he'd decided exactly what he was going to make of his relationship with Sophie. He saw no point in adding more complications to an emotional stew that was already overspiced with his own neuroses.

He grabbed his briefcase and tucked the phone between his cheek and his shoulder, using his hip to shut the car door. "It's good to hear from you, Meg. How are you?"

"Hmm, let's see. Busy at work. Missing Wyoming. Hopelessly in love with Adam. Wishing he lived about a thousand miles farther away from his parents. Maybe a million miles farther away, actually."

He made a sympathetic noise. "That would mean living on the moon, Meggie."

"Yeah, well, that would work for me." Megan's laugh was rueful.

"I take it Mr. and Mrs. Fairfax Senior are still less than thrilled that their favorite son is engaged to Ron Raven's daughter?" Liam pressed the button to summon the elevator, which was currently ten floors away.

"Less than thrilled barely begins to describe it. Try frothing-at-the-mouth furious, interspersed with occasional patches of icy disdain just for variety. They'd have a hard time reconciling themselves to the fact that their Southern gentleman son is living in sin with a damn Yankee, but the fact that I'm Ron Raven's daughter sends them over the top."

"They'll come around, Meggie. Eventually, they'll get tired of hating our father."

"Will they?" She sighed. "Is that happy day going to arrive this century, do you think?"

"It'll arrive when their daughter and granddaughter stop hurting because of what Dad did to them. You need to give everyone a few more weeks, Meg. It's only three months since Avery Fairfax learned that her supposed husband was dead and that her marriage had never existed as a legal reality."

"You're right, I need to be patient, which is never my strong suit," she said. "I guess I'm feeling extra sensitive because Adam and I were in Wyoming with Mom last week and the tension at the ranch just never let up. And then we flew back to Georgia and found even more hostility waiting for us. After a while, having your prospective in-laws fall silent every time you walk into the room gets kind of old. Adam gets it from Mom in Wyoming and I get a double dose from the Fairfaxes in Georgia."

Liam was sorry to hear that their mother still wasn't at ease with Megan's choice of fiancé. He would have been more than willing to put in a positive word for Adam and his sister, but his own relationship with their mother was sufficiently rocky that interference from him was likely to do as much harm as good.

"Dad managed to mess with everyone's emotions," he said, giving another frustrated push to the elevator call button. "Even though Mom likes Adam and wants you to be happy, it still must seem to her as if you're siding with the enemy."

"You're so right." Megan smothered another sigh. "She tries hard, but she's really uncomfortable when she has to spend time alone with Adam. If she finds herself in the same room with him, without a cushion of other people around, it's obvious she's thinking about just one thing—"

"The fact that Adam is not only a Fairfax, but Avery's youngest brother." Liam had no trouble finishing his sister's sentence.

"You've got it. I know it's hard for Mom to accept that Dad was the only villain in what happened, but he was. Avery and Adam were both his victims, just like she was."

"Mom will accept that soon. She's coming around." Liam hoped he was speaking the truth. "Give it a bit more time, and I'm betting Mom won't see *Avery's brother* every time she looks at Adam. She'll see Megan's fiancé and a good guy."

"God, I hope so. By the way, speaking of fiancés—" Megan's voice turned a little breathless. "Adam and I are thinking of getting married at the beginning of next month. We thought we'd slip away for a few days over the Labor Day weekend."

"Hey, congratulations! I'll make sure to clear my calendar." Despite his general disdain for the married state, Liam was surprisingly happy for his sister. He'd met Adam three times now and really liked the guy. "Will you have the ceremony in Wyoming? At the community church or at the ranch?"

There was a slight pause. "Neither place," Megan said.

"In Georgia, then?" Liam was careful not to sound surprised by her choice. Megan loved Wyoming and the ranch; he'd simply assumed she would get married there.

"Adam and I can't get married in Wyoming or in Georgia," she said, and he could hear the regret in her voice. "And we can't invite our families to the ceremony. Think about it. If we don't invite the Fairfax clan, Adam will be sad and his family will be justifiably offended. If we do invite them, especially if we invite Avery, Mom is going to hate every minute of my wedding day."

She had a valid point, Liam thought grimly. Jeez, what a mess. The elevator finally arrived and he stepped in, pushing the button for the seventh floor. In a perfect world, the Fairfaxes and the Ravens would be so happy for Megan and Adam that the past would have no importance. In the real world, Ron Raven's bigamy cast a long and chilling shadow. It was unrealistic to expect the two widows to sit in church, smiling benevolently as Ellie's daughter married Avery's younger brother. And although Megan hadn't mentioned anything about the media, unless they hired armed guards to surround the church and the ranch, the whole ceremony would probably end up being filmed for some sleazy tabloid TV show. Ron's death had become one of those stories that the world of cable refused to let die.

"What are you going to do, then?" he asked. "Do you want to come to Colorado and get married in Denver? It would be easy for me to make all the arrangements and I might even be able to keep them secret, since I'm in the marriage business, so to speak…"

"Thanks. I appreciate the offer, Liam, but we've decided the best thing for us is to elope to Vegas."

In normal circumstances, Vegas would have been just about the last place Megan would have chosen to get married and Liam felt a spurt of resentment on his baby sister's behalf that the wedding of her dreams could never be. He was so taken aback at the thought of Megan in a wedding chapel on the Vegas strip that for a crucial moment he couldn't come up with a damn thing to say.

"I know what you're thinking," she said softly. "Don't worry, Liam. I'm not regretting the white dress and the flower girls and the endless family conferences about who gets to sit at which table—"

"Why not?" he asked, sending a silent curse in the direction of his dead father, the most recent in a long and useless line of similar curses. "It's a huge day in your life and it ought to be as special as you can make it."

"It will be special." Megan sounded completely sure of

herself. "I'll be marrying Adam, so it's bound to be wonderful wherever we have the ceremony."

The elevator clunked to a stop. Liam got out on his floor, amazed by his sister's quiet exuberance. "You really love the guy, don't you?"

"Yes, and fortunately he loves me, too." She laughed. "That kind of puts the where-shall-we-have-the-ceremony issue into perspective. Before I met Adam, I used to fantasize about the perfect wedding. The only problem was that I had this huge hole where I was supposed to have a mental image of the groom. Now I realize the only thing that matters about a wedding is having the right person as your partner when you make your vows. The bridesmaids, the cake, the fancy dress and all the rest of it are basically irrelevant."

"Speaking as a divorce lawyer, I can only say that I'm sure you're right. I wish more people were as smart as my little sister."

"No, you don't, or you'd be unemployed!"

Liam laughed but there was a lump in his throat. Since he couldn't deal with his emotions, today of all days, he spoke with deliberate briskness. "Adam seems like a good guy. Nowhere good enough for you, of course, but almost in the ballpark. Be happy, Meggie."

"He's a great guy, and I plan to be." She broke off. "Oh my gosh, wait! We're wading so deep into the sentimental stuff that I almost forgot the reason I called you in the first place. It's about Dad."

Liam winced, stopping outside the entrance to his offices. "Please don't tell me Adam has uncovered more financial problems."

"None that we didn't know about already, thank goodness. Between the platinum mine in Belize and the disputed wills, I couldn't take another financial disaster, or more documents to sign and send off to the probate court. No, this is something quite different. Do you remember Tricia Riley? She's a distant cousin on Dad's side of the family. Her grandmother and our grandmother were sisters."

"I have a vague image from Grandma's funeral." Liam wrinkled his forehead. "She's got curly hair a bit like yours, right? She was on the ditzy side, but smart in a geeky sort of way. As I recall, she used to work for a dot-com in Houston. She must be in her fifties by now."

"Yes, that's the one. She still does work in Houston, apparently for a company that manufactures household robots. She asked me to call her back when I had time to talk. She claimed she had something important she needed to discuss with me."

"That sounds ominous. If she's asking you to invest in her robots, I recommend you ask for a demonstration first."

"That was precisely my thought, but we're both offtrack. I called her back this morning and what Tricia had to say turned out to be a lot more worrying than robots designed to scrub the floors. Liam, she told me that she'd seen Dad in a shopping mall in Houston."

"*What?* You're kidding. She's claiming to have seen Dad *recently?*"

"She says she saw him last week."

"Good lord, she must be even more ditzy than she looks. So is she claiming to have seen him for real, in the flesh? Or are we talking visitations by a ghost?"

"Absolutely not ghosts. Tricia says she saw Dad going into Nieman Marcus in Houston. She called his name and hurried to catch up with him, but he ignored her. By the time she got into the store, he'd vanished."

"Obviously she suffers from an overactive imagination," Liam said, not sure whether to be irritated by his cousin or to pity her. He never understood why some people felt the need to turn commonplace events into major dramas, with themselves as the stars. "The guy didn't turn around because he had no idea he was being called. He didn't respond to somebody calling Ron Raven for the simple reason that wasn't his name!"

"You're singing my song. That's exactly what I suggested to Tricia, but she wasn't persuaded. She says she's *sure* the man she saw was Ron Raven, or else his double. I pointed out that she didn't know Dad all that well and that she hadn't seen him in the twelve years since Grandma's funeral, and she informed me that I was wrong. She'd had dinner with him in San Antonio a couple of months before he died. Apparently they discussed the possibility of Dad investing in her darn robots! She claims that she knows exactly what Dad looked like right before he was murdered and that this man—quote—had Dad's way of walking."

"That's what Tricia's basing her identification on?" Liam was torn between laughter and exasperation. "The way this man walked? She saw him at a distance, from the side at best and possibly even from behind, and now she's positive it was Dad?"

"Apparently. That and the fact she insists the man saw her and recognized her. According to Tricia, he dodged into the store in order to avoid her."

"She's paranoid. Not to mention delusional."

"Very possibly. But she's already called the police in Miami to tell them they've made a mistake in assuming that Dad was murdered. Cousin Tricia has informed them he's alive and they need to refocus their investigation."

Liam rolled his eyes. "And what did the cops have to say?"

"Nothing that satisfied Tricia." Megan groaned. "They thanked her for letting them know what she thought she'd seen and said they would investigate her claim as time and manpower permitted. In other words, they totally blew her off."

"Are you surprised? My sympathies are with the cops on this one. They'd never get any work done on the real cases if they allowed themselves to get distracted by reports like Tricia's."

Megan hesitated for a moment. "You don't think we ought to follow up with a private detective?"

Liam leaned against the wall outside his office, wanting to finish the call before he went inside. "Follow up what? How? There's nothing to follow up."

"That's true, I guess."

"You sound uncertain."

"I am. Tricia may be nuts—"

"Tricia *is* nuts."

"Okay, I'll grant you that much. But there are problems with the official police account of what happened the night Dad disappeared. The cops in Miami have closed the investigation, except for a half-hearted effort to track down Julio Castellano. But as I already told you, when Adam and I were in Belize, we met Castellano and spent quite a bit of time with him. He swore he wasn't the killer."

"I know. And you told me you and Adam are both inclined to believe him."

"We'd be dead if not for Castellano," Megan pointed out. "He put himself significantly at risk for our sakes, which makes it hard to see him as a brutal killer. And if he didn't kill Dad, who did?"

"Well, if Tricia saw him in Houston, apparently nobody! Did she have any suggestions as to why Dad hasn't let anyone know he's still alive?"

"She suggested he might have amnesia."

"If he has amnesia, why would he have run when she called his name?"

"You're right. Her story is incoherent." Megan hesitated for a moment. "Unless Dad deliberately chose to disappear."

Liam's stomach lurched, then quickly righted itself. "Why would Dad walk away from every penny he possesses? Does that seem likely to you? Or even remotely credible?"

"No," Megan conceded. "But we have to face the fact that the cops in Miami have no idea what really happened the night Dad died."

Now it was Liam's turn to hesitate. He was much less convinced than his sister that Julio Castellano was as innocent as he had claimed, despite the fact that the guy had definitely helped to rescue Megan and Adam from the dangers they faced in Belize.

"We talked about this when you first got back from Belize," he said in the end. "I agree the cops might have screwed up on the details of what happened the night Dad died, but their basic outline seems to be correct—"

"Sure. Apart from the minor detail that they have the wrong name pinned on the hit man."

"In a sense, that *is* a detail. From what you told me about your trip to Belize, it seems that Uncle Ted knew plenty of people who wouldn't have hesitated to kill Dad for quite a small sum of money. If not Julio Castellano, then take your pick of a dozen or so other smugglers and thieves hanging out in Las Criandas."

Liam found it depressing to think about his Uncle Ted, a maternal uncle with as few ethical scruples as his father. Poor Sophie was certainly inheriting a package of unpleasant genes from the Raven side of her family, he reflected grimly. For her sake, he hoped to God that the scientists who claimed nurture was more important than nature were correct.

"The cops in Miami aren't going to rethink their entire investigation without a stronger inducement than a vague sighting by a woman who didn't know him all that well," he said, forcing his thoughts away from his daughter. "It's convenient for them to have Julio Castellano as the chief suspect. Who could be better to accuse of murder than a man who's already been convicted and imprisoned for a previous killing?"

"Maybe a private investigator would find something powerful enough to turn the cops' attention in new directions," Megan suggested.

"But what could an investigator find? And how would he find it? Tricia hasn't given us anything new to work with. She didn't give you an address or a car registration for this guy she spotted. She didn't even get a make or model of the car he was driving. All she gave us was the way he walks! Where the hell is that going to lead us? Nowhere."

"You're right." Megan sounded wistful.

"You don't sound entirely convinced."

"No, I am. Of course, you're right…"

"Look, if you want us to hire a detective to reexamine the events surrounding Dad's disappearance, we should go for it. Except…what exactly are you going to instruct the guy to do? Even if we sent him to Belize, there's nobody to question. Uncle Ted is dead. We haven't a clue where to find Julio at this point—"

"I know. Tricia didn't provide any new information we can follow up on and there are no other leads. Rationally, I knew that even before I called you."

"There's a melancholy note in your voice. What's that all about, Meg?"

She hesitated for a moment. "I guess I realized when I was talking to Tricia that I haven't quite accepted the finality of Dad's death. He left so many issues unresolved that part of me feels mad at him for being at the bottom of the Atlantic Ocean, where I can't demand answers. I wanted Tricia to be right. I wanted Dad still to be alive. After a while, it eats at you to be angry with a dead person."

"You're right. But for my sake, I hope he's not alive," Liam said coolly. "Because if he ever did come back, I'd be tempted to kill him, and I have no desire to spend the rest of my life in prison."

Megan gave a wry laugh. "I think you'd have to stand in line. Ellie and Avery would both want to take the first shots." She paused for a moment. "Tricia told me the cops in Miami have received four hundred and twenty-seven reports from people claiming to have seen our father. Isn't that astonishing?"

"Not really. Police reports are generated in direct proportion to the amount of media attention. For a couple of weeks after Dad died, there was coast-to-coast, wall-to-wall TV coverage. The four hundred reports don't mean anyone's seen him, or even that they've seen a man who looks like him. It just means lots of lonely people like to feel connected to a celebrity murder."

"It totally amazes me how much media attention our family is still attracting. I caught a snippet on the news just last night. They were doing a special report on the increase in cases of bigamy and polygamy, and they dragged out all the facts of Dad's situation again."

Liam had a suspicion it would be a while before the Ravens and the Fairfaxes could sink back into welcome obscurity. In life, Ron Raven had been rich and successful; in death, he was mysterious. The combination was irresistible to news outlets and his two families were suffering all the notoriety that really ought to have been Ron's.

On the other hand, he wasn't in a position to be judging other people's failings right now, Liam reflected as he said goodbye to his sister and entered his office. His own choices and decisions over the past four years certainly didn't stand up to scrutiny. Four years ago he'd spent the night with a woman dressed as Cleopatra whose real name he didn't know and hadn't made any effort to find out. That fact alone put last night's careless seduction of No-Name into a new and unpleasant perspective. Clearly, he'd been pursuing a problematic lifestyle for several years. And what was his excuse? Four years ago, he'd been angry at the world because his father was a bigamist and the following year he'd had the bad luck to fall in love with a woman who'd murdered her husband. It was past time for him to admit that plenty of other people survived far worse. He'd chewed out Chloe this morning because she'd been unfaithful to her husband. Talk about the pot accusing the pan of being dirty! Okay, Chloe's adultery had been reprehensible, but his own behavior would clearly not stand up to any sort of ethical scrutiny.

Awareness of his own culpability—that he'd behaved like a major dick—did nothing to improve Liam's mood.

In retrospect, he wished that he hadn't been so damned smug this morning.

Chloe was already waiting for him in the small reception area, sipping water from a paper cup. She'd changed her ratty T-shirt for a soft cotton blouse that looked new, and her hair was combed into a smooth ponytail, held in place by a pewter-colored barrette. He felt a sharp jolt of sexual attraction as she crumpled the cup and tossed it into the trash, rising to her feet.

He pushed the attraction aside. God knew, where Chloe was concerned, sex had already gotten him into more than enough trouble. From now on, he was going to concentrate on thinking with his brain, a significantly smarter portion of his anatomy than his penis. Giving her a quick nod, he put the Cellini file on Jenny's desk and tried to sound like a man in full control of his life.

"We're finished with this case, Jenny, so you can send out the final bill."

"Did we win?" Jenny asked.

"We did." Liam gave a thumbs-up. Then he opened his office door and beckoned to Chloe. "Come on into my office," he said. "I'm glad you made it back safely." He was pleased with the casual courtesy of his opening gambit. "Since you're here, I'm assuming you didn't run into any trouble with the cops? Or the press?"

"I didn't even see a squad car, thank goodness. And no journalists."

"You got lucky. Quite often the journalists are more difficult to shake than the cops."

Chloe followed him into his office. "I did what you instructed. I went to the mall at Park Ridge and watched a movie, although I couldn't describe a single scene of what

I supposedly saw. The worst thing about having the police believe I killed Jason is that I've been left with no time to mourn him. So every time I'm alone and quiet, I feel paralyzed with grief."

Liam damped down another unwelcome rush of sympathy. Emotion and sound legal advice rarely went together. Besides, Chloe's comments could be carefully calculated to evoke sympathy.

Until he took Sherri Norquist out for a celebratory dinner in the wake of the jury's acquittal and she'd dropped her bombshell, he'd arrogantly assumed he would always know at some gut level whether or not his clients were guilty. Sherri had proved how ridiculous that assumption was. His feelings for her had also proved that he was quite capable of falling in love with a woman of dubious morals who lied easily and often. Sherri, it turned out, had murdered her husband because she wanted his money, and as far as Liam could tell she felt no remorse that the man was dead. Her only regret was that she hadn't been clever enough to avoid arrest. Worst of all, she had assumed Liam would be delighted that he'd persuaded the jury to return a verdict of Not Guilty, despite the fact that she was guilty as charged. She'd even offered to marry him as a reward for his superior professional skills. She'd been offended, not to mention furious, when he declined the honor.

At least Sherri had provided a crash course in humility. Liam considered himself a wiser, as well as more cynical, man these days. His basic assumption post-Sherri was that all his clients lied, at least some of the time. Many of them lied all the time. He didn't doubt for a moment that Chloe fitted right into the general pattern, at least as far as the events surrounding her husband's murder were concerned.

If he was to provide effective legal counsel, his task was to find out where there were holes in her story that the prosecutor's office might take advantage of and then find ways to plug those holes without encouraging her to commit perjury. A task that wasn't likely to be easy.

"Let's get right to the point, shall we?" He sat behind his desk and turned a deliberately distant gaze toward Chloe. He had to ask these questions, even though he placed no reliance on the accuracy of her answers. "Did you kill your husband?"

She flinched, but answered steadily enough. "No."

"Did you pay somebody else to have him killed?"

"No!"

She sounded surprised by his question, rather than outraged, which made him marginally more inclined to believe her. Murderers falsely protesting their innocence tended to go heavily for moral indignation.

"Do you still want me to represent you?" he asked.

"Yes, I do."

"Let me explain just one of the reasons why that isn't a smart decision on your part. Here are the facts of your situation as I understand them. Your husband is dead, stabbed through the heart. The stabbing occurred last night, while you were in the house. It also occurred after you and Jason had been arguing. You were found next to the body, holding a bloody knife. As if that's not trouble enough, your daughter is not Jason's biological child. I already advised you that it's essential to notify the police of this fact. At which point, I can almost guarantee the first question the cops will ask is the identity of Sophie's father. What are you going to tell them?"

"Nothing?" Chloe said, but her voice rose in a question.

He allowed himself a small smile. "I'm glad you were

listening this morning. Nothing is a very good choice. However, the cops are going to press you for a name. The detectives working this case will be smart, and they'll utilize every trick of the trade to persuade you to give them a name, because they'll want it. Badly."

"Why? Why in the world would they care?"

Liam's smile turned bleak. "Because the police will suspect Sophie's father—which would be me, of course—of being involved in the murder. They'll want to question him. In other words, they'll want to question me."

She stared at him, eyes wide with shock. He was almost a hundred percent sure that such a possibility had never crossed her mind. "But that's crazy! You had no idea about Sophie. You had absolutely no motive to want Jason dead."

"True. But the police aren't going to believe either one of us just because we happen to be telling the truth. Fortunately, I wasn't alone last night so I have an alibi." Depending on precisely when the mayor had been killed, Liam might still have been in the bar, in which case there were dozens of potential witnesses. If Jason Hamilton had been killed after 2:00 a.m., he had No-Name as proof that he'd been in an apartment on Alameda Avenue, and definitely not in the mayoral residence. Thank God he'd gone back to No-Name's apartment last night and not to a motel. Otherwise, he'd have had no sure way to track her down, given that he had no clue what she was called. He grimaced in disgust at yet another reminder of the caricature that passed for intimacy in his life.

Chloe linked her fingers, gripping tightly. "If you have an alibi, your personal connection to the case is irrelevant. The police will know you're not involved and it's okay for me to hire you as my lawyer."

He shook his head. "The fact that I'm not likely to be arrested doesn't mean that I would be a good person to represent you in court. You came to me because you thought I'd be the lawyer who would work hardest to keep you out of prison, that I'd have a vested interest in keeping you safe because Sophie is my daughter. Unfortunately, you could hardly have chosen a worse person to approach than the man who fathered your child. If this case ever comes to trial, the D.A.'s office would use the connection to blow us away. You wouldn't be the only person on trial in that situation. I would be, too. Almost before you could say *cheating wife* and *sleazy lover,* you'd be facing a jury who wouldn't believe a word I was saying, and a judge who would question my professional ethics. And their doubts would be justified, given the circumstances." The lingering stench from the Sherri Norquist trial wouldn't help, either.

"Then what am I supposed to do?" Chloe sounded as if she'd passed beyond the point of despair and had moved well into apathy.

"I've already given you the answer to that. If you actually reach the point of being arrested, you need to hire either Robyn Johnson or Bill Schuller. I'll call both of them on your behalf if you like. In the meantime, until Robyn clears her calendar or Bill gets back in town, I'll do everything in my power to keep you and your daughter safe. I'll try very hard to insure that the police don't arrest you until one or other of them agrees to represent you."

Chloe's head jerked up, and it was only when Liam saw the hope dawning in her eyes that he realized just how despairing she'd been previously. "Thank you," she said. "I really appreciate your help."

Now that he'd given her hope, he'd better live up to it. Liam quickly assessed and discarded options. It was important to avoid crossing paths with the police until he knew exactly what had happened last night. On the other hand, the widow of the murdered mayor of a major city didn't have many options open to her if she wanted to disappear. She was highly recognizable, and the press corps was going to be hunting her as hard as the police.

"What's the name of your husband's chief of staff?" he asked.

"Frederick Mitchell. Frederick Ambrose Mitchell."

"Is he a good guy?"

She nodded. "He's a friend, as well as Jason's chief of staff."

"Do you remember the number for his direct line?"

She nodded again and he pushed a scratch pad toward her. "Write it down for me, please."

Chloe wrote the number and he depressed the intercom. "Jenny, here's the number for the late mayor's chief of staff. His name is Frederick Mitchell. Call him, please, and tell him that Mrs. Hamilton is grief stricken and exhausted. She plans to spend the night at a friend's house, where she hopes to avoid any run-in with the media. She'll be back at her home in Park Hill tomorrow morning around eleven. For the next few hours, Mrs. Hamilton would appreciate it if Frederick Mitchell would run interference for her with the cops and especially with the media."

"Can I give him a number where he can reach Mrs. Hamilton if there's an emergency?"

"Tell him that Mrs. Hamilton isn't taking any phone calls tonight. Give him my cell number, and tell him I'll pass on any urgent messages from him to Mrs. Hamilton and vice versa. Encourage him to tell the press that she's not going to be returning to the mayor's home tonight so that they pack up their cameras and go home."

"I'll take care of it. I'll call right now."

Liam made sure he'd cut the intercom connection before speaking again. He didn't want Jenny to have any idea where Chloe was actually staying so that his receptionist would neither be required to stonewall or to lie if anyone happened to ask her.

"It's better if you don't return to your sister's house tonight," he said to Chloe. "The police don't have enough manpower to stake out dozens of places, even in pursuit of the mayor's murderer. But since they already know Sophie is staying with your sister, they've almost certainly spared at least one cop to watch her front door. I'll bet they're hoping to snag you for questioning when you come to pick up your daughter. In the circumstances, it would be best if you simply left Sophie at your sister's."

"I can't do that." Chloe was quiet but adamant. "I'm not going to leave her all night with Alexia. You're forgetting it's Sophie's father who just died. She's scared, she's sad and I've already left her for much too long."

"I'm not asking you to abandon your daughter, but you have to consider the big picture. She isn't going to be reassured if you're arrested when you go to pick her up."

Chloe paled. "Maybe my sister could drive her to a hotel?"

Liam shook his head. "The police will follow your sister. Same result, except at a hotel with plenty of witnesses instead of at your sister's house." He thought for a moment. "I'll have to pick up Sophie myself."

"But how will you avoid the police? What's the difference between you driving her to a hotel and my sister making the same drive?"

"I've had some practice in evading both the cops and the media. Above all, nobody will be looking for me. At this point, the police and the media have no idea there's any connection between the two of us." He held out his cell phone. "Use my phone to call your sister. Did you say her name is Alexia?"

"Yes."

"Tell Alexia I have your permission to pick up your daughter. If she asks where I'm taking Sophie, or where you plan to spend the night, explain that you can't tell her. That way, Alexia can't be tricked into revealing your destination."

"If the police ask her where I've gone, what should she say to them?"

"She should tell them the truth—that she has no idea if you're even still in town. If they press her, she should insist that she'll say nothing further unless she has a lawyer present. If the police decide she's hiding relevant information, they could be persistent enough to be unpleasant. Having a lawyer present will prevent that."

Chloe fiddled with the cell phone, looking troubled. "I had no idea I'd be dragging my sister into the middle of such a mess when I asked her to look after Sophie. Isn't there some less complicated way to do this?"

"Trust me, this is a lot less complicated than having you spend the night in jail."

"In jail?" She stared at him, eyes wide. "Surely they wouldn't put me in jail!"

"Why not?" He was deliberately brutal. "Because you're pretty? Because you won an Olympic medal? Because you married an important man?"

"I didn't mean that. I wasn't implying I deserved special treatment. But I assumed I could post bail even if they arrested me..."

"You can. As soon as a judge *sets* bail. If the cops arrest you tonight, you'd be required to stay in jail until court is in session tomorrow."

He'd managed to scare her to the point that her cheeks were now dead-white. "You really think I'm going to be arrested, don't you?"

He shrugged. "It's a high-profile case. That works for you and against you. The cops will be more careful building their case, and they'll make sure it's strong before they seek any warrants. On the other hand, they can't possibly let the murder of the mayor go unsolved, so there's going to be a lot of pressure on them to make an arrest."

"But how in the world can I prove that I didn't kill Jason?"

"I don't know that yet. If I'm going to help you, I need to find out everything that happened last night in painstaking detail. That's why I need you and Sophie to stay with me at my apartment so that you and I can take as long as we need to discuss the case. I can only work out a strategy once I know everything you know about what happened last night."

"I understand." Chloe straightened her spine, almost visibly girding herself for battle. Liam saw the return of some of the fire and strength of mind which he knew must be an integral part of her character. Any woman capable of achieving gold medal status in an Olympic event as challenging as downhill skiing must have courage to spare.

"I appreciate the offer of safe haven in your home, Liam. That's far more generous of you than I could expect."

"You're welcome." That was more true than he would have liked.

"There's one thing we have to get clear, though." Chloe's mouth firmed into a straight, determined line. "You do understand there's no way I can allow you to tell Sophie you're her biological father—"

"Not tonight. Of course not."

"Not tonight, and perhaps not ever."

There was no way in hell he'd allow a child of his to grow up not knowing the truth about her parentage. He'd seen what happened to families built on a foundation of well-meaning lies and it wasn't pretty. But that was a battle for another night, and he completely agreed with Chloe that a few hours after Jason's death was no time to be burdening a three and a half year old with the knowledge that the man she loved hadn't been her biological father.

"I agree that we need to protect Sophie," he said. "Tonight we're going to do that by developing a strategy for keeping you out of jail. Telling Sophie that I'm her father—"

"Jason was her father."

He dipped his head in acknowledgment. "Telling Sophie that I'm her biological father is a discussion for another night. We need to take this one logical step at a time. Right now, that means we need to get Sophie back to my apartment without alerting the cops. Go ahead, Chloe. Call your sister. Let her know I'll be leaving to pick up Sophie within the next ten minutes."

Four

Paul Fairfax climbed onto the stationary bike in his custom-designed exercise room and grunted in annoyance when he saw that his wife had altered the settings. This was *his* favorite piece of equipment and Julia knew it. He wished she'd stick to the treadmill, for Christ's sake, since she was the one who'd insisted on spending thousands on the fanciest damn treadmill manufactured in the entire United States. Probably the fanciest treadmill in the entire goddamn world, Paul reflected morosely, since Julia's ability to spend money reached a level that came close to high art.

God forbid that she should change her spending and shopping habits now, he thought sarcastically. He'd warned her repeatedly since Ron Raven died that things were tough and the business was going through a little rough patch. He might as well have been telling the wind blowing over Lake Michigan to stop ruffling the surface of the water.

Not that he expected his financial problems to last for long, Paul reassured himself. He was twice as shrewd as Ron had ever been, and the fact that he'd been unable to raise any new investment capital since Ron's disappearance didn't mean that the Chicago business community thought that Ron had been blessed with better instincts for turning a profit. How could anyone think that? Paul would never accept that good ole boy Ron, dragged up by a ranching family in the wilds of Wyoming, had been smarter than him—the eldest son and heir to a fine Southern family with roots growing three hundred years deep in the rich Georgia soil.

Changing the bike settings back to his liking, Paul flicked the switch and started pedaling. The challenging routine he'd designed for himself was so ingrained by now that he would have to put in at least fifteen minutes of intensive effort before he felt the rewarding tug of muscles that meant his workout was paying off. It was a never-ending struggle to keep his fifty-three-year-old body looking and behaving ten years younger than his calendar age, but it was a struggle Paul was determined to win.

God forbid that he should ever get a paunch of the sort Ron Raven had developed over the past couple of years. Paul despised people who didn't have sufficient discipline and willpower to keep their bodies in shape. Ron had no real willpower where his physique was concerned. He'd constantly bemoaned his weight problems, but he'd loved gourmet food and vintage wines far too much to stick to a diet.

Paul had always been mystified by the way Avery had fallen instantly in love with a man as crude as Ron Raven. He was even more mystified by the fact that his sister had apparently remained in love, right up until the day a

Chicago cop came and informed her that Ron Raven was not only missing from his Miami hotel room, but that he had another wife and family living in the godforsaken hick town of Thatch, Wyoming. As a crowning insult, the woman in Thatch was actually Ron's legal wife. Avery, a flower of Southern womanhood, had been nothing more than Ron Raven's long-term mistress.

Ron had been downright rough around the edges when he first came into Avery's life but for some mysterious reason, she'd been captivated by Ron's self-confidence and aura of bravado. When Avery announced her engagement, Paul pointed out to her that Ron was as brash as he was bullheaded. Avery had laughed and replied that her fiancé's brashness was one of the things she liked best about him. She'd claimed it was refreshing after too many years of being surrounded by men whose energy had been sapped by generations of keeping up appearances under the merciless Georgia sun.

Paul had to admit that Ron had been handsome enough back in those days. It was infuriating, though, that Ron's magnetism hadn't faded with the passing years as his waistline expanded and his hair grayed. What the hell had been the root of his appeal? True, the guy had been blessed with bedroom eyes. True, his bluff manner somehow conveyed a hint of the intellectual power and business smarts hidden behind the jovial facade. But Ron had looked every one of his fifty-seven years. What's more, he'd developed the beginning of arthritis in his knees and he'd lost his springy stride. His hands had been stubby and gnarled with calluses. He'd looked, in fact, as if he actually *worked* on his damned cattle ranch.

The memory of Ron's frequent trips to the Wyoming

ranch and the rival wife he'd kept there was enough to make Paul's heart pump fast with rage. He still couldn't believe how Raven had fooled them all. To think that Ron had spent twenty-seven years with his legal wife tucked away at the Flying W Ranch, while Avery stayed in Chicago, living in a fool's paradise with no legal claim to the wealth and prestige that her skills as a hostess had helped Ron secure. And all the time he, Paul Fairfax, had been adding class to Raven Enterprises—not to mention lending legitimacy to the scam of Ron's second bigamous marriage—by acting as business partner to the cheating son of a bitch.

Even if Paul could have forgiven Ron for deceiving Avery, he could never forgive his former business partner for the fact that he'd exposed the entire Fairfax family to public humiliation. Ron's bigamy shamed everyone it touched, leaving Paul to go through life knowing that people he met were sniggering behind their hands because his sister had never actually been married to the man she lived with for over a quarter of a century. Paul's blood pressure had skyrocketed in the wake of that humiliating discovery and he'd never been able to bring it down since. Another injury to lay directly at Ron's door, Paul thought angrily. Taking blood pressure pills was something only a loser should have to do and he was absolutely not a loser.

He mopped away the first welcome beads of sweat, admiring his own elegant fingers and buffed, neatly-trimmed nails as he did so. Unlike Ron, he would never be confused for a man who worked with his hands. The thought comforted him slightly. What the hell. Ron was officially dead and Paul was very much alive, which gave him the last laugh after all. Best of all, he was finally in charge of Raven Enterprises, after years suffering as Ron's junior partner. He'd run into a couple of financial rough spots over the past couple of months, but he'd soon be raking in the big bucks. To hell with all those tight-ass bankers who wouldn't lend him fresh investment funds. When the Arran project came on line, they'd be singing a different song.

His mood lightening as the endorphins kicked in, Paul clicked the remote fastened to the exercise bike. He muted the sound until the ads finished and the news came back on. The weather forecaster promised a day of high temperatures, low cloud and lots of humidity. Paul pulled a face. Jeez, what a miserable climate the city of Chicago had to endure. The summer was barely more tolerable than the winter. Thank God for air-conditioning.

"Let's go now to our affiliate in Denver," the anchor said, "where we're following a breaking story."

Paul frowned, irritated by the interruption. He tuned in to the local Chicago news precisely so that he wouldn't have to be taken to Denver, or anywhere else. Who the hell cared about breaking news a thousand miles to the west? He resigned himself to watching pictures of forests burning because some idiot had thrown away a lighted cigarette.

"It was reported just before dawn that the mayor of Denver has been murdered," a reporter for the affiliate intoned, standing in front of a large Tudor-style home on a sunny street lined with huge old trees.

"The police department is now confirming that the violent death of Jason Hamilton, one of the nation's most popular mayors, was caused by multiple stab wounds inflicted by an unknown assailant. The mayor was struck quote several times, the blows landing in the general area of the heart and lungs. The police department isn't saying anything more about the precise cause of death until the preliminary autopsy results are complete, which should be some time tomorrow morning. In the meantime, there are no official suspects, but the chief of police has confirmed that the mayor's wife, Chloe Hamilton, was found by the couple's nanny with a bloody knife in her hands, kneeling beside her husband's body.

"Chloe Hamilton won the gold medal for downhill skiing in the 1998 Winter Olympics, as well as a silver and a bronze in the same Olympics. In addition, she won a bronze medal during the 1992 winter Olympics in Albertville, France, when she was only sixteen. Before being elected mayor of Denver, Jason Hamilton successfully developed property in Telluride and Steamboat Springs...."

Jason Hamilton was dead! Paul stared at the screen and the bike jerked to a halt as he forgot to pedal.

His stomach roiled and for a dreadful moment he was afraid he would throw up. What a fucking disaster. He had every cent he could scrape up invested in Sam DiVoli's new building project, and with Jason Hamilton dead, they could probably whistle their chances of rezoning approval into the wind.

Paul switched off the power to the bike and listened intently to the rest of the report from Denver, where it was still only six-thirty in the morning. You didn't have to search too hard for a subtext to realize that Chloe Hamilton was the prime suspect in the death of her husband. Paul didn't put as much faith in the news reports as he would have three months earlier. Having lived through the media frenzy that followed Ron Raven's disappearance, he knew better than to believe everything he heard on any news program. It was possible that Chloe Hamilton had killed her husband, but he wouldn't put money on it. Personally, he would be more inclined to believe Edgar Showalter had ordered the hit. God knew, Edgar was ruthless enough. Not to mention furious that Sam DiVoli had bought the Arran property out from under his nose, acting on a tip that came directly from Jason Hamilton.

Slinging his towel around his neck, Paul hurried into the library, barely noticing his wife when he passed her coming out of the master bedroom.

Julia gave him a nervous smile. "Paul, do you remember that we're having dinner with the Feldmanns tonight? It's black tie. Eight o'clock."

He didn't remember because Julia had never mentioned the invitation until right now. She knew how much he disliked the Feldmanns, so she had clearly hoped to corner him into accepting an invitation he would otherwise have insisted on refusing.

"Why the hell are we having dinner with the Feldmanns? You know the only reason they ever invite us is because they want a donation for one of their damned charities."

Julia's thin, pointed face took on the mulish expression he so disliked. There was a price attached to keeping a forty-nine-year-old body fitting into size four designer clothes, and Julia's face was paying it. "The Feldmanns know everyone who's anyone in Chicago. There are going to be lots of people there with money to invest—"

There was so much else going on right now that he couldn't be bothered to disabuse Julia of her naive notions of how capital was actually raised. "Okay, okay. I'll be home at seven."

Julia was shocked into silence. He shut the library door before she could find her voice. His wife speechless was a rare enough occurrence that he needed to savor the moment. He had Sam's number on his speed-dial, and he barely waited for the door to cut off the view of Julia's startled expression before he pressed the appropriate key.

"Hello." Sam picked up the phone right away, but he sounded both sleepy and disgruntled.

"This is Paul Fairfax. You need to switch on your TV right now. Jason Hamilton's dead. He's been murdered."

"Jason's dead? *Murdered?* Christ almighty. There has to be a mistake!"

"It's all over the news. He was killed last night. Stabbed to death in the mayoral mansion."

"Jesus H. Christ, that's impossible! I just had dinner with the mayor last night. I had some friends in from D.C. and we were talking about Jason running for the Senate—"

"Well, he's dead now." Paul wasn't interested in hearing how close Jason and Sam had been, and even less interested in hearing about the mayor's ambitions to hold national political office. Bottom line, Sam's friendship with the mayor meant zilch now that the guy was dead. It could even be a negative as political factions lined up behind new players.

"I guess that means we can kiss goodbye to getting the Arran property rezoned any time in the next year or two." Paul didn't bother to hide his resentment that Sam DiVoli had taken so goddamn long to get the zoning variances he'd promised to deliver when Paul forked over money he goddamn couldn't afford. "The zoning committee is stacked with Edgar Showalter's people, and they'll never grant us a variance."

Sam swore with truly remarkable variety and fluency.

"They'll stonewall us at best," he said when he finally ran out of curses. "And every day we can't get started is costing us money. Worst case, they'll flat out reject the rezoning, and then the project is dead."

Paul's stomach knotted with dread. He simply couldn't allow this project to turn sour. "There's going to be a couple of weeks of confusion in the wake of Jason's death," he pointed out. "We need to get to somebody powerful on the zoning committee before Showalter has them lined up and on the record as opposed to the Arran rezoning."

"Yeah, great idea." Sam's voice oozed sarcasm. "Which councilman do you suggest we approach while they're all busy issuing statements mourning the loss of the mayor." He broke off. "Damn, Jason was a good guy. I'm sorry he's gone. He would have made a truly fine senator."

Paul couldn't spare time to waste mourning the mayor. "What's the name of the annoying little Nazi who guarded access to Jason as if he was in charge of the gateway to heaven?"

"Fred Mitchell," Sam said. "He is…correct that. He *was* the mayor's chief of staff. Jesus! I can't believe Jason's dead. Son of a gun, he was right here, enjoying dinner, less than twelve hours ago. He was smart and honest, too. You don't get many politicians like that. Especially not with approval ratings like Jason was getting. Dammit, his death is a real loss to the community."

Not to mention a real loss to the Arran project. Sam needed to get his thinking focused on what was important here, namely that there was nobody left to get their project the zoning variance it needed and that Paul's financial future was on the line. It was a hell of a nuisance that he had to rely on Sam, Paul reflected, but he really had no choice. The man had a knowledge of the inner workings of Denver city government that was second to none. Paul sure as hell hoped the guy would be able to put that knowledge to good use and pull a rabbit out of the hat. The financial consequences of an implosion of the Arran project were more than Paul could bear to contemplate.

"I'm going to fly out to Denver right now," Paul said. Sam might know Denver politics, but when the going got really tough, Sam backed off. He would apply pressure, but only so much. Paul, on the other hand, had discovered that if bribes didn't work, a touch of polite blackmail could usually turn the trick. Sam was one of those naive, old-fashioned types who scorned bribes and didn't understand blackmail—although he knew exactly where all the bodies were buried.

"I can maybe catch the ten-thirty flight." Paul was already walking toward his bedroom. "With the time difference, I could be in Denver before noon. I'll go straight to your offices. We need to plan our strategy."

"What are you smokin', Paul? Nobody in the mayor's office is going to be meeting with developers today. For Christ's sake, Jason Hamilton's dead! Show the man some respect, will you?"

"I'm sure he was the best mayor in the country. But showing him respect isn't going to get the Arran zoning sewn up before Edgar Showalter can fuck us over. We need to get somebody on the zoning committee to sign off on the paperwork. Today, if possible. I'll see you this afternoon, Sam." Paul hung up the phone before DiVoli could object some more. Maybe the millions at stake didn't matter all that much to Sam, but they sure as hell mattered to Paul.

He walked through the empty bedroom and into the shower. Julia was already dressed. He could hear her down in the kitchen, grinding beans for their thousand-fucking-dollar super-deluxe espresso machine. He wouldn't tell his wife he was going to miss the Feldmanns' dinner, Paul decided. He'd call once he landed in Denver. That would teach her to try to manipulate him into accepting invitations from people she knew he didn't like.

Paul turned the water on full blast and calculated how much he and Sam DiVoli might have to shell out in bribes to get the rezoning sewn up. Right now he was so strapped for cash that it might even be difficult to come up with a bribe big enough to do the trick. Maybe they should bag the idea of bribery and move straight on to blackmail. If that was the route they took, Sam would be crucial to their success. If you were important enough to have a secret, and you lived in Denver, Sam knew your secret. He was a useful business partner to have, Paul reflected, provided he didn't get sidetracked by an annoying attack of civic responsibility. Sometimes Sam DiVoli was just too damned honest to be reliable.

Paul couldn't afford to let this become one of those occasions on which Sam was afflicted with a conscience. The entire financial future of Raven Enterprises was riding on the success or failure of the Arran project.

He'd already suffered the public humiliation of being identified as the business partner of a bigamist. He sure as hell wasn't going to go bankrupt because that same damn bigamist wasn't around to tell him where to invest his money. Whatever the business and financial communities might think, Paul Fairfax was every bit as smart an investor as Ron Raven had ever been. The Arran project would prove that to all the doubters and then Raven Enterprises could be renamed Fairfax Enterprises, which it should have been from the first.

Bottom line: the Arran project simply could not be allowed to fail. It was Paul's ticket out of a deep financial hole and into a promising future.

Five

Liam drove slowly along the twists and turns of Coyote Lane, looking for 356, the house belonging to the Mallorys, Chloe's sister and brother-in-law. The road was narrow and gravel-surfaced, in keeping with Conifer's past as a frontier town, but the houses still managed to project an aura of yuppie success with front yards expensively landscaped to look untamed.

In keeping with the phony rural atmosphere, there were no sidewalks, no mailboxes and the house numbering seemed expressly designed to be invisible from the road. This last feature would have been infuriating except that it provided Liam with an excuse to brake often and scope out his surroundings, all the while creating the impression that he was simply searching for his destination.

Once he had the house located, Liam checked again for any cops in the vicinity. There were only three vehicles within sight and two of them seemed harmless: an empty Mercedes parked in a driveway and a landscaping truck at the far end of the cul-de-sac. Liam could hear members of the landscaping crew calling out to each other in Spanish as they loaded equipment onto the truck in preparation for leaving. The men were working too hard and much too efficiently to be undercover cops, Liam decided.

By contrast, the phone company van parked a couple of houses down from the Mallorys struck him as highly suspicious. In his experience, phone companies no longer made service calls after six, whatever type of emergency the customer pleaded. In addition, there was no activity around this particular vehicle. The man in the driver's seat had been staring at the same clipboard of papers ever since Liam first noticed him. Eighty-twenty the guy was a cop, Liam decided. Thank goodness there was no reason for him or his car to provoke any special interest.

Taking care not to glance back toward the cop, he parked his BMW right in the driveway and jogged up the front steps. The Mallorys' front door was opened by a man about Liam's own age, holding a small boy in his arms. The boy's nose was painted blue and he had green stars stuck on his cheeks, but otherwise he seemed a pretty regular kid bordering on the cute, in fact. Not that Liam considered himself an expert on toddler cuteness. His attitude toward kids was pretty similar to his attitude toward tiger cubs: they looked adorable, were incredibly difficult to raise and could bite off chunks of your flesh if you didn't treat them right.

"You must be Liam," the man said, shifting the toddler to a different arm so that he could shake Liam's hand. "I'm Tom Mallory, Chloe's brother-in-law."

"Hey, Tom. Good to meet you."

"And this is Peter, our son. Chloe's nephew." Tom jiggled his arms, bouncing Peter, who didn't crack a smile.

Liam told himself it was ridiculous to feel intimidated by a toddler with a blue nose. "Hi, Peter, how are you doing?"

The toddler stared at him in silence. Not hostile, exactly, but definitely assessing. Liam decided that a tiger cub would have been easier. At least nobody would have expected him to hold a conversation with a tiger.

"Come on in," Tom said, stepping to one side, apparently not expecting his son to speak. "This is a terrible situation, isn't it?"

Liam nodded, relieved to turn his attention back to a grown-up. "Yes. It's bad enough that Chloe's lost her husband, but it's worse that she isn't getting a moment's peace and quiet to grieve for him."

"Jason was a good guy and a terrific mayor. His passing is a terrible loss for a lot of people." Tom frowned and then shook his head. "Anyway, it's great to know you're on Chloe's team. Her whole family is very relieved that she's moved quickly to get the legal help she needs instead of relying on the fact that she's innocent to protect herself."

Liam certainly agreed with that. "Innocence is a lousy defense if it's all you have to bring to the table. But I'm hopeful we'll soon find concrete evidence to point the cops in another direction."

"God, I hope so. And it can't be too soon as far as I'm concerned. Anyway, Lexie's just finished feeding the kids their dinner, so Sophie is good to go whenever you're ready to take her." Tom shoved a plastic horse out of the way with his foot, sending it skittering toward the staircase. "Sorry about the mess. Dinner time is always chaotic around here and tonight Lexie is trying to give Sophie a bit more one-on-one attention than usual, so clearing up has to wait."

"Don't apologize. I'm awestruck by people who can cope with even one child, let alone multiple preschoolers."

"You don't have kids of your own?" Tom asked.

"I've never been married," Liam responded, as if that answered the question. He had known the truth of his fatherhood for less than twelve hours and already he could see that everyday conversation was going to be filled with booby traps. His choice seemed to be constant lies or a head-on clash with Chloe. At some point she would have to accept that he wasn't willing to abide by her wish that Sophie should spend her life in the mistaken belief that Jason had been her biological father. But for tonight, he'd given Chloe his word and he would stick to it. Eventually he would have to decide whether to be actively involved in Sophie's life. He was pretty sure he'd make a lousy father, but at least he wanted his daughter to know his name, for God's sake.

The parallels to his own father's life were too powerful to ignore, and not at all attractive. In the wake of their father's death, Megan had suggested that it might have been a desire to protect his existing family that had propelled Ron into a twenty-six year pattern of criminal deception. Liam had found that explanation incredible two months ago. Now he was having second thoughts. Had the whole bigamous mess of Ron Raven's life started as innocently as his father not wanting to hurt the people he loved? It was possible, Liam conceded grudgingly. After all, that was exactly what Chloe had chosen to do for Sophie—hide the truth beneath a more palatable sugarcoating. And

Chloe's ploy would have worked, if her husband hadn't been murdered—just as Ron Raven's ploy had worked for more than two decades.

Liam circled a giant plastic tub of toys deposited in the center of the hallway, not willing to cut either Chloe or his father any slack. Ron had screwed up, literally, and then lied to cover his ass. Ron's possible desire to protect his wife and children from being hurt didn't excuse either his initial adultery or the next quarter century of deception. Chloe's choices, in Liam's opinion, had been just as wrong.

He followed Tom into the family room, his breath catching in his throat when he saw a little girl sitting on the floor surrounded by an array of Barbie dolls. Chloe had claimed that Sophie was an amazing child and it seemed she hadn't been exaggerating. This little girl was picture-perfect, from her mop of golden curls to her tiny button nose and petal-soft rosy lips.

She jumped to her feet and greeted them both with a beaming smile the moment she noticed them. His daughter seemed to be friendly as well as adorably cute, Liam thought with a stab of irrational pride.

"Hi," she said to him, waving the naked Barbie clutched in her left hand. "I'm Morgan. I'm four. Soon I'll be five." She held up four fingers on her right hand and then pointed toward Peter. "My bruvver is three. It's a long time till his next birfday." She adjusted her fingers to provide Liam with a demonstration of the number three.

The child's name was Morgan? The delectable little girl was not, it seemed, Chloe's child or his daughter. Liam pushed aside a twinge of regret and tried to decide how he was supposed to respond to Morgan's overture.

"I'm thirty-five," he said finally, since age seemed big in her life at this point.

Morgan's eyes opened wide. "That's old," she informed him. "That's *very* old."

"Er...yes, I guess it is."

"My grandpa is old. My grandma is old. My nana is old. My poppa is old. Miss Rose is old—"

"Who is Miss Rose?" Liam asked, interrupting what threatened to become an endless litany of the aged. "Is she your teacher?"

"No!" Morgan chuckled at his ridiculous mistake. "Miss Rose is my dog. She frew up on Mommy's shoes 'cos she ate Peter's chicken nuggets. Mommy shut her in the laundry room."

Liam had no idea how to respond to this wealth of information. Tom, on the other hand, simply laughed.

"The bit about throwing up on Mommy's shoes might have been more than we needed to know, Morgan, love. Peter, you can play with your sister for a while." He set his son on the floor and dragged a box of wooden blocks into the center of the room. "Build a house for Morgan's dolls," he suggested. "Build a red house."

Peter, clearly a man of few words, sat down without complaint and carefully selected a dozen or so red blocks. "He's very good with his colors," Tom said proudly. "He knows them all."

"Er...great." Liam felt as if he'd been plunged into a foreign country where he spoke only a textbook version of the language and didn't quite grasp the native customs. According to Morgan, Peter was three years old. Didn't all three year olds know their colors?

"Do you like how I fixed Barbie's hair?" Not wanting

to be overlooked, Morgan extended her naked doll for closer inspection and Liam noticed that the stiff blond hair was haphazardly decorated with glittery pins.

"Er...very nice," he said.

Tom smiled. "Barbie is beautiful, honey bun. I love all those pink diamonds. Why don't you try dressing her in a skirt to match? Then she can go to the ball."

Morgan frowned. "She's not Cinderella. She's Barbie."

"Right. But Barbie can go to a ball if she wants."

Morgan considered this in silence for a second or two, then shrugged. "Daddy, tell Peter not to pull the heads off of my Barbies."

"Peter, are you listening? No chopping off Barbie's head, okay?"

Peter interrupted his turret building long enough to give a reluctant nod.

"Okay, be good both of you. Don't fight. I'll be right back." Tom appeared unaware of anything in the least strange about his conversation with his kids. Maybe discussion of head-removal was a normal exchange when you were dealing with preschoolers? Since he'd been thirteen by the time Megan was four, Liam had spent very little time playing with his sister but for sure he couldn't recall harboring any murderous impulses toward her Barbie dolls.

Liam followed Tom out of the family room, trying to remember when he'd last spoken to a human being under the age of twelve. He supposed it must have happened at least once or twice during the past fifteen years, but he'd be damned if he could remember the occasion.

A slender, pretty woman sat at the kitchen table across from a tiny little girl with poker straight, mouse-brown hair who was coloring with magic markers. The child's head was bent so intently over her task that it was impossible to see her face. The little girl didn't send a single glance toward the newcomers, but the woman rose to her feet, her smile not quite hiding both fatigue and worry.

"Liam?" She pushed her chair away from the table and stood up, holding out her hand. "Hi, I'm Alexia, Chloe's sister. I'm so glad you've agreed to help us. I've seen you on TV several times and your glowing reputation precedes you."

Liam let the possible reference to Sherri Norquist's trial slide over him. Surprisingly, it barely stung. "With any luck we'll be able to get Chloe's problems squared away fast," he said. "Then your sister won't need my help or anyone else's."

Alexia didn't look reassured. "I'm not optimistic about this being resolved quickly," she said, her voice low. "The whole situation is made-for-TV perfect and, boy, are they reveling in the mess." She glanced quickly toward Sophie, who gave no sign that she'd even noticed Liam's arrival in the room, much less that she was paying attention to the conversation. Once again, Liam was forcefully reminded of his own family's situation only two months earlier. Media intrusion then had been a nightmare for his mother and sister. He could barely imagine how much worse it would be if you were trying to shield young children from a brutal reality.

"I have a couple of questions for you," Alexia murmured, walking over to the sink where she stood staring at the dish detergent as if she couldn't remember why she was there.

Liam followed, gesturing toward Sophie when Alexia

didn't speak. "Is your niece going to be upset at being picked up by a complete stranger?"

Alexia shook her head. "I've told her the truth—that you're here to drive her home—so I'm sure she'll go with you willingly. She's taking the loss of her father very hard. She's been frighteningly quiet today." She gave a quick shrug. "Although I guess that's a dumb thing to say. How else could she take Jason's death except badly?"

"It's a difficult situation all around and the media attention makes everything that much more difficult." Liam winced at the platitude but he was sneaking covert glances at his daughter and didn't have much brain power to spare for conversing.

"Especially in our family. Did you know that our father—Chloe's and mine—is the deputy superintendent of schools in Colorado Springs?"

"No, I wasn't aware that Chloe had parents in the state."

"We all moved here in the late eighties, when Chloe started serious training for the Olympics. Once we were here, we fell in love with Colorado and never left."

He'd been ignorant of that, along with virtually every other fact about Chloe's life. "Is your father's profession significant for some reason?" he asked.

"Well, just that he's such an important figure in their community and the notoriety of Jason's murder is already proving horribly difficult for him and my mother." Alexia sighed. "Dad always tries so hard to set a good example for his students. Family is really important to him and to my mother. This is just the pits."

Tough for dad, maybe, but the situation wasn't exactly easy on Chloe, either. "I'll do my best to prevent the situation getting any worse than it already is," Liam said coolly.

"I recommend, however, that you and your parents avoid piling any more burdens on your sister's shoulders, even by implication. She's carrying a heavy enough load as it is."

Alexia flushed. "I'm sorry. I must have sounded like a jerk just now. That's what comes of listening to my mother cry into the phone all afternoon. She's terribly worried about Chloe, of course."

But not worried enough to have driven up from Colorado Springs, apparently. Liam stowed that fact away for future reference. "I'm optimistic that I'll be able to keep your sister out of jail," he said. "You can pass that information on to your parents if it will make them feel any better."

Alexia stared at him in mute horror and he realized that, despite everything, the possibility of her sister ending up behind bars hadn't hit home until this moment. She rubbed her forehead, as if trying to send away a sudden headache.

"The talk show hosts have been salivating at the possibility of Chloe in prison for the past couple of hours," Alexia admitted. "The fact is, I was so angry at their outrageous comments that I dismissed everything they said as ridiculous."

"Most of what they said probably was. Still, we have to manage the timing of your sister's arrest—if it comes—in such a way that the police have no excuse to hold her in jail overnight while we wait for a bond hearing. That can be trickier than it sounds. Accused murderers are usually required to wait trial in custody, but I'm optimistic we can persuade a judge not to lock Chloe up."

Alexia took a few seconds to absorb the horrifying

prospect of her sister awaiting trial behind bars. Apparently, she couldn't handle the implications and changed the topic. "It's mind-blowing that the media can use Jason's murder as entertainment," she said. "Chloe was the most loyal wife you could imagine, but the TV reporting today managed to make her sound like a nympho on steroids. They interviewed every guy in Colorado she ever dated from the time she was sixteen and edited the sound bites so you'd have thought she spent her life hopping from bar to drunken party and back again. How the hell do they think she won her Olympic medals? By falling out of bed and whizzing down the ski slopes between parties? Have they any idea—any remote clue—what it takes to train for such dangerous and grueling races?"

The annoying thing about the media, Liam reflected cynically, was not that they were so often wrong, but that they were occasionally dead right. Alexia seemed to think Chloe was a saint; Sophie's existence proved she was, at the very least, capable of breaking her marriage vows and committing adultery. He sneaked another glance at the top of his daughter's head, which was all he could see since she was still coloring with fanatic concentration. He doubted if Sophie could hear what was being said and he reassured himself that there was no chance that a three-year-old—an age level that apparently had trouble distinguishing red from blue—would be able to grasp the significance of the conversation.

Liam forced himself to turn away from his daughter. There was no point in shattering Alexia's glossy image of her sister. In fact, from a defense attorney's point of view, family and relatives who firmly believed in a suspect's innocence were valuable assets and he needed to bolster Alexia's good opinion of her sister.

"The reporters are probably annoyed that they haven't been able to find Chloe to interview her," Liam said. "Unfortunately, when they can't get hard information, they tend to move on to speculation."

Alexia grimaced. "Yes, we learned that when Chloe was part of the Olympic ski team. In fact, I was thinking the best way to counteract the harmful publicity might be to choose one of the more sympathetic reporters and give them an exclusive interview."

"Bad idea," Liam said quickly. "Trust me, any sort of family interview right now would be a very bad idea."

"Why?" Tom had joined them. He put his arm around his wife's shoulders and she leaned against him gratefully. "That's what Chloe used to do when the sports journalists got on her case. Her PR rep would call a few journalists and get some positive articles out there."

"This is different." Liam tried not to sound impatient. "We're not talking about putting a stop to rumors that Chloe is overtrained, or having a hard time with her left knee joint. We're talking about avoiding an arrest for murdering her spouse."

"We could find somebody friendly," Tom persisted. "Somebody from ESPN who remembers her warmly—"

"Take my advice on this, no reporter is genuinely sympathetic to a suspected murderer. Worse, when the piece airs, the police would be watching and analyzing every word that comes out of Chloe's mouth."

"But all she's going to say in an interview is that she's innocent!" Alexia protested. "And she can't be tripped up because she *didn't do it!*"

"The first lesson for you to learn right now is that innocence doesn't count for much in a court of law, and even less in the court of public opinion." Liam spoke flatly, no longer trying to win over Alexia and her husband. On the question of media contact, he was adamant. Chloe had spent most of her young adult life in the spotlight and it was natural for her family to think they knew how to handle reporters. They didn't, not in the wake of a celebrity murder.

"I'm giving you advice based on my experience trying other high profile criminal cases," Liam said. "I guarantee that there are plenty of secrets concerning her marriage that Chloe doesn't want revealed, whether or not they relate to Jason's murder."

"But—"

"No buts. As long as I'm her defense lawyer, Chloe will refuse any and all interviews. I can't force you two to do the same, but I'm strongly requesting it. If you want to help your sister, don't speak to the press. Or the police, for that matter. Your only smart response to any and all questions is no comment, whoever is asking—friendly neighbor, church minister, cop, reporter, one answer fits all. No comment. Practice saying it until it's a reflex. Advise your parents to do the same."

Tom started to protest again, but Alexia put her hand on his arm, silencing him. "Then what options do we have? Sit back and wait for Chloe to be tried and convicted by the media?"

"We can't tackle the media or the cops in a vacuum. We need a comprehensive strategy. I'll have a better idea of exactly what we're facing when Chloe and I have had a chance to talk."

"You haven't discussed the case with Chloe yet?" Tom sounded incredulous. "What have you been doing all day, for Christ's sake?"

"Serving my existing clients." Liam kept his voice level. "I spent most of today in court. Consequently, I don't know enough of the facts of this case to have even the outline of a strategy."

"I'm sorry." Tom gulped in air and shoved his hand through his hair. "This situation is getting to me. I didn't mean to criticize."

"That's okay. It's stressful for everyone. However, right now we're wasting valuable time. I need to get your niece back to her mother."

"Like I said, the poor little thing has barely spoken since she got here." Alexia dried her hands on the dishtowel, although she hadn't actually washed them. "Normally she's as chatty as Morgan and the two of them love to play together. But not today."

Liam followed Alexia's worried gaze toward the child at the table. Sophie was still coloring. Despite his inexperience with kids, even he was able to recognize her extreme focus as an avoidance tactic.

Ignoring the roller coaster that had begun operation in his stomach the second he walked into the kitchen, he crossed the room and drew up a chair next to Sophie. Next to his daughter.

"Hi, Sophie," he said, hoping she couldn't hear the squeak in his voice. He cleared his throat. "My name is Liam. I'm...um...a friend of your mom."

Sophie said nothing. She continued to color exactly as if he hadn't spoken—as if he didn't exist. By comparison, blue-nosed Peter had been positively friendly.

Liam felt sweat gather under his shirt collar. He was astonished to discover that he wanted, quite desperately, for Sophie to acknowledge his presence.

"Your mom asked me to pick you up and drive you home," he said. "Well, not home exactly. I'm going to take you to the place where your mom is staying for the night."

Silence.

"Your mom is really anxious to see you." He wondered if *anxious* was too hard a word for Sophie to understand. "She's waiting for us," he elaborated. "If you've finished your picture, we need to get going."

Sophie finally looked up from her coloring. Her face was pale and pinched with worry, but that wasn't what made Liam feel as if he'd been kicked in the stomach. It was her eyes that had him gaping. They were huge, long-lashed and green. His sister Megan's eyes staring out at him from his daughter's face. Megan's eyes, displaying Sophie's heart-wrenching grief.

"Mommy isn't waiting. She's gone away," Sophie said with unsettling calm.

"Well, yes, I know she went away," Liam agreed. "She's kind of busy right now. That's why she sent me to fetch you."

Sophie's expression remained shuttered, as if she struggled to hold an unbearable weight of sadness inside. "Mommy is wiv my daddy. They're in heaven. That's far away."

"Sweetheart, no!" Alexia swooped across the kitchen and hugged Sophie to her chest. "My God, I had no idea she was thinking that." She rocked her niece back and forth, tears wetting her own cheeks although Sophie didn't cry. "Sweetheart, your mommy is fine. She's waiting to see you, I promise!"

"She's in heaven," Sophie repeated, but this time there was a faint question in her voice. "Wiv my daddy."

Liam knelt beside Sophie's chair, reaching instinctively for her hands. They were ice-cold and he chafed them as he spoke. "Sophie, I promise, your mom is waiting for you in Denver. She's sad that your father is..." *Dead? Murdered? Gone to heaven?* Jesus, what euphemisms did you use to explain death to a three-year-old? Liam swallowed. "Your mom is waiting for you," he finished lamely.

"We should have realized Sophie wouldn't understand if her mother vanished almost the moment we told her about Jason," Tom said. He rubbed his hand across the stubble on his cheeks. "Jeez, we really blew that, didn't we?"

Alexia combed her fingers through her niece's flyaway hair. "Sophie, sweetie, your mommy isn't in heaven. She's right here, I promise."

"No, Mommy isn't here," Sophie said with incontrovertible logic. "Only you and Uncle Tom are here. And the other man." She nodded toward Liam, finally acknowledging his existence.

"Well, she's not right here in the kitchen, but Mommy is very close by. She isn't with your daddy in heaven, I promise. She's in Denver, like Liam said, waiting to see you."

Sophie slowly put down her marker. "If my mommy isn't in heaven, why did she go away?"

"She had grown-up stuff she needed to take care of." Alexia chose her words with visible care. "She wanted to stay with you, but she just couldn't. That's why she sent Liam to get you."

"I don't know him." Sophie kept her gaze fixed on her aunt.

"He's a good friend of your mommy's. Can you say his name?"

Sophie nodded. "Liam. It's easy-peasey."

"Right. Liam will take you in his car. It'll be a little way to drive, but not nearly as far as going to Nana and Poppa's house."

Sophie said nothing, but Liam thought he detected a slight reduction in the tension that had held her spine straight and her tiny, skinny body so rigid that it looked brittle. The oddest ache was lodged in the pit of his stomach and he fought the urge to push Alexia aside and take his daughter into his arms. It was physically painful for him to see her so miserable.

He coped with the pain the only way he knew how, by becoming even more practical than usual. "It's clear we need to get Sophie reunited with her mother as quickly as possible," he said briskly. "Let's get moving, shall we? Chloe said to be sure I didn't forget to bring the stuffed rabbit Sophie takes to bed."

"She's talking about Bobby Bunny," Alexia said at once. "He's in Sophie's backpack. I'll get him—"

"Wait. There's one more problem." With an effort, Liam moved away from his daughter. "There's a phone company van parked opposite your driveway. I think the repairman is really an undercover cop, watching the front of your house."

Tom's brows creased in fury. "The hell there is!"

Liam grabbed Tom's arm before he could pull back the kitchen curtain. "Don't! Whatever you do, don't let the cop know he's been spotted."

Tom shrank back as if he'd been scalded. "Sorry. I wasn't thinking. Which seems to be an ongoing problem for me right now." He pounded his fist into the palm of his hand.

"Okay, Liam, since the cop's parked out front, and so is your car, how can you avoid being seen when you leave?"

"I can't. If I walk out of the front door with Sophie, the cop will guess right away that I'm taking her to her mother and he's going to tail me straight back to the safe haven I've established for Chloe."

"So what the heck can you do?"

"My plan is to leave via the front door, but I won't take Sophie with me. That way, the cop will have no reason to follow me. I'll drive my car to a nearby street. Somewhere close, but safely out of sight of the cop. I suggest you sneak out the rear of the house carrying Sophie. You can cut across your backyard on foot—maybe you'll need to cut through a couple of neighboring backyards as well—and meet up with me at some designated point to hand off Sophie."

"Yeah, that will work," Alexia said. For the first time, the glance she directed at Liam was entirely approving.

"I hope so," Liam said. "You two know the area around this house, and I don't. Where do you suggest we meet up? Where's the nearest place that's invisible to the cop, but reasonably easy to access from your backyard?"

Tom thought for a moment. "The properties in this neighborhood aren't fenced, so I can cut through the yard of the house behind us and come out on Blue Spruce Court. It's almost no distance."

"I'll get a sweater for Sophie while you and Tom work out your exact meeting place." Alexia held out her hand. "Sophie, honey, come with me. We'll find your backpack and you can say goodbye to Morgan and Peter. Maybe Morgan can come and play with you tomorrow or the next day?"

"When is it tomorrow?" Sophie asked, but she slid off

the chair and took her aunt's hand almost eagerly. Liam could see a gleam of hope in her expression that had been totally absent before.

"Tomorrow comes after you've been to sleep for one whole night."

"Bobby wants to sleep in our own house."

"I know he does, honey. But Bobby likes the place you're sleeping tonight almost as much as he likes your house. He thinks it's a great place for a vacation."

"Are we going to Disney World?" Sophie said with what struck Liam as breathtaking lack of logic.

Alexia, however, had no difficulty following her niece's train of thought. "It's not that sort of a vacation, sweetie. Tonight you're going to be with Mommy. That's even better than Disney World, isn't it?"

Sophie nodded vigorously. "Yes."

Alexia was already out of the kitchen when she suddenly swung around. "I just thought of something. Do you have a car seat, Liam?"

"No." He frowned. "Damn, that's a problem. Apart from the safety issues, if Sophie isn't properly strapped in, the cops have a valid reason to stop me."

"We have a spare car seat in the garage," Tom said. "You can borrow it."

"Great, but how do we get the seat into my car?"

"I could carry it…" Tom suggested.

"In addition to Sophie?"

"Sophie weighs less than thirty pounds and this particular car seat is pretty light." Tom turned to his wife. "But we'd better bag the backpack, honey, at least for tonight. Sophie and Bobby Bunny plus the car seat are about my limit."

"There's nothing in the backpack that's essential anyway." Alexia held out her hand. "Liam, it was great to meet you. Ask Chloe to call me ASAP, please."

"I will, but remember that the two of you should only use cell phones and be careful what you say to each other. Don't discuss the case. You, too, Tom. From now on, don't say anything on a phone call that you wouldn't want to hear played back in a court of law."

Muttering under her breath, Alexia took Sophie to retrieve Bobby Bunny. Tom looked shell-shocked, as if the warning about the phone had been the final straw that brought home to him the seriousness of his sister-in-law's plight. "Chloe's really in trouble, isn't she?"

"When a murder investigation is under way, it helps not to have been found kneeling next to your dead husband with a bloody knife in your hand." Liam tried not to sound irritated, but Tom and Alexia's almost willful naiveté was beginning to wear on him. "Okay, we need to pick up the pace here, Tom. Give me directions on exactly where you're going to meet me, please."

Tom managed to give clear, detailed instructions and left the house through the garage carrying Sophie at the same time as Liam exited alone via the front door. The phone company van, he saw, had moved down to the end of the cul-de-sac and was now parked alongside a gray metal junction box. The supposed repairman was talking into the sort of big phone with dangling wires that repairmen usually carried for testing purposes.

All very authentic, Liam reflected cynically. However, the guy had made the mistake of directing the beam of his powerful flood lamp not onto the switch box, but toward the Mallorys' driveway. That pushed the odds the guy was a cop to about ninety-nine to one, Liam concluded.

He resisted the temptation to walk over and ask when phone service was going to be restored. Playing games might provide short-term satisfaction but tended to piss off the cops and cause long-term harm.

He got into the car and drove to the end of the road, swinging around a hilly curve, and coming back up along Blue Spruce Court, a short road that more or less paralleled Coyote Lane. According to Tom, the backyard of 2771 Blue Spruce abutted directly onto his own backyard, separated only by a ditch, a few pine trees and some brambles.

Fortunately, the phone company truck hadn't attempted to follow him. Maybe he'd exaggerated the risk, Liam mused, although he didn't regret his precautions. He slowed down as he reached 2771, realizing that his heart was actually pounding. He was taking this case way too personally, he reflected grimly, but it was hard to contemplate the mother of his child spending the remainder of her life in prison, especially for a crime he wasn't at all sure she'd actually committed.

He scanned the side yard of 2771 intently, but the sun was sinking fast and he didn't see Tom and Sophie until they were caught in the beam of his headlights only a few feet away from the road. He opened his side window and greeted them without getting out of the car, leaving Tom to slide the safety seat into the car and buckle Sophie in.

"All set." Tom shut rear door of the BMW and leaned down to talk to Liam. "Drive safely, and give our love to Chloe. Tell her we're thinking of her, and we hope to see her over the weekend."

"I'll pass on the message. Ready to go, Sophie?" As Liam spoke, a squad car from the Jefferson County police force turned off the main road and came barreling onto Blue Spruce, emergency lights flashing.

Tom muttered a curse under his breath. "What the hell's all that about? Do you think they're looking for us?"

"We're clearly about to find out." Liam jerked his head toward the squad car. "If the cops approach us, don't say *anything*. Leave the talking to me."

"Why are they wasting taxpayer money harassing us? What the hell do they think *we've* done? They'd better be polite, or I'm calling my congressman." Tom scowled as two cops, both in uniform, emerged from the squad car. They had parked so that the headlights shone directly through the windscreen of Liam's BMW into his face. The emergency lights on the squad car continued to revolve, red and white beacons of intimidation.

"Move away from the vehicle, sir." The younger cop gave Tom the brusque instruction. His older partner stood off to one side, his hand ostentatiously resting on his gun holster.

"Why the hell should I?" Tom was clearly spoiling for a fight. "We're doing nothing wrong. You have no right to order law-abiding citizens—"

"Tom, it's best if you move away from the car. Let me handle this." Liam spoke quietly, relieved when Tom did as he'd been asked. Technically, Tom was in the right, but practically, the cops could invent a thousand reasons to make life difficult for people they thought were obstructing an investigation.

"What's the problem, officers?" He forced himself to speak politely.

Neither cop responded. The older guy, Joseph Ramirez according to his name badge, stepped closer and directed his flashlight to the rear of the car. The powerful beam rested for several seconds on Sophie's face. Liam discovered that it wasn't only Tom who was in danger of telling the cops to piss off. He found himself gripping the steering wheel with white-knuckle force: a wiser choice than punching Ramirez on his short, fat nose but a lot less satisfying.

"Show me your license and registration, sir." Ramirez finally aimed his flashlight at the front of the car, away from Sophie. Liam could see her in the rearview mirror, rubbing her eyes.

Clenching his teeth, Liam produced his license. Ramirez read it slowly, as if committing every word and number to memory.

"Vehicle registration?" The cop held out his hand again.

"The registration and insurance documents are in the glove compartment." The last thing Liam wanted was to make any movement that would give Ramirez an excuse to draw his weapon. "Do you want me to get them out?"

"Yes. Go ahead."

Liam pulled his registration. Ramirez took the plastic wallet with a curt thank-you and handed it to his partner, along with Liam's license. The younger cop took everything back to the squad car and Ramirez strolled over to plant himself foursquare in front of the BMW, as if he expected Liam to drive off at any second.

"What the hell burr does he have up his ass?" Tom said, barely pretending to lower his voice so that Ramirez wouldn't hear.

"Who knows?" Liam shrugged. "We'll soon find out."

"What's he doing now?" Tom's gaze was glued to the younger cop's back.

"He's calling in my license and registration."

"Why?"

The cop was undoubtedly hoping against hope to find some excuse to haul all of them into the local police station, Liam thought grimly. He would only need a couple of unpaid parking tickets and he'd be able to justify it. Thank God, he wasn't going to find anything.

"It's just routine procedure," he told Tom.

"Jesus Christ!" Tom paced angrily. "The cops need to get their priorities straight and go chase a few actual real live criminals."

"That's what they think they're doing," Liam said wryly. Sophie's silence worried him. He twisted around to look at her. She was huddled behind the seat belt, Bobby Bunny clutched to her chest, her face buried between the rabbit's floppy ears. Liam muttered a string of inaudible curses, glad that Ramirez couldn't read his murderous thoughts or he'd be arrested for sure.

He patted Sophie's leg, the only part of her he could reach. "We'll soon be home, sugar plum." The silly endearment popped into his mind from out of nowhere. Then he remembered it was what his father had always called Megan. His mouth tightened. He'd had more than enough reminders of Ron Raven for one day and he didn't need another.

The young cop returned and murmured something to Ramirez, who strolled around the car and bent down at the window again. "Do you mind telling me where you're going, Mr. Raven?" It was clearly damn near killing the guy that they hadn't been able to dredge up an excuse to bring Liam in.

"Yes, I mind." Liam spoke crisply, but added a polite smile. There was probably a dashboard camera in the cop car taping the scene and he was going to play this by the book. "Why have you stopped my car, officer?"

"It matches the description of a vehicle seen fleeing the scene of a crime committed in this neighborhood."

"Yeah, I'll just bet it does."

Ramirez's expression didn't change by so much as a flicker. Liam, though, could feel the anger vibrating beneath the superficial calm. The guy was itching to bring him in.

"We understand that you've agreed to act as Mrs. Chloe Hamilton's attorney in the matter of her husband's death," Ramirez said, finally cutting to the chase.

How the hell did they know that? "Is that a question, officer?"

"Yes. Answer, please. Are you currently Mrs. Hamilton's attorney?"

"Mrs. Hamilton undoubtedly has many attorneys—"

"But you're the only criminal lawyer she's visited since the mayor of Denver was murdered."

So much for all his clever precautions. Liam allowed himself the luxury of another string of silent curses. Now the cops had confirmation that Sophie was in his car, they'd undoubtedly trail him all the way home. Taking Chloe to his condo had seemed such a safe decision when he made it. Now it seemed more like a trap leading Sophie's mother straight to jail. He piled on a few more curses for good measure.

"I'm no longer practicing as a criminal defense attorney," he said finally, wondering how the hell he was going to reunite Sophie with her mother if the cops were stuck to his butt.

"Since when?" Ramirez demanded.

"If your partner checked back with headquarters when you ran my license, and I'm sure he did, you must know that I've been working as a divorce lawyer for almost three years now."

Ramirez pounced. "Did Mrs. Hamilton ever discuss divorcing her husband with you, Mr. Raven?"

"You know I'm not going to respond to that."

Ramirez grunted. "I take it that means she did."

"It means that I'm not going to respond to any more of your questions. Just that, nothing more. You've established that I'm a law-abiding citizen, going about my legitimate business. Now, if you'll excuse me, officer, I need to get going. And my friend Tom here needs to get back to his wife before she's worried enough to call in a missing person's report."

Ramirez finally allowed some of his frustration to show. "Tell your client not to leave town, Mr. Raven. We'll be in touch. You can count on it."

Liam resisted the urge to score points, or to make smart remarks of any sort. It was enough that the cops had lost this battle, even though the war might still be theirs for the plucking. "Good night, officer. Tom, why don't you jump in the car? I'll drive you back to your house."

"Thanks, I prefer to go on foot. I need to run off some steam. See you, Liam." Tom was clearly burning to report to his wife what had happened.

"Remember our earlier discussion about phone calls." Liam hated to give the instruction while the cops were listening, but Tom struck him as a gun half-cocked and likely to explode at any moment. Unfortunately, if Tom fired, Chloe would be the person taking the bullet.

Tom acknowledged Liam's warning with a quick salute. Instead of cutting across the neighbor's backyard, he set off at a fast jog along the side of the road. It was a safe bet that the cops were going to follow him back to his house and try to question him. Liam was pretty sure neither Alexia nor Tom had anything relevant to say. Above all, thank God, they had no idea where Chloe was spending the night.

"Can we go home to my mommy now?" Sophie's voice, very scared and small, spoke from the back of the car.

"We're going right away," Liam said. "We'll be with her in just a little while."

"How long is a little while?"

"It means a few minutes. Less than an hour."

Liam hoped like hell he was telling the truth. He needed to come up with a brilliant plan some time very soon or else he'd end up returning to his condo with half a dozen of Denver's finest trailing in his wake. How the hell was he going to avoid leading the cops straight to Chloe and the arrest he was now very much afraid they planned to make?

Six

Liam drove sedately down the hill—no way he was going to provide the cops with an excuse to stop him again—and joined the traffic on the main road out of Conifer. Sophie was so quiet that he hoped she'd fallen asleep, which left him free to devote his addled wits to coming up with a brilliant escape plan.

Five minutes stretched to fifteen without a glimmer of inspiration. He strained to identify which cars might be following him, but it was impossible to make out what type of vehicle was concealed behind any given set of headlights. The cops had the advantage at this time of night. They merely had to keep his license plate in view, he had to single out potential tails when dusk made colors and shapes impossible to discern. Bottom line: the only safe way to proceed was to assume he was being followed, which meant he couldn't go home. The cops wouldn't expect Chloe to be at his house and he couldn't give them any reason to suspect the truth.

It was Sophie who provided him with an idea of how

he might be able to shake his tail. "Bobby Bunny feels sick," she announced as they rounded a sharp curve in the mountain road. "He's going to frow up."

Liam had zero experience with small children, but he was a fast learner and he already realized that Bobby Bunny and his daughter had interchangeable identities. If the stuffed rabbit was going to throw up, then so was Sophie.

"Tell Bobby Bunny he needs to hold on for a few minutes," Liam said, trying not to think about the gray glove leather of his car seats. "We'll stop in just a very little while."

"How long is a little while?"

Conversations with kids apparently tended toward the repetitive. He was quite sure they'd had this conversation before. "It means a few minutes."

"You said that before."

It hadn't occurred to him that Sophie would also remember their earlier discussion. Desperation provided him with inspiration. They had already crossed over C-470, the highway that circled the west and south of Denver. A giant shopping mall at Southwest Plaza was no more than half a dozen miles down the road.

"How about if we stop at the mall in another five minutes?" he asked. The mall would not only provide Sophie with the chance to stretch her legs and—please, Jesus—avoid puking, it would also be the perfect place for him to arrange a rendezvous with another car and driver. If he could switch to a car that the police didn't recognize, with a license plate they didn't have on record, he'd be in great shape for evading them. Or at least significantly better shape than he was right now.

"Do you think Bunny can hold off being sick for five more minutes?" he asked.

"I don't know." Sophie was silent for a moment, then performed another of the conversational leaps Liam found so disconcerting. "I didn't see you before."

"See me where?"

"Nowhere. I didn't see you. Not ever."

After some thought, Liam translated this to mean that Sophie was asking for confirmation of the fact that they'd never met until tonight. "No, you didn't meet me ever before. But I've known your mommy for a while."

"How long is a while? Is it five minutes?"

Oh boy. He tried a clarification. "I've known your mommy since before you were born." Telling the truth could have its ironic moments.

"Did you know my daddy, too?"

"Yes, I knew your daddy, too." He wasn't exactly lying. He and the mayor had been at the same fund-raisers on a couple of occasions, not to mention the fact that they'd spent several minutes chatting one-on-one at the infamous New Year's Eve party when Sophie had been conceived. That, of course, would have been right before he had sex with the man's wife, Liam thought sardonically.

He tried to make amends for his mental sarcasm since the guy was dead and unable to stick up for himself. "Your daddy was a very good mayor of Denver. He worked hard to make Denver a great town for people to live in." Liam had no idea if Sophie could understand what he was saying, but it sure beat Bobby Bunny's likelihood of puking as a topic. Not to mention defining the precise time parameters of *a little while.*

"Where's the TV in this car?" His daughter executed another one-eighty switch in the conversation.

"There isn't a TV. Usually I drive alone, and you can't drive and watch TV at the same time."

"My mommy's car has a TV. So does my daddy's."

"Great. I'm happy for you."

"My favorite movie is *Finding Nemo*. What's your favorite movie?"

"Marlon Brando in *On the Waterfront*."

"I never saw that movie."

"And I haven't seen *Finding Nemo*."

"Nemo is a fish. He gets lost and his daddy has to find him." She paused for a moment. "Can you find my daddy for me? I don't want my daddy to be in heaven."

So there'd been a connection between the mayor's death, TVs in the car and Sophie's favorite movie after all. If he'd seen the movie, he'd have realized that sooner. His daughter's obvious sense of loss stabbed Liam through the heart.

"I'm sorry, Sophie. I wish I could bring your father back, but that's what going to heaven means. It means that you can't come back."

"Not ever?" Her voice wobbled.

Liam was angry that there was no way to make her feel better. "No," he said, his voice rough. "Your daddy is never coming back. I'm sorry."

Silence descended, thick and absolute. It was really hard to look at her and drive at the same time, but Liam craned his neck and got a glimpse of the top of her head in the rearview mirror. Sophie's little pointy face was once again buried between Bobby Bunny's ears.

"I have to make a phone call," he said, unable to deal with any more emotion. How could somebody so small, whom he'd barely met, have the power to wring out his guts with no visible effort on her part?

"Hang on, sugar plum." *That stupid endearment again.* "We'll soon be getting out of the car."

He pulled out his cell phone and pressed the speed-dial for Helen, his paralegal. Helen was married and had two children, the youngest of whom had been barely a year old when Helen joined his practice two years ago. Surely that meant Helen's car would come equipped with a car seat? Best of all, he knew Helen lived in a town house only a couple of minutes from Southwest Plaza.

He finally got lucky after an evening of disasters and near-disasters when Helen answered the phone on the first ring.

"Hey, what's up, boss?"

"I have a big favor to ask," he said. "I need you to meet me at the mall as soon as you can get there."

"Southwest Plaza, you mean?"

"Yes. I'll explain everything when I see you. I need to borrow your car."

"How will I get home from the mall? Will you drive me?"

"No. I want to borrow your car for the night. You can drive home in my car."

"In *your* car? You're volunteering to let me drive your seventy-thousand-dollar *convertible?* Your baby? Your pride and joy?"

He winced. "Yeah, that's the one. And don't joke about it, Helen. I'm already traumatized just visualizing you behind the wheel."

Helen, treasure that she was, dropped the subject and merely asked where they should meet.

"You choose," he said. "Tell me where to park my car, and what store to meet you in. Something small enough that we can't miss each other but big enough that we won't be too conspicuous."

"Park in the west lot and meet me in Treasure Trove."

"Treasure Trove?"

"Yep. It's next door to the movie theater, and it sells decorative items for the home. Mirrors, giraffes you can hang your hat on, that sort of thing."

Who knew that there were stores devoted to such oddities? "Thank you, Helen. I'll be there in about fifteen minutes. And I owe you big time."

"Yes, you do. How about a day off next week for my daughter's third birthday as a reward?"

"You've got it. And Helen, bring a child car seat with you that you don't need for your own kids."

"You have a *child* with you?" Helen couldn't have sounded more shocked if he'd told her he was taking a boa constrictor out for a spin.

"Yes. A little girl who's not yet four. I guess that means I need to keep the car seat for the next twenty-four hours."

"Okay, you've got it. I'll see you in twelve minutes with my trusty Subaru and a spare car seat."

"Thanks, Helen."

"You're welcome. And I deserve a raise for not having asked a single question about *why* you need me to do this."

"I'm ignoring that remark about a raise, seeing as how I already pay you a small fortune. Take your day off and be happy. Oh, and Helen?"

"Yes?"

"Park somewhere that isn't visible from the west lot."

Helen's voice sobered. "Liam, seriously, are you okay?"

"I am now that you've agreed to meet me. Bye."

He found a space to leave his convertible under a bright light in the west parking lot. Neither Sophie nor Bobby Bunny had thrown up on his leather seats, which he considered a definite sign of divine favor. He couldn't see any cops tailing him, but that didn't mean there were none out there, merely that the cops might be good at their job.

He hurried into the mall, carrying Sophie, her body bird-light in his arms. Bobby Bunny made the trip squashed between her body and his, apparently a traveling spot the rabbit was well accustomed to.

Once inside, Liam quickly made his way to the menswear department of the store anchoring the west wing of the mall. If there were cops on his butt, it was imperative to shake them right now. He dodged rapidly through the cosmetics counters, emerging through women's shoes and immediately ducking into the gourmet kitchen equipment store next door. Hiding behind the espresso machines, he watched to see if he could spot any cop still on his tail.

Either there was nobody following him, Liam decided, or they were brilliant at keeping out of sight. Optimistic that he'd shaken loose from any unwanted escort, he took the precaution of dodging in and out of another two stores before carrying Sophie into Treasure Trove.

Helen was already there, seemingly enraptured by a display of pottery elephants. "Thanks for making the trip," Liam said. "I really appreciate it." He touched his daughter's soft cheek. "This is Sophie Hamilton, by the way."

"Hi, Sophie." Helen gave a friendly smile, although she threw him a quick sideways glance, indicating that she'd recognized the name and now was even more curious than before. "It's nice to meet you. My name is Helen."

"Hi, Helen." Sophie produced a shy smile that lit up her whole face. The first smile he'd seen from her, Liam realized.

"What do you think of this handsome fellow?" Helen

patted the trunk of a painted elephant whose back had been flattened to accommodate a tray top.

Sophie studied the elephant. "I like him," she said. "His name is Barney."

"An excellent name. Like the dinosaur on TV. Do you watch that show?"

"Sometimes."

Helen gave the elephant another pat. "Barney looks a bit sleepy, don't you think?"

Sophie tipped her head sideways and considered. "No," she said. "He's not tired. He's hungry. He wants a peanut butter san'wich."

Helen laughed. "You know, you could be right."

Liam cut in. "We need to get out of here, Helen."

"Sure. Where's your car? I'm already salivating…"

He grimaced. "I'm sorry, Helen, but I've changed my mind about having you drive it home—"

Helen snorted. "Yeah, that figures."

"I think the police have my car under surveillance," he said quietly. "If you attempt to drive away in it, they're going to question you long enough and hard enough to make the rest of your evening very unpleasant. Plus, I don't want you having to lie in order to cover for me. It's better if I drive you home in your car and drop you off."

"How will I get into work tomorrow morning?"

"Hire a limo. The tab's on me."

The look Helen directed at him was uncomfortably shrewd. "I won't ask any questions right this minute," she said, her attitude suddenly a lot more sober. "But you'd better explain everything as soon as we're in the office tomorrow, or I'm likely to explode from curiosity."

"It's a deal. But now we need to get out of here before the cops track me down again. Thanks again for doing this, Helen. You're a lifesaver."

Seven

They arrived back at Helen's Subaru wagon without any sign of a tail, which suggested that Liam's maneuvers at the mall had succeeded in shaking off his pursuers. Nevertheless, he was glad to have Helen around to carry Sophie back to the car and buckle her into her safety seat. The fact that they were now a threesome made him and Sophie less easy to identify at a distance. Hopefully the cops had no clue where he'd gone and would waste at least an hour or two milling around his abandoned BMW, waiting for him to return.

At this time of night traffic wasn't a problem and Liam dropped Helen off at her front door a scant ten minutes after leaving the mall. He looped around a couple of side streets to be doubly certain his rear was still free of hangers-on and made it back to his condo by eight-fifteen.

The sleek building overlooking Confluence Park had rarely seemed more appealing and he drove into the basement parking garage with a sigh of profound relief. The latch on Sophie's safety belt gave him some problems, but in the end he managed to spring her from confinement without totally humiliating himself.

"It's dark in here." She put both her arms around his neck, squashing her stuffed rabbit between them. She sounded grouchy, but Liam picked up on the fear lurking beneath the surface. "This isn't a nice place to live."

"It's just the parking garage. Your mommy's waiting for you upstairs and it's nice there. We're going to take the elevator up to my condo."

"What's a condo?"

"It's like a house without a garden. It's where I live."

Her head lifted a notch. "I like elevators."

"Good." He ransacked his scant store of childhood memories. "Do you want to push the buttons? I live on the fifteenth floor. If I show you the right button, will you press it for me?"

Sophie perked up enough to nod, and although she wasn't smiling, she seemed reasonably happy when they walked into his condo a couple of minutes later.

The front door opened straight into the living room, where Chloe was waiting for them. She tossed aside the magazine resting on her lap and ran across the living room, scooping Sophie up and smothering her with kisses. "Thank goodness you're here, honey bun! I missed you so much. I'm so glad you're home now."

Liam saw to his bewilderment that Sophie wasn't laughing and happy now that she was reunited with her mother. She was crying, her body shaken by huge, shuddering sobs.

"You were gone," Sophie said between sobs, burying her face in her mother's neck. "You were gone a long time."

"Yes, I was. I'm so sorry, Sophie. I thought you'd have fun with your cousins and Aunt Lexie."

"I wanted to be with you," Sophie said, scrubbing her eyes with her knuckles. "I was sad."

Chloe pushed her daughter's hair away from her face and tucked it behind her ears. "Well, I'm here now, and I'm not going away any more, I promise, so you don't have to be sad any more."

"Promise you'll stay all the time?" Sophie clung to her mother, her sobs subsiding, although her body still quivered with the occasional aftershock.

"I promise. I totally promise." Chloe's arms tightened and the worry in her expression intensified. Probably because she realized what an incredibly rash commitment she was making, Liam reflected.

"Guess what?" Chloe squished Sophie's nose. "We're even sleeping in the same bed tonight. Can you believe it?"

"All night?"

"All night," Chloe confirmed. She looked at Liam over their daughter's head. "I'm going to bathe her, if that's okay with you. It might make her bedtime routine seem a bit more normal. I'll be with you as soon as I have her settled."

"Fine. There are extra pillows in the closet. The pullout bed in the sofa is made up, I think. My cleaning service takes care of that."

"Yes, I already checked it out. Everything looks great, thank you."

Liam knelt alongside his daughter and gave her a quick, awkward hug. "Goodnight, Sophie. I'll see you in the morning."

She looked at him solemnly, her green eyes—Megan's

eyes—still sparkling from the tears. "Good night. Sleep tight."

Liam's stomach clenched. He made his way to the kitchen, speaking to Chloe without turning around. "Did you find something to eat while you were waiting for us?"

"Thanks, but I wasn't very hungry."

He shrugged. He was her lawyer, barely an acquaintance, and certainly not a friend. If she wanted to skip a meal, he had no reason to argue with her.

"There are TV dinners in the freezer if you change your mind. Help yourself any time." He went into the kitchen and popped the cap on a bottle of beer, taking a satisfying slug while he waited for the microwave to nuke his macaroni and cheese. Dammit, ever since his father died in May he'd been fighting to keep his emotions on an even keel. Between them, Sophie and Chloe had the power to unravel just about every shred of tranquility he'd managed to rope together. His emotions felt raw, painful to even the lightest touch, and he couldn't think of a single damn way to build some protective cover.

He'd finished eating and was working on his second beer when Chloe finally came back into the living room. "Sophie's asleep," she said. "Thank you for picking her up, Liam. My sister called before you got home and explained what a difficult time you had with the cops. I can't believe they had Lexie's home staked out!"

"I warned you that they probably would. Having lost track of you this afternoon, it was the logical place for them to pick up your trail again. But I didn't reckon on them being aware that I'm acting as your lawyer. I didn't expect to be tagged the moment I arrived at your sister's house, and clearly that's what happened."

Chloe suppressed a shudder. "I was afraid the police might follow you back here."

"I took care that they didn't." She was making him angry, and he wasn't sure why. Something to do with the reasonableness of her attitude, maybe. As if their relationship was that of old friends with an intimate knowledge of each other's lives, whereas their real relationship had nothing to do with friendship. Not now, and not when they first met. His surprisingly vivid recollection of their time together in the motel room involved lots of hot, sweaty sex and a couple of truly mind-blowing orgasms. There had been nothing remotely reasonable about what happened between the two of them. Add the fact of Sophie's existence and Jason's murder to those memories of anonymous passion and what you got was a royal mess.

"Let's cut to the chase, shall we?" He was almost glad that the question came out sounding curt to the point of aggression. There was a time and place for sugarcoating reality beneath social courtesies and this sure as hell wasn't it. "Apparently the police know that you've selected me as your lawyer. Maybe they didn't know that this morning. Maybe they only decided to bring you in later in the day. Whatever the reason, you got lucky this afternoon and somehow sailed under their radar. We need to take advantage of the extra time that gives us and develop a comprehensive strategy, as well as some tactics for coping with the next few days."

Chloe's face was white with exhaustion and she had to hold her hands tightly in her lap to stop them shaking, but he didn't allow himself to feel sympathy. "If the cops find me—"

"Not if," he corrected. "*When* they find you."

"*When* the police find me, can you convince them not to arrest me?"

"Not a chance if they've already obtained a warrant."

"Then what can we do?" Chloe's question was flat with despair. "You saw Sophie. She can't take too much more disruption in her life. Losing me would devastate her. And whoever else might be to blame for the mess I'm in, it certainly isn't my daughter. I have to do whatever I can to protect her. Maybe I should just take Sophie and catch the next flight to New Zealand..." She was half rising from her chair as she spoke.

Liam pushed her back down. "Don't even think about running unless you want to completely screw up your daughter's life. Not to mention your own."

Chloe's face lost the last dregs of color. "Then how do you propose to keep me out of jail?"

"Your best bet is to have me call the police chief first thing tomorrow morning and tell him that you're voluntarily coming in to answer any questions his team might have. With any luck, if the warrant isn't already issued, that will give them pause."

"How does it make a difference if I surrender voluntarily?"

"Because we'll be controlling the timing, and that's crucial. We'll go early in the day so that if the cops are determined to arrest you, we can at least arrange bail right away. Even if you're at home, waiting for trial won't be easy, especially if you have the media sitting on the sidewalk in front of your door, but it beats the hell out of waiting for trial in the Denver county jail." He didn't add that in murder cases, the suspect had to fight hard to be allowed out on bail and judges were becoming less and less sympathetic to a defense lawyer pleading for leniency and compassion.

Chloe rested her head in her hands. "This is a nightmare and I know I'm going to wake up soon."

"There isn't a chance of waking up until you explain to me why the police are so sure you killed the mayor."

"Other than the fact that I was found next to the body with the murder weapon in my hand?" Chloe asked bitterly.

Liam thought for a moment and then shook his head. "That's not enough. The cops know innocent people do foolish things when they find dead bodies. Especially dead bodies of people they love. They also know any halfway competent lawyer is going to claim you found your husband lying in a pool of blood and that it was instinctive to attempt to remove the murder weapon from his body. Did you recognize the knife, by the way?"

"Recognize it?"

"Yes. Was it Jason's favorite hunting knife, for example?"

"Jason doesn't hunt. I didn't really pay any attention to the knife—"

"Was it big? Small?"

She paused. "Medium sized. But not a kitchen knife, I think. Jason actually likes to cook more than I do—" Chloe's teeth started chattering, and she clamped them together. "I wanted to stop the bleeding, that's all I was focused on…and I couldn't unfasten Jason's shirt with the knife in the way."

"Was the wound still bleeding?" Liam asked sharply. "Was Jason still alive when you found him? Did he have a pulse?"

"I didn't think to feel for his pulse." Chloe's voice was heavy with self-blame. "There was so much blood I just automatically tried to mop it up. I don't recall if it was still gushing, though. I took off my T-shirt to make a pad for the wound and then Trudi...Sophie's nanny...came downstairs, looking for me. She insisted we should go into the kitchen. I didn't want to leave Jason. I could see the hole in his chest...but Trudi dragged me away and my hands were dripping with blood—"

She suddenly sprang to her feet and dashed in the direction of the bathroom, her hands pressed hard against her mouth. She came back ten minutes later, droplets of water still clinging to the hair around her face. Her pallor was now tinged with green.

"I'm sorry about that. I don't seem to remember a lot of what happened this morning, but I guess there are some parts I remember much too clearly."

Liam reminded himself that Sherri Norquist had been a master at evoking his sympathy whenever he asked a tough question. In fact, he'd probably be smart to assume that every time Chloe pretended to be overcome, that meant he'd asked a question she didn't want to answer.

Opening his laptop, Liam busied himself fixing up his voice recorder, steeling himself not to react to the pain in Chloe's eyes. "I need to hear what you did yesterday. I want a complete schedule."

He gestured to the mike plugged into the computer's recording device. "I'll record what you say, but don't worry, that's only so that I can go over the details afterwards to see if there are events or incidents the police are going to latch onto. I'm not trying to trip you up, but I can't afford to be surprised by anything that emerges during the investigation. Don't try to decide what's important and what's trivial. Don't second-guess my reactions, or try to sugarcoat the truth. Just tell me everything. Okay, please start talking now."

Eight

It seemed such a reasonable request, Chloe thought despairingly. Except that if she told him everything, she might as well go straight to jail without passing Go, much less stopping to collect two hundred dollars.

The silence pulsed with Liam's impatience, but she didn't know where or even how to begin. She'd had hours today to invent a crisp, believable story and here she was, still bumbling around the edges of the truth. Her brain felt as if it were pieced together from wads of sodden cotton and her body ached with the pain of Jason's loss. Life had seemed to sparkle with such promise on their wedding day. She had no idea how they had ended up in such a terrible place only seven years later.

"You're thinking too hard," Liam said. "This isn't a trap, or even a test. Just start at breakfast and go through your schedule for the rest of the day. Remember, I'm on your side."

She wondered if he had the faintest inkling of the effect his voice had on her. Cool, always shaded with irony, his detachment pricked at her, a challenge to her battered femininity. The night Sophie was conceived Liam had been a passionate and skillful lover, but his passion had been controlled. Ever since that night she'd wanted to see him when he was ruled by his passion rather than the other way around.

It bothered her that she could have a sexual reaction to another man less than twenty-four hours after her husband had been murdered. Although, God knew, it was more than four years since she and Jason had put themselves through the torment of pretending to have sex, so her response to Liam might be nothing more than the accumulation of pent-up physical need: her body's way of asserting that she was alive in the face of another human being's mortality.

But she had to start talking, or Liam would become even more suspicious than he already was. She began with the easy stuff: yesterday morning, when Jason had been at his downtown office, rushing from meeting to meeting and she'd been blissfully free to pursue her own schedule.

"It was just a normal day," she said. "I worked out first thing—"

"Where?"

"In the basement exercise room. I'm a bit obsessive about working out each day after all those years of intensive training. Then I paid bills and spent an hour with the caterer going through the arrangements for a couple of big events Jason had scheduled for next week. I ate lunch with the chairman of this year's United Way campaign and promised to attend a kickoff fundraiser in the fall. That meeting lasted just over an hour. I spent the rest of the afternoon with Sophie. She goes to a local, summer day camp in the morning, but we always spend the afternoons together."

"What did you and Sophie do yesterday afternoon?"

Liam was typing, and the screen of his laptop placed a barrier between the two of them that made it a little easier for Chloe to talk. "We didn't have anything special planned. Sophie has a sandbox in the backyard. She had fun building lopsided sand castles for an hour, but it was really hot by midafternoon, so we came inside and read stories for a while."

"Which books did you read?"

She couldn't imagine why Liam cared, but recounting the details of her afternoon with Sophie helped to calm her. At least everything she was telling him was a hundred percent accurate.

"We read *The Mitten* and *The Very Hungry Caterpillar.* Sophie's at the stage where she loves lists. She likes to count how many animals crawled into the lost mitten and how much food the caterpillar ate on each day of the week. Reciting the long list of crazy food is almost as much fun for her as having the caterpillar turn into a beautiful butterfly at the end of the book. After that, I helped her make some dinosaurs out of Play-Doh, and then it was time for her to eat dinner with Trudi, who'd just returned from her afternoon off. Trudi usually takes a few hours off in the afternoon."

"You didn't eat with Sophie?"

"No, I went to get changed. Jason and I had a cocktail party and a dinner to attend last night."

"I expect you and Jason had functions to attend almost every night?"

Chloe nodded. "The social demands on a big city mayor are relentless. I tried to keep at least two nights a week clear, but it didn't often happen. That's the main reason we have a live-in nanny, so that we don't...didn't...have to play hunt-the-babysitter four or five times a week. We couldn't have kept up with Jason's obligations as mayor without Trudi to help care for Sophie. She's been a godsend."

Liam glanced up from the keyboard. "You still say that, despite her accusation that she saw you stab Jason?"

"Trudi is only reporting what she thinks she saw. She's mistaken, not vindictive." Chloe shrugged. "If I end up getting arrested, I may not be quite so noble and understanding."

Liam made no further comment about Trudi but Chloe was sure he intended to check everything she'd said with the nanny. Fortunately, he wasn't going to uncover any discrepancies.

"Was there anything special about the dinner you and your husband attended last night?" Liam asked.

She found his short, simple questions oddly unnerving. That, undoubtedly, was the point. He offered no complexities and no subtexts. No way, in other words, for her to weasel out of giving a direct response.

"The dinner was anything but routine as far as Jason was concerned," she admitted. "The Senate majority leader was in town yesterday and had specifically asked to meet with Jason." Chloe fell silent, absorbing the incredible fact that only a little over twenty-four hours ago the biggest problem in her life had been her husband's desire to run for the United States Senate.

Money was always the huge issue for candidates, and for the past couple of months she'd been counting on the fact that Jason's personal fortune wasn't large enough to bankroll a successful campaign and that he wouldn't be able to raise the enormous sums he needed. But in an ironic twist on the adage that no good deed goes unpunished, his tenure as mayor of Denver had been so successful that he'd attracted attention not just from local Republicans, but from the party big shots in Washington. Several of the most powerful movers and shakers in Colorado politics had arranged a cocktail party for Jason to meet with the visitors from Washington, D.C.

Everyone had been up-front about the fact that Jason was being vetted as a potential Senate candidate and that Chloe was on trial, too. The fact that she'd won an Olympic gold medal was considered a definite asset; the fact that she was suspected of being a closet liberal was a problem, but probably not a deal-killer provided she demonstrated willingness to keep her mouth shut. In the political world, her value as a PR hook trumped her annoying belief system every time.

After the cocktail party, there had been a small dinner party at the home of Sam Divoli, one of those deep-pocketed businessmen whose names almost never appeared in the press but whose contributions kept the wheels of American political life spinning. By the end of the dinner, it was evident that Jason had passed inspection with flying colors. Short of pinning a badge on his chest, it couldn't have been made more obvious that he'd been awarded his party's official seal of approval.

Jason had returned home to the mayoral mansion high with excitement. Chloe had returned home so angry that you could have ignited a match on the sparks she was giving off.

"Were there any arguments at the dinner?" Liam asked. "Heated exchanges? Serious differences of opinion?"

"On the contrary, the evening was a huge success, a regular lovefest, in fact." She struggled not to sound bitter.

"Jason got the promise of financial backing from the national party if he decided to campaign for Colorado's vacant Senate seat."

"Good news, then."

"For Jason, yes." Chloe added a few details, all honest, to demonstrate how upbeat the mood at the dinner had been. It had often surprised her during the past five years how much truth could be woven into a picture that was fundamentally a lie.

She even acknowledged that she was reluctant to have Jason run for national political office. Better to get that out on the table since she'd voiced concerns about Jason's political ambitions to several friends and family members. By exposing her reservations up front, she could make them seem trivial, rather than a monster snapping at the heart of her marriage.

Liam, unfortunately, wasn't nearly as easy to hoodwink as most people. He just kept typing away and asking his seemingly low-key questions. "You mentioned this morning that you and your husband argued last night. If this dinner was so wonderful, what precipitated the argument?"

He was smart enough to leave the question open-ended, forcing her to try to remember precisely what she'd said earlier about her disagreements with Jason. Had she admitted that they'd been fighting about his political ambitions? She was quite sure that she wouldn't have acknowledged the depth and intensity of the struggle, but she might have touched on it. Dammit, she'd been so stressed this morning that she couldn't remember exactly what she'd said.

She also had to consider the likelihood that Trudi had overheard at least some part of their argument. When you had employees sharing your home, there was no such thing

as guaranteed privacy, not even at midnight. Not even in
the master bedroom where she and Jason had continued to
sleep together in their king-sized bed, despite the distress
that caused both of them. No way could Jason afford even
a hint of sexual dysfunction in the marriage to seep out via
whispered reports from the twice-weekly cleaning crew.

"It's an open secret that I wasn't too happy with my
husband's desire to run for the Senate," Chloe said, playing for time.

"You don't enjoy political life?"

"I loathe it." That came out with a bit too much honest
fervor. Chloe tamped down her feelings. "I dislike having
to watch every word I say in case some political enemy
uses my statements as a weapon against Jason."

"And yet you were a big part of your husband's campaign when he was running for mayor of Denver." Liam
leaned back in his chair, flexing his fingers. "You appeared
enthusiastic enough about politics then."

She nodded. "I was genuinely enthusiastic, not just
faking it. But Jason promised me that his political career
would begin and end with two terms as mayor of Denver.
I was willing to put my life on hold for a few years because
I felt there was so much good Jason could do for the city
of Denver. I lived up to my end of the bargain, but he
reneged on his part of the deal."

"You sound very angry."

She drew in a deep breath. Since it seemed that she
couldn't disguise her feelings, then the smart move was to
admit them. "I *was* angry," she said. "I told Jason flat out
that I wasn't willing to play second fiddle for another
dozen years while he tooled off to Washington. Quite apart
from the fact that I wanted to get started on my career here

in Colorado, Jason and I had different political views. In today's hardball climate, it's not only the candidate who has to be constantly on message, it's everyone in his family, especially his wife. I was sick and tired of being on somebody else's message."

"Did Jason expect you to change your political views?"

"No, but he did expect me to keep quiet about them. I could have caused serious damage to his political career if I ever expressed my real views on various hot-button social issues."

"What issues would those be?" Liam kept his gaze on the computer screen, but Chloe knew he was paying close attention and would pick up on the slightest tremor in her voice.

"Gun control, abortion, capital punishment, that sort of thing." She forced the list to trip glibly off her tongue. "Actually, Jason shared my opposition to capital punishment. He always felt that keeping a few dozen murderers locked up for life was a small price to pay for avoiding the risk of executing one innocent person. Of course, capital punishment wasn't an issue that he had to act on one way or the other in his capacity as mayor. As a senator, though, he would have been out of lockstep with his party leaders. It was something the people from Washington really grilled him about at the dinner last night."

She was pleased with the way she managed to switch the subject from hot-button social issues to Jason's views on capital punishment. The deft shift in focus helped to conceal that one of the most important and divisive social issues had been omitted from her initial list.

If she'd hoped to divert Liam into a discussion of capital punishment, she failed miserably. "I guess I still haven't grasped the dynamics of your marriage," he said. "You came to me a few months ago and discussed the steps you needed to take before filing for divorce. Then you changed your mind and went back to Jason."

"People have second thoughts about ending their marriage all the time. I was one of them."

"But now you're admitting that you and your husband had ongoing disagreements about how the two of you should spend the next twelve years of your life. These weren't minor differences, they were fundamental. Divorce seems an obvious solution in the circumstances. Was that option discussed last night?"

She saw that she was rubbing the pad of one thumb against the nail of the other, a sure sign of stress, and quickly stopped the betraying gesture. "Voters tend to be hard on politicians who get divorced..."

"Only if the divorce is messy." Liam's cynicism was more pronounced than usual. "A male politician can discard his wife and marry a new one with almost no punishment from the voters, provided he's discreet and the ex is willing to keep quiet. In fact, from Jason's perspective, staying married to you was a high risk proposition, given that you might take flight at any minute. He'd have been much better off ending the marriage months ago and getting a compliant new wife in place before he rolled out his senate campaign next spring."

"Your suggestion might be practical as a campaign strategy but it pays no attention to people's feelings. Unfortunately, Jason wanted to be married to me, not to somebody else."

"Unfortunately?"

Dammit, she'd slipped up—and Liam had jumped right

on it, of course. She shrugged. "I just meant that finding a new and improved Mrs. Hamilton wasn't something Jason wanted to do. He liked the family he had. He *loved* the family he had."

Liam, no surprise, wouldn't let the issue drop. "I notice you didn't actually answer my earlier question."

"Which question was that?"

"Whether you and your husband discussed the possibility of getting a divorce last night. Did you?"

They were right here, at the place she had known would arrive. Right at the crucial point where she should have worked out exactly what she was going to say. But instead of being prepared with a tidy story, she was mentally floundering. Chloe shut her eyes, dispelling the image of Jason's stricken expression as he made his final, ugly threat. They had managed to remain such good friends right up until the moment a year ago when she first talked about getting a divorce. Since then, though, they'd slithered and slipped down the jagged slope of their broken relationship, ending up in a swamp of shared pain. It struck her as tragic that on the last night they would ever spend together, they had both done their utmost to be as cruel as possible.

"I did talk about getting a divorce last night," she acknowledged. "But in the end we shelved the whole discussion. As I already explained, terminating our marriage was the last thing Jason wanted."

"Second to last thing," Liam pointed out. "He apparently wanted to be the junior senator from Colorado more than he wanted to stay married to you."

She didn't let herself rise to the bait. "Jason wanted both. He was confident he'd eventually bring me around to his point of view. Quite apart from the fact that he loved me and Sophie very much, he was honest about the fact that being married to somebody who has as much name recognition with the Colorado voters as I do might make the difference between defeat and victory in a close election. Olympic skiers tend to resonate more here than they do in other states."

"You're right, they do. Another reason your reluctance to support his political goals must have been very frustrating for Jason."

"Well, yes, I'm afraid it was—"

"In fact, more than frustrating," Liam interrupted. "Infuriating. Exasperating. Maddening. Because the bottom line is that Jason had no legitimate way to prevent you getting a divorce if that's what you decided to do. And you were clearly walking right on the edge of that decision."

If only you knew, Chloe thought bitterly. *If only you knew.* She rubbed her hand over her forehead, which felt as if it might split in two with the force of the headache pounding inside her skull.

"You're absolutely correct that I could have ended our marriage at any time." She hoped the lie came out with a convincing ring of honesty. "Which is why I'm puzzled as to why my argument last night with Jason is even relevant to the tragedy of his death. It hurts a lot to remember that the last words the two of us exchanged were angry, but our disagreement has no connection to his murder. No relevance to anything, in fact."

"I wouldn't say that." Liam's tone of voice struck her as alarmingly mild. In her limited experience, he wasn't a man much given to soothing platitudes. "If you wanted a divorce and Jason wouldn't agree, I'd say his death is very relevant."

"How so?" She asked the question even though she knew the answer perfectly well.

"The cops are going to leap to the conclusion that you murdered him as the only path out of a marriage you could find no other way to end."

"That's crazy." She hoped her voice didn't shake. "You were the person who said just a minute ago that Jason had no power to stop me getting a divorce. This is a no-fault state. I can...I could have divorced Jason whether he agreed or not—"

"You'd have lost access to his money," Liam pointed out. "Jason was a successful real-estate developer before he became mayor and judges are reluctant to award alimony these days. On the other hand, as his widow, you inherit a tidy sum. At least a couple of million, I'm guessing, quite apart from that lovely nineteen-thirties mansion you live in."

"Even assuming I'm a person who's stupid and immoral enough to kill my husband for money, I don't *need* his money. I have my own. Skiing didn't make my fortune, but winning the Olympic gold opened the door to enough endorsements and other opportunities that I have no need to stay married just because I'm too poor to leave. And that house in Park Hill was important to Jason, not to me."

"Okay. We'll stipulate that you weren't desperate to inherit the house and that you had no interest in Jason's money." If Liam's smile was meant to be reassuring, it didn't do the trick. "Let's move past the argument the two of you had last night and carry on with the actual chain of events once the two of you stopped yelling at each other."

Liam was being deliberately snide. Unfortunately, he was also being accurate. She and Jason *had* yelled at each other, despite all her vows to remain polite and civilized. Chloe pushed the sad memories aside. In the interest of shifting Liam's focus away from the reasons why she hadn't divorced Jason, it was even worth bringing another troublesome piece of evidence about the murder to his attention.

"So far, you haven't touched on the subject the police kept hammering at this morning."

"What subject was that?" Liam asked.

"They wanted to know about the security system and how difficult it would be for an intruder to get into the house. You don't seem to have considered the possibility that Jason was killed by an intruder."

"I haven't considered that theory or any others, Chloe. That's because the police are responsible for solving this murder, not me. I just have to make sure that you—my client—don't end up convicted. That being the case, I'd like to think that you told the cops no comment when they asked about the security system. Unfortunately, I'm assuming you told them everything you know?"

"Yes, I answered all their questions as best I could. That was before you informed me I wasn't allowed to say anything except *no comment* or *I want my lawyer.*"

"That figures." He faked an exaggerated sigh and she was surprised into returning the faintest of smiles. "Okay, you wish I hadn't said anything, but I still don't understand what harm it does for me to have told the cops that the security system is state-of-the-art and there are cameras in several of the rooms, including the room where Jason was murdered. If I hadn't told them, they could have found that out for themselves in about a minute and a half."

She'd finally managed to surprise Liam. He shot a startled look in her direction. "If there's a security camera in the basement, doesn't that mean there's a record of who killed your husband right on camera?"

"There should be, but there isn't."

"Why not?"

Chloe drew in a shaky breath. "The entire security system, including the cameras, was disarmed last night around 2:00 a.m. It wasn't a failure or a power outage, it was deliberate sabotage."

"And the security company didn't realize their system was down?" Liam sounded justifiably incredulous. "How is that possible?"

"The sabotage seems to have involved sophisticated tampering with the electronics, not smash-with-a-tire-iron assault. The security company records show everything as functioning all night without a hitch."

"Are you telling me somebody deliberately programmed the security system to convey false information to the security company?"

"That seems to be what happened, yes."

Liam didn't speak, but his forbidding expression suggested that he not only understood why she had shot right to the top of the cops' suspect list but that if he were in charge of the investigation, he would put her there, too. Clearly, she was one of the few people who had both the knowledge and the opportunity to disarm the security system in her own home. In the wake of her bitter argument with Jason, it wasn't unreasonable to conclude that she had a motive, too.

She pounded another nail into her own coffin. "The cops kept asking me if I had any reason to disarm the system. I told them no." She shrugged, feigning a casualness she didn't feel. "I'm pretty sure they didn't believe me. I think that's why they're so convinced I'm guilty."

"Given the apparent focus of their investigation, I'm assuming the police found no signs of a break-in?"

"They didn't tell me much about their investigation." With a masochistic urge to fill him in on all the damning details, she pointed out all the reasons it would have been difficult for any intruder to gain access to their home.

"I expect that's why the TV pundits haven't suggested that the killer might be a burglar, or a drug addict hoping to score some quick cash," she concluded, sounding a lot calmer than she felt. "Bottom line, there's no getting around the fact that since the security system was sabotaged, whoever killed Jason must have known how the system functioned. He must also have planned the murder well in advance."

"Not necessarily. It could simply mean that somebody planned a robbery and your husband was unfortunate enough to get in the way."

"Oh. I never thought of that. Our safe is in the basement, so it's logical a burglar would have been down there." Hope crept back. "It's possible Jason was killed by somebody who broke into the house after all! I need to get back home and check to find out if anything was stolen. Maybe robbery *was* the motive—"

"Maybe." Liam's gaze was oddly reassuring, given that she couldn't detect the smallest hint of sympathy in his eyes. "Look, you can drive yourself crazy speculating about the motives for this crime. My advice is not to waste the mental energy, at least not right now. Instead of wondering who might have a motive to kill Jason, let's work some more on finding out who had the opportunity. Tell me exactly who was sleeping in the house last night. Do you have any other live-in help besides Trudi?"

"No. The cleaning crew comes in twice a week, and we use a catering firm when we entertain. But Trudi was there last night, of course. Her room connects to Sophie's through their bathroom. Other than Trudi, it was just the three of us—Jason, Sophie and me."

"And the murderer, of course."

She couldn't tell if he was being sarcastic. "And the murderer," she agreed.

"Could an intruder sneak into your house during the day and find somewhere to hide where he wouldn't be noticed?" Liam asked. "That strikes me as an easier thing for a murderer to plan than somehow breaking into your home at two in the morning without triggering any of the alarms."

Chloe thought for a moment, and felt briefly more cheerful. "You're thinking about somebody from the cleaning crew, or a repairman or something?"

"Yes, exactly."

"It would be more than possible. It would be relatively easy." Chloe hoped with all her heart that this would turn out to be the explanation for Jason's death. Bad as it was to imagine her husband dying at the hands of a brutal stranger, it was better than visualizing him dying at the hands of a so-called friend. "We have the entire attic where an intruder could hide with almost no likelihood of anybody going up there to look. Somebody could even hide in a closet or in the basement furnace room, if they were prepared to run a very slight risk of being caught before nightfall. Our house is big, and since Jason became mayor it's inevitably become more of a public venue, despite the fact that Cableland is where the mayor is supposed to do most of his official entertaining. People come and go all day long."

Cableland, a sprawling mansion in the Hilltop neighborhood, had been donated to the city as an official mayoral residence by a benevolent billionaire and was loaned out on a regular basis for nonprofit and civic functions. However, no mayor had ever actually lived there, since the vast house, with its eighty-eight televisions, pink grand piano and condos for the resident tame squirrels, was more reminiscent of a Disney fantasy set than it was of a home.

"The ease with which an intruder could hide in your home is good news in the circumstances. We need to remind the police of that." Liam's voice was dry. "At the moment, it seems we have a choice of pinning this crime on you, or on the babysitter or on a mysterious stranger hiding in a closet." He gave a bleak smile. "I'm casting my vote for the mysterious stranger. How about you?"

Chloe couldn't summon up an answering smile. "I guess it's not hard to see why the police suspect me," she said. "I'd suspect me if I was a cop."

"You're an easy suspect, but not necessarily the correct one," Liam said. "Yes, your marriage had its rocky moments, but there are no doubt plenty of Denver citizens with reason to dislike their mayor. And yes, you had access to the internal security system, but from what you've told me, there seem to be dozens of people—possibly hundreds—who could have found a way to gain access to the house last night if they really set their minds to it. The cops aren't going to get a free ride pinning this on you."

She sent him a wry glance. "You have a contrary nature, Liam. I'd have to say that the manipulation of the security system points almost directly to me as the culprit, but you brush it away. On the other hand, when I gave you an innocuous account of my schedule for yesterday afternoon, you seemed ready to turn me over to the cops in handcuffs with a guilty placard hung around my neck."

He smiled at her and, for the first time, his smile held genuine warmth. "We defense lawyers are a strange breed. Evidence the prosecution calls damning pushes us into instant combat mode. And the funny thing is that by doubting what might appear certain at first glance, we often discover that things are nowhere near as clear-cut as they seem."

"That's lucky for me, I guess."

Liam's momentary warmth faded. "Perhaps. Unfortunately, however good your defense lawyer is, he can only work with the facts, and I seem to be having a hard time getting those from you."

"I just told you about the security system."

His smile tightened into mockery. "Yes, because for some reason you wanted to divert my attention from the details of your schedule last night. Something happened between you and Jason that was so incriminating you're willing to discuss the sabotaged security system as a better alternative. What was it you were trying to hide?"

Chloe felt her cheeks burn. She'd wanted Liam as her lawyer precisely because he was smart. Right now, though, he was too damn smart for comfort. "I've told you what happened last night," she said. "Jason and I argued about his senatorial campaign. We couldn't agree. We went to bed."

"Together?"

"No. I was exhausted and went to our room. Jason went downstairs to talk to Freddy Mitchell—"

"By phone, I assume?"

"Yes, of course. It was late, but in addition to being Jason's chief of staff, Freddy had already been designated as chairman of his senatorial election campaign and I expect he was waiting for the call. As you can imagine, he was extremely interested in the outcome of last night's dinner. But I don't know if they actually talked or not. As I explained, I went to bed."

"It'll be easy enough to ascertain whether Mitchell and your husband actually spoke. I'm assuming that right after midnight was the last time you saw your husband alive?"

"Yes." Chloe was caught off guard by the sense of loss that suddenly swept through her. "That is, unless he was still alive when I found him…found him outside his office."

She wished she didn't remember the last words she'd ever spoken to Jason with such crystal clarity. *If you wanted to make me hate you, you've found the perfect method. Go away, for God's sake. I can't bear to look at you.*

She bit her bottom lip, fighting back the tears she'd been waiting four years to shed. If she started crying now, the chances seemed excellent that she'd never stop.

Liam leaned back in his chair while she regained control. Not for him the reassuring pat on the arm or murmured words of comfort. He had to be amazingly in tune with her mood, however, because almost at the second that she had her emotions under wraps again, he asked his next question.

"What time was it when you found Jason this morning? I'm still fuzzy on the timeline."

"The police asked me that, too. I told them it must have been just after three-thirty."

"Was there some special reason why you were wandering around the basement of your home at three-thirty in the morning?" Liam's bland tone of voice did nothing to disguise his underlying skepticism. Apparently after his brief moment of warmth they were right back to their previous adversarial relationship.

"I was having a restless night, worrying about the whole campaign issue." Another truth that wasn't quite what it seemed. "I thought I heard Jason call my name but when I sat up and discovered that he wasn't in bed, I decided I must have been dreaming."

"And that's when you went to check on your husband's whereabouts?"

"Not right away. Jason is a night owl. He doesn't need more than five or six hours of sleep and he often stays up late or wakes up early to get a jump start on the day. In fact, the strange thing is that I went looking for him at all. It would have been much more natural for me just to turn over and go back to sleep."

"So why didn't you go back to sleep? Why did you go looking for him?"

"Because the minute my head touched the pillow, I became convinced that I really had heard Jason call out for me." Chloe hesitated, knowing that Liam would assume she was inventing excuses to explain her presence at the scene of the crime. In fact, she was telling the whole truth and nothing but the truth.

"I don't believe in premonitions, but that's what I seem to have experienced last night. Something compelled me to go looking for Jason. I couldn't get rid of the feeling that he'd called for my help. So I went searching—and you know what I found."

"So basically, your explanation for being discovered

next to your husband's mortally wounded body is that you had a psychic connection to his soul and as he was dying, his spirit called out to you."

Anger enabled her to meet his gaze head on. "Minus the heavy sarcastic overtones, yes, that's pretty much what happened. Or else he really did call out my name loudly enough for me to hear."

"Any particular reason you went looking for him in the basement?"

"A very good reason. I searched for him in the basement because that's where he had his home office and that's where I assumed he'd gone in order to call his chief of staff."

"Great." Only a faint trace of color along Liam's cheekbones suggested that he wasn't quite as detached as he sounded. "I can already see how much fun the D.A. will have ripping that statement to shreds. Three floors in your house, and at least twenty rooms, but you go straight to the basement."

"Where else would he have been? Conceivably the library on the first floor, but we use that more as a sitting room than an office. The wood paneling is eighty years old and neither of us wanted to drill holes in burled walnut in order to bring in cables and computer wires, so Jason automatically headed for the basement whenever he was doing anything work related. Maybe you and the police need to consider the possibility that the truth often sounds a lot less credible than a clever lie."

Liam laughed. "Funny you should bring that up."

"What do you mean?"

"Simply that I've decided during the past hour that you're a talented liar." He leaned back and pushed his laptop away, swinging his chair around so that he was looking straight at her.

"What does that mean?"

"It means now that you've given me the carefully doctored account of what happened last night, how about we start over? Why don't you tell me what really happened?"

"I already told you—"

"No, you didn't *already tell me.*" Liam snapped the denial. "You have thirty seconds, Chloe. Tell me exactly how Jason was blackmailing you to remain married to him, or I'm no longer your lawyer."

Nine

"Jason wasn't blackmailing me. That's crazy." The denial was not only pathetic, it was transparently untrue. Chloe regretted the feeble words the moment they spluttered out of her mouth.

Liam leaned forward, his eyes blazing. "Anybody else and I'd already have walked," he said softly. "This is your last chance, Chloe. What was the hold Jason had over you? It had to be something pretty powerful or you'd have ended this marriage back in the spring. Was his hold powerful enough for you to kill him to get out from under?"

"No." Her reply was as soft as his question, but not from weakness. Surprisingly, Liam's anger actually stiffened her mushy backbone. "Nothing would have persuaded me to kill Jason. Nothing."

"That's it? That's all you have to say? Just *no* and *nothing?*"

She leaned forward across the table, mimicking his actions, her focus as intense as his. "The details of my relationship with Jason are irrelevant to his murder. There's

only one thing you need to know, Liam. I…did…
not…kill…my…husband."

"No, that's not all I need to know. Dammit, Chloe! Keep
up this attitude and you're going to smart-ass yourself all the
way into a jail cell. Tell me what hold Jason had over you!"

Her stomach churned. "I'll admit that Jason was
blackmailing me to remain in the marriage. There, are
you satisfied?"

Liam gave a short, hard laugh. "No. In fact, I'm about
a thousand light years away from satisfaction."

A sudden electric tension arced between the two of
them. Chloe reached out and touched his arm, an instinctive move she'd never have made if she'd retained even a
few functioning brain cells after the stress of the previous
twenty-four hours. She felt his muscles tense beneath her
touch. Then, very deliberately, he took her hand and lifted
it from his arm.

"I'm sorry—"

He cut into her mumbled apology. "My fault. I
shouldn't have made a remark that was easy to misinter-
pret. But just to get something straight—you're probably
aware that I previously defended another woman accused
of killing her husband."

Liam spoke in an aloof voice that ought to have repelled
her but instead had the effect of making her want to rip off
his clothes and tumble on the nearest bed. God, what
wouldn't she give just once to feel that she was in control
and he was the person floundering in a pool of emotions
he didn't understand, didn't especially want and didn't
know how to deal with.

Chloe folded her hands in her lap. "Yes, I'm aware.
You're talking about Sherri Norquist."

"What you may not know is that Mrs. Norquist decided her chances of getting away with murder would be considerably enhanced if she seduced her attorney. I fell right into her trap and felt damn foolish when I finally woke up and found myself there. As you can imagine, having made a complete horse's ass out of myself a mere three years ago, I'm now somewhat immune to sexual invitations from my clients."

Chloe hung onto her temper—just—but she rose to her feet, too angry to remain seated. "You seem to be suffering under several misapprehensions. For your information, I wasn't extending any invitations to you, sexual or otherwise. And for the record, let me assure you that if I had been inviting you to have sex with me, you wouldn't be left in any doubt about the invitation. I wasn't. I'm not. More importantly, unlike Sherri Norquist, I'm not guilty of killing my husband. Since I'm not a murderer, I don't need to seduce my lawyer. I merely need you to keep me out of jail long enough for the police to find the real killer."

Chloe was relieved that she somehow managed to keep her voice as flat and distant as his. "Do you think you can handle that reasonably simple task, Mr. Raven?"

"Only with your cooperation. Which I sure as hell haven't had so far tonight." Liam pushed back his chair with an angry scrape of metal on slate, looming over her by several intimidating inches. "I'm tired of asking you this question, but I'll repeat it one last time. Tell me what threat your husband used to keep you married to him. What could be that powerful? Is it something to do with Sophie?"

"No." Anger made her reckless. "It was nothing to do with Sophie. Besides, it's irrelevant to Jason's death. Absolutely and completely irrelevant."

"If it kept you shackled to his side when you wanted to be free, it's extremely relevant. In fact, it's an excellent motive for murder. I need to know what it is."

"Didn't we have a discussion a moment ago about motives for murder not being important?" She made an impatient gesture. "No, don't bother to answer. We're wasting time here. The bottom line is that Jason accepted last night that there was nothing in the world powerful enough to keep me married to him. When we returned home from dinner, I let him know our marriage was over. I made it clear there was nothing he could offer me—or threaten me with—that had the power to keep me inside a marriage that had been a sham from the beginning."

"Were you telling the truth? And did he believe you?"

"Yes, to both questions."

Liam was so close to her that she could see the stubble of beard growing along his jaw. "Why was your marriage a sham, Chloe?"

The lies that had built her marriage up were being torn down, brick by brick. Soon the illusion would be destroyed, leaving a tired and unhappy man behind the curtain where once there had been the wonderful wizard of Oz. "My marriage was a sham because Jason was gay," she said flatly. "Not bisexual, not ambivalent, not questioning his sexual orientation. He was gay, plain and simple, and he knew it from the time he was a freshman in high school. Unfortunately, he chose not to share that crucial piece of information when he asked me to marry him. And to save you wondering, yes, we'd slept together before I agreed to marry him and yes, the sex seemed okay. Not earth-shattering, but okay. And yes, I was twenty-seven at the time and I'd had other relationships and I ought to have known better. I was moronic not to have realized."

"You're doing a great job of blaming the victim," Liam said quietly. "Jason really did have a politician's silver tongue if he managed to convince you it was your fault that he lied about his sexuality. How did you discover the truth?"

"Our sex life degenerated from not so hot, through pretty dreadful to not happening. When I suggested counseling, he told me the truth. At one level it was a tremendous shock. At another level, it simply confirmed what I'd been suspecting for months."

Instead of responding, Liam went into the kitchen and came back carrying two ice-filled glasses and a can of Coke. He poured soda into one glass and handed it to her.

"Here. Since you won't eat, take a hit of sugar."

"Thank you." She sipped with surprising gratitude.

He nodded, and filled his own glass with the rest of the soda. "The fact that Jason was gay explains a lot, but it doesn't explain why you were afraid to divorce him. Was it because you didn't want to risk Sophie finding out that Jason wasn't her biological father?"

He'd given her the perfect opening, and Chloe was sorely tempted to take it. How would it hurt anyone to pretend that she'd kept silent for Sophie's sake? Except that for the first time in years she felt the lifting of some of the burden that had oppressed her and she yearned for the freedom that would come from admitting the whole truth.

"You've hesitated too long," Liam said. "That means it wasn't Sophie that kept you locked into your marriage. It was something else." He set his glass down on the table and then looked up, holding her gaze. "I'm your lawyer,

Chloe, and I'm one hundred percent on your side. On top of that, I'm bound by professional ethics to keep anything you say relating to Jason's murder confidential. You have no special reason to trust me, but you can. I promise. Remember, I've worked as a criminal defense attorney *and* a divorce lawyer." He gave a small smile. "Believe me, with that kind of experience, there's almost nothing you can reveal about your life with Jason that would shock me."

It was his smile and his unexpected kindness that threw her for a loop. She'd done a pretty good job keeping it all together as long as Liam treated her as an antagonist. His offer of something close to friendship was a straw that her overburdened emotions couldn't tolerate.

She hurriedly broke eye contact and swung away, but it was already too late. The tears she'd been holding at bay—for months, not just for the past few traumatic hours—gushed out in a mortifying flood. She wept for Jason and her marriage and for secrets carried too long. She wept for the fear that she might end up in prison, unable to care for Sophie who needed her so badly. Most of all, she wept for the unbearable sadness of knowing that love didn't conquer all. She'd once loved Jason. She still loved Sophie. Her love hadn't been enough to keep either of them safe.

For several agonizing seconds there was no sound in the room beyond the shuddering heaves of her sobs. Then Liam spoke from behind her. "Don't cry, Chloe. For God's sake, don't cry. Here." He put his hand on her shoulder, urging her around and simultaneously thrusting a stack of tissues into her hand.

She turned because she didn't have the emotional or mental reserves to resist, but even though the move brought her face-to-face with Liam, her sobs refused to stop. It was bad enough to be wailing like a banshee; it was more humiliating than she could bear to know that Liam was watching her make an idiot of herself at close quarters. She shoved past him, aiming for the bathroom where she could at least stick her idiotic head under the cold water tap, but he put out his arm, stopping her in her tracks.

"Don't run and hide," he said quietly. "There's no shame in grieving for Jason, or for mourning that your marriage didn't turn out the way you'd hoped." He paused for a heartbeat. "Tell me how Jason blackmailed you into staying married to him, Chloe. Tell me and break the hold he exercised over you."

"I can't…" She made a sound, half sob, half hiccup, wholly inelegant. "I wish I could, but it's not my secret…"

"Maybe it wasn't your secret in the beginning. But it's become your secret because you refuse to reveal it. The longer you keep it to yourself, the heavier the burden of carrying it will become."

The temptation to tell him was enormous. Chloe smothered the temptation with an effort that left her physically and mentally drained. She wasn't in a fit place right now to be making decisions that would affect so many other lives. That meant her only safe choice was to remain silent. She started to resume her trek to the bathroom, chiefly because she had no more explanations or excuses left inside her and she wanted to be alone.

Liam stopped her from leaving by the simple process of folding her into his arms and cradling her head against his chest. He wasn't holding her tightly and she could easily have moved away, but it was a long time since anyone except Sophie had hugged her and she discovered how much she'd been craving the solace of friendly human contact in the hours since Jason was murdered.

For several seconds she was aware of nothing more than the thud of Liam's heartbeat and the rock solid strength of his body. She was so relieved her tears had stopped and she was in control again that it took her longer than it should have to register that while her attention had been elsewhere the soothing sensations of warmth and comfort had somehow transformed themselves into the heat and edginess of sexual desire.

Liam tilted her chin upward and used his thumbs to wipe away the last streak of tears. "It's been a very long day," he said. "Maybe we've done enough talking for tonight. Would you like to get some rest now? We can pick up again first thing tomorrow morning."

"You're right, I am tired." She closed her eyes, afraid of what he might read there. Liam's sympathy had exposed the underbelly of her motives for seeking his help, and she could no longer hide from the truth of her attraction. She was exhausted, and yet her body felt more alive than it had since the night Sophie was conceived. Heat coursed through her veins, flushing her skin. Her breasts ached with the need to be touched. She yearned not just for sexual gratification but to be held by a man who found her desirable. After seven years as Jason's wife, she'd almost forgotten what it was like to feel wanted as a woman and sexual partner.

She wasn't sure what she did that allowed Liam to recognize her feelings. He suddenly tensed, but he didn't say anything. He didn't move away, either, and she felt the same subtle changes in his body that she'd already felt in her own. His eyes darkened and his body moved against hers, hard with sexual demand.

My God, she thought. *I remember now what desire feels like. This is how a man and a woman are supposed to be.*

For a wonderful, terrifying moment she thought he was going to kiss her, but the thought barely formed before Liam's eyes blanked and the ironic mask that seemed to be his trademark descended. He stepped away from her, reasserting control with an ease Chloe could only envy.

"For the second time tonight, we seem to be heading in a direction neither one of us really wants to go," he said. She was relieved that at least his voice didn't take on the biting note that had become all too familiar over the past few hours. "Let's take this discussion back to where we were a couple of minutes ago. Do you want to call it a night, or would you prefer to get started on developing a plan of action for tomorrow morning?"

"I'm not sure…" Chloe was so distracted by her lingering state of arousal that it took her a moment to realize the violent banging she heard wasn't inside her head, but a physical reality. Somebody was pounding on the front door.

"Police! Mr. Raven, are you there? We need to have a word with you!"

Liam immediately covered her mouth with his hand, pushing hard enough to compel her silence. "Don't make a sound or move a muscle," he murmured, speaking right into her ear. "If the cops don't have a warrant, they can't come in."

The banging began again, along with another demand to open the door. "We want to talk to you about your car, Mr. Raven. We found it abandoned in Southwest Plaza. We want to make sure you're okay."

Chloe glanced at the clock on the corner bookshelf. Nine-thirty. The mall had barely closed half an hour ago, so the car was obviously an excuse for the police visit, and not the true reason. She was the only reason the police would have for wanting to talk to Liam, she thought despairingly. Did they have a warrant for her arrest? Would that be sufficient legal cause for them to batter down Liam's front door in search of her?

Please God, don't let them come in. Not yet. Not tonight. Each knock felt like a hammer blow falling on her heart. Despite everything that had happened today, she still found it incredible that the police could believe she was capable of killing Jason. How could they imagine she would stab him, not just once, but multiple times? Chloe might have laughed at the absurdity if she hadn't been so completely terrified.

The banging continued. She would have sworn nothing worse could happen, but at that moment Sophie appeared in the door leading out of the guest bedroom. Her eyes were wide with fear and she had Bobby Bunny pressed to her mouth, his ears parted to make a resting place for her nose—a position he only ended up in when Sophie was seriously upset. Liam noticed her at once and swept her up, holding her so that she was cradled between their two bodies. Sophie's terror must have been overwhelming because she didn't speak or make even a whisper of sound. Instead, she buried her face against Chloe's chest, and drew Liam's arms into a protective circle that stretched around her and encompassed Chloe, too.

They stood in their huddled threesome until the banging stopped and the police finally went away. "Will they come back?" Chloe whispered when silence had reigned for a full minute. She was shaking from head to toe, but Sophie probably couldn't feel the tremors because Liam was still holding them both. Chloe wondered how in the world she had managed to arrive in a place where the most reassuring thought she could come up with was that Sophie was so scared herself that she might not realize how afraid her mother was.

"I don't know." Liam kept his voice low and gently rubbed Sophie's back. Somehow, he managed to convey the impression that the subject they were discussing was nothing to worry about. "Normally I'd say the cops wouldn't waste time coming back, but for obvious reasons they're putting a lot of resources into this case."

"Can they break the door down if they have a warrant?"

"They can exercise reasonable force, whatever that means, but they didn't have a warrant to search this condo or they'd have said so. Did you notice that they only said they wanted to talk to me, not that they had a warrant to search the premises?"

She hadn't noticed a thing. Hadn't even distinguished the precise words the cops were calling out. "I can't subject you to this sort of harassment," she said despairingly. "I should leave. Go to a motel—" Her teeth were chattering so violently that it was difficult to form the words.

"Unless you want to walk straight into the arms of a waiting police officer, you should stay right here. I'll lay odds they've left a cop downstairs in the lobby."

"I scared," Sophie interrupted, her voice thin with fear. "Mommy, I scared."

Her daughter was about the only thing in the world that could have grounded Chloe at that precise moment. "It's nothing to worry about, sweetie." She kissed the top of her daughter's head, breathing in the reassuring smell of shampoo and talcum powder. "We'll be fine."

"Bobby Bunny is scared." Sophie's voice still trembled.

"I have a great idea," Liam said. "Why don't we all sleep together in my big bed tonight?"

Sophie's head popped up for the first time since the banging started. "Bunny, too?"

"Definitely." Liam nodded. "You and Bunny can be in the middle, Sophie, and your mommy and I will sleep one on each side so that whichever way you turn, there will be a grown-up right there to look after you."

"Yes." She nodded, clearly relieved.

Liam met Chloe's eyes over their daughter's head. "I don't think the cops will come back," he said softly. "But if they do, I want both of you right where I can see you."

If the cops came back, that was exactly what Chloe wanted, too. It was a measure of how much fear the cops had inspired that her reaction to the prospect of sleeping with Liam was simply a feeling of increased safety, nothing remotely to do with sex.

"Thanks for the offer," she said tiredly. "I do appreciate all you're doing for us, Liam. It's way more than I could have expected."

"You're welcome." He gave an almost imperceptible smile. "Just to let you know, my bill is going to be enormous."

"You've earned it." She took Sophie's full weight into her own arms and forced herself to speak cheerfully. "Okay, sweetie, let's get you and Bobby Bunny settled in Liam's great big bed."

"I want you to stay wiv me, Mommy."

"I will, sweetie." Now that the adrenaline rush caused

by the cops' assault on Liam's front door was fading, Chloe felt wrung out, emotionally flattened. She yearned for sleep, not just because she was tired but because she craved the luxury of a few hours of oblivion.

If this was going to be her last night of freedom, it seemed oddly appropriate that she should be with Sophie's father. The night their daughter was conceived, she and Liam had spent their time together consumed by sexual activity, so this would be the first time they'd ever actually slept together. Their first time was also likely to be their last, she reflected wryly, since the cops seemed determined to get her inside a jail cell at the earliest possible opportunity.

Chloe suspected there was a moral lesson hidden somewhere in that crazy jumble of circumstances. Her mother was fond of quoting the biblical warning about people who sow the wind reaping the whirlwind. At the moment, though, Chloe felt as if she were reaping a monster hurricane without ever having enjoyed the fun of sowing even a mild spring breeze. Now, when it was much too late, she realized that her mistake hadn't been to threaten to leave Jason. Her mistake had been that she lacked the courage to carry out her threat months and months ago.

Too late. Whoever said that those were the two saddest words in the English language had known exactly what he was talking about.

Ten

Paul Fairfax fought to keep hold of his temper. Almost nothing had gone right since he landed in Denver after a god-awful plane ride. He'd actually been forced to fly economy in order to get a seat on the early flight out of Chicago. Now he was being forced to brownnose Frederick Mitchell, a political hack who probably planned to use the excuse of the mayor's death simply to increase the size of his payoff. Because in Paul's experience of politicians, there was always a payoff.

Swallowing his resentment, Paul directed an ingratiating smile toward Mitchell, the tanned and glossy aide to the dead mayor. If there was one group of people Paul despised even more than elected politicians, it was the parasites who hid in the background behind the pols, pulling the strings. Still, he wasn't about to offend the guy by letting his dislike show. Paul's particular skill at Raven Enterprises had always been to put a smiling, socially charming face on the not-so-charming economic reality of Ron's business deals. He could sure as hell disguise his true feelings for this little turd. This was crunch time, and with twenty-five years of successful hypocrisy under his belt, he wasn't about to be thrown for a loop by a lowly mayoral aide in a third-rate city like Denver.

In fact, the more control the prick had actually exerted over Jason Hamilton the better. If Mitchell truly had been the power behind the mayoral throne, that might mean he still had sufficient clout to get the Arran project approved swiftly. According to Sam DiVoli, Fred was an insider's insider who enjoyed excellent relations with everyone who mattered on the zoning committee. If Sam was right—and he usually was—all they needed to do was convince Mitchell to act on their behalf and the Arran project would be rubber-stamped through the committee.

Paul really needed Fred Mitchell to work that sort of magic. During this morning's tedious plane ride he'd forced himself to confront the bleak truth: whatever it took, he couldn't afford to let Jason Hamilton's death screw up the Arran project. The financial situation at Raven Enterprises had gone from bad to worse in the four months since Ron Raven fucked up everything by disappearing. Total, humiliating financial disaster loomed if he and Sam couldn't get the zoning variances for the Arran project put on a fast track through the appropriate committees. That meant getting Fred Mitchell on board—before Edgar Showalter poisoned people's minds with his constant wailing about the environment, forest fires and mud slides. Mud slides, for God's sake! Denver was a *city* and its major environmental feature was concrete. How the hell could a hotel and luxury residential condos impact the environment in an area already full of buildings? The people of Denver ought to be begging him to rehab one of their run-down inner-city areas. Instead, Showalter kept trotting out new roadblocks simply because the houses that would need to come down happened to have been standing for ninety years. Ninety years, for God's sake! In Georgia, in a town like Fairfax, ninety years was considered no more than a blink of the eye. But in this part of the country people acted as if tearing down a few ramshackle houses signaled the doom of Western civilization.

Adjusting his face into an expression of heartfelt sympathy, Paul waited for Sam to finish offering condolences on the mayor's death. He spoke the minute Sam stopped.

"Thanks for talking to us, Fred, when we know you must be run off your feet. We really appreciate the fact that you've taken time out of your busy day to meet with Sam and me. We were horrified to hear about Jason Hamilton's death, and we certainly appreciate how difficult the situation is for everyone who worked with him."

"It's not just difficult, it's devastating." Annoyingly, Fred Mitchell didn't seem willing to get off the subject of Jason's death. They'd exchanged variations of the same condolences at least three times. Enough already, Paul thought, swallowing a sigh of irritation.

"Everyone agrees that Jason was the best mayor Denver's ever seen." Mitchell's fingers tapped a restless rhythm on the stack of papers in front of him, and his eyes actually filled with tears. "I can't wrap my mind around the fact that he's gone. Jason told me about his dinner with you last night, Sam, and we spent half an hour talking about the launch of his senatorial campaign. I was over the moon, as you can imagine, and Jason was so much looking forward to taking his vision for the people of Colorado to Washington. He would have been a shoe-in for senator and now it's all over." His voice dropped. "I can't believe I must have been the last person to speak to Jason before he was killed."

Mitchell still looked on the verge of tears and Sam produced another string of condolences. Maybe the guy really did care about Jason's death, Paul thought. The aide had just seen his own career wash down the sewage pipes, at least until he could clamber aboard some other politician's bandwagon. When you got right down to it, the mayor's murder posed a bigger problem for Fred Mitchell than almost anyone else.

Paul waited for Sam to finish his latest round of condolences. "The best tribute we can make to Jason's memory at this point is to insure his favorite projects don't get stalled in committee," he said, as soon as Sam paused for breath. It was past time to broach the subject he'd actually flown in from Chicago to discuss, for Christ's sake. "Jason couldn't invest directly in the Arran project, of course, because that would have been a conflict of interest and we all know how ethical he was. However, it's no secret that he was very interested in seeing it through to completion as part of his vision for a renewed and revitalized downtown for the city of Denver. He assured Sam only a couple of days ago that getting the necessary permits and zoning variances was right at the head of his agenda for next week."

"I'm aware of Jason's interest in the Arran project," Fred said stiffly. "And I understand that you want to get construction under way before winter sets in. But we can't afford to be seen pandering to big business interests and trying to rush something shady through committee while the city's in a state of shock—"

"You need to watch your words, my friend." Sam leaned

across the desk and patted the aide's arm. "For a start, Fred, there's nothing in the least shady about the Arran project. It's high class, high quality and totally aboveboard. Second of all, Paul and I aren't *big business*. We're just a couple of hardworking entrepreneurs trying to do something good for Denver and make an honest buck in the process. Heck, we're a couple of little guys who started out with nothing. Yes, we want to make a profit. Of course we do! But basically we're trying to build something that will benefit the people of Denver, that's all."

Mitchell didn't blink an eye at Sam's characterization of himself as a little guy, and a self-made man, despite the fact that Sam's personal fortune was in the range of forty to fifty million bucks—the first two million of which he'd inherited from his grandpa, both facts Mitchell was aware of.

"I understand that you and Paul have the best interests of our city at heart," Mitchell said. "But I have to persuade the committee members to stand up to Edgar Showalter, and that's not easy. Bottom line, for your project to work, we'll not only have to condemn eight houses that were built almost a century ago, we'll also have to bulldoze an apartment building that houses forty-two low income families."

"Those houses you're talking about haven't got a lick of architectural merit and everyone knows it," Sam said. "They're just old. More to the point, the plumbing's shot and the electric wiring dates from 1950. Since when has the city of Denver been in the business of preserving ramshackle houses for no better reason than the fact they were built a long time ago? As for the apartment building, I recognize you've got a problem with affordable housing in the city, Fred, but we're willing to work with you on that—"

"How?" Mitchell asked boldly. "I need something

concrete to take to Showalter. And frankly, I'm tired of developers making a profit on the backs of low income families who've been pushed out of their homes."

"That's not what we're planning," Sam said smoothly. "Not at all. Remember the town houses Jason and I went into partnership to build at Stapleton? That would have been a couple of years before he ran for mayor the first time."

Mitchell nodded. "Yes, I do remember. It was one of Jason's most successful projects."

Sam smiled. "It sure was. And since you're familiar with it, you probably know we included thirty units of affordable housing in our final design."

"Yes, you did. But Stapleton was already zoned for redevelopment—"

Sam spoke right over the interruption. "As you know, Fred, that Stapleton development not only turned out to be one of the projects Jason was always real proud of, we won a passel of awards for it."

"How about including fifty similar low income units in the Arran project?" Fred suggested. "That would make the project a lot easier for me to sell to the zoning committee."

Paul just managed not to laugh. *The guy had to be kidding!* He wanted them to build apartments for slum dwellers in the midst of their fabulous Arran project? Paul opened his mouth to protest, but Sam spoke first.

"That's certainly one option we'd be happy to consider." Sam leaned forward, his smiles fading now that they were getting down to the nitty-gritty of negotiations. "Not fifty units, that's out of the question, but maybe we could see our way clear to providing twenty units without undercutting the financial viability of the project. We can work with the city on this, Fred. Just give us the go-ahead and we'll build a legacy Jason and everyone associated with him can be proud of. I had an idea this morning—how about we call that four star hotel we're planning Hamilton House? That has a nice ring, don't you think? And it would be a real nice memorial to Jason. Maybe that's the way you should present it to the zoning committee, as a special memorial in honor of the best mayor Denver has had in fifty years."

To Paul's annoyance, the phone rang just when Mitchell looked as if he might be edging toward a commitment. "It's the police chief," Mitchell said, glancing at his caller ID. "Excuse me, I need to take this."

His conversation lasted for several minutes and when Mitchell hung up the phone he was shaking his head. "The chief seems to think that the fact Chloe Hamilton can't be found must mean that she's guilty of killing Jason. I'm a big admirer of our police chief—hell, I was the person who pushed Jason to appoint him—but he's chasing the wrong trail in this instance. I keep telling him there's no way she killed her husband. He was asking me if I had any idea where she might be, but of course I don't."

"Innocent people don't usually cut and run," Paul interjected. In his opinion, Ron Raven was the ultimate proof of that. Ron had been involved in one too many shady enterprises and he'd met the fate he deserved. According to the story Adam had brought back from Belize, Ron Raven had run to Miami because he found out that Ted Horn was planning to kill him. Ron had died because he hadn't run fast enough to escape Ted Horn's hired killer. Paul hadn't bothered to argue with his brother, but he knew that story had a ton of holes in it. He knew, for example, that Ron had been preparing to run before Ted Horn put his murderous plans in motion. How else to explain that the corporate bank accounts for Raven Enterprises had been almost completely cleaned out in the weeks preceding Ron's disappearance? When the police arrived with news of Ron's murder, it was as if the missing piece at the center of a giant jigsaw puzzle had suddenly been slotted into place. Paul had gone straight to the company accounts and what he'd found there—or not found—had left him in a state of near panic. The company coffers had basically been cleaned out.

Not that Paul had breathed a word about the missing money to anyone, least of all the police. He knew too well that in business, money flowed to money, and a single word suggesting that Paul Fairfax had been left with a shell of a company but no actual investment funds would have sunk him quicker than Ron's body bag had disappeared into the Atlantic Ocean.

"But Chloe *hasn't* cut and run," Fred Mitchell protested in response to Paul's earlier comment. "She's trying to avoid the media frenzy and I don't blame her. The cops have had to divert the traffic on Seventh Avenue because the TV crews and roving camera vans are stacked three deep along the road leading to her home. Her husband was just killed—of course she wants to avoid having cameras and mikes shoved in her face every time she turns around. And as for the fact that she's hired Liam Raven as her attorney, well, so what? The guy has a reputation as a brilliant courtroom attorney. He saved Sherri Norquist when she was accused of killing her husband. Why wouldn't Chloe want him to save her, too?"

Sam made a comment about the TV coverage of the

mayor's murder, but Paul didn't hear it. His ears were ringing and he could honest to God feel his blood pressure climbing. "Who did you say Chloe Hamilton hired as her lawyer?" he asked. "Did you say *Liam Raven?*"

There had to be a mistake, Paul though feverishly. The long arm of coincidence couldn't stretch far enough to have Ron Raven's only son defending the woman accused of murdering Jason Hamilton.

Fred looked at him with evident surprise. "Do you know Liam Raven?" he asked.

"Yes." Paul couldn't manage to dissemble enough to avoid having the acknowledgment emerge in a hard, angry monosyllable.

"And judging by your expression, I'd have to guess he's not one of your favorite people." Sam chuckled, clearly trying to cut the sudden tension in the room. He, of course, was the sort of dirt-digger who would undoubtedly have known all along of the connection. It had simply never been useful or relevant before. Paul was relieved that he couldn't imagine any way Sam could exploit the connection even now. Sam cared about three things: political power, money and the Denver Broncos. The fact that Liam was Ron Raven's son provided no leverage for acquiring more of any of the three.

However, the last thing Paul wanted to talk about was Ron Raven's son. In the interest of switching everyone's attention back to the Arran project, he forced himself to speak dismissively. "I have reason to question Mr. Raven's ethics, that's all."

"Interesting you should say that," Fred Mitchell commented. "He's raised a few red flags here in Denver, too. As I mentioned, he defended a local TV personality, Sherri

Norquist, when she was accused of murdering her husband. Lots of people who followed that case thought he pushed the envelope so far he was lucky not to be accused of professional misconduct."

Paul filed away the name Sherri Norquist for future reference. Thank God for laptops and the Internet. He'd be able to find everything he needed on the case as soon as he got back to his hotel room. Bad enough that Chloe Hamilton was a murdering bitch who'd killed her husband at a moment of maximum inconvenience for Paul and the Arran project, but it was intolerable to know that Ron Raven's son was out there, working to help her escape just punishment for her crimes.

Still, he needed to stay focused. Right now Paul's task was to bring Fred Mitchell on board with the Arran project. Money, after all, took priority even over revenge. But once Mitchell was squared away, Paul would make damn sure Liam Raven paid a price for defending Chloe Hamilton.

He had nothing on Liam he could take to the police, of course, but he would be more than happy to free up a couple of hours of his valuable time to help the media connect all the dots between Ron Raven, criminal bigamist, and Liam Raven, defender of the guilty. The public deserved to know what sort of man Chloe Hamilton had hired as her lawyer. It would be a real pleasure to expose Liam Raven for the charlatan he was. In fact, finding a new way to make life difficult for Ron Raven's son was the most pleasurable thing that had happened to Paul since he stepped on the treadmill this morning and learned that Jason Hamilton had been inconsiderate enough to get himself murdered. Leaving Sam free to hammer out the final details of their deal with Fred Mitchell, he allowed himself the luxury of contemplating what lies he might tell to insure that Liam Raven and Chloe Hamilton blistered in the white hot heat of media notoriety.

Eleven

His father's death had provided Liam with plenty of opportunity to see the press corps at its frenzied worst. He'd anticipated being greeted by a mob scene when he drove Chloe and Sophie back to their home early the next morning, but even his experiences in the wake of Ron Raven's disappearance and at the Sherri Norquist trial hadn't prepared him for the crush of vans, camera crews and hangers-on crammed into every available inch of space in the road outside her house. In the wake of her husband's murder, Chloe seemed to be climbing at breakneck speed up the celebrity ladder of shame.

"Are you ready for the attack of the media ghouls?" he asked, not allowing his sympathy to show. Chloe's behavior last night suggested sympathy was more destructive to her self-control than hostility and he needed her to hold it together when she was in front of the TV cameras.

"This is no bigger than the crowd of reporters waiting for me after I won the Olympic gold." She drew in a defiant breath. "I'll be fine."

That was clearly more a statement of will than an accurate assessment of her feelings, Liam thought. "Whatever questions anyone calls out to you, don't answer," he said. "That's really important, Chloe."

"I know. Don't worry, I've been listening to all your dire warnings. I understand those people out there aren't my friends."

A small voice piped up from the rear. "Why aren't they your friends, Mommy?"

Chloe winced and then glanced back at Sophie who was staring out of the car window, her body language suggesting more curiosity than fear at the noisy, jostling crush of people. "Well, I've never met any of these people before," Chloe said. "You have to meet somebody and get to know them before they can become your friend."

"It's too many people." Sophie frowned. "Why are they here at our house?"

"They're here because they're sad about Daddy," Chloe said. "They wish Daddy was still here so that he could carry on being the mayor."

"I wish Daddy was here, too." Sophie subsided into silence, pressing her nose against the window for a closer look at the crowds.

"She seems basically okay with all this, don't you think?" Chloe said, low-voiced, turning back to face Liam. "And I don't see any way we could have avoided exposing her to the crowds. Not if she wants to be with me."

"I'm not an expert where kids are concerned, but she seems to be doing at least as well as could be expected, all things considered."

"Fortunately, she has no clue what this media circus is about, which helps."

Liam gave a wry smile. "I'm not sure *I* know what this media circus is all about."

"That's easy." Chloe lifted her shoulders in a resigned shrug. "They want to take pictures of me being arrested and marched off to jail in handcuffs. They're willing to hang around in order to get the shot."

Liam admired her calm, even if it was only skin deep. "We're going to be asked to show identification," he warned as they approached the police barricade guarding access to her home. "As soon as the cop stops the car and asks for my driver's license, somebody is almost certain to recognize you. Get ready for the onslaught."

She gave a small, tired smile. "How could anyone ever be ready for this much hostile attention? But don't worry. I won't go to pieces."

"No, I'm sure you won't."

She didn't respond and Liam realized that although he'd intended the comment as a compliment, to Chloe it might well have sounded like another of his endless criticisms. In retrospect, it occurred to him that he'd been a little too willing to pile on the insults yesterday. Yes, Chloe had committed adultery, but her husband had married her under egregiously false pretenses, which had to be something of an excuse for her behavior. And he was far from blameless in Sophie's procreation. He, after all, had been willing to sleep with a woman dressed in a Cleopatra costume without even bothering to find out who she really was, and his recent night with No-Name suggested that his dating habits hadn't improved much in the four years since that encounter. Chloe wasn't going to be chosen as the poster child for a chastity campaign, but then, neither was he.

The bottom line was that he didn't really believe Chloe had killed Jason Hamilton. And that, far from being a relief, was actually the root cause of much of his hostility. He was afraid he was being duped again, as he had been by Sherri Norquist. The solution to that problem, however, was not to lash out at Chloe; he needed instead to accumulate sufficient hard facts either to confirm his gut instincts about her innocence or to refute them. Above all, he needed to stop reacting to Chloe as if she were nothing more than a Sherri Norquist clone. Everything that had happened since her first phone call early yesterday morning suggested that she was about as different from his former client as it was possible for two women to be.

He watched as she twisted around and reached into the back of the car so that she could squeeze her daughter's hand. *Their* daughter's hand. Chloe's gesture was casual and yet full of love, and Liam was aware of a totally unexpected surge of desire.

"Are you and Mr. Rabbit okay, honey bun?" Chloe's voice was gentle, her eyes warm.

In the rearview mirror, Liam saw his daughter nod, her tiny, solemn face breaking into a smile that caused the strange clenching of his stomach muscles that seemed to occur on at least half the occasions he looked at her. "He's not Mr. Rabbit, Mommy. He's Bobby Bunny."

"Oh, yes. I keep forgetting."

Sophie smiled again. Name-the-rabbit was obviously a familiar game, one of those silly exchanges that wove a reassuring web of intimacy. Liam switched his gaze back to the road. Both Sophie and Chloe were seriously messing with his head and he didn't much care for the sensation.

They had reached the police barricade and a police officer gestured to indicate Liam should roll down his side window and then asked to see Liam's driver's license.

"I have a meeting arranged with Captain Dexel," Liam said, naming the chief of police as he produced his license for the cop. "This is Mrs. Hamilton, the mayor's widow, and I'm her lawyer. Can you arrange to get us inside the house with as little fuss as possible? We have Mrs. Hamilton's daughter with us and we'd obviously like to avoid frightening her."

The cop peered into the car, presumably to satisfy himself that Liam wasn't a reporter hoping to win an inside advantage. Liam was still driving the Subaru borrowed from Helen and the cop seemed to be having trouble wrapping his mind around the idea that the mayor's wife and daughter really were traveling to their home in a battered Subaru with a ding on its left rear door.

The cop eventually decided they were who they claimed to be. "Wait here, please, Mrs. Hamilton. Don't move, Mr. Raven." He left to confer with higher authority and returned a minute later with another man, not in uniform. Liam recognized the newcomer as Detective Kenneth Murphy, a grizzled veteran of the Homicide Bureau who'd been in charge of the investigation into the murder of Sherri Norquist's husband.

Unfortunately, Detective Murphy had been infuriated by Sherri's acquittal and had made no effort to disguise his contempt for her lawyer. Liam had no particular respect for the detective, either. Even now, even knowing that Sherri Norquist had been guilty as charged, he was still convinced that the detective had perjured himself on the stand in an abortive effort to guarantee a conviction. Not all the sins committed during the Sherri Norquist trial could be laid at his door, Liam reflected.

He schooled his features into an expression of polite neutrality. If he wanted more than tepid police cooperation in assisting Chloe and Sophie into their home with a minimum of press interference he was going to have to eat a large slice of humble pie. "Good morning, Detective Murphy."

"Mr. Raven." The detective inclined his head in the barest of acknowledgments.

"We'd like to drive this car straight into Mrs. Hamilton's garage to avoid the media circus," Liam said. "Could you arrange to have the garage door opened for us? We don't have an opener in this car."

"I'm sorry." Detective Murphy didn't look in the least sorry. "I'm afraid you and your client will have to walk from here into the house, counselor. There are police vehicles blocking the entrance to the garage and with all the TV cameras on the street there's no way for us to move them."

And if there were, Murphy sure as hell wouldn't move them anyway. The detective could barely conceal his glee at the prospect of Chloe—and Liam—having to run the gauntlet of at least a hundred rabid reporters.

Liam hid his anger behind another polite smile and turned to Chloe with a casual attitude that suggested the detective was being entirely reasonable, instead of a major dick. "You should stay in the car until I have Sophie out of her car seat," he said. "No point in giving the reporters extra time to yell questions at you that you don't plan to answer."

"All right." The fact that she agreed without protest indicated to Liam that she was well aware that Detective Murphy was throwing her to the wolves. He could see, too, that she was no longer anywhere near as confident as she'd tried to appear earlier. It bothered him that there was nothing he could do to protect her except to use his body as a physical barrier to shield her from as many cameras as possible.

Seething behind the smile he had pasted in place for the benefit of the cops, he got out of the car and leaned through the rear door so that he could release the straps on Sophie's car seat. Her arms clutched him hard as he lifted her out and she burrowed close to him, cringing away from the raucous crowd. She might be very young, but she realized as soon as she saw the crowd without the intervening barrier of a car window that it was composed of people who were anything but friendly.

The yelled questions started, one of top of the other, with nobody waiting for Liam to answer, even if he'd been willing to do so. *"Look, isn't that the mayor's daughter?"*

"Who's the man?"

"It's the attorney who defended Sherri Norquist!"

"Over here, Mr. Raven! Mr. Raven, is it true that you've agreed to defend Chloe Hamilton?"

"Has your client been officially named as a suspect in the mayor's murder?"

Sophie buried her face in Liam's neck as the groundswell of noise hit them like a monster wave breaking on the beach, the individual questions bursting like splashes of foam above the background roar. The shouted questions quickly reached a frenzied pitch and, either by accident or design, one of the police barriers broke just as Chloe got out of the car. The resulting rush of people, cameras and microphones threatened to degenerate into a stampede. If he hadn't braced his back against the car, Liam would have been swept off his feet.

"I want Mommy." Sophie sounded desperate, gripping Liam's shoulders as if her life depended on it. For a moment, the crush was so great that Liam wondered if perhaps it did. "I want my mommy. Where is she?"

"I'm here." Somehow Chloe had pushed her way to their side. She reached to take Sophie into her arms.

"Have you got her?" Liam asked, one arm around Chloe's waist to prevent the rear end of a TV camera from being shoved into her back. "Can you hold on to her?"

She nodded and Liam handed Sophie over, his anger so powerful that he literally couldn't see the reporters through the white hot cloud of his rage. It was one thing for the police to decide a bit of rough handling by the press corps might serve as a useful softening up tool before they interrogated Chloe. It was another thing entirely to subject her daughter to the same treatment. He'd told Captain Dexel that they would be bringing Sophie with them, so the cops had no excuse. They couldn't plead ignorance, merely rank indifference.

"Get my client and her daughter out of here right now," he said to Detective Murphy, no longer bothering to conceal his fury. "And Murphy, unless you want to find yourself slapped with the biggest lawsuit the police department in this city has ever faced, you'd better make sure that Sophie doesn't get so much as a broken fingernail as a result of your cynical decision to deny Mrs. Hamilton access to her home through her own garage."

Even with uniformed cops on either side clearing a path, they had to fight their way across the street. By the time they made it into the house, Liam was ready to take Detective Murphy apart, bone by bone. He had just sufficient control left to remind himself that however tempting it might be to contemplate punching out every cop and reporter in the vicinity, getting arrested for bodily assault wasn't going to help Chloe or his daughter.

The captain was waiting in the entrance hall. A young woman, not in uniform, stood at his side. "I apologize about that," the captain said with patent insincerity. "The media these days is damn near out of control, isn't it? I didn't expect them to break through the barricades though."

"Why not? You only used a plastic ribbon and there were no cops assigned to crowd control. Short of issuing an open invitation to manhandle my client, I don't see what else you could have done to put her and her daughter at risk."

"I didn't anticipate the number of people who would be interested in seeing Mrs. Hamilton return to the scene of the crime." The captain didn't wait for either of them to respond to that obvious absurdity. Instead, he gestured to the young woman standing at his side. Apparently she wasn't a cop.

"Trudi Laniken has made herself available to take care of your daughter for the rest of the morning," he said to Chloe. "She'll take the child now and we'll get started on our interview."

"No, she won't take *Mrs. Hamilton's daughter* now." Liam stepped forward, interposing himself between Chloe and the babysitter. It occurred to him that if Chloe hadn't killed her husband, Trudi was the most likely suspect—or at least the person who'd had easiest access to both Jason and the alarm system. He sure as hell didn't want a potential murderer taking care of his daughter.

The captain flashed a smile that was all teeth and no friendliness. "I wasn't making a suggestion, Mr. Raven. I was telling you how it's going to be—"

"And I'm telling you that Trudi Laniken is not going to be taking care of Sophie this morning. Clearly, I need to remind you that we're here as a gesture of goodwill. We've come because Mrs. Hamilton is extremely anxious to have her husband's killer identified and for no other reason. As you know, Mrs. Hamilton has been away from her home since yesterday morning, trying to secure a few hours of peace and quiet in which to recover from the shock of her husband's murder. She needs to change her clothes and take a few minutes to get her daughter settled down. We'll be ready to talk with you in half an hour. I'll help my client take care of Sophie until then. Chloe, will you lead the way, please?"

"You're going to escort Mrs. Hamilton into her bedroom? While she's changing her clothes?" Captain Dexel pounced. "You have an interesting way of conducting your professional relationship with your clients, Mr. Raven."

The malicious sexual innuendo was precisely the sort of attitude Liam had warned Chloe to expect from the police and the public when she first approached him. The fact that his behavior with Sherri Norquist justified the police captain's jibes didn't make him feel one bit better. He realized with sudden, piercing clarity that he'd done Chloe a huge disservice when he agreed to act as her lawyer. She hadn't been in any fit state to be making rational judgments yesterday morning, and he'd known it. That left the burden of decision making with him. Since Bill Schuller was off fishing, he should have insisted on contacting Robyn Johnson. True, Robyn rarely took on clients these days, but she had always given him more respect than he deserved and he could have persuaded her that Chloe genuinely needed her expertise. Instead, he'd allowed his professional judgment to be overridden by a toxic cocktail of emotions that revolved chiefly around his own hang-ups about fatherhood. Unfortunately, Chloe was the person now suffering for his lapse.

His rash decision to act as her lawyer brought the issue of Sophie's paternity front and center of the investigation into Jason's murder, Liam acknowledged silently. Yesterday, in the comfort of his own office, it had been easy to insist that they needed to reveal up front that Sophie was his child. That decision had been correct in theory, since there was at least a chance of the autopsy revealing that Jason was sterile. In practical reality, however, Captain Dexel was going to make mincemeat of the information and serve it up for their dinner—probably with a charge of murder as relish on the side.

Liam was pretty confident that his expression revealed nothing of what he was thinking. Control of his body language and facial expressions was a courtroom skill at which he'd always excelled. Right now, though, that was only a small consolation for having made decisions that basically screwed Chloe over.

He spoke to the captain with icy politeness, not because he felt in the least courteous but because at this point it was his best weapon. "We'll be with you in thirty minutes, Captain Dexel, at which time Mrs. Hamilton will be happy to respond to any questions you might have for her." He walked away as if the issue had been settled, ushering Chloe ahead of him. To his huge relief, nobody stopped them.

Chloe led him upstairs to the master bedroom, a room decorated in a soothing blue-and-mauve palette. She set Sophie in the middle of the bed and gave her a smacking kiss. "I'll be right back," she said. "I'm just going to get you a few books and some puzzles. Okay?"

"Okay." Sophie dropped her rabbit onto a pillow and wriggled into a more comfortable position. "That man is mean."

"Which man, sweetie?"

Sophie thought for a moment. "All of them," she said finally.

"You're right, Sophie." Liam gave a short laugh and turned to Chloe. "We have a very perceptive daughter."

Chloe's gaze locked with his. "Yes, Sophie is very smart. You need to remember that." Her voice lowered. "You heard in the car how she picks up on things adults say. Be careful, Liam."

"I'm sorry." He looked away, since eye contact with Chloe tended to make him uncomfortable. "I won't tell her anything about our relationship until you're ready. You have my word."

"Thank you. I'll be right back." She returned in a couple of minutes and spread the books and puzzles across the bed. "Here you are, sweetie. Would you like Liam to read you a story while I change my clothes?"

"Yes." Sophie nodded. She selected a book and handed it to Liam. "This book is called *Brown Bear, Brown Bear, What Do You See?*" she told him. "You'll like it. It's a very good story."

"I'll read it in just a minute." Liam turned to Chloe and gestured toward the bathroom. "I need a few moments alone with you. Could we talk in there?"

She nodded and quickly followed him into the palatial bathroom. "What is it? Is there a problem with Sophie?"

"Not with Sophie, but indirectly about her." He hesitated for a moment, and then decided there was no way to make what he needed to say more palatable.

"The police are even more hostile than I expected and I'm afraid they'll go after you with no holds barred if we tell them that Sophie is my biological daughter. In the current circumstances, I don't believe there's any way to convince them we were never really lovers. The fact that you've selected me as your lawyer is simply going to confirm their suspicion that we had a long-term adulterous relationship. Which, I'm sure I don't have to point out, gives you an excellent motive for getting rid of Jason."

"Then what should we do? Not tell them about Sophie? I have no problem with keeping quiet about her paternity. We both know it has absolutely nothing to do with Jason's death, so why do the cops need to know?"

Liam shook his head. "That's a high-risk strategy. Too risky. Sophie's paternity is a potentially explosive secret and we want to detonate it before the cops get to pull the trigger. My advice is to tell them during your interview this morning that Jason was sterile, and that he'd known ever since you became pregnant that he wasn't the biological father of the child you were carrying. Make sure you emphasize that he adored Sophie. There are probably plenty of witnesses who can testify to that."

"Wait, let me get this straight. You want me to reveal the fact that I had an extramarital affair, but keep *your* identity protected?" Chloe didn't bother to hide the mockery in her question.

"Yes, that's what I'm recommending," Liam said quietly. "That's for your sake, Chloe, not for mine. Detective Murphy is one of those cops who's been on the job so long he's gotten tired of seeing thieves and murderers and rapists escape just punishment for their crimes. Once he decides you're guilty, he's going to do whatever he thinks is necessary to obtain a conviction against you. He's furious that Sherri Norquist walked free, and he blames me for what he sees as a blatant miscarriage of justice. He's bringing all that baggage to this investigation and making you carry it. If you tell him this morning, while I'm still acting as your lawyer, that Sophie is my daughter, he's going to tear both of us apart."

"You mean he's going to accuse us of conspiring to murder my husband?" Chloe asked. She choked out a tiny laugh. "That's so crazy I can barely ask the question."

Shocked into silence, Liam could only stare at her. "Would you believe that I never once considered such a possibility?" he said when he recovered his voice. "But you're right. That's exactly what the cops are going to suspect."

"Thank God you have an alibi."

"Yes, I have an alibi for the actual time Jason was murdered. That won't stop Detective Murphy accusing me of helping you plan to get rid of Jason. He can slap a conspiracy charge on me in a heartbeat."

She shook her head. "Now you're going beyond crazy—"

"Maybe. But the bottom line is that I can't represent you in this case, Chloe. You need another lawyer. I'm going to call Robyn Johnson as soon as we leave here. She's an icon in Denver, and the mere fact that she's agreed to represent you will give the police department pause."

"*If* she agrees to represent me."

"I interned with her when I was in law school. I'm optimistic she'll take the case. Meanwhile, the moment I'm out of the official picture you need to discuss the question of Sophie's paternity with Robyn and take her advice as to how it should be handled."

She started to protest, and he silenced her with a quick shake of his head. "Chloe, you came to me because you wanted solid legal advice in a difficult situation. I'm giving you really good legal advice right now. You need to be represented by somebody else for this case. I can't act as your lawyer."

"Based on what you've just said, the police are going to suspect me anyway, whether you're my lawyer or not. And no other lawyer would have done for me what you did last night."

"But another lawyer might well have been able to convince the cops to treat you a lot more kindly and then you wouldn't have needed my help." Liam put his finger under her chin and tilted her face upward. "I'll still offer you any support you want or need Chloe, but it will be unofficial. Trust me, I can be much more use to you if I'm not operating under the rules governing lawyer-client relations."

"I understand the difficulty of your current position," she said with weary formality. "Thank you for your help last night and this morning, Liam. I appreciate everything you've done for me…"

Liam realized she didn't believe his offer of continuing help was sincere. He had no idea that he was going to kiss her until his mouth was touching hers. She didn't resist, even for a moment, perhaps because she was too stunned. Her lips were soft and she smelled of his soap and shampoo, the masculine scent mysteriously transformed by her skin into something quintessentially female.

She was a beautiful woman, and he was often attracted to beautiful women, so Liam wasn't surprised to feel a surge of desire the moment his mouth touched hers. The intoxicating sensation of flying off into space was more intense than he was accustomed to these days, but not entirely unexpected. It was the accompanying rush of tenderness that caught him completely off guard. That, and a hunger so deep that it made him realize how empty he'd been for the last four years. At the same time as part of him was drowning in the sheer physical pleasure of their kiss, another part of him was marveling at the idea that he not only wanted to have sex with Chloe, he also wanted to protect her, and talk to her, and ski down a mountain with her when the snow was a crisp white powder and the sun was beating down out of a clear Colorado winter sky.

His head shouted a warning to back off, that he was getting in much too deep, much too fast, but his body was sending an entirely different message. He held Chloe tightly, his hips grinding against hers and the kiss becoming more and more demanding, in part because whatever he sought from her—and he didn't quite know what it was—she seemed to give back without hesitation.

He broke away about one millisecond before the kiss changed from merely passionate into sexual foreplay leading inevitably to naked bodies on a horizontal surface. When they separated, he stole one final quick glance and saw that she looked as dazed as he felt. She also looked flushed and incredibly beautiful.

With significant effort, Liam resisted the temptation to take her back into his arms. He touched his finger very lightly to her lips. "That's another reason why I can't be your lawyer," he said. "Sherri Norquist taught me my lesson. These days, I never have sex with my clients."

Twelve

The Flying W Ranch, Thatch, Wyoming, August 8

Eleanor Horn Raven took a pan of apple raisin muffins from the oven and gave a nod of approval to their golden brown perfection. Holding the dogs at bay with her foot, she levered one hot and crumbly muffin onto a plate and poured herself another mug of coffee, her last one of the day. She was turning into a parody of the earth mother ranch wife, she thought, not sure whether to be amused or disgusted by the coping mechanisms she'd developed in the months since her husband was brutally attacked and killed in his Miami hotel room.

Her thoughts began their familiar spiral into questions about her marriage and Ellie quite deliberately pushed them away. Ron was dead. Her brother had committed suicide. There was nobody left who could explain why her husband had been a bigamist, or why there had been a woman in Ron's hotel room the night he died.

Actually, that last bit wasn't entirely true, Ellie mused. Megan and Adam had discovered Ron's link to the platinum mine at Las Criandas where her brother had worked. They had even been able to give the mystery woman from Ron's hotel room an identity. She was Consuela Mackenzie, former mistress to Ellie's own brother. The sordid facts of the tragedy were all out in the open now. She supposed that the short way to sum up Ron's death was to say that it had been about money. Money, and the power it bestowed on men like Ron who had the knack of accumulating it. Ellie hadn't been too surprised to learn that Ted, her brother, had been pathologically jealous of Ron's financial success. What remained as much a mystery to her as ever was why Ron had needed the attention of two wives and a mistress all at the same time.

Still, at least she'd moved past the point where she blamed herself for being inadequate, as if Ron's crimes could somehow be laid at her feet. Her willful blindness to the problems in her marriage had been stupid, but at least she hadn't been downright immoral, which was more than could be said for Ron.

Ellie took a comforting bite of muffin and turned on the TV. She'd gotten into the habit recently of sharing her breakfast with Diane Sawyer and *Good Morning America.* This morning she was tuning in later than usual and the headlines had long since been dealt with. Diane Sawyer had moved on to fluff and was talking with a hair stylist who'd invented a new system for coloring hair.

A discussion of hair color was just about the level of seriousness that she preferred in her news programs these days, Ellie reflected. Although maybe it wasn't just her personal situation that had affected her viewing habits. Sometimes it seemed that the politicians were making such a mess of things that the only rational thing to do was to ignore them.

She watched the hair stylist flutter around the set and wondered what percentage of Diane's viewers could afford to spend three hundred bucks on a hair color job that would need renewing at least once a month. The stylist was touting the fact that his new patented product not only left hair color looking *entirely natural* but took a mere five minutes to work its magic.

Personally, Ellie thought natural was overrated. These days she sometimes felt a defiant streak stirring that had her understanding why teenagers went out to the mall and came back with purple hair and studs through their eyebrows. She wasn't quite ready for purple, but she was seriously considering the possibility of becoming a platinum blonde. Not discreetly highlighted to a muted gold, but bleached to a brazen hussy, brassy blonde. It would be liberating to have her hair dyed to a color that Ron had never seen—and certainly would never have imagined on his boring homebody first wife.

The doorbell rang. Ellie brushed muffin crumbs from her fingers, muted the TV sound and went to open the front door, the dogs huffing and puffing at her heels. Harry Ford, the local sheriff, waited on the front porch.

He greeted her with a smile, reaching out to scratch behind the ears of both dogs simultaneously. "Hey there, Ellie, how're you doin' this morning? Belle, Bruno, you're good dogs, now get your paws off of my pants."

"Nice to see you, Harry." She gave him a big smile before glaring at the dogs. "Belle, Bruno, for goodness' sake, sit. You're too old to get that excited." Surprisingly, the dogs obeyed her. She stood back and gestured to invite Harry in, glad for the company. She'd known Harry since they were in high school together. These past few months, she'd come to value his quiet, no-nonsense strength more than she'd have imagined possible, despite all those previous years of friendship. Just being with him always made her day brighter.

"Come on through to the kitchen, Harry. I've got some coffee and I made fresh muffins just a while ago. They should still be warm."

He groaned and patted his stomach, which was actually quite flat, with no excess flesh hanging over his Western-style turquoise belt buckle. "You know I swore off your cakes, Ellie. I've gained five pounds these past few months. If you keep on feeding me that stuff, I'll soon be bustin' out of my uniform."

"These aren't cakes, they're muffins."

"What's the difference?"

"Well, there's no frosting." She smiled at him, shooing the dogs ahead of her. "Seriously, the recipe doesn't call for much sugar. There's even a bit of bran in the mix."

"That makes it all okay then." He kept a poker face. "I guess the bran takes the calories right out of the flour and the butter."

She laughed. "At least it helps pass the flour and the butter through your system a bit quicker." She poured him a big mug of coffee, handing it to him black without needing to ask. Harry had shared quite a few breakfasts with her over the past four months and she liked the easy routine of it.

She popped a muffin onto a plate and set that next to

the coffee. "You're not in uniform, so I guess this isn't an official visit?" She always needed to get that question out of the way, since back in May and June there'd been too many official visits and far too much bad news.

"Nah, Jerry's on duty today. I'm off for forty-eight hours."

Ellie snorted. "Jerry's a nice man, but he's about as qualified to be a sheriff's deputy as one of my steers."

Harry grinned. "Yeah, well, I'm not expecting a crime wave today. I put three drunks in jail last night. They were busting up the chairs down at the bar, so that pretty much takes care of the crime scene in Stark County until next Saturday."

Unless there's another secret bigamist in town. Ellie didn't give voice to her thought. At least she'd reached the point of mental health where she recognized when she was being neurotic.

Harry took a bite of muffin, washed it down with a sip of coffee and sighed contentedly. "You're a fantastic cook, Ellie." He leaned back in his chair and his gaze was caught by the television. "They're doing a sports segment," he said. "You mind if I turn up the volume to listen to the baseball scores?"

"Of course not." Ellie handed him the remote, which was sitting on the draining board for some reason. "Here."

She busied herself putting the muffins into plastic bags and then storing the bags in the freezer. She was going to have to stop baking as therapy, she thought wryly, eyeing shelves filled with her previous endeavors. Or maybe she should take all these packages to church on Sunday and get rid of them that way.

The baseball scores were reported, apparently not to Harry's satisfaction. For reasons lost in the mists of time, he was an ardent New York Yankees fan, and his loyalty remained unwavering despite everything the team did to disappoint him. He muttered a couple of expletives that Ellie ignored, and the dogs gave him a comforting snuffle or two, as if fully aware that the Yankees hadn't been living up to expectations.

The program switched to a news update. "An amazing scene outside the home of the murdered mayor of Denver…" Ellie heard, before Harry muted the sound and the reporter's voice cut off into silence.

"That's a bad business," Harry said. "Not just losing the mayor, but having his wife as the chief suspect. It's a real shame."

"Don't spouses kill each other all the time?" Probably a lot more often than they committed bigamy, Ellie thought cynically.

"Yeah, but the mayor of Denver's wife is Chloe Hamilton. You remember her?"

"The pretty little thing who won all those Olympic medals for skiing back in the nineties?" Ellie shook her head. "She always seemed a nice kid."

"Yeah. I sometimes wonder if we're going to have any sports idols left, the way things are going. Ever since OJ—"

"Press the freeze button! I mean stop the program!" Ellie spoke over him, and when Harry didn't instantly react, she grabbed the remote and halted the broadcast herself.

"Well, I'll be damned," Harry said, staring at the image she'd captured on the screen. "It's Liam. Turn up the sound so's we can hear what they're saying, Ellie. For gosh sakes, what's that boy got himself into now?"

Ellie heard the sheriff speak, but she couldn't make

sense of his words. Her attention was fixed with hypnotic intensity on the image of her son, holding a little girl in his arms. The child was clinging to Liam for dear life and a moment before she froze the picture Ellie had seen the little girl bury her face in the hollow at the base of Liam's neck. By a quirk of timing, she had stopped the program on a frame that had the little girl with her head lifted again. The child was staring straight into the camera, green eyes wide with fright.

"Ellie." Harry stepped in front of the TV, waving his hand. "Ellie, what is it? You look like you've seen a ghost, honey. It's just Liam, and he's fine. You can see he's fine."

Ellie didn't answer. She couldn't. She went into the living room and came back holding a picture of Megan, taken on her fourth birthday. In the picture, Megan was riding her new pony, a gift from her dad, and she was staring straight into the camera lens, her unusual green eyes wide with excitement.

Ellie handed the photo to Harry, and nodded her head toward the TV screen with its big, frozen image of Liam and the little girl. "Do you notice…" She stopped and cleared her throat. "Look at the picture of Megan," she said to Harry. "Now look at the little girl on the screen. Do you notice anything?"

Harry gave the familiar picture of Megan an affection- ate glance. "Well, your Meggie always was cute as button, wasn't she? Those curls of hers are something else." He glanced up at the TV screen. "That kid's cute, too, but she sure doesn't have to worry about curls! You don't often see hair that poker straight. Not even a tiny kink at the ends."

"Don't fixate on the hair, Harry." *Men!* Why couldn't they see what was in front of them unless it reached up and socked them in the jaw? Ellie smothered her impatience. "Look at Megan's picture. Then look at the little girl's eyes. Look at the shape of her chin. And remember, it's Liam who's holding her."

Harry glanced at Megan's birthday picture again and then up at the TV screen. "What in the world are you suggesting, Ellie?" He spoke slowly, his gaze switching back and forth one more time. He drew in a sharp breath, his gaze focusing on the child's eyes. "You're surely not suggesting that...you can't believe that the kid—"

"That the little girl Liam is holding is actually his daughter?" Now that the words were out, Ellie felt surprisingly calm. "Well, yes, Harry. I guess that's exactly what I'm suggesting. And you must have seen the similarity to Megan, too, or you wouldn't be instructing me not to jump to conclusions!"

"I told you not to jump to conclusions because I know how you think," he said. "It doesn't mean I see any likeness between the two kids just because I cottoned on to why you ran to grab Megan's photo!"

"Now you're rationalizing your own reaction—"

"Let's sit down and listen to what the TV is reporting," Harry suggested. "The first mystery is why Liam would be anywhere near the mayor's home, and why any TV cameraman would be taking pictures of him even if he was."

"That's not the first mystery," Ellie retorted. "The first mystery is why Liam's holding a little girl who can't be much more than three years old. If you'd have asked me, I would have said that he hadn't been around enough young children to recognize which end is up on a three-year-old." She pressed the button on the remote, and the newscast jolted back into action.

"Crowds around the residence of the mayor of Denver were out of control an hour ago when Chloe Hamilton, Olympic gold medalist and widow of Jason Hamilton, returned to her home. Liam Raven, a well-known Denver lawyer who specializes in high-profile murder trials, drove Chloe Hamilton back to her home and even provided baby carrying services for Sophie Hamilton, the three-and-a-half-year-old daughter of Chloe and the late mayor.

"Denver's chief of police refused to name Chloe Hamilton as a person of interest in the investigation of the mayor's brutal murder. He would only say that the investigation is ongoing and that his department is waiting for the preliminary autopsy results before moving forward with any public announcements. He refused to speculate on a possible motive for the crime, but he did acknowledge that preliminary examination of the crime scene revealed hints both of premeditation and passion on the part of the killer. He refused to expand on this statement."

Chloe was a beautiful woman, Ellie thought, watching her son hand over the little girl to her mother. Liam bent down to say something, speaking right into Chloe's ear. He probably needed to lean in so close to be heard over the noise of the crowd. Still, Ellie saw a level of intimacy in Liam's body language that suggested something more than lawyer and client in a tight spot together. And since when had Liam taken up the practice of criminal law again? Last she'd heard he was still making pots of money helping Denver's elite unravel their wedding vows. Or, more accurately, unravel their marital finances.

She wished that she knew her son well enough not to be wondering what sort of law he was practicing these days, but being estranged from Liam was just one more sad consequence of her late husband's bigamy. Ellie wasn't sure whether Liam had stayed away from her because he was afraid of revealing the truth about his father's other wife in Chicago, or because he had suspected Ellie already knew and was angry with her for continuing the charade. In fact, she'd been ignorant of Ron's bigamy—not complicit. Still, the result was the same. In the years immediately preceding Ron's death, Liam had avoiding coming to the ranch when there was any possibility of encountering his father. Until Liam came home this spring in the wake of Ron's death, Ellie had only been in touch with him through very rare visits and dutiful monthly phone calls where he avoided talking about anything even remotely personal.

Harry waited for the reporter to finish his recap of the murder, together with the news that the city of Denver had declared the following Saturday to be an official day of mourning for the late mayor. "Chloe Hamilton's been married for seven years, according to that piece," he commented when the program switched to commercials.

Ellie nodded and muted the sound, but she still didn't say anything. That had always been one of her problems, she thought. When she was emotionally overwhelmed she took too long to find the right words to describe her feelings. Far too often, things that were important ended up never being said at all.

Harry scraped a few muffin crumbs from the table and brushed them off his hands onto his empty plate. "If Chloe and Jason Hamilton were married seven years that means the little girl must be his."

"She must be the mayor's, you mean?"

"Yeah. He was Chloe's husband, after all. If the kid wasn't his, he'd have divorced her."

Ellie shot him a withering glance. "Harold Jonas Ford, since when did you turn into a blithering idiot?"

"I don't know." He grinned. "But I get the feeling you're about to tell me."

"The day you decided you needed to tell stupid lies in order to protect me." Ellie managed to answer his smile, although it cost her. "Don't patronize me, Harry. A woman can trick her husband into believing he's the father of her child, which Chloe quite possibly did. And we both know my son is perfectly capable of having an affair with a married woman."

"Sure he is. We're all capable of being unfaithful, if the temptation's strong enough. But I know you too well, Ellie. You're thinking *like father, like son,* and you're wrong. Everything I know about Liam suggests that he's tried hard not to follow in his dad's footsteps."

"Assuming my son got Chloe Hamilton pregnant, he's not following in Ron's footsteps. Ron got Avery Fairfax pregnant when he was married to me, then married Avery, as well. Liam isn't married to anyone. If Sophie's his daughter, the only similarity to his father would be his inability to keep his fly zipped." She blushed as soon as she'd spoken. When she was growing up, she'd been taught that a good woman never used crude language.

Instead of looking shocked, Harry laughed. "Now I know you're riled up," he said. "Next thing you know, you'll be saying *damn.*"

"I'm not likely to step that far onto the wild side." She smiled again and discovered that this time she meant it.

"You know what?" Harry didn't wait for an answer. "It's

crazy for us to be having this conversation. We've constructed the two-hour pilot for a TV drama on the basis of a single picture of a kid who looks a bit like Megan."

"A kid who looks *a lot* like Megan and was being carried by Liam, who had his arm around the kid's mother, and who is defending that same mother against a charge of murder, despite the fact that last I heard, he was a divorce attorney."

"It's not surprising if he switched back, Ellie. Liam's heart was never in divorce law. He only chose that area of the law to piss off his dad and now Ron is gone there's no reason for him to continue."

Ellie looked at her old friend, not really surprised at his insight into Liam's character and motives. Harry's sun-lined face wasn't handsome, but it was wise and incredibly dear to her. She trusted this man, she realized, with a depth and a confidence she'd never felt for Ron in thirty-seven years of marriage. Emboldened by her insight, for once she allowed herself the luxury of expressing just exactly what she was feeling. "I'm so tired of living in the middle of a bad soap opera, Harry."

"It's not a bad soap opera, it's a good one. Personally, I like the way it's playing out right now."

She wondered exactly what he meant. Instead of asking, she retreated into the comfort of her usual tart remarks. "You mean you think I should enjoy playing Guess Who's a Granny?"

He reached across the table and covered her hand with his. "There's an easy way to find out whether you're a grandma or not," he said. "Go to Denver and ask Liam."

"Oh my goodness, I couldn't do that—"

"Why not?"

That was a darn good question. Why in the world couldn't she ask Liam if he had a child, for gosh sake? Worst case, he'd tell her no. Or maybe it was worst case, he'd tell her yes. Either way, it was better to know. There were four or five flights a day from Jackson Hole to Denver and she had more than enough money for a plane ticket and a few days in a hotel, even though Ron's estate was still tied up in legal limbo. She had a manager to take care of the ranch and the dogs. When you got right down to it, there wasn't a soul who needed her to be in Thatch, Wyoming if she wanted to be somewhere else.

"You're right," she said. "Thanks for helping me to see the light, Harry. I don't have a thing on my agenda this week except taking all my excess baked goods to church on Sunday. That being the case, I guess I'm going to visit my son."

"Today?" Harry asked.

Ellie drew in a deep breath. "Why not? It's still early and it won't take me but a few minutes to pack."

"I'll drive you into Jackson Hole," Harry said. "Hell, it's my day off. We should have time to eat lunch together before you leave. I might even live it up and spend the night in Jackson."

"Come with me to Denver." As soon as she'd spoken, Ellie wondered if seeing that newsreel clip had sent her over the edge. How awful it would be if Harry thought she was propositioning him…

Far from looking disgusted, Harry actually seemed pleased by the invitation. "That would be real nice," he said. "We'll swing by my place, I'll pack my suitcase, and we should be in Jackson Hole by noon."

"You're coming then?"

"You betcha." He grinned and gave her a hug that warmed her with a pleasant, tingly feeling, although Harry had been giving her friendly hugs for the past thirty years. "Now I'm officially invited, I wouldn't miss it."

"I'll get packed," was all Ellie said, but she had to turn away so that Harry wouldn't notice how she was beaming from ear to ear for no real reason. Well, no reason except that for the first time since he brought her the news that Ron was missing from his Miami hotel room, she was not only happy, she was also excited. After three months in limbo, she was finally looking forward instead of back. It was a real nice feeling, Ellie decided.

Thirteen

A uniformed cop tapped on Chloe's bedroom door and announced that Liam Raven was downstairs and asking to speak with her. Chloe felt a wave of relief that Liam had returned. She was probably setting herself up for some hideous emotional trauma a few weeks down the road, but for right now, Liam felt like her only anchor in a sea blowing gale force winds. However many different ways she tried to wrap her mind around the fact that she was on the verge of being indicted for murder, the sheer craziness of it always stopped the truth sinking in. The formless fears, however, were strong enough to keep her teetering on the edge of panic.

Her momentary lightening of spirits must have communicated itself to Sophie, who immediately stopped her desultory attempt to finish a puzzle and jumped to her feet. "Oh, goodie, Liam! Can we have dinner at Wendy's, Mommy?"

For the past two days, Chloe seemed to have denied every request Sophie made, big or small. Just in time, she stopped herself from apologizing for saying no. Sophie

loved eating fast food and she'd asked to go to Wendy's
on an almost daily basis even when Jason was alive. Nine
times out of ten, Chloe had refused. From Sophie's perspective, tonight would just be another one of those times
when she refused. No need to explain about unfriendly
crowds, or reporters, or the terrors of being front and center
in the hostile media spotlight. A simple no would suffice.

"We can't go to Wendy's tonight. Let's see what Liam
has planned for dinner. He probably knows somewhere
even better than Wendy's." Too late she realized there was
no reason to assume Liam planned to eat dinner with the
two of them. Their personal relationship had never existed
unless you counted a single night of hot sex and their professional relationship was now over. It was entirely possible that he'd come to formally end his collaboration on
the case.

Since the cop was staring right at her, Chloe didn't
allow her worry to show. It was ridiculous to be so dependent on a man who at his best was icily polite and at his
worst was downright insulting. She reached out to take
Sophie's hand. "Come on, sweetie. Let's go downstairs
and find Liam, shall we?"

The cop positioned himself in the middle of the doorway to prevent her leaving the room. "There's still a lot of
people milling around down there, ma'am. This is a big
house, and it's taken the crime scene techs a while to…
well, it would be better all around if you stayed right where
you are, ma'am."

"You were the person who said Liam Raven was here
to see me," Chloe pointed out.

He nodded. "Yes, ma'am. And now I know you want to
see him, I'll send him up."

Two minutes later, Liam tapped on her open door. "Hi, Liam!" Sophie ran to the door and grabbed Liam's hand with a lack of inhibition Chloe could only envy.

"Hi yourself, sugar plum." Liam strode into the room, bringing energy and vitality with him. He scooped Sophie up and tickled her briefly under her chin, making her giggle. "How was your day? Has Bobby Bunny been good while I've been gone?"

She nodded and pointed to her mother's bed. "He's sleeping."

"Already? What a good bunny."

"I drew you a picture." Sophie wriggled out of Liam's arms and ran to the bedside table where she'd stacked the day's artwork. "Here." She returned carrying a drawing consisting of many red and purple lines, with a few green circles and hearts. "Here's my name." She indicated a backwards S and pointed to the clusters of letters scattered randomly around the page. Chloe hoped that Liam wouldn't say anything cutting. Sophie could recite the letters of her name in order, but hadn't yet absorbed the idea that writing them down required the same quantity and order.

Liam looked briefly bewildered, then turned the page sideways. "S for Sophie!" he said. "I see it now. Here's an O, too. And a P."

"There's a frog." She pointed to a blob. "And a flower."

"I see. A yellow flower. My favorite color for flowers. It's a great picture."

"I like frogs."

"I like frogs, too."

She nodded graciously. "You can keep the picture."

Chloe's opinion of Liam skyrocketed when he expressed heartfelt thanks and tucked the messy drawing into the pocket of his two-thousand-dollar suit.

"Did you find my daddy?" Sophie asked him, the question shooting out of nowhere.

Liam directed a startled glance at Chloe, clearly unsure how to respond. She gave a slight shake of her head and knelt down so that she was eye level with her daughter. "Sophie, honey, I'm sorry, but you know Daddy isn't going to come back. We've talked about this, remember? Daddy isn't lost. Liam didn't go away to look for him. Your daddy is in heaven."

Sophie's eyes filled with tears. "I don't want him to be in heaven."

Chloe wrapped her tightly in her arms. "I know, sweetie. Neither do I." There was nothing more to say. Nothing would make Jason's death easier to bear, so she simply waited for a minute with her arms around her daughter, offering silent comfort. Then she stood up, keeping hold of Sophie's hand.

"Thank you for stopping by," she said to Liam. "Was there something you needed to say to me?"

"Lots of things." Liam's gaze met hers above Sophie's head. "Business first. Robyn Johnson told me she was in touch with you this afternoon, and that you hired her as your attorney?"

"Yes. Thank you for persuading Robyn to take my case. She seems very competent."

"Robyn is more than competent. She's brilliant. She passed the bar in the days when most law firms only allowed women to make coffee and answer the phones. She's also kind and ethical. She'll do a great job of representing you, Chloe."

"She seems to think I'm safe for at least one more night.

Her impression is that the cops aren't ready to issue a warrant for my arrest, although she didn't seem optimistic that they'd hold off for much more than another twenty-four hours."

"A lot of new information could come to light in the next twenty-four hours," Liam said. "The autopsy will give us more information. There's a good chance that the killer left DNA evidence behind."

"Is that why the cops have held up on arresting me?"

"Probably. So let's hope the killer messed up and left a huge hunk of skin or hair behind."

"Preferably both," Chloe said wryly.

"Wouldn't that be great? However, that's for tomorrow. Captain Dexel did warn me that you shouldn't leave the Denver metro area tonight."

"That doesn't mean I have to sleep here, does it?" Chloe hadn't realized quite how much she wanted to get away from the house she'd shared with Jason until the prospect loomed of having to stay there.

Liam shook his head. "No, it just means you can't go to your sister's or your parents' because they live out of the Denver metro area. If you'd like to go to a hotel downtown, I'll be happy to drop you off wherever you choose. Or you could spend the night at my condo again. My place would offer you a little more privacy—more protection from the press."

There were so many secrets she needed to hide from the press, Chloe thought. As soon as she found out that Jason was gay she'd urged him to step forward and publicly acknowledge the reality of who he was. Jason had refused, not only because he believed honesty about his sexual orientation would destroy his political career, but also because his father—a retired Marine Corps general— would have been utterly devastated to learn that his eldest son was gay. Jason's political career no longer mattered, but Chloe wasn't ready to burden her father-in-law with the truth about Jason's sexuality when he was grieving for his son's loss. And that was only one of the secrets she couldn't afford to let the press discover.

She wished with all her heart that Jason hadn't been killed, but Chloe had already decided that whatever else might result from his death, she was never again going to trap herself in a relationship where everything important was hidden beneath a thick veil of silence. She was so desperately tired of keeping other people's secrets.

She forced herself to hold Liam's gaze, although she always found it difficult to look into his unusual hazel eyes without betraying how attractive she found him. "I really appreciate the offer, but you're not my lawyer anymore, Liam. You have no obligation to share your home with us."

"You're right. I have no obligation. I made the offer because I'd like to help you. I've been the focus of enough negative media attention to know that a hotel room isn't going to be a comfortable place for you and Sophie to spend the night."

Liam spoke with his usual coolness, but Chloe understood him better now and she'd begun to realize that there was little correlation between the flatness of his expression and the intensity of his feelings. "Thank you," she said softly. "I really appreciate your kindness, Liam."

"I'm not kind. I'm possessive." He hoisted Sophie onto his shoulders and she laughed delightedly. Liam swung around so that he was looking straight at Chloe. "Don't say you haven't been warned."

Fourteen

Liam had always cherished the order and quiet of his condo. Above all, he loved the privacy of it, the sense that this was his safe haven where he could relax and be completely himself without reference to another living soul. He'd bought the condo immediately after the Sherri Norquist trial and he'd never invited any of his subsequent sexual partners to spend time here; he either slept in their homes or he took them to a hotel. Last night, with Sophie tucked into the center of his bed and Chloe perched decorously behind a barricade of pillows, was the first time he'd ever shared his bed with anyone. In fact, it was the first time any visitor to his condo had stayed for longer than a couple of hours.

His invitation last night could be explained away as the result of a major emergency: Chloe had been his client and she was in danger of going to jail. He wasn't sure what had prompted tonight's repeat. He supposed Sophie's well-being was the major reason. Perhaps the fact that Sophie was his child also explained his strange compulsion to protect Chloe even though he was no longer her lawyer. Clearly Sophie would be utterly bereft if her mother went to prison. In practical terms, she would be homeless. He tried to imagine her growing up with her aunt and uncle in Conifer, or living with her grandparents in Colorado Springs. Either placement would be a life many kids with mothers in prison would envy. Still, Liam felt slightly sick at the thought of his child as the outsider in somebody else's close-knit family group.

Fortunately, having Sophie around meant that Liam had no time to spare for contemplating the future. His daughter had no idea she was invading a sanctuary; she simply seemed pleased to be back in his condo. She bounced through every room, pointing out that Liam had three TVs as if he might not have noticed and hopping onto his bed as if it were familiar and cherished territory. She arranged her stuffed rabbit against a stack of pillows, covered it with the edge of a sheet, and announced that Bunny wanted to sleep in the big bed again tonight.

To his surprise, Liam discovered not only that he rather liked the idea of sharing his bed with Chloe and his daughter, he also enjoyed seeing his home through Sophie's eyes. His minimalist décor didn't impress her, but his electronics did and she was fascinated by his intercom system. He left her standing on his bed so that she could reach the speaker and conduct a giggly conversation with her mother in the living room.

He went into the kitchen to prepare dinner. Unlike most of his friends, he cooked meals for himself quite often. He'd had a girlfriend when he was in law school—back in the days when his sexual partners lasted months rather than hours—who decided to teach him to cook as a step on the road to matrimony. He and the girlfriend had never made it anywhere close to the altar, but he'd put her cooking lessons to good use ever since.

His dinner plan involved a simplified version of chicken Alfredo, which struck him as a reasonably kid-friendly meal, followed by ice cream for dessert. He used the microwave to defrost some sautéed chicken breasts he'd stored in the freezer along with a parmesan cream sauce. Then he set some broccoli florets on the stove top to steam. Just as he put the lid on the vegetable pot he realized he was humming the chorus to the "Wheels on the Bus," a song he hadn't heard or thought about in thirty years until Chloe and Sophie sang it in the car tonight. Apparently his taste in music was turning to mush right along with the rest of his brain. He switched to humming a Jack Johnson hit just to prove to himself that he hadn't totally lost it.

Sophie eventually tired of the intercom and pursued him into the kitchen. "What are you doing?" she asked, watching with interest as he dropped noodles into a pot of boiling water.

"I'm making dinner. Are you hungry?"

"Sort of." Sophie clearly needed to know more about what was being served before committing herself. "I like noodles," she admitted.

"Good. How about chicken and broccoli? Do you like them, too?"

"What's brocklee?"

He picked her up to show her the pot, warning that the glass lid was hot. She viewed the broccoli without enthusiasm. "Mommy makes me eat those trees." She wrinkled her nose.

"That's because your mommy is smart and knows what's good for little kids."

"I'm not a little kid. Soon I'll be four."

"You're right. You're a very big kid. Broccoli is still good for you."

"I can take her away if she's bothering you." Chloe leaned against the arched entrance to his kitchen. "Do you want me to lay the table?"

"That would be great. There are place mats and cutlery in the sideboard."

"Me, too," Sophie volunteered. "I'll help!"

"Thanks, sweetie." Shooting Liam an amused glance, Chloe handed her daughter some paper napkins. "With Sophie helping, it shouldn't take more than three times as long to get the job done."

Liam grinned. "Yeah, but your chances of eating a meal where I don't forget the salt or burn the noodles just doubled."

Chloe laughed and it occurred to him that for three people who'd had their lives turned upside down over the past couple of days, their current activities seemed amazingly normal. He contemplated the strange fact that cooking dinner for a small child and her mother struck him as among the more pleasurable ways he'd spent an evening in the past two years.

He shouldn't have tempted fate with his contentment. He'd barely registered his strangely happy mood when the intercom buzzed. A light flashed on the panel indicating that the security guard in the lobby wanted to speak to him. Sophie squeaked with delight at the intercom activity.

Reporters or cops, Liam thought grimly, not sharing his daughter's pleasure. He flicked the intercom switch up. "Yes?"

"Mr. Raven, you have a visitor."

"I'm not interested. Ask them to leave. I'm not seeing anyone—"

"Liam, it's me. I just flew in from Jackson Hole. May I come up?"

"*Mom?*"

"Yes. Actually, Harry Ford is with me, too, if that's all right."

Of all the inconvenient times his mother could have chosen to pay him a visit, this would have to rank close to the top. And the fact that Harry Ford had accompanied Ellie was the icing on the cake. Still, his sister had informed him more than once that it was past time for him to be a grown-up and repair his battered relationship with their mother, so sending Ellie and the sheriff away didn't seem a viable option unless he wanted to cause serious offense. Liam hoped that the sheriff's presence didn't mean there was some new and even more dreadful revelation about his father that needed to be passed on. Although he couldn't imagine what fresh revelation there could be to top the horrors of platinum smuggling, embezzled millions, bigamy, suicide and murder.

"Come on up, Mom. Harry, too." He did his best to sound delighted. "Remember to turn left when you get out of the elevator."

"My mother's just arrived in Denver for an unexpected visit," he told Chloe, clicking off the intercom. "Apparently she flew in from Wyoming a short while ago. She has an old friend with her. They've known each other since high school." He decided not to mention that Harry was the sheriff of Stark County. Chloe must have had her fill of law enforcement officers over the past couple of days.

"Your mother will want to stay here with you," Chloe said quickly. "Sophie and I should go to a hotel. Do you want us to leave now? We can call a cab."

"And have every reporter in Denver on your tail within five minutes? Besides, there's no need for you to leave. I doubt if Mom wants to stay here, especially since she has a friend with her. She knows I only have the pullout sofa in the den to sleep on. Plus she had her own unpleasant spell in the crosshairs of media scrutiny earlier this spring. She would understand better than most people what you're going through right now in terms of harassment by reporters and publicity hounds."

It was the first time he'd made any mention of the scandal surrounding his father's death to Chloe. She started to ask him something, but she had no time to complete her question before the front doorbell rang. Liam let his mother in, greeting her with a hug. He'd always liked Harry and admired the absence of bullshit and dash of compassion with which he administered the law in Stark County. The two of them exchanged friendly thumps on the shoulder.

"Sorry to spring a surprise on you," Harry said easily. "I had some unexpected vacation time and your mom was tired of staring at the cows, so we decided to hit the bright city lights for a couple of days."

"We were just about to have dinner." Liam spoke more to Harry than to his mother. After years of wondering if Ellie knew about his father's bigamous marriage to Avery Fairfax, he'd forgotten how to converse naturally with her. Recently, he'd become convinced that Ellie had been as much a victim of Ron's deceptions as everyone else, but the years of estrangement and awkwardness didn't seem to have been wiped away by the fact of his father's death.

"Will you stay and eat with us?" he asked politely. Too politely. When you invited your mother to dinner, you were surely supposed to sound more enthusiastic.

He tried again. "There's plenty of food. I always cook too much. It's probably a hangover from law school and all my starving friends." Now he sounded way too hearty to be sincere.

Harry gave a decisive shake of his head. "We appreciate the invite, Liam, but we never meant to intrude on your evening. We have reservations for some fancy nouvelle cuisine place downtown. Your mother's promised me I won't have to eat anything that once had suckers or tentacles, so I'm willing to give it a shot."

"Anyway, you already have company." His mother nodded toward Chloe and Sophie, clearly expecting an introduction.

What in hell was he supposed to tell his mother about Chloe? Had Ellie already heard about the murder of the mayor of Denver? And what, if anything, was he going to say about Sophie? His mother had been dropping hints about wanting grandchildren for the past half dozen years. Now he had the longed-for grandchild standing a yard away from Ellie's nose and he wasn't allowed to mention the relationship. In a sitcom, this would definitely be time to cue the canned laughter.

Never apologize, never explain. Since he couldn't figure out where to begin his explanations, he'd do better not give any, Liam decided.

"This is Chloe Hamilton," he said, drawing her forward. "And this is Sophie Hamilton, Chloe's daughter. They've come for dinner, as you can see."

Chloe extended her hand first to Ellie and then to Harry, producing a smile that Liam recognized as one of her PR specials: bright, shiny and hiding a lot more than it revealed. "It's a real pleasure to meet both of you." Chloe did a great job of sounding sincere. "I hope you had a good flight?"

If he hadn't known better, he would have sworn that Chloe didn't have a care in the world. He tended to forget just how much experience she had in concealing her true feelings from members of the public. He would be smart to start remembering, Liam reflected grimly. The stakes were high and she had every reason in the world to manipulate him into feeling that she needed him—that he was uniquely important to her. So far, if she was manipulating him, her ploy was working well. He *did* feel that he was uniquely important to her and to Sophie right now.

"It sure is a pleasure to meet you," Ellie said, shaking Chloe's hand. "And the flight wasn't too bad, thanks, considering what a nightmare plane journeys can be these days."

His mother's gaze was searching as she looked Chloe over, but that didn't necessarily mean she had heard about the mayor's murder. Ellie had been trying to get him married off for the past decade, despite all the evidence that he had no desire to change his bachelor status. She was no doubt wondering if Chloe was a marital candidate worth adding to her skimpy list of prospects.

"I recognize your name, of course," Harry said, pumping Chloe's hand enthusiastically. "I must have been one of your biggest fans when you were skiing in the Olympics. Man, you sure kicked some serious butt tearing down those mountains. That gold medal run of yours was thrilling just to watch, so I can't imagine what it must have been like for you, actually skiing it."

"Thrilling," Chloe said with another smile, although

this one reached her eyes. "When you've trained for years, it's a fantastic feeling to win your event. And standing on the podium to receive your medal, with the crowd cheering and the 'Stars and Stripes' booming over the loud speakers... Well, it's something you never forget."

"The hard thing must be deciding what to do with the rest of your life when all the training and single-minded focus suddenly stops," Harry said. "Not to mention all the limelight and the adoring fans. How did you cope?"

"I got married and had Sophie." Chloe's smile had a brittle sheen again.

"Having a baby sure must have brought you down to earth with a bang." Harry chuckled, taking the sting from his comment.

"But in a nice way." Chloe's arm tightened protectively around her daughter.

"There's nothing like having a baby to make your world change focus, is there?" Ellie bent down so that she was closer to eye level with Sophie, although since she was barely five feet she didn't have to bend too far.

"Hello," she said. "It's very nice to meet you. How are you doing today, Sophie?"

"Fine." Sophie edged closer to her mother, uneasy in the presence of two strangers.

"How old are you, Sophie?" Ellie kept her voice soft and friendly. "You look as if you might be four."

"I'm nearly four." Sophie cheered up at the topic of her age, which Liam was beginning to recognize as one of the staples of conversation with preschoolers. "On my birfday I'll be four. My birfday is October."

"Only two months away. That's not long to wait," Ellie said cheerfully. "Are you going to have a party?"

Sophie nodded. "We're going to the zoo. I can have four friends 'coz I'm four."

"Sounds like the perfect party. And I can see you were helping your mommy set the table for dinner. You're doing a great job."

"We're having noodles." The discussion of her birthday seemed to have thawed Sophie's reserve. "This is my seat," she said, indicating the chair where she'd sat at breakfast time. "We're going to sleep over tonight. Liam has a big bed and Bobby Bunny can sleep with us. My mommy sleeps with us, too. Liam knowed my mommy before I was borned."

Silence descended over the room, thick as a shroud. "The broccoli!" Liam exclaimed, grasping at a lifeline. "Excuse me, I have to drain the broccoli."

Sweat pooling at the base of his spine, he ignored Chloe's look of desperate appeal and escaped into the kitchen. Okay, so he was a coward. It was one thing to fight the D.A. and the Denver Police Department, or even the occasional murderer who decided to take out his frustrations on his attorney. It was another thing altogether to face down his five-foot-nothing mother. And all over a daughter he wasn't allowed to acknowledge and a woman he hadn't actually had sex with in four years. And then it had only been for one night! Sometimes life was incredibly unfair, Liam thought, tossing the broccoli with the drained noodles to justify his continued absence.

Murmured voices floated into the kitchen from the living room. The topic, thank God, seemed to have switched from the proposed sleeping arrangements to Harry and his mother's plans for the following day. Liam concentrated fiercely on finishing his dinner preparations and storing the food in such a way that it would remain hot for the ten minutes or so that his mother was likely to linger. Please God, she would only be staying for another ten minutes.

When he was confident that the conversation was not going to stray from the beauties of the Botanic Gardens and the splendors of the Flatirons shopping mall, he ventured out of the kitchen.

"Dinner's ready," he announced, hoping his voice didn't sound as ridiculously chirpy to everyone else as it did to him. "Are you sure you can't stay, Mom? Harry?"

"If I said yes you look as if you'd have a heart attack on the spot," his mother said tartly. "Don't worry, I'll take pity on you and leave you to enjoy your company."

Thank you, Jesus. "I'm sorry you can't stay—"

"I'm here for a couple of days. I'll look forward to having lunch with you tomorrow, if you're free?"

He should have known he wasn't going to escape with one fifteen-minute meeting. "Er...yes...I'm free. I'd... er...love to have lunch with you."

"Good. I'll come to your office at noon. I assume you haven't moved locations?"

"No, I haven't moved." Liam made rapid mental plans. Tomorrow he'd make darn sure Chloe wasn't with him, which would at least provide some hope of directing the conversation with his mother to a less harrowing subject than his sleeping arrangements. "I'll look forward to seeing you, Mom. There's a nice sandwich shop just around the corner from the office."

"It's the company I'm looking forward to, not the food—"

"We'd better get going, honey." Harry stood up. Liam had the impression that for some reason the sheriff was almost as anxious to get Ellie out of the condo as Liam was to see her go. "Our dinner reservation is for seven-thirty, and the way they puffed and huffed when I called in, seems like they don't hold the table if you're late."

"All right, Harry, I'm coming right now." Ellie shook hands with Chloe. "It's been nice meeting you, Chloe."

"You, too." Chloe's smile had wilted over the past ten minutes. Even if the conversation had focused on innocuous subjects such as shopping and botanical gardens while Liam hid in the kitchen there had apparently been an undertow that had stressed her. Liam refused to feel guilty. Dammit, he'd have stuck around and helped out if Chloe hadn't imposed such ridiculous rules regarding what he could say concerning his daughter.

Ellie bent down to say her goodbyes to Sophie, brushing her fingertips lightly across the little girl's cheek. "It was very nice to make your acquaintance, Sophie. I hope I'll have the chance to meet you again real soon. I'd love to talk to you about your school and your friends."

Liam wondered why his mother wanted to meet Sophie again. He might not have a clue about the conventions of conversing with a four-year-old, but it seemed to him his mother's interest was more than casual. A lot more. He hoped like hell he was misreading the signals, but he was very much afraid he wasn't.

"Goodbye. Come again soon." Unlike Ellie, Sophie was clearly doing nothing more than repeating a stock phrase. She gave Ellie a friendly wave before climbing onto her mother's lap and looking up wide-eyed at the visitors from the safety of her mother's arms.

Oh, shit. Liam thought. That's done it.

Ellie stared at the child, transfixed. Then she drew in an

audible breath and started to speak. Harry placed a warning hand on her arm. "Not now," Harry said. "Ellie, not now."

Ellie visibly bit back whatever it was she'd been on the verge of saying and abruptly swung around so that she was no longer looking at Sophie. Unfortunately, Liam knew what his mother was bursting to ask. He'd been almost fifteen when Megan was four and he had clear memories of how his baby sister had looked. The delicate bone structure of Sophie's face was very different from Megan's chubby baby cheeks, and her dead straight, light brown hair couldn't have been more different from his sister's riotous auburn curls. Her eyes, however, were uncannily similar to Megan's, not just in color but in their shape and the way they were set into her face with an exotic, almost Asian tilt. When Sophie looked up at a certain angle—as she just had—the likeness to his sister was close enough to send shivers down Liam's spine. His mother couldn't possibly have avoided noticing the similarity.

There was something deeply ironic about the fact that his mother was so wrong to suspect an ongoing extramarital affair between him and Chloe, Liam thought, whereas she was entirely right to suspect that Sophie was her grandchild. At this precise moment, however, he was not in the mood to appreciate the multiple ironies that fate seemed determined to fling in his direction. He was merely anxious to get his mother and Harry out of the condo before anything was said that might upset Sophie.

With single-minded resolve he managed to usher the two of them out at top speed while maintaining a semblance of courtesy and goodwill. His mother's parting shot—that she would be at his office tomorrow promptly at noon and they had lots to talk about—indicated that he'd delayed the inevitable confrontation but not avoided it.

Liam's earlier carefree mood was not only scattered to the winds, its lack of foundation was cruelly exposed. His mother wasn't going to be put off with evasions or even outright lies. She would demand to know if Sophie was his child. Meanwhile, Chloe was insisting that nobody could know the truth. In other words, an irresistible force was about to meet an unmovable object and he was the sucker in the middle. As if facing down his mother wasn't enough potential disaster for tomorrow's schedule, he also had to confront the depressing fact that unless they were saved by the autopsy report, then Chloe was likely to be indicted within the next twenty-four hours.

For Sophie's sake, he tried to maintain a pleasant atmosphere while they were eating, but Chloe was as aware as he was of the dose of reality that his mother's visit had injected into the fantasy world the two of them had constructed. It was a struggle for both of them to prevent the tension spilling over.

He cleared up from dinner while Chloe bathed Sophie and put her to bed. His fear toppled over into anger and then switched back again to fear in a nerve-wracking spiral. He would have liked to pile all the blame onto Chloe, but he couldn't quite ignore the inescapable fact that she wasn't the only person who'd behaved badly the night of Sophie's conception. He reminded himself that it was counterproductive to dwell on the past and even less useful to bother about assigning blame. He needed to concentrate on the future and try to develop a workable action plan. What was he going to tell his mother tomorrow? And what in *hell* would he do if Chloe was arrested?

"Come and say good night. I'm in your big bed."
Sophie's giggling command burst from the intercom.

"Coming." Liam shut off the intercom, tossed the dishtowel onto the counter and went into his bedroom.

Chloe greeted him in the doorway. "She really wanted
to sleep here again. She says she's scared to be alone
tonight." Her voice lowered. "She's usually very good
about staying in her own bed. This need to sleep with you
must be a symptom of how upset she is about Jason."

"It's no big deal. I guess this room feels familiar since it's
where she slept last night." Liam sat on the edge of the bed,
emotions roiling. Sophie looked impossibly small and
fragile against the backdrop of his king-sized pillows and
mahogany headboard. His heart lurched. God, she was too
tiny, too vulnerable and much too young to lose both her
father and her mother in the space of a few days. How in the
world was he going to protect her from what might lie ahead?

He kissed her good night and she snuggled under the
covers, Bobby Bunny positioned with his floppy velvet
ears across her mouth. Liam brushed the ears away and she
pulled them back. "She always goes to sleep like that,"
Chloe murmured.

Liam gave a curt nod of acknowledgment and walked
through to the living room. His emotions churned in a
speeded up cycle that left his stomach knotted with dread.

Chloe followed him into the living room five minutes
later. "Sophie seems settled, thank goodness. As soon as
she's firmly asleep, I'll move her into the den."

"There's no need. Why disturb her?" Liam realized he
was pacing and flung himself into a living room chair as if
that was what he'd intended to do all along. "Where Sophie
sleeps seems to be the least of our problems right now."

"Yes, but at least it's a problem we can solve."

He was perfectly well aware that Chloe's calm was no more than skin deep. Nevertheless, her attitude fueled his simmering anger, perhaps because he so often hid his own turmoil behind a mask of faked serenity. Seeing your own coping mechanisms in another person was not a pretty sight.

"You need to get a grip on reality, Chloe. We've been doing a great job of practicing avoidance for the past few hours and it needs to stop."

"I'm not sure I have the mental stamina to go over Jason's death one more time."

"Then you're going to have to dig deep and find some stamina." He was deliberately cruel. "Trust me, finding some stamina beats the hell out of spending the rest of your life in the tender care of the Department of Corrections."

She paled. "You're right. I have been trying to ignore what's really going on." She sat on the edge of the seat opposite him, her body once again stiff and angular with tension. "What do you need to know?"

"Let's start with something easier than the events preceding Jason's murder. We need to talk about Sophie. My mother is meeting me for lunch tomorrow and I can guarantee she's going to ask me why I haven't told her for the past three years and ten months that she's a grandmother. How do you propose that I should answer her?"

Chloe's eyes widened in astonishment. "Why on earth would she suspect for a moment that Sophie is your child?"

"Apart from the fact that the three of us were cozily playing house, you mean? Chiefly because she looks a lot like my sister, Megan. Sophie and Megan have identical eyes. Same shape. Same color. Same everything. That shade of green with barely a hint of hazel is unusual."

"Your mother isn't going to leap to the conclusion that Sophie's your daughter on the basis of the color of her eyes! That's crazy."

"You underestimate the likeness between Sophie and my sister. Besides, from my mother's perspective, everything she saw here tonight must confirm the idea that you and I are long-time lovers. Sophie managed to do a great job of suggesting that we're a snug threesome. It's a damn good thing there were no cops around to hear her riff on our sleeping arrangements."

Chloe pressed her hands against her stomach as if she was afraid she might throw up. "Liam, you can't tell your mother about Sophie. You promised that you wouldn't tell anyone."

"No, I didn't. I promised that I wouldn't tell *Sophie* until she'd had more time to recover from Jason's death. That's the only promise I made you."

"Well, for sure she hasn't recovered yet. It takes more than twenty-four hours to come to terms with losing your father!"

That was true even if you'd despised the guy as much as he'd despised Ron, Liam acknowledged silently. Months after Ron's death had been confirmed, he was still struggling to work out how he really felt about his father. For Sophie, who had loved Jason with a childish intensity, the loss would be a raw wound for a long time.

"I never considered telling Sophie the truth tomorrow," he said. "I realize it's too soon for her to know. The only person I'm planning to tell is my mother. And in case you're wondering, I'm not looking forward to explaining tomorrow why I haven't mentioned the fact that she's a grandmother for the past four years. Right off the top of my head, I can't come up with any explanation that doesn't make you look like a scheming bitch and me look like a witless fool."

"Then don't say anything. Honor your promise."

"Honor my promise!" Liam swung around in the chair, frustration and fear combining to ratchet his anger up a notch. "You're such a hypocrite, Chloe. You claim that you don't want Sophie to know the truth, but your actions reveal something quite different. You just want to be in a position where you can blame me for doing your dirty work."

"That's too ridiculous even to answer."

"No, it's not. It's the simple truth. The secret of Sophie's parentage was entirely safe with you. I had no idea we'd had sex, much less that I'd impregnated you. If you didn't want Sophie to know I'm her father, all you needed to do was to keep away from me. Instead, you came to my office—"

"Because I was desperate! Because I knew I was in real danger of being arrested!"

"And what was your reason for coming to me when you were considering divorcing Jason? There must be a hundred attorneys handling divorces in the Denver area, but you picked me. Why?"

"I don't know!" Chloe's façade of calm finally shattered. "Maybe because I wanted to see if there was any chance that the sex we'd had was as great as I remembered it—"

"Thanks for the compliment."

"Don't thank me. It wasn't much of a compliment." Her sarcasm was as thick as his. "When you haven't had sex in over four years, the last time it happened tends to stick in your memory."

He was the last person Chloe had had sex with? That meant she'd been celibate since before Sophie was born. Liam shook off an emotion he didn't want to deal with and settled for more sarcasm. "You should have told me you were looking for sex, not legal advice. I'd have been happy to oblige and we wouldn't have wasted so much time pretending to work on your divorce."

She flushed. "The divorce wasn't a pretense. I intended to go through with it, until Jason threatened—" She stopped abruptly.

"Until Jason threatened what?" Liam demanded. "I seem to recall that we've been at this point in our discussions several times before. You need to tell me the truth, because I suspect it has a lot to do with the reason Jason was killed. What hold did your husband have over you, Chloe?"

"It's not relevant to Jason's murder. I swear—"

He gave a quick, harsh laugh. "The D.A. will really enjoy hearing you say that in court. Or, of course, you could try trusting me for once, in which case you might never have to explain yourself in court. Where, let me remind you, there are likely to be hundreds of reporters watching the proceedings, all eager to pass on your revelations to their millions of viewers and readers. I'm the best hope you have of keeping your secret, Chloe."

"It isn't my secret to reveal." She sounded despairing.

"Then trust me to keep it. For God's sake, why is it so hard to trust me?"

Chloe remained silent for a long moment and then raised her shoulders in a weary shrug. "My father is the deputy superintendent of schools in Colorado Springs…"

"Yes, your sister told me. A pillar of the community, so she informed me."

Chloe's smile was bitter. "A pillar of the community who has…who had a gambling problem. His house has a second mortgage and his credit cards are all maxed out, or at least they were last year when his creditors were coming after him. My parents' home was about to go into foreclosure, so he embezzled more than a hundred thousand dollars from school district funds. Then he approached me for an urgent loan because the district auditors were about to come in and uncover the loss. He was desperate to make restitution..."

"You gave him the money?" With difficulty, Liam refrained from suggesting that her father was a thief rather than a pillar of the community, and that paying back the stolen money with borrowed funds didn't exactly amount to restitution. On the contrary, borrowing money from your daughter was nothing more than a save your ass weasel out of the consequences of your crime.

Chloe gave a dismissive shrug. "My parents sacrificed much more than a hundred thousand dollars to help me pursue my Olympic dreams. I had the money and it seemed a small way to repay them for all they'd done for me."

"I hope you're charging your father interest at the prevailing rate." The slimy bastard.

She ignored his comment. "I made Dad promise to enroll in Gamblers Anonymous and he swore he would never put another nickel in a slot machine, or sit down at a blackjack table. According to my mother, he's lived up to his side of the bargain."

"Has he paid you back the money he borrowed?"

She flushed. "Some of it. It's not as if Sophie and I need it right this minute."

If Chloe's father had returned a couple of thousand, he'd be astonished, Liam thought grimly. And he wouldn't be so damn sure that the guy had stopped gambling, either. He'd handled several divorces where one of the spouses had a serious addiction problem, and in his experience it took a lot more than a single near-disaster to force an addict to confront his problems. So far, Chloe's father had paid no real price for his gambling or his theft; Chloe was the person who'd paid. And since her parents still hadn't bothered to make the ninety minute drive up from Colorado Springs, he assumed they weren't all that grateful for her sacrifice. More than likely they were following the familiar pattern of feeling resentment toward the person who'd bailed them out of their difficulties.

"I assume Jason found out about your father's theft and then threatened to expose him if you didn't agree to call off the divorce." In Liam's opinion, Chloe's husband was almost as despicable as her father.

"That makes Jason sound like a much crueler person than he was—"

Liam shrugged. "Not cruel necessarily. Just unforgivably self-centered."

"He didn't set out to develop a plan to blackmail me into staying married," she said, as if that excused him. "It just happened."

"My heart bleeds for Jason. Damn, the poor guy was almost *forced* to blackmail you."

"The timing of my decision to divorce him was a disaster for Jason's political ambitions." Chloe's body language pleaded with him to understand. "One of his biggest backers, Sam DiVoli, had heard a rumor that Jason was gay and he was threatening to pull both his money and his support with the leaders of the national party. Jason simply asked me to stay married through the campaign season. No blackmail, just a request. He felt that a divorce would confirm every suspicion Sam had and that without Sam's support, his senate ambitions were dead."

"At the very least, a divorce would have deprived your husband of what he and DiVoli undoubtedly considered a major asset of Jason's campaign, namely the fact that you're a well-known Olympic champion."

Chloe shrugged. "You make it sound as though there's something unethical about Jason exploiting my name recognition among Colorado voters. I wouldn't have had any problems with that if our marriage had been as advertised. But after a lot of soul-searching, I decided I wasn't willing to go along with the charade any longer. Voters weren't being asked to elect me, they were being asked to vote for Jason. And the fact is that Jason is...he was gay. That's an important part of who he was. He was also hard-working, thoughtful, well informed and a brilliant politician with a real talent for helping different groups understand how to work together for the greater good. It seemed to me that Jason owed it to himself to be honest. He could admit to the world he was gay and see if he could get elected despite the admission. After all, he had his track record as Denver's most successful mayor in his favor. Or, if it turned out that a Senate career wasn't possible, then he should find some other way to use his talents. I suggested maybe he needed to become active in the Gay Rights Movement. At least that would have allowed him to be true to the person he really was."

"I take it Jason didn't like your analysis of the situation," Liam said dryly.

Chloe looked bleak. "No, he didn't. When I told him I'd consulted you about a divorce, he retaliated by informing me he had documented proof of my father's embezzlement and he'd take it to the authorities if I didn't agree to stay married until the end of his campaign for the Senate. He pointed out that it was only six months until the election, and that six months wasn't much to ask for."

"You'd already given him seven years. That seems a pretty significant payment to me."

"But not seven years of knowing the truth about his sexuality. I only discovered he was gay the night Sophie was conceived and for at least a year after she was born I was so wrapped up in caring for her that I had zero interest in getting divorced. In fact, I considered myself in Jason's debt because he was such a terrific dad to a child who wasn't biologically his."

"Being a great father doesn't make up for being a lousy husband. Not to mention the fact that he was also a blackmailer."

Chloe spread her hands as if to ward off his attacks on her husband's memory. "I'm not sure Jason would really have carried out his threat to expose my father's embezzlement if I'd left him."

"But you were sufficiently afraid not to take the chance," Liam pointed out.

"Because the stakes were so high. My father would have been fired if the school district ever found out about his embezzlement. In fact, since he's a public official, they'd have been compelled to prosecute him and he'd most likely have gone to prison. At an absolute minimum, he'd have been put on probation and lost his pension. My parents are so close to retirement, I decided I couldn't buy my freedom from Jason at the expense of ruining their whole lives. After all, Jason wasn't asking me to stay married forever. He only wanted me to stay married until after the next election. At the time, six months didn't seem like such an outrageous demand."

Chloe's problem was that she was carrying too much weight for all the people around her, Liam reflected, and giving her own wants and needs nowhere near enough attention. She'd probably fallen into the habit of taking on too much responsibility when she was an Olympic contender and the life of her family had, of necessity, orbited around her star.

"What about *your* life? For God's sake, Chloe, you were a young woman, trapped in a marriage that was a complete sham, and you're still protecting and apologizing for every damn person except yourself."

She tried for a smile but didn't quite make it. "Thanks for the outrage, but I'm not quite as noble as you think. The dinner we attended the night Jason died was a real eye-opener for me. I realized Jason was right and that the leaders of the party would never endorse him as their candidate if he admitted publicly to being gay. I also realized that in November he would still need the protection of our marriage, whether he won or lost. He'd make another excuse to keep me as his wife and another after that until my whole life had been frittered away playing second fiddle to his political ambitions. I guess my patience snapped. I told him that I didn't care if he told the entire world that my father was a gambler and a thief. I wasn't staying married to him any longer."

"Did Jason take your threat seriously?"

She nodded. "Absolutely. Jason knew I meant what I said."

As a lawyer, Liam knew he ought to be worried by her admission that her patience had snapped. The way Jason had been murdered suggested precisely that—blows inflicted by someone who knew him intimately, whose patience in a long-running dispute had finally snapped. As a man, however, he found himself wanting to find ways to protect her from her own honesty.

"You say he knew you were serious this time in threatening to leave him. Did that make him furious? Maybe even violent?"

As usual, she picked up on exactly where he was heading. "You're wondering if I killed him in self-defense. Nothing could be further from the truth. Jason *was* angry— we both were—and he said some terrible things. But he would never in a million years have used physical violence to make his point."

She shook her head, as if clearing away the mist from her memories. "I've just this minute remembered something about our argument the night he died. When Jason realized there was nothing he could do to persuade me to change my mind, at some level I believe he was almost relieved. It was as if the burden of an enormous deception had been lifted from him and he didn't have to struggle to carry it any more. I promised him that I had no plans to tell anyone that he was gay, that the choice to lie or be honest was his to make and I'd do anything I could to support his political ambitions from the sidelines."

"So you're suggesting the two of you were reconciled right before he died?"

"God, you've no idea how much I wish we had been." Chloe rubbed her eyes, looking worn out. "But we weren't. It was more that in those final few moments we both accepted that our marriage was truly over."

She was either brilliant at deception or she was telling the simple truth. She had given herself the perfect opportunity to claim that she and Jason had been reconciled before he died, but she hadn't taken it. On the contrary, she'd made a statement that any prosecutor would have jumped on with glee. Perversely, Liam found himself more convinced than ever that she had nothing to do with her husband's murder. That being the case, since Robyn Johnson was now in charge of Chloe's legal problems, tomorrow morning he needed to move on to phase two and start trying to determine who else might have had means and opportunity to kill the mayor.

"Did Jason believe your promises to keep quiet about his sexual orientation?" he asked.

"I'm not sure. He was frustrated…and sad, I think, that despite the glowing commitments all those important Washington people had made at dinner he was probably never going to become the senator from Colorado." She drew in an unsteady breath. "We were so cruel to each other. Jason called me a cold-hearted bitch who'd ruined his life's dream. I told him that if he really wanted to do something to make me happy, he should just go away…far away. That I never wanted to see him again." Her breath caught. "And then he walked out of the room and the next time I saw him he had a knife sticking out of his chest."

She stared straight ahead, her face pale and her eyes brilliant with unshed tears. "I'd give almost anything in the world if I could see him one more time…to tell him that I didn't mean what I said. That I would always consider him a friend, even though I didn't want to be married to him any more."

Liam had a horrible vision of Chloe leaning over Jason's mortally wounded body and pouring out heartfelt apologies as she tried to wrestle the murder weapon from his corpse. He could just visualize Trudi, the au pair, watching from the doorway and hearing Chloe say how she hadn't meant it, and she'd never intended to hurt him, and a dozen other incriminating comments. He knew the justice system well enough to recognize that she was in real danger not just of being arrested but also of being convicted and he was ice-cold with fear on her behalf.

His reactions right now were completely different from the period when he'd been defending Sherri Norquist, he realized. In the weeks preceding Sherri's trial, he'd been full of energy, running on adrenaline, bursting with bright, innovative ideas about how to defend her. With Chloe, his feelings kept getting in the way of his strategic planning. Sherri had turned him on sexually. Chloe tore at his heart and he hadn't the remotest idea what he was going to do about it.

He walked over to her and drew her to her feet, intending to do nothing more than suggest they should go to bed since Chloe looked several stages beyond exhausted. Entirely without conscious decision, he found himself leaning down to kiss her. His lips touched hers and he was instantly caught up in the same rush of desire as yesterday.

Chloe's arms reached up and she linked her hands at the back of his neck, her breasts pressed enticingly against his chest. He heard the telltale rasp in her breathing and felt the deliberate pressure of her lower body against his erection. The urgency of her kisses confirmed she was experiencing the same lightning-swift arousal as he was. But for all the familiar symptoms of sexual need, he realized there was something more racing like a current beneath the waves of desire, something both unfamiliar and vaguely terrifying.

Better not to get too analytical. He had enough problems right now without attempting to define exactly what his feelings for Chloe might or might not be. His hands slipped down to her thighs. There was nothing more effective than hot sex for turning off the wheels spinning in a man's brain and it seemed obvious that with Chloe the sex would be as hot as he cared to make it.

"Come to bed," he murmured when it became apparent that they were in desperate need of a horizontal surface. Shedding clothing as they walked, he propelled her toward his bedroom.

"Not there. Sophie. Remember?"

Chloe's voice was so husky that she had to speak her daughter's name twice before he registered what she was saying. Damn! He'd forgotten that Sophie was asleep in his bed.

"The den. There's a couch." He could barely make the sounds coherent.

Still locked together, they lurched into the den. Chloe had opened the pullout bed yesterday before she and Sophie transferred to his bedroom and it was still open. They tumbled onto the thin mattress, precipitating a wave of protesting squeaks from the metal frame. Liam barely heard a thing, except as meaningless background clutter. His senses were filled with Chloe; not just the wonders of her lithe and athletic body, but the subtle essence of her. He couldn't have defined exactly what it was that he found so sexy, but something about the way she kissed him and held him and touched him was erotic beyond belief.

Usually he was a considerate sexual partner. He didn't talk too much—he'd discovered many partners ago that it was a myth that most women wanted sex accompanied by a running patter—but he was normally polite enough to toss off a few sincere compliments if it was at all possible and if not, to invent a few soothing lies. He realized as he ripped off Chloe's panties, the only piece of clothing she still had on, that he hadn't said a single word since he first kissed her except to grunt directions to the den.

He made the mistake of stopping for a moment and actually looking at her while he searched for something appropriate to say. Chloe's face was flushed and her lips swollen from the pressure of his mouth. Her hair was tumbled over the pillow and her chest rose and fell swiftly with the shallow intake of her breath.

He was blown away by how beautiful he found her arousal, but his mind seemed to be blank and he couldn't construct even a simple sentence to tell her…to tell her what? That she was great at kissing? That her body was hot? That she turned him on big time? Every one of his stock phrases sounded trite to the point of insult.

Chloe looked up at him, her blue eyes darkened by a sheen of desire. "Don't stop," she said, moving feverishly beneath him. "Make love to me, Liam."

He bent his head and covered her mouth in a kiss forceful enough to make any more speech impossible. His desire rose and peaked in an overwhelming, crushing wave. From the convulsive shuddering of Chloe's body, he was pretty sure her climax was equally shattering.

He was glad that he'd been able to avoid responding to her in words, chiefly because he was very much afraid that making love was exactly what he had been doing. He waited a couple of minutes to catch his breath, and then slowly began to bring Chloe back from quiescence to quivering need.

Thank God for the conversation-destroying power of hot sex. Words not spoken couldn't be used against you. A piece of lawyerly advice he had never before experienced any difficulty in remembering.

Fifteen

Ellie barely glanced at the menu before setting it to one side. "What are you going to have?" Liam asked her. "The avocado on a wheat roll is usually pretty good—"

"I'll have chicken salad on a croissant," she said. "I'm on vacation so I might as well not even pretend to stick to my diet."

She waited while the waiter took their order and then leaned forward across the table, her tiny, capable hands playing nervously with the salt shaker. "We need to talk, Liam."

"I know." He forced a smile. "That's why we're here, isn't it?"

"I don't mean the way we've been talking for the past few years. I mean really *talk.*"

Today of all days, Liam could hardly think of anything he wanted to do less than indulge in a heart-to-heart with his mother. Soul searching was never his favorite pastime; right now it ranked up there with root canals and water torture on the pleasure scale. He'd spent the morning handling the client appointments he'd been forced to cancel over the past two days. In his few seconds of spare time, he'd attempted to process exactly what had happened between him and Chloe the previous night. So far, his processing kept leading him to places where he resolutely refused to follow. Now his mother was waiting for him to explain a relationship he didn't begin to understand.

"I guess I'm not big on revealing my inner confusions, Mom. Nothing personal, but it's just not my thing…"

"I know and I sympathize because it's not my favorite way to spend the day, either. But sometimes you have to gather up your courage and decide that you're going to let the people who love you actually share what's going on in your life."

"I've always kept you up to date with what's going on in my life," he protested.

"No, you haven't," Ellie said crisply. "You've kept me up to date on your career moves and your new phone numbers, the dry facts of your existence. You haven't told me a thing about what's making you happy, or what has you worried. You may look a lot like your father on the outside, but inside I've always known you're like me. Basically, you'd prefer to have your nails pulled out with pliers than admit to having feelings you don't know how to cope with."

He gave a wry smile. "That's a slight exaggeration, Mom. I'm not into pain."

"Hmm. Only a slight exaggeration, I'm guessing." She met his gaze, her eyes gleaming with acknowledgment of their mutual inhibitions. "I'm going to start the ball rolling and say a few things I probably should have told you months ago, right after Ron went missing. First off, just to clear the air, you need to know that I never for one split second suspected that your father was a bigamist. Sometimes I thought he might be having an affair, or more likely a series of affairs, but I took care not to probe too deeply, and Ron was much too clever to slip up and make a mistake that would have forced me to confront him. So we trudged on, deep in our rut, and pretended everything was fine. What I realized after he died was that I'd wasted almost thirty years of my life being a coward, and for no good purpose. The humiliation of finding out for certain that my husband was having an affair wouldn't have come close to the humiliation of discovering after he died that he'd been married to another woman for twenty-seven years."

He understood exactly what sort of cowardice his mother was talking about, Liam reflected, because he'd succumbed to much the same thing in the years right before Ron died. He'd attempted to protect Ellie and ended up subjecting her to exactly what he'd been trying to avoid. He'd allowed his father to blackmail him into keeping silent, and the only person who'd benefited from that silence had been Ron.

"I should have told you as soon as I found out about Dad's other wife and daughter," he said. "In retrospect, I can see it was a terrible mistake to have kept quiet."

"It's real easy to be wise in retrospect, so I'm not holding it against you. But why didn't you tell me?"

Because Ron would have chosen his other wife. Even now, the temptation to protect his mother by lying was strong. It was also totally misguided, Liam realized. Ellie needed to know just how despicably her husband had behaved.

"Dad blackmailed me," he said flatly. "He told me that if I forced him to choose between families, he'd choose

Avery and Kate in Chicago. On top of that, he threatened to make sure that you lost the ranch in any divorce settlement. I should have called his bluff, but I was arrogant enough to assume I knew what was best for you. I decided you were happy with your life, and that you especially loved the Flying W, so I chose to keep silent."

"You decided I would want to stay at the Flying W even at the cost of being in the dark about your father's bigamy?" Ellie sounded more puzzled than angry.

It was painful to admit the truth. "Yes, I guess I did." Liam forced himself to meet his mother's gaze. "Dad was rich, and life at the ranch was very comfortable."

"I can't believe you have such a low opinion of me." Ellie's cheeks had lost their normal healthy pink.

Despite the fact that his mother looked devastated, Liam resisted the urge to back off and smooth things over. "It wasn't much of a stretch for me to conclude you already knew the truth, Mom. You're smart, you're perceptive and Dad was away from Wyoming far more often than he was there. You must have been alone two nights out of three. It sometimes seemed to me it would be impossible for you not to know. I was afraid to rock the boat if you were trying hard to keep it stable."

Ellie waited while the server brought their sandwiches and asked them if they wanted more ice water. "I can see how it might have looked," she conceded when they were alone again. "But from the inside of our marriage it was another story. I'll admit I should have seen that our relationship wasn't quite normal. But Ron seemed to love being at the ranch and we enjoyed each other's company well enough. We'd been married for a long time and when we were alone we spent as much time talking about you and Meg as we did talking about ourselves. It wasn't as if we were fighting every time we were in the same room, or even that we never talked. We did talk, and pleasantly, too. Yes, there were a few hints and clues that Ron was keeping stuff hidden from me, but nowhere near as many as you'd expect, given all that was going on. Was our relationship superficial? I guess it must have been. But it sure doesn't feel that way when you're sitting together across the kitchen table, talking about your kids and years of shared memories."

"I guess a lot of married couples don't realize just how superficial their relationships are," Liam said. "I'm amazed at how little communication there often is between the couples who come to me for their divorces. I've had more than one couple where the spouses didn't even know where their partner worked, much less where they really were when they claimed to be away on a business trip."

"You pay a price for looking the other way," Ellie said. "Apparently part of the price I paid is that I lost your respect."

"No you haven't. I've always admired you."

"How can you say that when you thought I stayed married for the sake of Ron's money?"

"Not exactly for the money. For the lifestyle his money provided."

"How is that better?"

He shrugged. "It just is. I know how much you love Wyoming and the ranch and how proud you are of what you've achieved with your cattle breeding program—"

"Nowhere near as proud as I thought I was," Ellie said. "That's another thing that's a lot clearer now Ron's dead than it was when he was alive. In fact, Megan and Adam have talked to me about converting the ranch into a resort and I'm considering doing just that." She smiled, albeit a little bitterly. "Ron conned Adam into believing he was already converting the ranch into a resort. There's something mighty appealing about making a reality out of one of Ron's biggest scams, don't you think?"

"Megan mentioned something about your plans the other day. I have to admit I was surprised you'd consider getting rid of your cattle, even for the worthwhile purpose of thumbing your nose at Dad. You've spent the past twenty years working so hard to build up your herd."

"That's true, and it's been fun, and I like that I've been successful. But maybe it's time to move on and spend the next twenty years building something else. When Ron died, I realized that the ranch had been my crutch. And why did I need a crutch? Chiefly because there was a gaping hole in my life where my marriage ought to have been. Learn from my mistakes, Liam. Don't ever imagine that not talking about something will make it go away, much less make it better."

"Does Adam think you can raise the money to convert the ranch into a resort?" Liam asked, deciding it was much safer to gloss over his mother's advice. Was that what he was doing in regard to Chloe? Imagining that his feelings for her would go away as long as he didn't put them into words, even in his thoughts? He hurriedly switched back to discussing the future of the ranch. "I've often thought the location of the Flying W is so beautiful it deserves to be shared. But it would cost millions to do it right, wouldn't it?"

Ellie nodded. "Yes, but Adam seems optimistic that we can pull it off. Megan's working with a developer who's built a couple of successful hotels in Jackson Hole, and Adam's talked to several money men. So far, nobody's told us we're crazy. A few people have even suggested they'd be willing to invest half a million or so."

She paused, ostensibly to take a bite of her sandwich, but really to regroup her forces. "What about you, Liam? Have you got any major life changes in the works right now?"

He decided that if his mother could share some of the difficult truths about her marriage, he could share a few equally uncomfortable truths about his relationship with his father. "I've been doing some thinking myself since Dad died and I realize that it's a hell of a waste to spend the rest of my life rebelling against a dead man. I'm planning to return to practicing criminal law. It's what I always wanted to do, and my battles with Dad diverted me. I went into matrimonial law as a way of insulting Dad for his failure to get his life in order. Well, he's gone and it's time to stop fighting with a dead man."

"I'm glad you've worked that out, Liam, because when you think about it, I'm not sure your dad was worth rebelling against, dead or alive. And I can't think of a sadder epitaph than that, can you?"

Liam gave a small grin. "Dad would hate it, that's for sure."

"He would at that. Well, enough about Ron. I can't believe I'm saying this, but he strikes me as unimportant at the moment. Are you going to tell me what was going on last night with you and Chloe Hamilton?"

"Not what you think," Liam said quickly.

"You have no idea what I'm thinking. Talk to me, Liam. If you have a problem, I would like very much to help."

He realized the moment had come when he either had to explain about Sophie or retreat into a silence that his mother could only view as an insult.

He drew in a deep breath, and then another. "Well, you probably know that Chloe Hamilton was married to the mayor of Denver and that he's been murdered."

"I saw pictures of you with Chloe Hamilton on the news yesterday morning," Ellie said. "You were carrying Sophie and the reporter was talking about the mob scene outside the mayor's home when you and Chloe returned there. To be honest, those pictures of you and Sophie are what brought me to Colorado."

If that was the case, then the chances of him being able to lie about Sophie's paternity were receding by the second. "You want me to tell you about Sophie," he said reluctantly.

"That would be nice."

"It's difficult...there are a lot of people's lives involved, not just mine..."

"Does it make things easier if I tell you I already know Sophie is your daughter? I was suspicious when I saw her on TV and I was certain once I'd seen her in person. Right now, if you showed me a DNA test proving that Sophie's father was the former mayor of Denver, I'd send the swabs back to the lab and tell them to try again."

"I hope to God my relationship to Sophie isn't as blatant as you're suggesting or we're in big trouble."

His mother examined his features appraisingly. "You lucked out. She doesn't favor you all that much. But to somebody who knew your sister when she was the same age as Sophie, the relationship's crystal clear. What I don't understand is how you came to be the father of Chloe's child when she's been married to Jason Hamilton for the past seven years."

"It's really complicated, Mom..."

"Yes, adultery usually is."

Liam stared at the ketchup bottle as if he'd never seen such an object before. He hadn't felt this awkward and guilty since his senior year in high school when his mother returned home early from a church meeting and discovered him and a cheerleader named Tiffany making out on the family room couch.

"I don't know where to start."

"Try starting at the beginning and going on from there," Ellie suggested. "That usually works real well."

He shook his head. "Not this time. Everything is complicated by the fact that the mayor has been killed and Chloe is the prime suspect in the murder."

"Are the police right to suspect her? Did she do it?"

"No." Liam was no longer shocked either by the question, or by the certainty with which he could make the assertion. "No, she had nothing to do with Jason's death, but unfortunately she is the most logical suspect."

"Is she going to be arrested?"

Liam pushed away the remains of his sandwich, abandoning the pretence that he was eating. "Yes, I'm afraid she is."

"Are you in love with her?"

"No." His denial was too quick and too emphatic. He shrugged, trying to recapture some tattered remnants of privacy. "I barely know her."

Ellie shot him a disbelieving look. "That wasn't the impression Harry and I got last night. And even though I realize nowadays people often have sex first and introduce themselves afterwards, I assume the two of you must have had some sort of a relationship before you decided to hop into bed and make a baby."

Liam was silent too long and his mother spoke again.

"It's bad enough to accept that you would have sex with another man's wife. I surely hope that you didn't do it casually. I really hope I raised you better than that."

This conversation was about three times more horrible than his worst imaginings. "Mom, you have to trust me that when Chloe and I...well, the night Sophie was conceived, I didn't know Chloe was married."

"You didn't know she was married?" His mother sounded justifiably skeptical. "Good grief, Liam, we even used to hear about her and the mayor in Wyoming. And you live right in Denver! How could you not know Chloe was married? She and the mayor were featured in gossip columns all the time. *The beautiful Olympic champion Chloe Hamilton and rising star of Colorado politics Jason Hamilton.* I'd like a hundred bucks for every time I heard or saw that phrase over the past few years."

"It's complicated..." Liam seemed to remember that he'd said that several times in the past ten minutes.

"It sure seems to be. And even if you didn't know Chloe was married, presumably she knew! Or was she suffering from temporary amnesia while you had your affair?"

He winced at his mother's sarcasm. "There's a lot going on that I can't tell you about." Liam was beginning to think that he really would prefer to sacrifice at least a couple of thumbnails rather than continue to discuss his affair with Chloe Hamilton across the too-small table.

He gulped in some air. "The bottom line is that Sophie has no idea I'm her biological father, and Chloe doesn't want her to be told the truth until she's recovered from the trauma of losing Jason. I'm counting on you, Mom. Nobody can know about Sophie for a while, not even Megan. The fewer people who have to keep this particular secret, the better, especially with the ongoing investigation into Jason's murder. Imagine what would happen if the media got wind of this particular wrinkle in the case they're all having so much fun building against Chloe."

His mother's forehead wrinkled with worry and it was a while before she spoke. "You're right, this is a complicated situation. Sophie's your child, and you have a responsibility you can't walk away from."

"I've no intention of walking away from Sophie."

"Good. And I hope things work out for you and Chloe, too. But speaking from my personal experience, I married Ron because he was handsome, charismatic and clearly going places. I didn't stop to think too much about his ethics, which I guess is easy when you're nineteen. Don't you make the same mistake, Liam. Chloe is beautiful, talented and she has the sort of presence that makes heads turn when she walks into a room. But what about her character? You ought to keep in mind that if she was willing to have an affair with you when she was married to Jason Hamilton, is there any reason to think she'd be faithful to you if the two of you were married?"

"There are reasons why Chloe wasn't faithful to Jason."

"Can't think of any that would prevent her getting divorced before she started up an affair with a man who wasn't her husband."

"It's complicat—" Liam cut off the lame excuse just in time. His mother's advice was well meant and she had every reason to be sensitive to issues of marital fidelity after discovering that her own marriage was a bigamous sham. It was surprisingly difficult, though, not to leap to Chloe's defense.

"I haven't even remotely considered the possibility of

marrying Chloe," he said curtly, hoping to put an end to the discussion.

"Having seen the two of you with Sophie last night, you could have fooled me."

He realized there was no point in getting mad at his mother. Her questions, after all, were entirely reasonable given that she wasn't in possession of several crucial facts. He forced himself to speak pleasantly. "At this point, Chloe can't afford to focus on anything other than finding out who really killed her husband."

"I understand. And I understand that right now *your* attention is fixed on keeping Chloe out of prison. But Sophie is my granddaughter, and I've already missed almost the first four years of her life. I want to get to know her, Liam. She's not only cute as a button, and smart as all get-out, she also seems to have a sweet personality."

Liam felt a warm glow of pride, as if he had something to do with Sophie's sweetness beyond accidentally donating sperm. "There's nothing I'd love more than to bring Chloe and Sophie to the ranch to spend time with you, Mom. I'm sure Sophie would love it, too. But right now, Chloe isn't even allowed to leave the state."

His cell phone buzzed and he quickly glanced at the caller ID. Robyn Johnson's office. "Sorry, Mom, I have to take this. It's Chloe's lawyer."

He flipped open the phone. "Yes, this is Liam Raven."

"This is Mike Potter, Robyn Johnson's assistant. She asked me to call to let you know that the D.A. has indicted Chloe Hamilton on a charge of first degree murder."

"He's gone for first degree?" Liam's worst fears were realized.

"I'm afraid so. He claims there are plenty of grounds

to believe the mayor's murder involved planning and pre-meditation. Robyn has arranged a voluntary surrender for Mrs. Hamilton. She's escorting Mrs. Hamilton to police headquarters now."

Liam had to swallow before he could speak. "Bail?" he said. "Is the D.A. going to oppose bail?"

"Hopefully not. That's one of the reasons I'm calling right now. Sophie has been left at the Hamiltons' home with her aunt—"

"With Alexia Mallory?" Liam asked, just to be sure.

"Yes, that's the one. Mrs. Hamilton has asked if you could go around to the house and reassure her daughter that everything is going to be okay. I understand her daughter is suffering from separation anxiety. Apparently Sophie specifically asked to speak to you."

Liam didn't kid himself that Sophie felt some primal bond with him. He supposed that having lost Jason, Sophie was in desperate need of a replacement father figure and he had fortuitously become it. He could only be grateful for the coincidence.

He had no idea how he was going to rearrange his schedule for the afternoon, but somehow he would manage it. Thank God he wasn't due to appear in court.

"Thanks for calling…" He'd already forgotten the guy's name. "If you can get a message to Robyn, please let her know that I'm going around to Mrs. Hamilton's house right now and I'll stay with Sophie until her mother is able to come home."

"I'll do that. Thank you, Mr. Raven."

"Thanks for keeping me informed." Liam hung up. "I have to go," he said, looking at his mother but not really seeing her. "Sorry, but it's an emergency."

"Has Chloe been arrested?" Ellie asked.

"Yes, and Sophie's been left with her aunt. Alexia's nice enough, but right now Sophie associates death and loss with being taken care of by her aunt. I need to get her away from there." Liam stood up with a noisy scrape of the iron chair against the tiled floor. He pulled a twenty dollar bill from his wallet, anchoring it to the table with the ketchup.

"Can you make your own way back to your hotel?" he asked. "You can ask the hostess to call you a cab."

"I could, but I'm not going to." Ellie followed him out of the restaurant, jogging to keep up with his swift strides, since her legs were at least ten inches shorter than his. "I'm coming with you."

Liam stopped short. "That's not necessary."

"I'm not coming because it's necessary. I'm coming because I want to help and because Sophie is my grand-daughter."

Liam had no mental energy to spare for devising arguments as to why his mother shouldn't come with him to Chloe's house. He pressed his car keys and popped the locks on his car. "Get in," he said. "And whatever you do, Mom, you have to promise that you won't tell Sophie or anyone else that you're her grandmother."

"I promise," she said, tucking herself into the car. "Now tell me exactly why Chloe's been arrested and what you plan to do about it."

Sixteen

Schooling his features into an expression that he hoped hid every trace of his anxiety, Paul Fairfax sat down across the desk from Fred Mitchell. Why the hell had the annoying prick invited him into his office today? More puzzling still, why wasn't Sam DiVoli here? The mayor's former chief of staff had made it plain that this was to be a one-on-one meeting. Why?

Fred Mitchell had his own set of smiles warmed up and on full display. Apparently they were going to be buddy-buddies, at least to begin with. "Thanks for stopping by today, Paul. Just let me switch my calls through to my assistant."

Fred fiddled with the buttons on his phone before leaning back and exhaling an exasperated breath. "I think I've done the right thing. Technology's great, except when you don't quite remember how it works." He leaned back in the chair, sucking in another gulp of air. "It's been a madhouse here today. Quite apart from all the civic business, I swear we've taken a hundred calls from various reporters, all panting for the inside scoop on Chloe Hamilton's arrest."

"You're certainly the man with the inside track to the hot gossip about the mayor's murder." Paul managed to make the comment sound like a compliment.

Fred made a dismissive gesture. "The local journalists already know that I never leak. The national media will soon learn the same. Anyway, it's my personal opinion that the cops have arrested the wrong person. I can't believe Chloe killed her husband. I saw the two of them together as much as anyone else in Denver, and I would have sworn they'd put their differences behind them and were happily married."

Paul picked up on the not-so-subtle hint that the mayor's marriage to Chloe Hamilton hadn't always been entirely happy. Personally, he couldn't care less whether Chloe killed the mayor or the deed had been done by an execution squad dispatched from the planet Krypton. His only interest in the mayor's murder was the delay it was causing the Arran project and the fact that Ron Raven's son was peripherally involved. That said, he would *really* like to see Liam Raven suffer the sort of public humiliation already inflicted on Avery and Kate.

"As you suggested, the police probably have their wires crossed," Paul said mildly. "They often do."

Fred tugged at his lower lip. "The D.A.'s office seems to think the evidence against Chloe is overwhelming, but I don't think we know the whole story yet, not by a long shot."

"It's early days, and the prosecution doesn't like to tip their hand by releasing all the details of their case." If he never heard another word about the mayor of Denver's murder he would be a happy man, Paul thought acidly. Even the hotel had been buzzing with conversations about it last night. Enough already.

Fred Mitchell seemed to realize he was losing Paul's attention. "Anyway, back to the business at hand. I know how tight your schedule is." He selected a file from the stack on his desk and pulled out a complex flowchart of forthcoming meetings. He pointed to an entry for the following Monday. "I'm happy to report that the zoning committee is convening next week, despite all the turmoil caused by Jason's death. As you can see, the Arran project is the first project scheduled for discussion."

"That's good news." Paul kept his smile relaxed, although it cost him. He couldn't think of any reason the mayor's former chief of staff would have called him in, except for a shakedown. And the stark truth was that if this was a shakedown, Sam DiVoli would have to come up with the cash because Paul was scratching the very bottom of the barrel, thanks to Ron Fucking Raven's depletion of the Raven Enterprises coffers.

He knew that showing weakness or fear would be fatal, so he concentrated on maintaining body language that suggested he didn't have a care in the world. "I'll look forward to hearing that the committee's given the project their final approval."

"Well, that's where we run into a problem." Fred leaned forward across his desk as if he were about to confide a secret that required Cosmic Top Secret security clearance. "There are a few committee members who don't see the benefits of allowing the Arran project to go forward as clearly as you and I do."

Here we go, Paul thought. Thieving little turd. He knew the rituals, however, and played along. "What could we do to help those committee members see the many advantages of our plan?" he asked.

"The councilors in opposition to the Arran project

happen to owe me a couple of favors." Fred relaxed in his chair, apparently satisfied that he'd hooked his fish. "If I call in my markers, I can say with confidence that your project will be approved."

"Great." Paul rose to his feet and extended his hand as if preparing to leave. Dammit, he wasn't going to roll over as easily as the mayor's chief of staff seemed to expect. He'd been dealing with political flacks in Chicago—not exactly small potatoes in the corruption stakes—when Fred was still worrying about zits on his chin. The guy needed to appreciate that he was dealing with a master, not an ignorant novice.

"Thanks for calling me in for an update when you're so busy, Fred. I appreciate your time. I'll pass on word to Sam DiVoli that you're going to be personally steering the Arran project through committee for us." Paul flashed a confident smile. "I know what an important figure Sam is in Colorado business, not to mention Colorado politics. He'll be glad we can count on you to call in those favors you mentioned."

"Well, now, we may be getting ahead of ourselves." Fred was visibly displeased to have his opening gambit so cavalierly ignored. "In order to call in my markers, I have a small piece of business that I need to bring to your attention."

Paul was tired of beating around the bush. "How much, Mitchell?"

Fred managed to look horrified. "Are you offering me a bribe, Mr. Fairfax?"

"Of course not," Paul said wearily. Sometimes these days he found himself wondering if he wasn't getting too old to tolerate all the bullshit that went along with an investment like the Arran project. "I'm simply asking what

I can do to facilitate moving this extremely beneficial development through your city's zoning committees."

"Well, here's the thing. I imagine you have quite a bit of experience dealing with the media, Paul." Fred's tone suggested they were finally getting down to brass tacks.

"I don't know why you'd say that. Frankly, I prefer to avoid reporters as much as I can. Half of them are vultures, and the rest are idiots."

"I sure can sympathize with that point of view. I'm also aware of the problems you had earlier this spring with the disappearance and death of your business partner, Ron Raven. That was a nasty few weeks of publicity you and your family went through. The revelation that Ron's marriage to your sister was bigamous must have been especially painful. I hope she's managed to move on with her life?"

God damn Ron to hell, Paul thought viciously. It was unendurable that this...this worm was in possession of such humiliating details about the Fairfax family, bastions of the Old South and founders of the historic and beautiful town of Fairfax, Georgia.

He responded with a cool disdain that took years of patrician privilege to get just right. "I don't see the relevance of my sister's marriage to anything we're discussing here."

"Not directly perhaps. But bear with me and you may see the link. I imagine you have no great affection for Liam Raven."

"Why are we discussing Liam Raven?" Paul was too smart a negotiator to reveal the sudden piquing of his interest.

Fred's smile was a miracle of blandness. "He does happen to be the only son of the man who contracted a bigamous marriage with your sister."

"I've never met Liam Raven," Paul said coldly. "We

have no dealings either professional or personal. However, it's public knowledge that Liam Raven has handled some rather sleazy cases."

Fred leaned back in his chair, looking pleased with himself. "He's a defense attorney, Paul. That means he defends *criminals*. It's his job. Chloe deserves the best, and rumor has it that Liam Raven is the best."

Paul decided it was time to stop dancing around and bring their negotiations to a conclusion, one way or another. "Fred, I have a plane to catch tonight, so let's cut to the chase. What do you want from me?"

"Nothing very onerous. In fact, I believe we can do each other a favor, always the best way to cement a business deal, don't you agree?"

"Yes."

"Good. So, here's the situation as I see it. You want to see Liam Raven burning in the glow of unfavorable media coverage, and I'd like to make sure that the cops have all the information they need to prosecute this case. Our interests coincide. How would you like to slip some information to the media that's really damaging to Liam Raven?"

"What information?"

Fred paused for a fraction of a second and for once Paul had the impression that the hesitation was genuine rather than calculated. "Chloe Hamilton's daughter isn't Jason's child," he said finally.

Could that possibly be true? "Then who is?" Paul realized he was holding his breath.

"Sophie Hamilton's father is Liam Raven."

Holy shit! He would never have expected such a gift. "What proof do you have?" Paul demanded, hoping Fred couldn't see his avid interest. "Even the tabloids would think twice about printing a story that huge without backup documentation. Liam is a lawyer, remember. If there's no truth to the report, he'll file a suit for libel in a heartbeat."

Fred pushed a slender blue file folder across his desk. "Would a DNA test satisfy your need for proof?"

Paul opened the folder. Inside was a report from a genetic testing lab certifying that Subject A was the biological child of Subject B. Neither subject was identified by name.

"There's nothing in this file to show who is being tested," Paul said, disappointed. "It could have been run on any father and daughter in the world."

Fred pushed another unmarked blue folder across the desk. Paul opened it and discovered two DNA profiles, one certified as belonging to Liam Raven, the other to Sophie Hamilton.

"Compare Liam's DNA profile to Subject B in the other file," Fred suggested. "And then compare Sophie's profile to Subject A. As you can see, they're perfect matches."

Paul found the comparisons hard to make, and it took him a while before he was satisfied that the four samples were of the same two people. "There's no way to prove that the DNA sample labeled as being Liam's actually is from him," Paul said, closing both files. "Same for Sophie, come to that. You have nothing here."

"On the contrary, I have proof positive of what I'm claiming. Those DNA tests are the real thing."

"Maybe. But Liam Raven can deny them."

"Not really. If Mr. Raven wants to dispute fathering Sophie Hamilton, he'll have to submit to another DNA test, at least if he takes his dispute to court. If and when he does, I can assure you the test will confirm he's Sophie's father."

Paul meditated for a moment. With these tests as

backup, he might have just enough to get the story reported, depending on the sleaze level of the media outlet he gave the story to. Chloe and Liam were both in the public eye already. When dealing with a public figure, journalists only had to prove that they acted in a good faith belief that they were telling the truth.

"How did you acquire this material?" Paul gestured toward the files. "And what makes you believe it's genuine? I certainly don't have the scientific training to judge whether it's bogus or not. Do you?"

Fred steepled his fingers. "It came with authentication already attached, so to speak."

"Meaning what?"

"The mayor gave it to me for safekeeping. Presumably, he would have a stronger interest than almost anyone else for making sure the tests are accurate."

"When did the mayor give it to you?"

"Some time ago. Look, Paul, I'm not about to reveal anything more about private conversations I might or might not have had with the late mayor. I'm sure this information is genuine and, for obvious reasons, I believe it's highly relevant to the investigation of Jason Hamilton's murder."

"Then hand it over to the police." From his brief acquaintance with Fred Mitchell, Paul was confident there was more going on here than met the eye. Probably a hell of a lot more. God knew, the information was explosive even if you just took it at surface value. That being the case, before he did Fred's bidding and passed this on to a reporter, Paul wanted to be damn sure he wouldn't be caught with his ass hanging out of his pants when the explosion was triggered.

"I can't give these files to the police because I don't want the information traced back to me." Fred was no longer smiling and his voice had acquired a new edge.

Did that mean Fred had stolen the files as opposed to being given them by the late mayor? Probably, Paul decided, relieved to have another hint that Fred was no moral purist. Moral purity left an opponent with no angles to work. He much preferred to go up against somebody with dubious ethical standards.

He spoke dismissively. "If it's too hot for you to handle, I see no reason why I should risk getting my hands burned."

"Then I'll give you a reason," Fred said tersely. "If you want approval for the Arran project, you *will* make sure that the information contained in those two folders is made available to a journalist from one of the major national outlets before you leave for Chicago tonight. Given your time frame, I recommend setting up a meeting at the airport. For your sake, I also recommend taking steps to preserve your anonymity. Fortunately, Denver International Airport is big enough for you to get lost in the crowd."

"And if I refuse?"

"Then, Paul, I'm sorry to say you are going to find yourself in a deep financial hole. We both know you need the Arran project to be approved or you're going to be forced into bankruptcy. Whereas I have no need whatsoever for the Arran project to make it through the council, except as a favor to you and Sam DiVoli. Without my help, the approval you're seeking will not be forthcoming and the Arran project will die in committee next week."

The more pressure Fred Mitchell applied, the less enthusiasm Paul felt for doing the little prick's bidding. He didn't like making moves when he couldn't see his way clear, and he was damn sure that right now he was wading into a swamp filled with the murkiest of waters.

"I've no idea where you get the idea that I have any particular need to get approval for the Arran project—"

Fred cut him off with an impatient sound. He threw yet another file in Paul's direction, the contents spilling out across the desk. This time Paul had no difficulty grasping what he was seeing: comprehensive financial reports not just on himself personally, but also on Raven Enterprises. Neither made for pretty reading, and it was terrifying to think that this information was out there for almost anyone to pick up. Sometimes a universally wired world was not a blessing.

"You're not even bleeding anymore," Fred said, giving a contemptuous flick to one of the report pages. "You've already bled dry, Paul. Financially speaking, you're one small step away from being a corpse. You need the Arran project, or you're going to lose everything. And I'm talking about your trophy wife, your trophy house and the designer shirt on your back."

Fred was one hundred percent correct and Paul hated him for it. Realistically, however, he knew that he had no more wriggle room left if he wanted to survive. He made a last ditch attempt to figure out what the mayor's former chief of staff was going to get out of the deal. Something political? Financial? Nothing clicked as likely. The trouble was, all the information sat on the wrong side of the desk. Even more unfortunately, all the power was there, too.

"*Why* do you want this information about Liam Raven to get out?" he asked. Since he had nothing left to lose, he posed a question he would normally have left unasked. "What's in it for you?"

"Nothing but the public good," Fred said and his smile was so damned smug even a complete moron would have known he was lying. "What other motive could I possibly have, Paul? Like you, I've never even met Liam Raven. I just don't want to see him get away with murder."

Fred wasn't going to tell the truth and Paul had no way to force him to be honest. Paul finally accepted the inevitable and gave up on pretending he was negotiating as an equal. They both knew he was going to pass the information to a member of the press corps. Only one of them knew why.

When you had no money, Paul reflected bitterly, you were helpless in the face of a brutal world. At moments like this, he really wished he'd been the person who pulled the trigger on the gun that killed Ron Raven.

Seventeen

When she finally got home after hours at police headquarters and at her bail-bond hearing, Chloe held everything together by focusing only on what needed to be done for Sophie. The process of being booked on charges of first degree murder had been terrifying, but she'd been almost as much troubled by the fact that she'd broken her promises to her daughter as she had been by any of the humiliating procedures surrounding her arrest. She'd promised Sophie not to leave her, and less than two days later she'd done just that.

The fact that she'd had no choice in the matter didn't seem an adequate excuse. If she'd been smarter…wiser… more devious… If she'd been less wrapped up in grief for Jason and her complicated feelings for Liam…if she'd been any of these things, surely to God she could have averted the disaster of being arrested for a crime she hadn't committed.

Thank goodness, it seemed that Sophie was less distraught tonight than she had been in the immediate aftermath of Jason's death, perhaps because she had spent the day in her own home. Chloe was grateful to her sister, and to Liam and his mother, who had clearly worked hard to keep Sophie occupied and happy. This time nobody had made the mistake of letting Sophie believe her mother was dead. Even so, she still clung to Chloe with a persistence that suggested her mother's second forced absence in the space of a few days had filled her with dread.

Sophie's fear was the final straw, as far as Chloe was concerned. The tension and sadness of the past two days dropped away, coalescing into a white-hot rage directed at life in general. She was angry with the universe for its blind lack of justice and with the police for not seeing beyond the obvious. She was angry with herself for having walked with so little resistance into the trap fate had laid. Above all she was furiously angry that she had never until this moment asked herself the most obvious question. Who had killed Jason? What was wrong with her that she'd wasted almost three vitally important days without ever wondering who had precipitated this disaster?

Her sister looked as if she'd been crying for hours, although she did her best to put on a happy face for Chloe's benefit. Chloe was sorry for her sister and grateful for the babysitting Alexia had provided over the past few days but she didn't have time or energy to cope with anyone else's emotional crisis right now. She had even less time for listening to her sister attempt to explain why their parents still hadn't managed to make the trip up from Colorado Springs. Later, when today's events weren't so raw, she might be upset by her parents' lack of support. Right now, though, she was too angry with the person who'd killed her husband to have energy to waste on a relationship that had begun to seem almost peripheral. Her parents had been enthusiastic supporters of her Olympic ambitions, and they liked the fact that she had been married to the mayor of Denver. But her parents didn't do well with failure or negative publicity, and she wasn't surprised that they were keeping their distance.

To her relief, Liam sensed her desperate need for solitude and managed to dispatch both Alexia and his mother without offending either one. In normal circumstances, Chloe thought she might have liked Liam's mother, but tonight she couldn't find anything to offer her beyond the most basic platitudes. Ellie, fortunately, seemed to understand at least some of what Chloe was feeling and merely commented how much she'd enjoyed spending time with Sophie and what a lovely child she was—about the only compliment with the power to penetrate Chloe's consciousness at this point.

Not surprisingly, Sophie took much longer than usual to settle for the night and it was past nine by the time she finally fell asleep after eliciting yet another promise from Chloe that she wouldn't *go away* before Sophie woke up. If the police came calling again, Chloe reflected grimly, they'd have to drag her bodily from the house before she'd leave. She hoped to God it wouldn't actually come to that. A mere four days ago it would have seemed borderline crazy to worry that she might not be able to stay with her own child, but Jason's murder had shoved her into an alien world where her sense of security had vanished and none of her old logic applied. If the police decided they wanted her locked up, she had a suspicion they would easily find excuses to claim she'd violated the terms of her bail bond and there would be nothing she could do about it.

She went downstairs feeling emotionally wrung out,

with every bone and muscle aching from weariness. The ache bore no resemblance to the muscle fatigue she'd experienced during her Olympic training. Worry, she discovered, was a lot more exhausting than skiing down a mountain.

"Drink first, talk later." Liam handed her a glass of chilled white wine as soon as she walked into the kitchen. She took a long swallow, not allowing herself to dwell on the gloomy thought that she might as well enjoy a few luxuries while she still had the chance.

"Sometimes drowning your sorrows in drink seems like a great way to go," she said, taking another defiant swig.

Liam touched his glass to hers in an ironic toast. "The rest of the bottle is waiting in the fridge. I didn't cook anything, but I've put some fruit and cheese on the table if you want to graze."

He didn't urge her to eat, and he didn't ask her what had happened this afternoon, for which she was exquisitely thankful. He already understood the process of being arrested for a major crime and didn't need her to recount the painful details.

"It's good to have you back," he said, leaning against the kitchen's center island. "I…missed you."

She knew Liam well enough by now to guess that the admission was huge on his part, although she was too numb to react with more than a nod of acknowledgment. She supposed the fact that she couldn't imagine getting through the rest of the night without him at her side meant that she had missed him, too.

He straightened and came to stand close to her, leaving a few inches of space between the two of them. She was glad he realized that she needed space. She craved a perimeter of privacy after the humiliating physical invasions of the arrest process. Did all criminal defendants react in the same hypersensitive way, or was he able to read her mood with an accuracy she would have found disconcerting in other circumstances?

He spoke softly. "Let go of what happened today, Chloe."

"I would if I could." She tossed back the rest of her wine. "It's hard to come to grips with what's happened. Until this afternoon, I'd only ever seen people arrested on television and I wasn't prepared for the reality."

"I can guess how rough it must have been, especially with the press crowding you every chance they could find. But you got through it with dignity and it's over now."

The arrest was over perhaps, but she was permanently changed. She might never view a police officer in quite the same way again, Chloe reflected. In future, there would always be a primal twitch of fear before she accepted that the cop standing guard at the intersection was just a regular guy doing his job, not an enemy waiting to pounce.

"The law may state that you're innocent until proven guilty, but the arrest process supposes the opposite." She tried not to sound bitter since everyone involved with booking her had been scrupulously polite. "The process assumes you're guilty. At some point this afternoon I realized that the system is going to fight hard not to let me go. They have me in their database. They want to keep me there."

Liam opened the fridge and pulled out the wine, topping up her glass. "The system is harsh because the reality is that at least ninety percent of the people arrested are guilty as charged."

"But that means one person out of ten could be innocent! And since it's hard to know upfront who might be one of the ten, shouldn't the pretrial system give people the benefit of the doubt?"

"In an ideal world," Liam agreed. "But in the real world, giving people the benefit of the doubt would mean a lot of dangerous criminals skipping out and never turning up for trial."

Chloe grimaced. "A week ago, keeping the criminals in jail would have seemed a lot more important than worrying about the few innocent people swept up in the system. It's funny how quickly your perspective changes when you're the person who spent the day being fingerprinted and having your mug shot taken."

"The best protection an innocent person has is a competent lawyer." Liam touched his hand to hers, brushing his thumb over her fingers where traces of black ink still clung to the cuticles of her nails despite all the times she'd scrubbed them. "Fortunately, Robyn is a lot more than competent," he said.

"You're right, and in a couple of days I may be able to count my blessings, but not right now. Right now, I'm still trying to come to terms with the insane fact that I've been accused of murdering Jason. The fact that I can afford to pay a competent lawyer seems almost trivial." She drew in a shaky breath. "The truth is, I seem to be doing a lousy job of coping with what's happened. I don't think my stomach has stopped churning for the past twelve hours."

"The criminal justice system is frightening if you haven't been in contact with it before."

"It's not frightening. It's terrifying." Words spilled out of her in an tormented rush. "Have you any idea how uncomfortable handcuffs are? I never thought about it before—never cared, I suppose. Now I can't stop visualizing a future in which every time I move out of my cell, somebody is waiting to slap steel shackles around my wrists and ankles."

Liam took her glass and set it on the counter next to the bottle of wine. Then he drew her into his arms. She resisted for a moment, still tense with the weight of the day. She'd been pushed and prodded and poked by so many different law enforcement officials during the afternoon that her body stiffened in automatic reaction to the slightest touch.

"You're not going to spend the rest of your life in a cell," he said quietly. He pulled her head down to rest against his chest. "We're going to defeat these charges, Chloe."

"How?" Despite everything, she discovered there was comfort in breathing the subtle scent of Liam's skin and feeling his clean, starched shirt beneath her cheek. "They're never going to acquit me unless we find out who really killed Jason."

"I agree we need to offer the D.A.'s office an alternative theory of what happened here the night Jason was killed. Robyn's already hired one of the best private investigative firms in Denver with instructions to examine every one of Jason's controversial decisions and to interview anyone who might have had a serious grudge against him. And first thing tomorrow, you and I can start work on analyzing Jason's more personal relationships. We'll put a name to the murderer, Chloe. All it takes is time and money. Fortunately, you have money and we have months before this case is going to come to trial."

"I don't think I can survive months of being an accused murderer."

"Hopefully, it won't take nearly that long. But first

things first. Right now, I'm prescribing a long soak in the tub followed by…"

An exclamation from the doorway behind her made Chloe jump. She swung around and saw Trudi, the au pair. The day must have been even rougher than she had recognized, Chloe thought grimly. She'd completely forgotten that the prosecution's star witness was still living in this house.

Liam kept his arm around her waist and, with a spurt of defiance, Chloe decided not to move away. Trudi had already misinterpreted what she had seen in the wake of Jason's murder; there didn't seem any point in worrying about the au pair coming to the accurate conclusion that Liam was more to her than a legal advisor.

"Did you want something from the kitchen, Trudi?" She asked the question as politely as she could.

"Have you no shame?" Trudi's eyes flashed and her voice cracked with disgust. Normally her English was fluent, but emotion put a guttural Finnish intonation to her words. "Your husband is not yet in his grave and already your lover has moved into this house. *Jason's house.* Is it not enough that you killed him? Must you flaunt your betrayal?"

Liam started to speak, but Chloe tightened her grip on his arm, silencing him. "I didn't kill Jason and Liam is a friend—"

"A friend does not hold you so." Trudi gave a scornful toss of her head. "You show no respect to Jason's memory, but I am not surprised."

Delving deep into her vanishing store of compassion, Chloe kept her anger on a tight leash. The real problem was that Trudi had fancied herself in love with Jason and was suffering from a sense of loss she had no easy way to express.

"Whatever you may believe, Trudi, the truth is I'm grieving for Jason. We all wish he was still alive, me most of all. I know you were in love with my husband and you're distraught that he was killed in such a horrible, violent way. But that doesn't give you an excuse to insult me."

Trudi flushed bright red. "It is true I have…had…much admiration for the mayor. He was a wonderful man. But if you think I had an affair with your husband, you are wrong. I did no such thing. I did *nothing* wrong."

"I'm quite sure you didn't." Chloe resisted the temptation to score easy points by saying that the reason she was so sure had a lot more to do with Jason's sexual orientation than Trudi's integrity. Jason was dead and there was no reason to inform Trudi she'd been in love with a man who could never have returned her feelings even if he had been single.

She realized that allowing the au pair to remain in the house was going to be impossible for both of them. "Look, Trudi, I appreciate the love and care you've shown Sophie ever since you arrived. You've always gone above and beyond the basic job requirements. Still, Jason's death has changed everything and we can't pretend otherwise. You've accused me of killing my own husband and that's too big a hurdle for either of us to ignore. I'd like you to leave first thing tomorrow morning."

"I have a contract, signed by the mayor, which guarantees me a year of employment."

"I know you have a contract, Trudi. I'll pay the balance of your year's salary and your airfare back to Helsinki—"

"Are you hoping that I will go back to Finland and not testify at your trial?" Trudi's eyes narrowed in contempt. "I have promised the police I will testify in court. Even if

I leave, I will fly back from Helsinki for the trial. I want everyone to know what I saw you doing to your husband. I *saw* you stab the mayor."

"No, you didn't," Chloe said. "What you saw was me trying to pull the dagger out of Jason's chest."

"You would have to say that. What else are you going to claim if you do not wish to go to prison?"

Liam stepped forward, his lawyerly instincts obviously aroused to the point that he felt compelled to intervene. "Mrs. Hamilton claims that she was taking the knife out of her husband's chest because it's the simple truth," he said. "But now I have a question for you, Trudi. How did you happen to see Mrs. Hamilton kneeling beside her husband's body? Why were you running around the house at three-thirty in the morning?"

"For no bad reason. I had been sleeping but I heard a noise…"

"You sleep on the second floor, don't you? Next to Sophie?" He waited for her nod. "That's three flights away from where the mayor's body was found at the entrance to his basement office. And yet you heard a noise that brought you running downstairs…"

"Well, it was not hard to know where I should go. Mrs. Hamilton was screaming for help. I followed the sound of her cries."

"So it was Mrs. Hamilton who woke you?"

"Yes, it was."

Trudi spoke emphatically and Liam waited for a moment to let the implication of what she had just said to sink in. "On reflection, doesn't it seem odd to you that Mrs. Hamilton should be screaming for help if she'd just murdered her husband? After all, you were sleeping, and so was Sophie.

She could have killed him and gone back to her own bedroom and nobody would have been any the wiser."

"I...don't know why she screamed." Trudi gave another toss of her head, although she looked suddenly less sure of herself. "It proves nothing that she called out for help. Maybe she regretted killing the mayor as soon as she'd done it. Her cries were instinct, perhaps."

"Did Mrs. Hamilton say anything to you when you found her holding the knife?"

"Yes, she said something. She told me to call 9-1-1."

"In other words, you were woken out of a deep sleep by Mrs. Hamilton's anguished cries for help. You found her kneeling next to her husband's body, desperately attempting to resuscitate him. As soon as she realized you were in the room, she asked you to call emergency services. Does that sound like the actions of a murderer to you? It doesn't to me."

"That's because you are her lover—"

"I'm a friend."

"On Court TV, they claim you are her lover. It is reported everywhere. Tonight in the news it is told that Sophie is not the child of Jason Hamilton. Many reporters are saying that you are Sophie's father and that there are DNA tests to prove the truth of this. Why should I believe anything either of you tells me?"

"*What?*" Chloe had been fairly sure the day could hold no more dreadful surprises. Apparently, she'd underestimated the malevolence of fate. How in the world had something known to so few people become the stuff of TV gossip? She turned inward, seeking shelter in Liam's arms, unable to bear the sight of Trudi's accusing face.

Liam recovered more quickly than she did. As a criminal lawyer, he must have had plenty of experience catching courtroom curve balls. Or perhaps he recovered so fast because he'd already known what was being reported on the news? For a moment, Chloe considered the dreadful possibility that he was the person who'd slipped the titillating information about Sophie's parentage to some avid journalist.

She dismissed the thought almost as soon as it formed but her split second of doubt must have shown on her face. Liam, perceptive as always, registered her suspicions and his own expression shuttered. She hated the cool, faintly ironic mask that immediately descended to veil what he was thinking. She hated even more that she didn't know the father of her child well enough to trust him implicitly. Everything between her and Liam was too new and too intense for comfort, she thought despairingly. Problems were inevitable, given that they were trying to build their relationship with the crushing pressure of life-altering events piling on top of them. Her body was already in love with him but her heart and mind hadn't yet decided if her body was an idiot. When your reason and your emotions were fighting a bloody battle, she supposed there were bound to be casualties.

Liam turned away from her in order to answer Trudi, or perhaps simply to avoid seeing her doubts. At least he kept his arm around her. "You don't want to believe everything you hear on television," he said, his voice as devoid of expression as his face.

"Is it not true, then?" Trudi asked. "You and Mrs. Hamilton are not lovers? Sophie was truly the mayor's child?"

For once Liam hesitated, leaving it up to Chloe to confirm or deny Trudi's accusations. "Sophie was Jason's daughter in every way that mattered to him and to her," Chloe said in the end.

Trudi gave a short laugh, not deceived by Chloe's equivocal answer. "I take it that means the news reports are true. You deceived your husband. He was not Sophie's biological father."

Chloe abandoned her last faint hope of preserving her privacy. "I would have preferred not to share the intimate details of my marriage with the entire world, but the truth is that Jason learned soon after we were married that he had a medical condition that would prevent him ever becoming a father. So if you and the reporters are assuming I killed my husband because he just recently discovered that Sophie wasn't his child, then you're all barking up the wrong tree."

"That is your story—"

"Yes, it *is* my story," Chloe said, no longer attempting to rein in her temper. "And it's easy to prove I'm telling the truth. Jason's doctors will not only confirm he was sterile, they'll also confirm he knew long before Sophie was born that becoming a biological father would always be impossible for him."

"If you speak the truth, then they are wrong on TV—"

"Well, that would be a huge surprise." Liam's sarcasm was sharp. "An error in television coverage of a crime! Who'd have thought it could happen?" He made an impatient gesture. "Look, there's no point in continuing this discussion. Mrs. Hamilton has asked you to leave her house and you need to respect her wishes. As a concession to the fact that it's already late, she would most likely be willing to allow you to spend one more night in this house. Is that correct, Chloe?"

She nodded and Liam continued briskly. "My advice to you, Trudi, would be to spend the next couple of hours packing your belongings. That way, you'll be ready to move out first thing tomorrow morning."

The au pair was silent for a moment. "You are right, it's better that I do not stay. I will go in the morning." She turned toward Chloe and her manner softened slightly. "I would like to say goodbye to Sophie at breakfast tomorrow. She is a lovely child and I will miss her very much."

"And she'll miss you, Trudi. Of course you must say goodbye to her. She'll be sad to learn that you're leaving."

A little more anger drained from Trudi's expression, replaced by genuine grief. "I am sad, too. I wish very much that the mayor was still alive. Poor Sophie." She turned abruptly and left the kitchen without saying anything more.

Eighteen

The silence once Trudi had gone was heavy with issues neither one of them seemed ready to deal with. Liam spoke first, and Chloe realized with a pang that his voice had reverted to the cool detachment of their early meetings.

"It seems I need to reassure you that I haven't been talking with members of the press. Let me state for the record that I haven't discussed Sophie's parentage with anyone except my mother. You may recall that I gave you my word not to talk about our relationship. I have, of course, kept my promise."

He sounded supercilious but even in her current battered state Chloe recognized the hurt beneath his apparent arrogance. If she blew it now, she suspected she could inflict permanent damage on their relationship. True, she had no precise idea of what she wanted their relationship to become. She did know, however, that she wanted the chance to build something more with Liam than mere acknowledgment of the fact that they were parents of the same child.

"I could pretend you misunderstood what I was thinking," she said finally.

"But you won't, because we both know the truth. You suspected me of notifying the press that I'm Sophie's father. Perhaps you still suspect me. In other words, you're wondering if I'm completely untrustworthy."

"How could I help wondering?" The question was torn from her. "I wasn't being paranoid, Liam. The facts force me to be suspicious. Apart from you and me, Jason was the only person who knew the truth. Jason's dead. I didn't talk to anyone. That leaves you."

"Jason's doctor knew he was sterile. Maybe the doctor talked."

"That's possible, I guess. But the doctor didn't know the name of Sophie's father. He assumed she was conceived through a sperm bank."

"Wasn't she?" he asked acidly. "That's exactly how you've treated me for the past four years—as a sperm donor, nothing more."

She recoiled and with visible effort Liam cut off another angry comment. "I'm sorry. That wasn't helpful."

She flushed. "Not helpful maybe, but at least partially justified."

"Only partially," he conceded. "Let's face it, there's plenty of blame to spread around. For a start, there's the fact that the night Sophie was conceived I made no effort to find out who you were."

"Neither of us have much to be proud of concerning that night." She drew in an unsteady breath. "It wasn't fair of me to keep your role in Sophie's birth a secret. But it wouldn't have been fair to Jason to admit it, either."

Liam shrugged. "I don't agree that you owed Jason

years of silence, just as I don't believe you owed it to him to stay married. He deceived you, Chloe, and then used your presence in his life to deceive the people who voted for him. But those decisions are past, and since we can't change them, we need to live with the consequences. In the meantime, you have to take my word that I haven't spoken to the press about Sophie. As I explained a moment ago, I haven't told anyone except my mother."

She hesitated, searching for the right way to reply and he burst into speech again. "Dammit, Chloe, only a little while ago you were blaming me for *not* wanting to tell the police that I was Sophie's father. Now you're accusing me of the opposite." He looked at her, his expression as close to vulnerability as she'd ever seen. "After last night I thought you might begin to trust me."

She finally admitted the truth, not just to him but also to herself. "After last night, I'm afraid to trust you."

He struggled to maintain his façade of control, but she could read both frustration and desire in his face. "This probably isn't a good moment for you to switch into cryptic mode, Chloe. What do you mean, precisely?"

"It means that the sex last night was fantastic. It means that even now, after three of the most horrible days of my life, I only have to look at you to feel aroused. There's a part of me that wishes you'd just sweep me off my feet and carry me into the bedroom and make love to me until I'm too exhausted to do anything except fall asleep."

He cupped his hands around her face, his hazel eyes already heating with desire. "You've no idea how happy I'd be to fulfill that particular fantasy."

When he looked at her in just that way she had to fight hard to remember why it wasn't a smart idea to tumble into bed and avoid the tough discussions. She forced herself not only to move away but to explain why.

"I made the mistake of marrying Jason because I liked and admired him and I decided it didn't matter if there was no sexual spark between the two of us." She gave a self-mocking smile. "You see how well that worked out. I don't want to make the opposite mistake with you and assume that because we're great in bed, then everything else will fall into place."

He was silent for a moment, considering. She'd noticed months ago, when she consulted him about her divorce, that he really listened to what people said. It was one of the things she liked most about him. Even so, she fully expected him to try to convince her that great sex was all that mattered. But he didn't say anything at all. Instead, he kissed her; hard enough to set her nerve endings tingling and sensuously enough to demonstrate that for all her attempts to be rational, it was Liam's self-control keeping them out of bed, not hers.

He stepped away from her, breathing hard. "You're right," he said, "This isn't the time to explore our relationship. We need to concentrate on discovering who killed Jason. That has to be our priority for now. I wish we didn't need to be sensible, but this murder charge isn't going to go away on its own."

"I just hope you have more ideas about where to start looking for Jason's murderer than I do." Chloe rubbed her forehead, trying to will a spark of creativity into her leaden, exhausted brain. At the moment, the only part of her with even a smidgen of energy was the gland pumping out hormones shouting the message that sex was the answer to everything.

"It just occurred to me that the leak to the media about Sophie might actually turn out to be helpful," Liam said. "The leak means that somebody else knows the truth about Jason not being Sophie's biological father. Who? And why did that person choose to inform the world? I'll call Robyn first thing tomorrow morning and make sure her investigators track down exactly which media outlet first floated the story. You never know, we might get lucky and find out who passed the information to the press."

"Reporters aren't going to give up their sources." Chloe's frustration bubbled over. "Besides, that brings us right back to the problem we talked about a few moments ago. Nobody else knew about Sophie. *Nobody.*"

Liam gave an impatient shrug. "Clearly, you're wrong. Somebody else knows the truth and the leak to the media proves it. Start from that premise and think again about who it might be."

"There's nobody—"

He cut off her denial. "Think positively. Somebody else knows I'm Sophie's father. Who is it?"

She hesitated for a moment. "Don't be offended, Liam, but the only person who springs to mind is your mother. The timing's right. She guessed the truth yesterday. You confirmed it at lunchtime. Could she have told the media some time this afternoon?"

"There's absolutely no reason in the world why my mother would talk to a reporter about Sophie," Liam said. "Why would she risk alienating you, or me for that matter, when all she wants is to spend time with her grandchild? Besides, she was hounded so badly when my father died that her opinion of most reporters ranks right down there with her opinion of con men and bank robbers. And, on a practical note, she spent the entire day with me. She not only has no motive, she had no opportunity. Not to mention no access to DNA tests."

"Then we're back to square one," Chloe said flatly. "I never told anyone. Not my parents, or my sister, or even my ob-gyn when I was pregnant. I didn't tell anyone except Jason. Until you." She rubbed her forehead again, where the headache that had been pounding all day had taken a forceful turn for the worse. "Maybe we're searching for somebody who doesn't exist. Maybe there was no actual leak. Perhaps one of the scandal sheets just took a wild flying guess."

"That might be a possibility—except they're also claiming to have DNA reports proving that I'm Sophie's father. That was what Trudi said, remember."

"And the DNA test is a mystery in itself," Chloe pointed out. "How did somebody get DNA samples from you and Sophie in the first place?"

Liam's forehead wrinkled in acknowledgment of the puzzle. "It has to be Jason who ran the tests, don't you think? Who else? He had unlimited access to Sophie—"

"But not to you."

"That's not quite true. Jason and I met at three or four parties and a couple of fund-raisers, maybe more. If he was determined to get a DNA sample, it wouldn't have been difficult. All he needed was to collect a glass I'd used, for example. I'd never have noticed, and he could have taken a DNA sample from the saliva left on the rim."

Liam spoke quietly, as if he disliked forcing yet another reminder on her of the threadbare bonds that had held her marriage together. If Jason really had been responsible for running the DNA tests it meant he hadn't trusted her to tell him the truth, not even about something as important as Sophie's paternity.

Chloe briefly closed her eyes, shutting out images of her dead husband that she didn't want to see. "Perhaps the media are claiming to have DNA tests just to cover themselves legally," she suggested.

Liam frowned. "You mean the tests don't exist? Or did you mean they might be faked?"

"More likely they're faked, don't you think? The reporter who first floated the story probably calculated that if he was sued, and forced to retract, he could claim he had every reason to believe the paternity tests were the real thing. That would provide him with legal cover, wouldn't it? And, to be honest, it's easier to imagine the tests are faked than to imagine Jason running around at a party stuffing used drinking glasses under his jacket. He was always under such intense scrutiny when he attended any public event. To be honest, I'm not sure how he could have done it."

"Fake tests are a possibility," Liam agreed. "And if those tests hadn't specifically identified me as the father, I'd assume you were right and some overeager reporter pulled the story out of his ass. But it's an awfully big coincidence that I'm the guy the journalist just happened to pick on as Sophie's dad."

"Maybe not," Chloe persisted. "You were with me yesterday when I first came back to this house. There were pictures everywhere of you carrying Sophie. If they wanted to pin fatherhood on somebody, you were as good as anyone else. Better than most."

Liam clearly wasn't convinced. "That just isn't enough to convince me the story's made up. I'm a lawyer. Pinning fatherhood on me without proof is a lawsuit waiting to happen and any reporter would know that. Besides, the TV stations all have lawyers of their own, and they'd be throwing fits. In my opinion, somebody talked to the press, and that reporter has authentic-looking DNA tests to back up his story."

She sighed. "Okay, but if you didn't talk to them, and I didn't talk to them, then bizarre coincidence is the only explanation we have left."

"There's one more," Liam said. "Jason could be the source of the story."

Chloe blinked, then stared at him. "Jason is dead."

"Yes, but he could have told someone the truth before he died."

Chloe shook her head. "He'd never in a million years have told a reporter that Sophie wasn't his biological child! He worked his butt off to convey the impression that our marriage was picture-perfect."

"I don't mean he personally talked with a reporter. But suppose he told the truth to his mother, or his favorite cousin—"

"Telling his family is only a fraction less likely than talking to the press." Chloe was adamant in her rejection. "Jason's father is a retired U.S. army general. He's an honorable person, but he's steeped in military culture. It would just about kill him to find out that his son was gay. Jason seized on Sophie's birth as one more piece of protective camouflage and waved it under the general's nose. *Look, I'm a dad! That proves I'm straight, doesn't it?*"

"How about his siblings? His mother?"

"He has one brother, who's with the Marine Corps in Iraq right now. Jason loved him, but they weren't close, for all the same reasons as with his father. As for his mom, she hasn't kept a secret from the general in fifty years. Jason would never have confided anything personal to her."

"Poor Jason." Liam sounded genuinely sympathetic. "It must have been tough for him growing up in a family determined not to acknowledge the person he really was."

"He told me once that the day he left for college was the happiest of his life until that point. Being away from his family meant that for the first time he didn't spend every waking hour in fear of betraying the simple fact that he found men more attractive than women." Chloe was overcome by a renewed wave of sadness for her husband and anger toward the unknown person who had cut short his life.

"I can't imagine how emotionally isolated he must have felt, even from me." Her voice dropped. "Perhaps especially from me."

"I'm willing to feel sympathy for Jason as long as you don't do anything idiotic like blaming yourself for the bad choices *he* made." Liam spoke briskly enough to snap her out of her maudlin mood before it could take hold. "Talking about Jason's emotional isolation has just given me an idea. There's one other group of people Jason might have confided in. He could have told one of his lovers about Sophie."

Chloe paused to consider. Jason talking to his lover struck her as a lot more likely than the idea of him confiding in any member of his birth family. Jason had maintained a monogamous relationship with one man for almost a decade and she had long since accepted that the two of them had probably felt an intimacy that far exceeded anything her husband ever felt toward her.

"As you can imagine, we didn't often discuss the details of Jason's sexual activities," she said finally. "But when he first admitted he was gay, I told him I couldn't understand how he'd avoided being outed. He was in the public spotlight and he had plenty of political rivals. It seemed incredible that there weren't even whispers about his sexual orientation, at least until very recently. He acknowledged that fear of hurting his family had made him super cautious, even when he was a teenager. He hadn't been promiscuous since his early twenties, and for the past ten years he'd had a single lover, a man he trusted completely never to reveal the truth. He didn't share the man's name with me, but he did say they'd known each other for years and that he was an ordained Catholic priest."

"A priest?" Liam looked startled. "Well, that explains why gossip about Jason's sexual orientation was pretty much nonexistent. His lover was breaking his vows of celibacy, not to mention indulging in sexual activity the church considers sinful. He'd be as anxious as Jason to keep the secret. Is there any way we could ferret out a name and address for this priest, do you think? Did Jason ever provide any clues about his identity?"

"We don't have to hunt for clues," Chloe said. "I know his name already. It's Father Matthias Hannity."

"That's fantastic news!" Liam tilted his head in a question. "But I thought you said Jason didn't identify his lover?"

"He didn't at first, and I never pushed because I wasn't sure I wanted any details. But when Sam DiVoli raised questions about Jason's sexual orientation earlier this year, Jason accused me of being the source of the rumors. That led, as you can imagine, to a lot of…discussion."

"Discussion?" Liam was incredulous. "How about flaming arguments? Weren't you furious with him? For

God's sake, Chloe, you'd stayed married to Jason. You'd kept his secrets. You'd totally subordinated your career to his—and his reward is to accuse you of betraying him to his most important political backer! Where's your outrage?"

"Dead, along with Jason," she said quietly. "I was angry at the time. Of course I was. His accusation was the final straw that pushed me into coming to you to start divorce proceedings. But in the meantime, Jason discovered that the rumors had almost certainly been put into circulation by Stephen Mackay, his chief political rival. Mackay was capable of resorting to whatever dirty tricks were necessary to get the nomination, and Jason eventually concluded that Mackay's political machine was simply flinging mud, hoping something might stick. Since there didn't seem to be any actual source for the rumors, much less proof that they were true, Jason decided to take a risk and deny everything to Sam DiVoli."

"Did you agree with his decision?" Liam asked.

"No, because I've been urging Jason to step out of the closet into the sunlight for years. But he didn't listen then any more than he had before. His own internal tracking polls suggested he'd easily win election to the Senate if he could just get the nomination. As he saw it, his life's ambition was in his grasp provided he quashed these rumors. He was desperate, so he used my father's embezzlement to blackmail me into staying married. Then he went back to Sam DiVoli and assured him that however deep Sam dug, he'd find the rumors had no validity."

"And he won his gamble," Liam said.

She nodded. "The more Sam DiVoli investigated, the more convinced he became that there was no basis to the reports beyond a vicious rival resorting to dirty tricks.

Stephen Mackay was disgraced, at least in party circles, and the flurry of suspicion went away, but by that time, in the course of one of our arguments, Jason had let slip the name of his lover."

"Let slip?" Liam queried, pacing angrily. "Even in a crisis, even when he'd wrongly accused you of betraying his secret, Jason still didn't want to share the truth with you?"

"No, he didn't. In his own way, you see, he loved me."

"Never telling your spouse the truth." Liam gave a grim laugh. "Yeah, that's what I'd call a real sign of true love."

"He thought he was protecting me." Chloe smiled sadly. "I've explained about his family background. You should be able to understand how difficult it was for him to trust anyone with intimate details about his sexuality. Jason's whole life was one long exercise in hiding the truth from everyone he cared about."

"You're way too forgiving. At a certain point, lies are destructive and Jason passed that point right around the time he asked you to marry him. It doesn't matter how noble his original intentions might have been. Endless lies build and compound. Eventually, they lead to disaster. In his case, they probably led straight to his murder."

"You might be right. Jason lied, and I enabled—"

"Dammit, Chloe, stop blaming yourself for Jason's rotten behavior!"

"I'm not blaming myself, just acknowledging that the lies couldn't have continued without my help. That's one of those insights that's blindingly clear in hindsight."

"Yeah, well, we'd do a much better job of life if we could look back and do it over." Liam brushed her hair out of her eyes, the gesture oddly tender. "Have you met this

Father Hannity person? Do you know which parish he's attached to?"

She shook her head, warmed by the feel of his fingers against her face. "I deliberately avoided finding out anything more about him. Even though Jason and I were never sexually involved after I got pregnant with Sophie, I didn't want to have too vivid a picture of the man he was in love with. So I've never met Father Hannity and I don't know where he lives or works. Jason did mention they'd first met in college and then lost track of each other. They met up for the second time at a fraternity reunion nine or ten years ago."

This meant, of course, that Jason had been involved in a long-term, established relationship with another man when he proposed to her, Chloe reflected miserably. If anything could make her angry with Jason even now that he was dead, that particular deception was probably it.

"Based on the fact that they met in college, presumably Jason and Father Hannity would be about the same age?" Liam asked.

"I imagine so. It shouldn't be too difficult to track him down, should it? How many Catholic priests called Matthias Hannity can there be in Colorado?"

"No more than one, I'm guessing." Liam moved away, radiating renewed energy. "I bet we could do a Web search and find him in less than five minutes."

Chloe pulled a face. "I hate to be a wet blanket before we even start looking for the guy, but I still have a major problem with this. Let's assume for a moment that you're right and Jason did confide the truth about Sophie to Father Hannity. That's already stretching it, as far as I'm concerned. Then you have to factor in the DNA test. Why in the world did Jason hand over a paternity test to his lover?

That's such a weird thing to do. And why on earth would a gay priest, who'd broken his vows of celibacy and was at risk of being thrown out of the church, take the risk of getting in touch with the media to reveal that Jason wasn't Sophie's father? He'd be exposing himself to a ton of awkward questions and I don't see what possible payoff there is for him."

"Maybe Father Hannity is honoring a request," Liam suggested. "Maybe Jason handed over the DNA tests and said that if anything ever happened to him, he wanted the world to know the truth about Sophie."

"I guess it's possible." But not probable, Chloe thought. She couldn't imagine a set of circumstances in which Jason would want the world to know that his much-loved daughter had been fathered by another man.

Liam gave her arm an encouraging squeeze. "Bottom line, Chloe, it doesn't really matter whether or not Father Hannity had anything to do with the leak about Sophie. Since we're trying to find out who murdered your husband, we can't possibly ignore as obvious a lead as the man who was his lover for the past ten years. Let's locate Father Hannity tonight and then, with any luck, tomorrow morning we can talk to him face-to-face. Better that the two of us make the contact rather than handing over the interview to Robyn's investigators. I imagine he's a lot more likely to talk to us than to them."

In order to track down Father Hannity, they would have to use a computer. Chloe could feel her stomach knot. "The computer's downstairs…"

Liam understood at once. "We don't have to go into Jason's office. I have a laptop with wireless capability. This house is wired, right?"

She nodded, grateful that she wouldn't have to venture down the stairs and past the bloody outline of Jason's dead body that still hadn't been cleaned up. She watched in silence as Liam cleared a space at one end of the breakfast room table, plugged in his laptop and fired it up.

"This should be relatively easy," Liam said, as soon as his Internet link was established. "I'll just Google *Father Matthias Hannity Colorado* and, with any luck, we'll get a hit right away."

The practicalities of finding Father Matthias Hannity might be easy, Chloe thought. However, the emotional impact of actually having an address and phone number—possibly even a photo—of Jason's true love would be harder to handle. She stared at the screen with a combination of dread and hope as Liam keyed in his query. Father Hannity might well be able to provide some clue to Jason's murder that she and Liam would never find from another source. The catch, however, would be persuading him to speak up. Given that admitting the truth about his relationship with Jason was tantamount to ending his career as a priest, there was a good chance they'd meet with nothing beyond a blank, high wall of silence.

Chloe peered over Liam's shoulder. "There he is," she said, hearing the slight shake in her own voice, whether from excitement or trepidation she wasn't sure. "Father Matthias Hannity, Ph.D., M.A."

"He doesn't appear to be attached to a parish," Liam commented. "It looks as if he teaches at the University of Denver, right here in town."

"That would have made it easier for him and Jason to meet without their friendship being noticed. College students are notoriously self-absorbed." She cleared her throat. "Is there…is there a picture of him?"

"No." Liam clicked forward and then back to the original screen. "They just list the details of his degree and the courses he teaches."

"American history," Chloe read. "His specialty seems to be the Depression era and World War II."

His laptop wasn't connected to a printer, so Liam took a pencil and paper from the kitchen and copied out the salient facts about Father Hannity, including an office phone number.

"We'll call first thing tomorrow morning," he said. "But since it's August and the school year hasn't started yet, we have to be prepared for the likelihood that he won't be there."

Chloe wasn't sure whether to hope that the priest would be at his desk or far away from it. After the past four years, such ambivalence shouldn't surprise her, she thought with a touch of self-mockery. If having conflicted emotions ever became an Olympic sport, she'd win another gold without a single day of practice.

Nineteen

Despite the fact that the university was operating on a summer schedule and there were few students around, Father Matthias Hannity was at his desk when Chloe, Sophie and Liam arrived on campus shortly before noon the next day. He stood up as they trooped into his office, a tall, broad shouldered man, with a shock of thick white hair. He was pleasant looking rather than handsome and carried a few extra pounds around his middle. He was at least sixty years old, Chloe registered with a start of surprise, and more likely older. That meant there had been close to a twenty-year age gap between the priest and her husband.

Father Hannity stepped out from behind his desk to greet them, his expression one of mingled warmth and compassion. "Mrs. Hamilton, I was so very sorry to hear of Jason's death. He was an outstanding mayor who struggled mightily to do what was right for the people of Denver. You've all been in my prayers for the past few days."

"Thank you." Chloe was disconcerted by the priest's friendly welcome. She'd expected at least a touch of wariness, or even outright hostility. "It's good of you to see us so promptly, Father."

"I'm not too busy at the moment." He gave a smile. "This is my last year of teaching before I retire, so I have my schedule of lectures down pat by now. Besides, Jason has told me so much about you and Sophie, I feel I'm meeting with old friends. It's a pleasure to see you both in the flesh at last, although I wish the circumstances of our meeting could have been different, of course."

Liam obviously shared her own sense of unreality at the priest's attitude. He stepped forward to take charge of the conversation. "Father Hannity, would you mind if I shut the door to your office? What we have to discuss is confidential."

"Of course, of course. Would you like me to find some paper and colored pencils to entertain your little girl? I'm afraid I don't have anything more exciting to offer her. I do have orange juice and bottled water in the cooler over there if you'd like some, though."

"No, we're fine, thanks. We brought a few toys," Chloe said, finding a patch of rug and putting Sophie on the floor with her Etch A Sketch and a selection of picture books. "We wouldn't have brought her, but she's been so sad and unsettled the past few days that it seemed cruel to leave her with a babysitter."

"I understand." Father Hannity directed an affectionate glance toward Sophie, who seemed reasonably content to doodle as long as her mother remained in sight. "Well, we'd better get right to the point," he said. "I'm the proud uncle of seven nieces and nephews, all grown now, but my memory is that five minutes of uninterrupted conversation is a major luxury when you have little kids around. How can I help you?"

Chloe exchanged glances with Liam, at a loss for words. Last night it had seemed relatively simple to confront Father Hannity. Now that she was actually in his office, it seemed almost impossible to stare him in the eye and demand to know if he had been Jason's longtime lover.

Liam took over, drawing on his years of professional experience in asking difficult questions to make his inquires sound less threatening. "Father Hannity, you're probably aware that Chloe has been arrested for her husband's murder."

"Yes," he said quietly. "I read the reports. I'm sorry."

His regret was open-ended, with no indication of whether he was sorry the police had made a mistake, or sorry that she'd committed the sin of murder.

"Chloe didn't have anything to do with her husband's death, but the circumstantial evidence against her is strong, which leaves us scrambling to find any clues that might point us in the direction of the real killer. We were hoping you might be able to give us some help in our search." Liam's face remained a picture of neutral courtesy, but Chloe could read him much better now and she saw that he was nowhere near as self-possessed as he might appear on the surface. He was a lot more worried about finding proof of her innocence than he'd been willing to share with her, she recognized.

"I'm not sure how I can help, but I'm willing to give it a try." Father Hannity's voice and expression remained polite and kindly.

Liam made a slight gesture toward Sophie, who appeared absorbed in her doodling. "Because of the small person in the room, it's difficult for me to speak plainly, but you may also be aware of recent news reports claiming that the late mayor was not the biological parent of his supposed offspring."

"Yes, I heard those reports on the local news last night." Father Hannity didn't ask whether or not the reports were true.

Liam plowed doggedly forward. "Until last night, Chloe was convinced that only three people in the entire world knew the truth about Sophie's paternity. Those three people were me, Jason and Chloe herself. And yet, somehow, this tightly held secret was splashed all over the news. Chloe has been aware of your relationship with Jason for some months now and although I appreciate that it's a very delicate situation, I hope you'll understand that we're determined to pursue every possible lead. That's why we're here. Not to cause trouble for you, but to ask for any help or information you might be able to offer us."

Father Hannity turned toward Chloe, his gaze still compassionate. "I wish I could help you, my dear, but the seal of the confessional is absolute, and that seal has been upheld many times in various courts. However, I believe it would be within the bounds of what's permitted for me to let you know that Jason never discussed these paternity issues with me, inside or outside the confessional. To be honest, I was stunned when I heard the news reports last night. Jason had always seemed such a very proud father."

Chloe stared at him. "You acted as Jason's confessor?" The dual role of lover and confessor struck her as so grotesque that she subsided into an embarrassed silence, unsure how to form her next question.

Father Hannity must have heard the distaste in her voice. For the first time, he looked uncertain. "I'm a bit puzzled as to why you're surprised," he said. "I hear a subtext in your question, but I can't decipher it."

"I would have expected Jason to choose almost anyone other than you as his confessor," Chloe admitted.

"Now I'm even more puzzled," Father Hannity said. "Why not me? It's true I've been active as a teacher for almost thirty years, but I'm a priest first and foremost. I've known Jason since he was in my history class at the University of Virginia. We've been friends for a long time and to a certain extent I believe Jason always regarded me as his mentor. It seemed entirely natural for him to turn to me as a spiritual advisor."

"But didn't you feel any conflict when you acted as his confessor, offering absolution of his sins?" Chloe no longer attempted to conceal her feelings. "I'm not a Catholic, but I thought confession was a sacrament—something to be taken seriously."

"It is indeed," Father Hannity said. "I'm afraid I still don't understand your problem. Why are you so shocked to hear that Jason chose occasionally to confess? He was a baptized and confirmed Catholic, after all."

Liam and Chloe exchanged glances. Father Hannity seemed blithely unaware of where they were heading with their questions. Either he was a consummate liar, or he was telling the simple truth. Before Chloe could bring herself to ask him point blank if he had been Jason's lover, Sophie interrupted them.

"My daddy is dead," she informed the priest, jumping up from her seat on the rug and coming to stand across the desk from him. Her chin barely reached six inches from the top of the desk. "My daddy is in heaven. I can't go there."

Father Hannity immediately got up and walked around his desk, using the back of a chair as an aid so that he could kneel down and be at eye level with Sophie. "You have to wait a little while before you can go to heaven," he told her gently. "But you can go there one day, I promise, and your daddy will be waiting for you. He'll be very happy to see you and you'll be happy to see him, too."

Sophie eyed him speculatively. "Mommy said I can't see my daddy any more. Not never."

"She meant you can't see him with your outside eyes. But you can see him with your inside eyes."

Sophie displayed definite interest. "I don't have inside eyes." She squinted at him to prove her point, her nose crinkling with the effort.

"Sure you do." Father Hannity touched his fingertips to her chest. "Your inside eyes are close to your heart. Just shut your eyes and think about your daddy very hard and you'll be able to see him inside your head."

Sophie closed her eyes. "I can't see him," she said after about three seconds of silence. "My inside eyes doesn't work." She sounded disconsolate.

"You need to be very still and quiet, like a mouse," Father Hannity said. "It's hard to see your daddy during the daytime. It might be a good idea to think about him just before you go to sleep at night. I'm guessing he might want to say good night and tell you how much he loves you."

"Okay." With one of the lightning swift mood changes typical of a not-quite-four-year-old, Sophie gave Father Hannity a sunny smile and then tugged her mother's hand. "Can we go for a walk?" she asked. "My books is boring."

"Why don't you come for a walk with me?" Liam suggested, rising to his feet. "Your mommy still has some things she needs to talk about with Father Hannity, but we could go to the coffee shop and buy an ice cream."

"Okay," Sophie said again. "I like ice cream." She put one hand in Liam's and waved the other one at her mother. "Bye. We'll be back soon."

"I'll be waiting." Chloe leaned across to give her daughter a kiss, relieved that Sophie was willing to leave the room and grateful to Liam for suggesting a walk. Most of what was being discussed with Father Hannity would have passed right over her daughter's head, but the mere fact that Sophie had suddenly jumped up and talked about her father indicated that she'd understood at least a tiny part of the conversation. It would be much easier for Chloe to speak freely with Father Hannity if they were alone.

There was no point in delaying asking the crucial question any longer, so Chloe drew in a deep breath and blurted it out before she could lose her nerve. "Father Hannity, I've known for several years that my husband was gay. A few months ago Jason told me that you were his lover. He claimed the two of you had been lovers for almost ten years. Was he telling the truth, or did he lie to me?"

Father Hannity shot to his feet so fast, his chair crashed backward. "He told you I was his...*lover?*" The color drained from his face and then returned in a rush of crimson. "He claimed we were lovers *for ten years?* Was he insane?"

His bewildered outrage surely couldn't be pretense, Chloe thought. Father Hannity not only looked shocked and scandalized but also hurt, as if he felt his friendship with Jason had been betrayed by the accusation.

"Jason told me more than once that the two of you were

lovers." Chloe pushed away a wave of despair at the re-alization that her husband, once again, seemed to have lied to her about something crucially important. "Jason explained that you met in college, years ago, and then lost track of each other. He told me you met up again at a fraternity reunion ten years ago." She hesitated for a moment. "The details that Jason gave me about how and when you two met agree with what you said to us a little earlier."

Father Hannity sat down with a thump. His face resumed a more normal color, but his eyes were tinged with sadness and his mouth was drawn down into what Chloe recognized as an unusually grim expression. In normal circumstances, this was a man who smiled a lot, she thought.

When he spoke again, Father Hannity sounded breathless as if the wind had been knocked out of him. "Whatever your husband may have told you, the two of us started out as teacher and student and we were never more than friends. Not that friendship is something I would dismiss lightly. I've often considered it among the greatest of God's gifts." His mouth tightened further. "I'm holding on to the memory that Jason and I *were* friends, who spent many pleasant hours together planning ways to put the world to rights. I'm also reminding myself that Jason was sometimes deeply unhappy. Otherwise, I believe I would be very angry, both that he has slandered me and that he has apparently lied to you, his wife."

"There's no truth to what he told me, then?"

"None." Father Hannity was crisp and adamant. "Let me assure you, Chloe, that I take my vows seriously. I'm not gay, and I was never sexually involved with Jason. I'm human, and I've committed many sins, some of them grievous, but breaking my vow of celibacy isn't one of them."

Unfortunately, Chloe believed him. "Did you know that Jason was gay before today?" she asked.

Father Hannity didn't reply immediately. He was probably wondering what he could say without breaking the seal of the confessional, Chloe thought bitterly. It was a pity her husband hadn't been as honorable as his mentor.

"I knew Jason struggled with his sexuality," Father Hannity said finally. "I also believed once he married you that he had made a conscious choice to put his past behind him. He yearned to enjoy all the blessings of family life, and he promised me that he intended to be a good and faithful husband."

"Perhaps he was sincere in believing he could change," Chloe said. "I'd like to believe he didn't deliberately deceive me from the very beginning."

Father Hannity hesitated. "I'm guessing you had no idea Jason was gay when you married him?"

"No, I had no idea." It was Chloe's turn to hesitate. "If you're wondering, and I'm sure you must be, Sophie was conceived after Jason told me both that he was gay and that he was sterile. That doesn't excuse what I did, but perhaps it helps to explain why it happened."

Father Hannity dipped his head in acknowledgment. "And yet you stayed with Jason. That's surprising in this day and age, when divorce is so easy."

"Jason always begged me not to leave him."

"Yes, I'm sure he did." For the first time, Father Hannity sounded cynical. "You were the perfect politician's wife. I understand Jason's motives, but that doesn't explain why you agreed with him."

"At first I stayed because I was so wrapped up in being pregnant that I didn't much care that the most we could feel for each other was companionship. After Sophie was born, I stayed because Jason was a wonderful father and it seemed to me that my greatest obligation was to my daughter. Even though I grew to be bitterly resentful of our sham marriage, I'll always be grateful to Jason for the love he showered on Sophie."

"When motherhood was no longer quite so all-consuming and you started to feel so bitter about your marriage, why did you stay with Jason then?"

"I stayed with him because he blackmailed me." She allowed her gaze to lock with Father Hannity's. "He wanted a wife in order to have a smoke screen that hid his true sexual preferences. As smoke screens go, I was about as good as it gets."

"Blackmail is an ugly word."

"Yes, it is. It was an even more ugly reality. I felt trapped and resentful and betrayed."

Father Hannity didn't ask what secret Jason had used to keep her tied to him against her will. "In the circumstances, I can imagine that you might have become almost desperate to escape from your husband."

She heard the unspoken question in his voice. "I *was* desperate," she admitted. "I was furiously angry with Jason, and resentful of his power over me. But I didn't kill him."

"Do you have any ideas about who might have wanted him dead? He always seemed so well liked." Father Hannity shook his head, as if disputing his own comment. "But then, I would have said he was a strong partner in a happy marriage, and clearly I would have been laughably off the mark."

"I wish I had some idea about who might have wanted

to kill him. There's all the usual suspects, of course—miscellaneous crazies who were annoyed because he raised the cost of parking in downtown Denver—or failed to fix a pothole outside their front door, but I don't see how they could have gained access to our house without showing up on any security cameras. Apart from that, I have no clue. Unfortunately, Jason's life is pretty much a mystery to me. We lived in the same house, we both cared a lot about Sophie, but apart from that, we've been strangers to each other for most of the last four years."

"It seems he was a mystery to me, too, and I imagined we were close friends." Father Hannity frowned, staring into space at some inner picture. "I admit, I'm finding it hard to reconcile the man I knew with the man you're describing. But when we were together, we talked mostly about politics, current events and the needs of the people of Denver. At one level you could say we had a true meeting of the minds. At another level, obviously, there were barriers in place that I made no effort to tear down…"

"Because you didn't know they were there."

"Because I didn't know they were there," Father Hannity agreed. He let out a sigh. "What a mess. What a terrible mess."

"At least you aren't facing charges of first-degree murder," Chloe said bitterly.

"No, I have the advantage of you there." He frowned as another perplexing thought struck him. "Why did Jason lie to you about our relationship, do you think? If he didn't want to disclose the name of his lover, he could simply have remained silent. After all, you had no power to force him to reveal the truth. Why did he need to implicate me?"

"I've been asking myself the same question," Chloe

said. "I've come up with an answer, although I don't like it very much."

"Would you share your insight with me?"

She gave a weary nod. "A few months ago rumors began to circulate in certain important political circles that Jason was gay. He accused me of being the source of those rumors. I denied it, but he didn't believe me. He thought I was leaking the truth in order to find a way out of our marriage. During the course of a heated discussion, Jason named you as his lover. At the time, it seemed a slip of the tongue. Now I'm convinced it was deliberate."

Father Hannity's forehead wrinkled in confusion "But why would Jason deliberately mislead you? For what purpose? As I said before, if he didn't want people to know the name of his lover, he could simply remain silent. Why lie?"

"Because he was testing me." Chloe felt the anger clawing inside her. "I had emphatically denied being the source of the rumors, but Jason didn't believe me, so he ran a test. He couldn't risk revealing the name of the man who truly was his lover, so he set you up as the fall guy. He mentioned your name to me, accidentally on purpose so to speak, and then waited to see if you suddenly figured in any of the rumors."

Father Hannity looked repulsed. "But why didn't he simply invent a name? That would have been just as effective in determining if you were behind the rumors."

"As effective in establishing my guilt, but not as effective in squashing the rumors." Chloe drew in a jagged breath. "You made for a much better protective shield than an invented person. Anybody checking into the rumor that you and Jason were lovers would quickly realize that you weren't gay, and that you'd never been anything other than Jason's friend and mentor. So the story about the two of you would have been totally discredited. From Jason's perspective, having the rumors investigated and dismissed was a much better outcome than having rumors that couldn't be proven true or false because the name he'd given me was for a person who didn't exist."

"If you're right, and I'm afraid you might be, there's only one conclusion for us to reach." Father Hannity was finally starting to look as angry as Chloe felt. "Jason didn't care much who got hurt, provided he protected his own political ambitions."

"And his real lover," Chloe added. "He always seems to have been very careful to protect him."

"Do you think his lover was a priest?" Father Hannity made the suggestion with obvious reluctance. "Or was that just another of Jason's lies?"

"I've no idea." Chloe gave a short, hard laugh. "I was married to Jason for seven years and it turns out I knew almost nothing about him."

"And I considered him my friend for more than twenty years, and it turns out I knew almost nothing about him either." Father Hannity glanced down and noticed that his hands were balled into two distinctly unpriestlike fists. He carefully unfurled his fingers. "At the moment, the most charitable thing I can find to say is that Jason was a man struggling with burdens he apparently wasn't strong enough to carry. I hope and pray he's finally at peace."

Chloe hoped that, too. She'd known for years that her marriage had been built on a foundation of lies, but it was still hard to come face-to-face with the many other deceptions that had been woven into the entire fabric of her life with Jason. She hadn't realized just how tawdry and thread-bare her marriage had become until it was so brutally ended.

"Is there any way I could be of help to you or to Sophie?" Father Hannity asked.

"I can only think of one thing," she said. "Jason always claimed he met his lover in college, that they were members of the same fraternity and that they ran into each other again here in Colorado almost a decade ago. It's a long shot to assume this was the one time Jason was telling the truth, but he often repeated that particular story. Is there anyone you can think of who might fit that description?"

Father Hannity leaned back in his chair, clearly trying to bring distant memories into sharper focus. In the end, he shook his head regretfully. "It's been a long time, and I've taught at least three thousand students over the past thirty years. Unfortunately, no names spring to mind."

"Well, thank you, anyway." Chloe tried not to sound disappointed. "I didn't really expect that you would remember anyone at this late date."

"Don't give up," he said. "My memory may not be up to the task, but I might be able to help you anyway. I still have many contacts at the University of Virginia. I'm sure I could find somebody in administration who'd be willing to fax me a list of all the students who were members of Delta Kappa Omega during the years your husband was a student there. The university won't reveal addresses or any other current personal information, of course, but perhaps you'll recognize one of the names on the list. It shouldn't be more than a couple of hundred entries. It might be a starting place, at least."

Chloe smiled her gratitude. "That's really kind of you,

Father. If anything Jason told me was true, a list of his fraternity brothers would be a big help in searching for a new lead." Chloe wrote down her fax number and handed it to the priest. "How long do you think it might be before you could get that list to me?"

"Most colleges are still on vacation, but school's about to start. That's good because the admin building probably isn't yet swarming with students, but it's fully staffed in preparation for the onslaught. I'll explain the urgency of my request without any details. With luck, I might be able to get back to you within forty-eight hours."

"Thanks again, Father." Chloe stood up and held out her hand. "I really appreciate the time you've given me, and especially your offer of help. I'm sorry Jason lied to me about you. I'm really sorry he turned your friendship into something it wasn't."

Father Hannity followed her to his feet. "You owe me no apologies, my dear. It's Jason who deceived us both and you need to place responsibility where it belongs, squarely on his shoulders. Christians are commanded to forgive. Fortunately, we're not ordered to pretend sin doesn't exist. Jason betrayed you. Acknowledge that, and you may actually find it easier to forgive him."

Chloe found an unexpected comfort in the priest's advice. She'd loved Jason once, and it might be easier to remember that past love if she allowed herself to be angry with the many ways in which he'd betrayed her.

"Don't give up," Father Hannity said, holding his office door open for her. "You have a murder charge to fight. Fight hard, search for the real killer and I'll keep you in my prayers."

Twenty

Helen reached across the desk and handed Liam a list of financial assets pertinent to the Maynard divorce case. He glanced through it, mentally highlighting the most important data. Far more interesting than the fact that Mr. Maynard was fighting for possession of a Wedgwood dinner service that had been in his wife's family for three generations was the fact that Maynard's casino in Black Hawk was losing money hand over fist.

Liam flipped to the supposedly certified accounts and recognized a financial pattern that had become all too familiar since he became divorce attorney to Colorado's rich and famous. Until two years ago, when the Maynard marriage first hit serious problems, the Black Hawk casino had raked in a sizeable annual profit. Now it was a losing proposition.

He sighed, wishing human beings weren't so predictably scummy. "Call Mrs. Maynard and give her a ballpark figure for how much it will cost to hire a forensic accountant," he told Helen. "Tell her my guess is that her husband is siphoning off almost two million a year in casino profits and hiding them in some sort of fancy shelter."

"Okay, will do. I thought those casino accounts looked fishy." Helen pushed the next file across the desk, not bothering to comment further on Mr. Maynard's shenanigans. By the standards of many rich men moving on to more glamorous second wives, Mr. Maynard was being quite generous. At least he was willing to pay child support and fund a trust for his kids' college educations.

"Next case," she said. "The Rauchmanns."

Liam groaned and Helen laughed. "Yep, it's as bad as you'd expect. Fortify yourself with another few sips of coffee."

"I need more than coffee for the Rauchmanns," Liam muttered, nevertheless taking a swig. "What have they done now?"

"Mrs. Rauchmann has served her husband with a restraining order. Mr. Rauchmann is very annoyed you didn't think of that tactic first. Now he wants you to get a restraining order for him, too. At no charge. He said it was the least you could do for having screwed up."

"Screwed up?" Liam rolled his eyes, wishing Mr. Rauchmann would grow up. Not all the way to adulthood—that was hoping for too much—but at least to somewhere past fourth-grade level. Personally, he considered the Rauchmanns ideally suited to each other. They both had a mental age of around ten, with personalities long on hostility and short on respect for others. The only good thing about their divorce was that there were no children left shipwrecked on the shore of their parents' failed marriage.

"Tell Mr. Rauchmann there needs to be grounds before a judge will issue a restraining order. Has his wife been harassing him? Stalking him? And so on, and so on. You know the drill."

"Yes, I know the drill." Helen sent a challenging glance in his direction. "Which is fortunate for you at the moment since your attention seems to be...elsewhere, to put it mildly."

"I'm sorry, Helen." Liam set his empty coffee mug on the desk and, with difficulty, pulled his wandering thoughts back from Chloe and Sophie. "Cut me some slack for a couple of weeks, will you? Right now, I'm about two steps away from drowning. And I know I'm taking outrageous advantage of the fact that you're one of the best paralegals in Denver."

"I respond well to flattery. A raise would work even better."

Liam leaned back in his chair, realizing he needed to have a conversation today that he'd been hoping to postpone for another couple of weeks. "Okay, let's take a few minutes to talk about your work here. I recognize that you're shouldering more than your fair share of the workload right now. Would a ten percent raise make you feel any better about the overtime?"

"It sure would." Helen grinned. "Extra money, despite what the psychologists claim, makes me feel better about everything."

"Good, then the raise is a done deal, at least for as long as you're willing to stay with me."

"Why would you expect me to quit? You're honest, you're smart and you give me lots of responsibility. Makes for a pretty good working environment."

Liam was surprised at how much the compliment

pleased him. Helen, notorious for her sharp tongue, was not the sort of woman to bestow praise lightly. Still, he owed her the truth about his plans. "I need to be upfront with you about some changes that are in the works, Helen. You know I'm not taking on any new clients right now. That's not just because I'm distracted by the murder charges Chloe Hamilton is facing. It's because I'm preparing to switch back to the practice of criminal law. Obviously, that's going to affect you more than Jenny. Her tasks are administrative, so it doesn't matter to her whether I'm working on divorces or criminal cases. But your training and expertise are in family law and I appreciate that you might be reluctant to spend the next several months studying the criminal code just because I've decided to make a career change. That said, I need you on the job right now, Helen. You're holding this office together, and if you could see your way clear to staying with me for the next couple of months, I'd be very grateful. When I make the switch to criminal law, I promise I'll call any divorce attorney in town that you want to work for and sing your praises."

"I appreciate the generous offer and I'd sure like to hear you sing." Helen flashed a smile. "Unfortunately, I may have to miss that treat. I want to work for you. God knows, that must prove I'm crazy, or at least a glutton for punishment, but there you are. I saw the writing on the wall a couple of days ago and guessed you might be planning to switch back to your old career as a defense attorney. I meditated about it for a couple of nights and I've decided I'll do the necessary studying to get familiar with the criminal code. What the heck. You were the one who said I'm smart, so it shouldn't take me too long to bring myself up to speed." She shot him a laughing glance. "I'll expect another raise, though."

"I'm willing to dip into my life savings to keep you." Liam was only half joking. "Thanks, Helen. I owe you one."

"Yeah, well, I'm a sucker for the wrongly accused, so criminal law should suit me just fine. Anyway, we'd better get back to business before somebody interrupts and you're tossed into crisis mode again. Here's the last case you absolutely must deal with today. The Borcellis."

The Borcelli divorce had gone quite smoothly until they got to the point of deciding how the three Borcelli children would divide their time between mom and dad. "Are the custody arrangements still causing trouble?"

Helen nodded. "Mrs. Borcelli insists her husband is a drug addict. She says he snorts coke regularly and she's refusing to allow their kids to stay at his place unsupervised. That means she's in violation of the temporary court order Judge Waide issued back in April, so this isn't an academic issue."

Liam flicked through the file. "I remember Mr. Borcelli agreed to drug testing at least six weeks ago, but I don't see the results."

"He says he's been too busy to get the tests done."

Liam looked up from the file. "Too busy? Has he been out of town on multiple business trips? Had a death in the family? Been in a car accident?"

"None of the above, or anything similar."

Liam closed the folder with a snap. "Does Mrs. Borcelli genuinely believe her husband's a user? Or do you suspect she's just getting back at her ex?"

"This isn't about revenge," Helen said. "It's about

keeping her kids safe. Mrs. Borcelli told me the last time she let the kids sleep over at their dad's new loft in LoDo, they came back to her starving. Literally. He'd neglected to buy any food, and he got violently angry when he caught them calling her to complain they were hungry. He ripped the phone out of the wall and locked them in the spare bedroom. Then he forgot about them for the next ten hours. The youngest Borcelli kid is only five and she's still having nightmares. Mrs. Borcelli is frantic, alternating with furious, at the prospect of ever having to send the children back to Dad."

Liam visualized a little girl, not much older than Sophie, cowering in the corner of a room while her dad yelled drug-fueled abuse at her. He was amazed at how intensely he reacted, in contrast to the cool efficiency with which he would have responded only a week earlier. He'd always sympathized in abstract with children suffering through a bad divorce, but now his reactions were visceral.

"I'll file a motion, requesting court-ordered drug testing for Mr. Borcelli," he said, his stomach still churning. "In the meantime, we'll ask for all unsupervised visits with Dad to be suspended. Do the paperwork, could you, and I'll get it hand-carried over to the court."

His cell phone rang and he checked the caller ID. Robyn Johnson. With an apologetic nod to Helen, he took the call.

"Robyn, hi. What's up?"

"Good news, I hope. Lenny, our investigator, had a breakthrough this morning. He discovered that the reporter who first floated the story about you and Sophie was Carter Kilgore."

Liam flashed onto an image of a handsome, fast-talking

news anchor. "Kilgore has his own show on MSNBC, right?"

"Yes. He specializes in covering crimes, as opposed to the political stuff, and he attracts a big audience as cable news shows go. He loves celebrity rapes and missing co-eds, especially if they're pretty. Kilgore and his staff all refused to answer Lenny's questions about where their boss acquired his information, of course, but then Lenny got lucky and managed to make an end run around the blockage."

"How did he pull off that minor miracle?"

"All these national news crews hire local go-fers when they move into town on a breaking story. It turns out one of Lenny's cousins was helping Kilgore's team with logistical support. Lenny eventually persuaded his cousin to admit that she'd driven Kilgore to meet his informant at DIA. The cousin either wouldn't or couldn't provide a name for the informant. I guess she was afraid of never getting hired again if word spread that she'd talked. Still, at least we have the name of the journalist who broke the story and confirmation that he did meet with a real live source. Carter Kilgore clearly didn't just dream up this report to boost ratings and then fake the DNA tests to cover his rear end."

"That's great work on Lenny's part." Liam kept his excitement in check. Robyn was a busy woman. Surely she wouldn't be making this call personally unless Lenny had managed to take the investigation a step further. "Did he succeed in identifying Kilgore's informant?"

"You're a demanding man, Liam." He could almost see Robyn's grin. "But yes, I have more." She paused for dramatic effect. "We have photos of the meeting between Kilgore and his informant."

Oh, man. Photos. "Clear enough for an ID?" Liam asked.

"Yep." Robyn sounded justifiably pleased with herself. "Fortunately for us, Kilgore met his informant at a place called the Sandwich Parlor. It's a café on the main airport concourse."

"Yes, I know it."

"Even more fortunately, the Sandwich Parlor uses a security company called Red Shield. Lenny has helped out Red Shield so many times he has multiple contacts inside the company. He persuaded one of his contacts to slip him a tape of Red Shield's security camera records for the appropriate time and place. And—hallelujah!—we've got several clear shots of Kilgore's informant."

Liam held his breath. "And his name is...?"

"I haven't a clue." Robyn didn't sound too upset by her lack of knowledge. "I didn't flash the photos around the office to see if anyone recognized the guy talking with Kilgore. In my opinion, there've already been way too many leaks in this case and we'd be smart to keep quiet about the direction we're heading. Anyway, here's why I'm calling you. I have to be in court on another case in less than five minutes from now, but I've already sent one of my assistants to hand deliver the pictures to Chloe. With any luck, she'll be able to identify the guy talking to Kilgore."

"It's definitely a man?" Liam asked.

"Yes. No doubt about that. He's tall, lean. Early fifties, I'm guessing. Dresses like a banker or a lawyer. A *rich* banker or lawyer. Caucasian. Probably has light brown hair, although it's hard to tell in a black-and-white photo. Ringing any bells?"

"Dozens. With that description, he could be ten percent of the men I meet during a typical workday."

"Well, get onto it, Liam. Don't let Chloe give up. Bring me a name. We need somewhere to go with this investigation that leads away from Chloe. And right now, this guy is all we've got."

Twenty-One

Robyn's assistant had already left by the time Liam reached Chloe's house. Sophie was at summer day camp for another two hours, so they had the house to themselves. Chloe had the security photos spread out across the breakfast room table but one glance at her face was all it took to warn Liam that she hadn't recognized Kilgore's informant.

"When Robyn called, I was so optimistic that we would soon have a new lead to work with. But I'm confident I've never seen this man before in my life." She picked up one of the pictures and handed it to Liam, angling a gooseneck lamp to give him more light. "This is the best shot, I think. Kilgore's informant is looking straight into the camera and the image is fairly clear. Clear enough for me to be sure I've never met him."

Liam gave her an encouraging smile. "Don't give up yet. Now that we have pictures, an ID can't be too far away."

"I sure hope you're right."

Liam glanced down at the photo and recognition hit him like a blow to the gut. For a moment it felt as if his whole body froze.

"What is it?" Chloe asked. "Liam, what's wrong?"

"I know this man," he said, when his facial muscles unlocked enough for him to speak. "I've never met him in person, but I've seen him on TV quite a few times. His name is Paul Fairfax."

"Is he a journalist? I've heard that name somewhere." Chloe frowned, then shook her head. "No, I can't place where I heard it." She picked up another of the photos, smiling in relief that Liam had been able to pin an identity onto the informant so quickly. Her smile turned teasing. "He's almost as good-looking as you, Liam. Older, of course, but still sexy."

He couldn't return her smile. All he could think of was that his connection to Chloe had brought her nothing but trouble. The police, he was sure, wouldn't have been so quick to arrest her if not for the fact that they hated his guts. As soon as they heard he was acting as Chloe's lawyer, they'd jumped at the chance to pay off old scores. The fact that he was Sophie's adulterous, out-of-wedlock father posed a clear conflict of interest, which he had arro-gantly—stupidly—ignored. He couldn't have predicted Paul Fairfax's malicious involvement in the case, of course, but he sure as hell ought to have been able to predict that hanging out anywhere near Chloe would make her life a lot more difficult.

He felt a strong urge to throw a punch—preferably at Paul Fairfax, but the wall wouldn't have been a bad sub-stitute. He had just enough sense left to realize that pum-meling an inanimate object wouldn't do a damn thing to correct his past errors of judgment, so he jammed his hands into his pockets and forced himself to speak like a rational human being. Something he apparently hadn't been for most of the past week.

"Unfortunately, I suspect this media attack was aimed at me, not you, so it may not be as helpful in solving Jason's murder as we'd hoped." He drew in a breath which did little to calm him. "Paul Fairfax wanted to cause trouble for my family and he took advantage of Jason's death to make his point. I'm afraid you were just collateral damage in a feud that has nothing to do with you."

"Fairfax is an enemy of yours?" Chloe's forehead wrinkled as she examined the photo again but she didn't appear as devastated as Liam would have expected. "Why does his name sound so familiar to me? You still haven't explained who he is. A lawyer? An ex-client with a grudge? Something worse?"

"Not a lawyer and not a client. He's a financial entrepreneur. He invests in start-up companies, construction projects, that sort of thing. We're not professional rivals. His dislike of me is strictly personal. Or I should say, transferred personal. He's angry with my father."

Liam steeled himself to explain about his father's bigamy, something he still had trouble doing despite weeks of intrusive publicity back in the spring. By the time the media had finished chewing over the spicy details of Ron Raven's life, there had been few secrets left. Still, his father's death remained a sore spot in Liam's psyche and he usually tried to avoid poking at the wound. Now, however, he had no choice.

"I expect you know my father was murdered earlier this year," he said finally.

"Yes, I was aware of his death. I'm sorry, Liam I know he disappeared from a hotel in Miami just a few days after I first consulted you about divorcing Jason." Chloe sent him a sympathetic look. "I saw the reports about your family situation on TV. It was hard to avoid, but to be honest, I was curious enough to go looking for coverage. Ron Raven was Sophie's grandfather, after all, and part of me wished that the two of them could have met."

The fact that Ron Raven was Sophie's grandfather hadn't previously occurred to Liam, except as a genetic fact. Since he had no idea how he felt about it, he fell back into bad old habits and simply avoided any direct comment. "If you saw the TV coverage, then you know my father was a bigamist. The TV news shows had a field day with that juicy item."

"Yes, I knew about Ron Raven's two wives, and the fact that you have a younger half sister in Chicago, as well as the sister you grew up with. It must have been painful for you to come to terms with your dad's years of deception."

"Nowhere near as painful for me as it was for my mother. For the first month after he died, my sister and I worried that Mom might go to pieces. But she seems to be doing much better recently, thank goodness."

"The sheriff...Harry...struck me as a nice man," Chloe said. "He seems kind as well as trustworthy."

Liam stumbled mentally over the seeming disconnect. Then he stared at Chloe in blank-eyed astonishment. "Good grief! Are you suggesting that my mother and Harry Ford are...involved?"

She was amused by his surprise. "Well, they clearly have feelings for each other. Whether they're actually dating... I guess that remains to be seen. Although they were in Denver together and that must mean something, don't you think?"

"I have no idea." Liam wasn't sure whether to feel aggrieved or awestruck by her insights. "What is it with you women? How come you notice these things that mere males remain totally clueless about?"

"Self-preservation, probably." Her smile turned rueful. "Until fifty years ago, women needed men in order to survive, so we worked hard to understand them. Men always had a lot more power, so they didn't need to work as hard to understand relationships."

"That was fifty years ago. What's my excuse now?"

"Well, in this particular case, I was looking at Harry and your mother with fresh eyes. I'd never seen them before, whereas you've seen them together often enough you don't actually notice them, certainly not as a couple."

Liam made a frustrated sound. "I suppose I ought to be grateful you didn't say I was oblivious because I'm a blind, self-centered moron."

She laughed. "Well, maybe a little bit blind, but not a moron."

When she laughed like that, he caught a glimpse of a younger, carefree Chloe. He would give quite a lot, he thought, to see that happier Chloe more often. Instead, he had to return their discussion to the subject of Paul Fairfax and extinguish her smiles.

"I was explaining that my father was a bigamist," he said, deciding there was nothing for it but to plunge back into the unpleasant subject. "My mother was his legal wife, but his second wife, the one who lived with him in Chicago, was…is Avery Fairfax."

"Avery Fairfax. *Fairfax,*" Chloe repeated, eyes

widening. "Oh my God, I'd heard her name, of course, but I didn't make the connection. I guess Paul Fairfax must be related to your father's bigamous wife?"

Liam nodded. "Paul is Avery's older brother. He was also my father's business partner in Raven Enterprises."

"Raven Enterprises is the investment partnership your father founded, isn't it? I remember commentators mentioning that it was very successful."

"Yes, it was. And Paul owned a quarter of the partnership shares. Unfortunately, though, Dad seems to have left his business in only marginally better shape than the ruins of his personal life. Which has always struck me as odd, since the one thing my father was really good at was making money."

Chloe's mouth twisted. "I can see why Paul might be a little angry with the Raven family."

"Yeah, one way or another, dear old Dad really worked a number on the Fairfaxes." Liam paced the length of the small breakfast nook, unable to walk fast enough to escape his self-reproach. "Dammit, Chloe, I've totally screwed up everything connected to this case. These public revelations about Sophie are my fault. You've been hurt and humiliated just because Paul Fairfax has a burr up his ass about my father—"

"Why are you responsible for Paul Fairfax's actions?" Chloe came and stood in front of him, halting him in his tracks. She took both his hands and cradled them against her chest. The warmth of her touch extended inward, banishing the icy chill of his self-loathing. He wondered how he'd reached the ripe old age of thirty-five without ever before realizing how much pleasure could be found in the simple act of holding hands with a woman you cared about.

"You're crazy if you're blaming yourself for the fact that I was arrested." Chloe's expression was oddly tender. "I'm sure the police were planning to arrest me almost from the moment the first cop walked in the door and saw Jason's body lying on the basement floor. You haven't caused me problems, Liam. It's the opposite. Don't you see that you're the only reason I haven't completely lost my sanity over the past few days?"

It scared him to realize just how much he wanted to believe she was telling the truth and not just offering comfort. But if comfort was all it was, he'd take it. Liam drew her into his arms, not kissing her, just holding her close. A stray wisp of her hair tickled his face and he shut his eyes, breathing in the light floral smell of her shampoo and the spicier scent of her skin. The feel of her body nestled against him caused an unfamiliar ache in the region of his heart. He'd wanted to impress her by playing Superman, he thought wryly. He'd wanted to storm into the courtroom and make all her legal difficulties vanish with a swirl of his magic cape. Instead of working miracles, he seemed to be causing her one problem after another. He would be the first to admit that right now his cape was looking distinctly tattered.

He wished with unexpected fervor that they could forget about death and murder trials and intrusive media hounds for the rest of the afternoon and simply relax together, enjoying each other's company in some humdrum way. He could drive with her to pick up Sophie from summer camp, then they could maybe order a pizza—and look forward to the moment when Sophie would be in bed and they would have the whole night to themselves. He wanted to make love to Chloe with an intensity that made his whole body ache.

Liam regretfully shut down his fantasy. "I wish Kilgore's informant had been somebody other than Paul Fairfax," he murmured.

"Why? Just because Paul Fairfax wanted to hurt you rather than me doesn't change the fact that he knew the truth about Sophie. Where did he get his information? Who passed him the DNA tests? And why?"

Liam stared at her, momentarily stunned into silence. He'd been so hung up on Paul's desire to get back at the Ravens that he'd ignored an entire list of blindingly obvious questions. "You're right," he said, giddy with relief that they still had a lead to work with. "Of course you are! I was so fixated on Paul Fairfax's dislike of my family that I couldn't see past it."

"That's understandable," Chloe said. "But the fact is, however badly Paul Fairfax wanted to screw you over, he needed information to do it. As far as I can tell there are only two explanations for how he found out you're Sophie's father. Either he was given those DNA tests directly by Jason, or he was given them by somebody Jason trusted a lot."

"Surely he wasn't given them by Jason." Liam wondered if it was mere prejudice on his part that made the idea seem so unlikely. "Why would your husband confide in Paul Fairfax, of all people? How did they even know each other?"

Chloe hesitated. "We've been trying to identify Jason's lover. Perhaps Paul Fairfax is the person we're looking for."

"*What?*" Liam stared at her, already shaking his head in denial. "You've got to be kidding! Jesus, Chloe, that can't be the answer. That would be stretching the long arm of coincidence a couple of miles beyond the breaking point. Besides, Paul went to Duke University, not the University of Virginia. On top of that, he's married and lives in Chicago—"

Chloe sent him a sardonic glance. "The fact that Paul is married doesn't mean anything. Jason was married, too, in case you've forgotten. As for Paul going to Duke instead of U. Va...." She shrugged. "Look how Jason lied to me about Father Hannity. There's no solid reason to suppose he told me the truth about first meeting his lover at college."

Liam ran his hands through his hair, a better alternative than tearing it out in frustrated hanks. "You're right, of course. But Chicago is a hell of a long way from Denver. How could Jason carry on a decade-long love affair with a partner who lived a thousand miles away?"

"It strikes me as...difficult," Chloe conceded. "On the other hand, your father managed to juggle two wives and two sets of children for twenty-seven years! So obviously it can be done."

Liam tried to wrap his mind around the possibility that the murdered mayor of Denver and his father's business partner had been lovers. His imagination couldn't stretch to the task.

"At least it's easy to decide what we need to do next," he said. "I must pay Paul Fairfax a visit."

Chloe looked at him, considering. "I can see the idea makes you uncomfortable. I'd go myself if I could—"

"And get arrested for breaking the terms of your bail bond and fleeing the jurisdiction? Don't even think of it."

"Perhaps confronting Paul won't be as difficult as you anticipate," Chloe said. "In some ways, his connection to your father puts you in a strong position to demand answers. You've got lots of background information to provide helpful insights."

Liam gave a short crack of laughter. "Finally, a reason to be grateful for my father's bigamy. I didn't expect to live long enough for that to happen."

Her answering smile was wry. "Where do you suppose Paul Fairfax is now? Still in Denver, or did he arrange to meet Carter Kilgore at the airport because he was scheduled to catch a plane back to Chicago?"

"We'll soon find out." Liam pulled out his BlackBerry and retrieved a phone number for Cody Holmann, the lawyer in Wyoming who was still attempting to work out the mess resulting from the fact that Ron Raven had left two different wills, both dated the same day and both apparently valid in the states where they were written.

"Hey, Cody," he said when the lawyer picked up the call. "This is Liam Raven. Sorry to bother you, but I need to contact Paul Fairfax urgently. Do you have his number at Raven Enterprises, by any chance? I don't have it, and I know you've been in touch with him over the past couple of months."

"Hey, Liam, how are you doin'?" Cody Holmann didn't seem to expect an answer to his question. "I have that number right here on my desk. Let me see….Yes, here it is. Office and home. Paul Fairfax." He read off the two numbers, and provided the street addresses for good measure.

"What's new with you, Liam? Keeping out of trouble, I hope?"

Cody Holmann didn't have an ironic bone in his body, so Liam could only conclude the lawyer hadn't watched any television for the past week. That was possible. In summer, Cody could find too many good fishing holes to waste time keeping abreast of what passed for news in the world outside Stark County.

"I'm fine," he said. "In a rush, actually. I have to catch a plane to Chicago this afternoon."

"Hmm. In view of the phone numbers you just asked for, it doesn't take a genius to work out that you're considering paying a visit to Paul Fairfax. He isn't an easy man to deal with, and he's mighty angry with your father."

"He probably has cause. However, I'm not my father."

"You're a fine substitute in Paul Fairfax's eyes. The fact that Ron is dead simply means he's more likely to take out his anger on you. I've heard rumors that he's in deep financial trouble, which would make him doubly mad at the length of time it's taking to get Ron's estate moved through probate. You're a lawyer, Liam, so I don't need to remind you that you shouldn't talk to him about anything even remotely connected to your father's estate. You're a beneficiary in one of the wills, so you need to steer clear of anything that could be considered unethical pressure on the opposing party."

"I wouldn't dream of discussing my father's wills," Liam said. "Especially since thinking about them makes me almost as hopping mad as it makes Paul Fairfax. You have my word, Cody. My mother is happy to leave that particular mess in your competent hands. Megan and I are equally happy. This is something else entirely. Look, I've got to run. Enjoy your weekend. Catch a few trout for me."

He hung up before Cody could ask any more questions and dialed the offices of Raven Enterprises. He was aware of how strange it was that he'd needed to call his mother's lawyer to find out the phone number of his father's company. Ron Raven had maintained a barrier between his two families by diverting phone calls to an answering service, so in all the years his father had been alive, Liam had never actually talked to anyone at the real office headquarters of Raven Enterprises.

He listened to an interminable electronic menu before finally being greeted by a chirpy human voice. The chirpy voice identified herself as Eileen, office manager for Raven Enterprises.

"Good afternoon, Eileen," Liam said. "Is Mr. Fairfax in the office today?"

"Who is calling, please?"

"I'm Sergeant Patterson, with the Chicago Police Department." The lie tripped smoothly from his tongue. "We've recovered a laptop that might once have belonged to Mr. Ronald Raven. I'd like to bring it around and show it to Mr. Fairfax to see if he can identify it." Liam had no idea where his story sprang from, except that Megan had often mentioned how strange it was that their father's laptop had never been found, despite the fact that his hotel room had contained all of his other personal belongings.

"Mr. Fairfax is in the office today," Eileen conceded. "But he's very busy. He's just got back into town after four days away…"

Today was Friday. Four days away meant Paul had been out of the office since Monday. Of course, Eileen wouldn't know if her boss had left Chicago over the prior weekend. Paul could have flown out of O'Hare last Saturday or Sunday. Either departure date would have given him plenty of time to arrive in Denver and kill Jason in the early hours of Monday morning.

Liam put a halt to his speculation. He was going too far,

much too fast. "I understand how busy Mr. Fairfax must be," he told Eileen, reverting to his role of cop. "In fact, I'm pretty busy myself and I may not be able to make it out there until after the weekend. Is Mr. Fairfax expected in the office next week?"

"Yes, he is. When would you plan on getting here, officer?"

"Early Monday afternoon, I guess. Let Mr. Fairfax know I'll be stopping by, will you? Thanks for your help." Liam hung up before Eileen started to wonder why a police officer was concerned about a laptop belonging to a man who'd already been dead for several months and whose killer had been identified to the entire satisfaction of the Miami Police Department, whose case it was.

"Isn't it illegal to impersonate a police officer?" Chloe asked him as he returned the phone to its stand.

"Yes." He didn't elaborate, just gathered up the photos and stuck them into his briefcase.

"The name Paul Fairfax has been striking a chord with me ever since you first mentioned it. I've just remembered where I heard it before, apart from in connection with Avery Fairfax. Remember Sam DiVoli, the businessman I mentioned?"

"Sure." Liam nodded. "He's the Republican party insider who gave your husband the official seal of approval as a senate candidate. You had dinner at his house the evening before Jason was killed."

"Right. Well, I'm sure I heard Sam DiVoli mention Paul Fairfax's name to Jason during the course of that dinner. I wasn't paying much attention to specific topics because I was feeling pretty self-absorbed that night. The realization that Jason and I simply couldn't go on with our fake marriage was a bit overwhelming. Still, I have a distinct memory of Sam talking about a business deal that he and Paul were involved in. A real estate development project, maybe? I think Sam was reminding Jason that the project had been delayed because the zoning committee hadn't issued the necessary permits." She lifted her shoulders in a shrug. "Mundane stuff, I guess, and I don't know if the connection matters, but I thought I'd mention it."

"Any information about Paul is useful at this point, especially business deals. If Paul's financial situation is as precarious as people are suggesting, that deal could be vitally important to him. And it's good to know about his connection to Sam DiVoli. I might be able to use that."

Liam tucked his BlackBerry into the zippered pocket on the side of his briefcase. "I'm off to Chicago, now that I've confirmed Paul is planning to be there through the weekend. If I can catch a flight around two, I can be in O'Hare by five."

"Will you see Paul tonight, do you think? Or wait until tomorrow morning?"

"Tonight, I hope. Seems to me, the earlier we confront him, the better. That way, the element of surprise is more likely to be on our side." Liam gave her a crooked smile. "With luck, I'll be back in Denver by tomorrow afternoon. Tomorrow night at the latest. Can you survive without me for twenty-four hours?"

"I hope so." She spoke soberly, as if his question had been serious.

"I'm not sure if I can survive without you." The admission sprang out of nowhere. Liam only knew that once the words were spoken, he recognized them as true. He put his briefcase down again and pulled Chloe back into his arms, kissing her as if his life depended on it.

Maybe it did, he thought. In retrospect—that phenomenal aid to clear vision—he could see that until Chloe came into his life, he hadn't been living. He'd simply been going through the motions, so busy protecting himself from repeating his father's mistakes that he'd withdrawn from all meaningful human relationships. Before Chloe, endless No-Name clones had been the best he could hope for as a substitute for intimacy. And a pale, cold substitute it had been.

He kissed her again, their kiss openmouthed, hot, passionate. It wasn't enough, but it would have to suffice for now. He reluctantly drew away. "Take care of yourself while I'm gone. Give Sophie a good night hug from me."

"I will." Chloe stepped back, but then reached up and curved the palm of her hand against his cheek. "Be safe, Liam."

His heart gave another of the disconcerting jumps he'd come to expect over the past few days. He ignored it. His emotions might have thawed some, but he still didn't believe in falling head over heels in love and other absurd romantic fantasies. He would be the first to admit that Chloe filled him with lust, and lust destroyed the brain's capacity to produce rational thought. So he left the house quickly, without looking back, before he could do something he would undoubtedly live to regret. Something totally crazy, like telling Chloe that for the first time in his life he was wondering if getting married and making a home with someone you cared about might not be the best shot at happiness a man could ever hope to get.

Twenty-Two

The Friday night rush hour traffic around O'Hare Airport was still moving sluggishly when Liam picked up his rental car at six o'clock. Hemmed in by commuters, he made slow progress across town, and it was almost seven-thirty by the time he reached Kenilworth, the upscale North Shore suburb where Paul Fairfax lived with his wife, Julia.

Paul's house turned out to be a brick and stone Tudor mansion, built on a cul-de-sac, and screened behind giant sycamore and hackberry trees that must have taken fifty years to mature. Kenilworth was the most expensive of the North Shore suburbs and everything from the manicured lawn to the gleaming mullioned windows reinforced the message that Paul's home was in the top price bracket, even for this exclusive town.

The upkeep of a house like this would consume the entire income of a middle-class family and Liam wondered how Paul was generating the cash to maintain his opulent lifestyle. Liam had very little respect left for his father, but one thing he had to concede about Ron Raven was that the guy had been a whiz at making money. After his death, plenty of Ron's business colleagues had been eager to inform the world that he had been both the brains and the driving force behind the success of Raven Enterprises. None of the commentators had shown much respect for Paul Fairfax, and the general conclusion had been that the company was likely to sink into rapid trouble now that Ron was dead.

The pundits' predictions seemed to be coming true. Cody Holmann had mentioned several times that, even in the short few months since Ron's death, the financial picture at Raven Enterprises already looked grim. Liam was sure that some of the animosity Paul felt toward Ron's Wyoming family was the result of resentment over his diminished financial prospects. The possibility that Paul was facing real financial difficulties would be his final leverage if the guy refused to part with the name of his source.

Liam parked his rental car a couple of houses down the street and made his way on foot up the long, flower-bordered driveway of the Fairfax home. With luck, nobody inside would realize he was approaching until he was at the front door.

He rang the bell, setting off chimes that rivaled Big Ben striking the hour. Thank God the Fairfaxes hadn't gone high tech with an intercom system to screen their visitors. After a brief wait, Paul himself opened the door. In the few seconds before he registered the identity of the person waiting under his polished slate portico, Liam stepped into the entry hall and positioned himself at the foot of an imposing staircase.

"Get out of my house." Paul was breathing hard, and his eyes narrowed with dislike and anger.

"I'll be happy to leave, as soon as you've answered a few questions."

Paul's mouth tightened into a thin line. "I have nothing to say to you, except—*get out.*"

"That's not true. You apparently have a lot to say to me. But for some bizarre reason, you prefer to conduct our conversations via the Carter Kilgore TV show."

"I don't know what you're talking about."

"Don't be tiresome, Paul. I'm in a foul mood and I don't have much patience for listening to you lie. We both know you're the man who tipped off Kilgore about my relationship to Sophie, so let's move on from there."

Paul spluttered another half-hearted denial and Liam made an impatient sound, pulling out a couple of the security camera pictures and jiggling them in front of Paul's nose. "Here are photos of you, deep in conversation with Carter Kilgore at the Sandwich Parlor on the second floor concourse of Denver Airport. Please, let's not waste time disputing the obvious when we have real issues that need our attention."

"There's no way to prove what Carter Kilgore and I discussed." Paul sounded sulky rather than guilty. He wasn't a man who leaped to take responsibility for his own actions.

"Are you sure?" Liam didn't have to feign his irritation. "Look, Paul, if you're determined to stick with your denials, we can go that route. But then, of course, I'll be forced to find another way to catch your attention. I have a few spectacular tidbits I could drop in Kilgore's ear concerning your relationship with the late mayor of Denver. Is that what I need to do in order to convince you it's time for the two of us to have a conversation?"

Liam had gambled that his threat would have teeth, and his gamble paid off, big time. Paul turned white, and then bright red. His reaction wasn't proof that he'd been Jason's lover, of course, but it was a strong indication he'd had dealings with the mayor that wouldn't stand public scrutiny.

"Come with me." Paul spoke through a clenched jaw, gesturing to a half-open door toward the right of the hallway. Liam had just started to move in the indicated direction when a petite, almost skeletal woman emerged from a room on the opposite side of the hallway.

The woman, presumably Paul's wife, smiled at Liam, stretching the too-taut skin of her face lift. "Paul! You didn't tell me we were expecting a guest."

"We weren't," he responded curtly. "Excuse us, Julia." Without another glance toward his wife, let alone an introduction, Paul ushered Liam into a library, heavy on the oak paneling and prints of English fox-hunting scenes. A single bookcase housed six shelves of leather-bound, gilt-embossed books. The books looked handsome, but their pristine state suggested they'd never been read or even taken off the shelves except to be dusted and returned.

Paul shut the door. "Tell me why you've come here," he said, standing behind his imposing desk and making no move to sit down.

"I want to know who told you I was Sophie's biological father and how you obtained the DNA tests to prove it."

"So you admit the information is accurate? Well, what do you know?" Paul made no effort to conceal his glee. His mouth twisted into a sneer. "You and your father are a fine pair. You should both have learned to keep your dicks in your pants and you'd have gotten yourselves into a lot less trouble."

Liam had already drawn plenty of unflattering comparisons between himself and his father, so Paul's taunt failed to find its mark. He wasn't doomed to repeat his father's mistakes, Liam realized. What mattered most was not the fact that he'd impregnated Chloe. What mattered was that as soon as he knew the truth about his daughter's existence, he'd tried to do the right thing for *her.* He wanted to be a part of Sophie's life, and he would work with Chloe to find the best way to do that. His father, on the other hand, had never tried to do the best thing for his children, or either of his wives. He'd merely tried to do the best and most convenient thing for himself.

More interesting than Paul's attempted insult was the fact that his question suggested he'd passed on the story about Liam and Sophie without being certain of its truth. Surely that meant Paul hadn't entirely trusted the person who told him the story? It also suggested he'd been willing to risk being sued for slander. The desire to wreak revenge on Ron Raven's son didn't seem adequate motivation for such perilous behavior. However much Paul disliked his late partner, surely he wouldn't risk facing a multimillion-dollar lawsuit unless the potential payoff was something a lot bigger than negative publicity for the Wyoming Ravens?

"You didn't generate those DNA tests yourself," Liam said. That, at least, seemed certain. "You've never been anywhere near Sophie or me, so you couldn't have obtained DNA samples from either of us, even surreptitiously. That being the case, how did the tests come into your possession?"

"They were mailed to me." Paul gave a smug smile. "Anonymously."

"Where was the package mailed from?"

"Sadly, I threw away the envelope before I realized it was my only clue about where the package came from." Paul's smirk intensified into triumph. He clearly relished the fact that there was no way to disprove his statement.

The balance of power between the two of them was weighted too much in Paul's favor, Liam thought grimly. He'd better do something fast to shift the balance or he'd be catching a plane home to Denver no wiser than when he'd flown in.

He rested his hands on the edge of the desk and leaned toward Paul, his stance deliberately menacing. "I'm debating whether or not to beat the crap out of you," he said conversationally. "That might persuade you to tell the truth. It might not, of course. But even if it didn't, the way I feel toward you right now, beating the crap out of you has a definite appeal."

Paul reached into the right-hand desk drawer. A second later, Liam was staring down the barrel of a Glock-19 pistol. "You've just made threats of physical violence against me," Paul said. "I can shoot you right through the heart, with a bullet to the brain for good measure, and there isn't a judge in the state who'll convict me of anything except protecting my home and my personal safety. Now get out of my home before I decide to pull the trigger."

Based on current Illinois laws about homeowner self-defense, it was probably untrue that Paul could shoot him with a handgun and escape prosecution. But Liam didn't care to debate the technicalities of the law, since he would be dead whether or not Paul was charged. Paul looked pissed enough to fire first and worry about the legal consequences later.

Liam backed up, raising his hands in a gesture of surrender. "Okay, you win. Your gun beats my fists. But now that you've made your point, you should put the gun away before somebody gets hurt. Speaking as a lawyer, I can tell you that trying to prove self-defense is a bitch, especially when you're known to have an adversarial relationship with the person you've shot."

"Fine." Paul lowered the gun but he didn't put it away. "Here's the deal. You leave right now and I won't shoot."

Liam slowly brought his arms down to his sides. "Let's start this conversation over. I'm not here to create trouble for you, Paul. I'm here because Chloe Hamilton has been wrongly accused of killing her husband and I need help proving that."

"What has that got to do with me? Besides, I can't think of a single reason why I might want to help you, of all people."

"Even if you can help me at no cost to yourself? You can point me in the direction of the real killer—"

"Like hell I can." Paul sounded distressed by the suggestion. "I had nothing to do with Jason's death. I was right here in Kenilworth when the mayor was stabbed and I can damn well prove it. I heard the report that the mayor was dead on the Monday morning news and that's when I decided to go to Denver. I left here on a ten-thirty United Airlines flight. With all the security checks there are nowadays, I'm sure I can prove it."

Liam was careful not to reveal his interest in Paul's flight information. The guy was so busy protesting his lack of involvement in the mayor's murder that he hadn't noticed what else he'd tacitly admitted. Apparently he had been sufficiently…upset? worried? alarmed?….by the news of Jason's death that he'd immediately flown to

Denver. Because the two of them had been lovers? It was possible but not likely, Liam thought. Nothing that Paul had done or said suggested that he was griefstricken by the mayor's death. Liam's gut told him that Paul had been more worried about his business deal with Sam DiVoli than the death of the mayor.

"I'm not accusing you of killing Jason," he said smoothly. "Absolutely not."

Paul snorted. "You could have fooled me."

"The information I want from you isn't directly related to Jason's murder. I simply want to find out who gave you the DNA tests you passed to Carter Kilgore on Wednesday night. Just that, nothing more. Until two days ago, Chloe Hamilton believed there were only three people in the world who knew I was Sophie's biological father. She was one of those people, of course, and her husband was the second person. I was the third. Neither Chloe nor I revealed the secret to anyone. That leaves Jason Hamilton as the only possible source of your information."

Paul shrugged. "I barely knew Jason Hamilton and I can assure you that on the few occasions we were together, he never mentioned his daughter. Or *your* daughter, I should say. Look, let's cut to the chase. You want to know who gave me the inside scoop about you and Sophie and I'm not going to tell you. That's pretty much the end of anything we have to discuss." Paul's hand hovered restlessly over his gun. "In the circumstances, this would be a good moment for you to leave."

"You seem to forget this is a murder case, and you're in possession of material information. You can't simply refuse to talk."

"Hah—watch me!" Paul's grip tightened around the gun. "You have no right to question me."

"You're absolutely correct. *I* have no right. However, law enforcement officials do have that right, and as soon as I leave here, I'm going to call one of my investigator friends in the D.A.'s office and tell him you're concealing material information." Liam hoped like hell that Paul wouldn't realize the D.A.'s office was conspicuously devoid of anyone he might call a friend. Not to mention the detail that Sophie's paternity might or might not have relevance to the mayor's murder.

Since he was bluffing, he might as well go full throttle. "In addition, if you aren't prepared to tell me privately how you found out about my relationship to Sophie, Chloe Hamilton's lawyer will have an official summons issued and you'll find yourself testifying in open court. And trust me on this, your bullshit story about receiving a package in the mail isn't going to hold up."

"Chloe Hamilton's trial is months away." Paul fell abruptly silent. He put down the gun and a flicker of annoyance crossed his face before he managed to reassert control over his expression. He turned a bland smile in Liam's direction, trying to cover his error. "As you know," he added.

Everyone and his dog already knew that Chloe's trial wouldn't start for several months—criminal trials were notorious for the length of time they took to come into court—and yet Paul was squirming as if he'd revealed a vital secret.

Liam had spent enough hours cross-examining lying witnesses to know when he'd hit pay dirt. Paul felt no great loyalty to his source and didn't care about protecting him for the long-term, Liam deduced. However, he felt the need to keep quiet for the time being, even if the cost for his silence involved testifying in open court a few months down the road. Paul might be betting on the chance that Chloe would enter into a plea bargain and the case would never come to trial. More likely, he had made a deal with his source. If Paul kept quiet, he was going to receive a payoff. And that payoff was going to come soon—long before Chloe's trial.

The fact that Paul's reward was going to be paid in the future ruled out the late mayor of Denver as his direct source. Dead men couldn't make payoffs. Whoever had given Paul those DNA tests was very much alive and available to provide the necessary reward, whether it was cash, favors or access to power.

There was no way for Liam to guess the precise nature of the deal Paul had struck. He didn't have enough information to guess why somebody wanted to publicize the fact that the late mayor hadn't been Sophie's biological father. The only thing he could do was threaten Paul with a greater penalty than anything he might hope to gain by keeping quiet. Time to spring the Sam DiVoli trap.

"Did you know that Jason Hamilton was gay?" Liam asked, his tone of voice deliberately conversational.

"The mayor was gay? Are you crazy?" Paul stared at Liam, wide-eyed with shock. "He can't have been gay! For God's sake, he was married!"

He and Paul both seemed to share a naive faith that gay people didn't marry, Liam reflected wryly. "News flash, Paul. Marriage isn't actually a guarantee that both parties to the deal are heterosexual."

"But Jason didn't look gay," Paul protested. "He

didn't act gay." He scowled at Liam across the desk.
"You must be wrong."

"No, I'm not."

Paul seemed to realize that his arguments lacked both
weight and logic and he lifted his shoulders in a dismissive shrug. "Who cares, anyway? Jason's dead. His sexual
orientation has nothing to do with anything. Not any
more."

Paul was either a world-class actor, or he'd been genuinely caught off-guard by the news that the late mayor
of Denver had been gay. Liam was fairly confident Paul's
acting skills were minimal, but it didn't much matter. His
threat depended only on how precarious Paul's financial
situation was, nothing else.

Liam once again braced his hands on the edge of the desk
and leaned forward. "I'm going to be more courteous to you
than you were to me. I'm giving you fair warning of what
I'm about to do. As soon as I leave here, I'm going to call
my assistant and arrange a meeting with Mr. Sam DiVoli.
He is the man you're working with in Colorado, isn't he?"

Paul turned white. "Why would you want to meet with
Sam?"

"I feel obligated to let Mr. DiVoli know that you were
Jason Hamilton's secret lover. That the two of you carried
on a ten-year love affair."

Paul started to speak, but choked instead. "Are you
insane? I wasn't his lover! Christ almighty, I didn't even
know the mayor was gay until two minutes ago!"

"Unfortunately for you, Sam isn't going to believe you."

"Of course he will!"

"No," Liam shook his head. "Sam will believe me."

"Why? Why would he believe something so crazy?"

"Because he already has a sneaking suspicion that the late mayor of Denver wasn't quite the straight arrow he seemed. Bad enough that his chosen candidate for the U.S. Senate got himself murdered, but it's a whole lot worse if word leaks out that the mayor was gay as a goose."

"But *I'm* not gay! I wasn't Jason's lover! Goddammit, the only time I even *talked* to Jason Hamilton, Sam DiVoli was right there!"

"That won't protect you. It'll just make Sam mad, thinking about how he was deceived. Not to pussyfoot around the facts, but the guy is a homophobe and he won't work with you if there's even the faintest chance that you and the late mayor were lovers. Sam is also richer than Croesus, so he doesn't need this project you're working on with him. But you do, Paul. You need it real bad. We both know that if Sam DiVoli cuts off his association with you, Raven Enterprises is going to collapse." Liam crossed his fingers and hoped like hell that was true.

"Sam DiVoli can't break off our deal," Paul muttered. "He's committed…signed on the dotted line."

Liam shrugged. "Sam DiVoli doesn't have to make a formal break with you. He's tied into every power line and power broker in the state of Colorado. He can just quietly put out the word and your project will fail. As soon as the project is dead, Sam is free and clear. He won't owe you a cent, and you'll be hung out to dry. The only question left will be whether the sharks get you before the vultures, or the other way around."

Paul no longer looked smug. In fact, he looked terrified. He glanced down at the gun and for a moment Liam was afraid he might use it on himself. The guy must be in serious financial straits.

"I can't give you the name you want." Paul's lips were so tight with tension he could barely form the words.

"Why not? Explain the problem, and maybe we can work something out. I know you won't believe me, but I have no interest in causing trouble for you. I figure my father already caused both of us enough headaches that we don't need to pile it on each other."

Paul remained silent.

"If you give me the name of your source, Paul, I promise not to disclose where I got it."

"My source isn't a fool. Even if by some unlikely chance you stick to your promise, he would guess where you got your information in a heartbeat."

"That's possibly true." Liam sensed Paul's weakening, and played on it. "Unfortunately, though, you have limited options. You can give me the name of your source and hope that I keep my promise to protect you as best I can. That way, there's a chance—a pretty good one—that Sam DiVoli will hear no unpleasant rumors and will honor your partnership agreement. Or you can refuse to give me the name I want. In which case, you can be one hundred percent sure that I'll be talking with Sam DiVoli. I'll let him know that you and the late mayor were lovers, and that you were the person who leaked the details of Sophie's parentage to Carter Kilgore. At which point, your business dealings with Sam will be over and you will have officially entered the financial dead zone."

Paul picked up the gun and stared at it for a few seconds. Then he slowly replaced it in the drawer. Walking over to the French door that led from the library into the side yard, he stared out into the darkness for at least a minute.

When he finally spoke, he did so without turning around. "Fred Mitchell," he said. "The person who told me about you and Sophie and gave me the DNA tests was Fred Mitchell, the mayor's chief of staff. Now get out of my house and don't come back."

Twenty-Three

The phone rang, and Chloe tensed reflexively. In the two days since her arrest for Jason's murder, she had received more than a dozen calls from people spewing such vile obscenities that she'd disconnected her voice mail service so that she wouldn't have to hear the hate-filled messages. She checked the caller ID and saw that this call originated at the University of Denver. After another moment's hesitation, she decided to risk answering.

"Hello."

"Mrs. Hamilton...Chloe? This is Father Hannity."

"Hi, Father Hannity. How are you?" She was so thankful not to be cursed as a whore that her voice sounded bubbly with relief. Her expectations about how she might expect to be treated had certainly taken a nose dive over the past few days, Chloe reflected.

"I'm well, and I hope you are, too." Father Hannity gave her no time to respond. "I have the list of your husband's fraternity brothers that you wanted, Chloe. Fortunately, it's not too daunting. Less than two hundred students were members of Delta Kappa Omega during the four years your late husband attended the University of Virginia, and that includes every student who overlapped with Jason even for a single semester."

"Thanks so much for contacting your friend and getting the list. I really appreciate your help, Father."

"All it required was one quick phone call, so I can't take too much credit. I can fax the information right now, if you like. It's only three pages."

"That would be great. Have you checked the list yourself? Do you recognize any of the names?"

"No, I haven't read it. I decided there was no point." Father Hannity's voice took on a definite edge. "It became quite clear to me during our meeting the other day that I have no idea who Jason's friends really are. To be honest, I'm worried about how you plan to utilize this list. I hope you won't resent the intrusion if I warn you to be careful."

"Careful of what? I'm not sure I understand, Father."

"You're dealing with people's lives and that's a big responsibility. Jason made false claims about his relationship with me. A great deal of harm could have been done although, thankfully, it wasn't. But make sure you don't leap to false conclusions about someone just because you find his name on this list. Jason, sadly, lied to both of us about vitally important matters. There's no reason to assume he was speaking the truth when he told you his lover was a former fraternity brother."

It was a sobering reminder. Chloe promised the priest that she wouldn't rush to judgment and thanked him again for his help. He responded politely but she got the impression that he was having second thoughts about the wisdom of having procured the list for her. Father Hannity, she suspected, had just enough faith in the possibility of her innocence that he was willing to provide help, but not enough faith that he felt entirely comfortable about doing so.

The three pages of names were already waiting in the collection tray when she went downstairs to Jason's office where the fax machine was located. It was the first time she'd visited the basement since discovering Jason's body and she had to steel herself to walk down the stairs. The carpet cleaners had removed all traces of Jason's blood from the floor. Their methods had been ruthlessly efficient and the carpet looked pristine, but there was a cloying smell of chemical deodorizer in the air. She wondered if it was just her imagination or if she really could smell the sickly, metallic tang of blood lurking beneath the too-heavy perfume.

The images from Monday morning were suddenly painfully fresh and she started to gag. She grabbed the faxed pages and ran back upstairs, desperate to escape from the demons of too-vivid memories. Back in the relative safety of the kitchen, she leaned against the wall and commanded her stomach to stop heaving.

Sophie chose this moment to decide that she was bored with her glue and glitter art project. Chloe was relieved to be jerked back into the mundane world of the here and now. She served her daughter an afternoon snack of juice and graham crackers, relishing the sheer normality of the task.

It was not that she wanted the cruelty of Jason's death to be forgotten, but for the sake of her sanity she needed to banish the worst of her memories. Despite everything she'd learned about Jason in the past few days, he had been a man who worked tirelessly to improve the lot of his fellow citizens, and his life amounted to much more than the brutal facts of his death. She wanted to get to a place where she could forget the bad and cherish the good.

Sophie was in a chatty mood, full of her morning's adventures in summer camp, including a complicated story about a dog in the swimming pool, but since Chloe needed half an hour of quiet to study Father Hannity's list of names, she broke her own rules and turned on the TV in the middle of the afternoon. It was such a rare treat that the TV worked instant babysitting magic and Sophie was soon curled up, hugging a pillow, absorbed in the adventures of Arthur and D.W. at the beach.

Chloe cleared away the juice and sat down at the table with Father Hannity's list. Jason's fraternity brothers were cited in alphabetical order, without addresses, but with two sets of dates after each name. According to the notation on the first page, one set of dates referred to the years in which the students had been registered at the University of Virginia. The second date showed when the student had pledged to the Delta Kappa Omega fraternity.

Chloe had expected to recognize at least one of the names. Nevertheless it was a shock when she realized that she knew the very first person on the list. Robert A. Attenheim had been a member of Denver's City Council for three or four years but he had stepped down last fall, citing pressure of personal problems. Jason had told her that Bob's wife was fighting breast cancer and since there were two young children in the family, Bob had needed to spend more time at home. Chloe had sent a gift basket of gourmet food to Mrs. Attenheim and another basket of kid-friendly snacks for the children. She had asked Jason for updates at regular intervals and had been delighted when she heard

that the surgery and subsequent chemo had been successful and Mrs. Attenheim would be well enough to return to
her job as a high-school English teacher next fall.

At no time during any of their discussions had Jason
mentioned that he and Bob Attenheim had been members
of the same college fraternity. Chloe checked the dates
again and discovered that Bob had graduated while Jason
was still a freshman. It was possible, she supposed, that
neither man remembered the other and that Jason hadn't
realized Bob was a fellow graduate of U. Va. It was even
possible that the Robert A. Attenheim elected to Denver
City Council was not the same Robert A. Attenheim who
had attended the University of Virginia twenty-five years
ago.

Possible, but not likely, Chloe thought bitterly. Attenheim was an unusual surname, after all. Looking back, she
wondered if every time she'd asked Jason for information
about Mrs. Attenheim's health, they'd actually been discussing the wife of his lover. The mere possibility was
enough to make her stomach knot with anger.

She'd known that she and Jason lived separate lives
while sleeping under the same roof, but until he died she
hadn't fully grasped the depth and breadth of the chasm
between the two of them. Anyone who said that spouses
needed to be friends more than they needed to be lovers
had never lived in a sexless marriage, Chloe thought acidly.
She wrapped her arms around her waist, pressing hard
against her stomach. She realized that the anger she felt
wasn't just directed toward Jason, but also toward herself.
She hadn't merely been complicit in Jason's elaborate lies
for the past four years, she'd been worse: she'd actively
constructed an entire edifice of evasions and half truths to

protect herself from confronting the empty reality of her marriage. What on earth had she been afraid of, she wondered. Had she bought into the PR image of the golden girl athletic champion so completely that she'd been afraid to let anyone see that the gold was tarnished and the interior hollow? Jason had been wrong to use her father's thefts to blackmail her but she'd been a complete idiot to give in to the blackmail.

Tamping down on her anger, she turned her attention back to the list, scanning the remaining columns of names. Her pencil stopped in the middle of the second page. *Frederick Ambrose Mitchell.* Frederick Mitchell and Jason Hamilton had started college at the same time, and they'd joined Delta Kappa Omega in the same year. Fred Mitchell, though, had remained a student at the University of Virginia for only one more semester after joining the fraternity. The date next to his name indicated that he had transferred to the University of Notre Dame in the middle of his sophomore year.

Chloe remembered Fred telling her that he had graduated with a degree in Public Service from Notre Dame, which seemed to confirm that the Frederick Mitchell who had briefly attended the University of Virginia was the same Frederick Mitchell who had later become Jason's chief of staff. Fred had joked with her about the football frenzy that afflicted Notre Dame students each fall and he'd mentioned several times how much he preferred the brilliant sunshine of Colorado to the damp, gray Indiana winters. Despite several such casual conversations about Notre Dame, Fred had never mentioned the fact that he spent the first three semesters of his college career at the University of Virginia. The fact that he'd pledged the Delta

Kappa Omega fraternity in the same year as her husband had never been mentioned, either.

Chloe read through the remainder of the list, forcing herself to concentrate on names and dates whenever she was tempted to wander off into conjecture about Fred Mitchell. When she reached the end of the list without spotting any other names she recognized, she leaned back in her chair and finally allowed herself the luxury of speculation.

If she had to choose whether Jason's lover might be Bob Attenheim or Fred Mitchell, Fred won hands down, no contest. She tried to follow Father Hannity's advice and not jump to conclusions, but Fred Mitchell fit everything Jason had ever told her about his lover so perfectly that it was hard to avoid feeling that she'd been willfully blind not to have detected the relationship years ago. Liam had called himself a moron for not noticing the emotional intensity between his mother and Harry Ford. Now she understood exactly how Liam had felt. Why had she never registered what—in retrospect—she could now clearly see? She had wondered how Jason managed to meet his lover on a regular basis without being spotted by friends, enemies or journalists. But if his lover was also his chief of staff, they already met daily. No need to sneak away to a secret rendezvous: Jason and Fred could meet right here in this house—and often did—without anyone ever questioning what was going on.

No wonder Jason had insisted on building an office downstairs in the basement. Her husband had long since trained her to believe that he suffered from insomnia and she simply accepted that he regularly went down to his office to work during the night. There was a basement door that led directly to the outside, which would provide extra easy access for Fred. Jason and his chief of staff could have spent hours together several times a week and she would never have noticed, or cared. Since Jason started to plan his campaign for the Senate, Fred, who was both chief of staff and campaign manager, had been a permanent fixture at his side. In fact, Fred was around so often that Chloe barely noticed his presence most of the time. Invisibility would be a valuable attribute for any lover in an extramarital affair, she reflected cynically.

Jason and Fred didn't even have to worry about the security cameras catching them in a compromising situation. They were both electronic whiz kids and they had complete access to all the security codes and design plans. They would have encountered no difficulties freezing the security cameras in the basement to display still photographs of an empty room. They could have had a party with a mariachi band down there seven nights a week and the security company would never have known, as long as the music didn't wake Chloe or Trudi.

It must have been Jason himself who disconnected the security system the night he was murdered, Chloe thought, a chill running down her spine at the simplicity of the explanation. Jason had gone downstairs to speak to Fred— he'd told her as much. She'd simply assumed that he meant to confer with his chief of staff by phone. What if Jason had, in fact, invited Fred to come over? Jason had realized she was deadly serious about filing for a divorce and he knew his Senate campaign was at risk once that happened. He might easily have wanted to discuss his options face-to-face with his campaign manager—his closest political ally. Knowing that Fred would soon be arriving in person, Jason had simply set the system to display an empty room.

Anyone back at the security company headquarters who happened to check the monitors would see exactly what was expected in the early hours of the morning: an empty basement. Ironically, Jason's need to protect the secret of his love life had enabled the murderer to kill him without photographic evidence of the deed.

"Arthur is ended, Mommy."

Chloe returned to the real world with a start and saw Sophie leaning over the back of the sofa, her chin resting on the cushions. She walked over and smoothed her daughter's hair away from her face. It was so soft and silky that this morning's neat ponytail had disintegrated into dozens of wisps around her face, her hairband barely hanging in there. Chloe tucked a few of the longest strands behind Sophie's ears and bent down to kiss her. This was one of those moments when she felt such an intense surge of love that her heart didn't feel big enough to contain the emotion.

"Would you like to watch *Little Bear?*" she asked, working a few more strands of hair into the blue band with a glittering plastic butterfly that Sophie had chosen that morning. Her daughter was at the stage where sparkle was her major definition of beauty. "Mommy has to make an important phone call, so it's okay for you to watch another program, just this once."

Sophie eyed her mother with evident puzzlement. "Is this a special day, Mommy?"

"Not really. Just a busy day for Mommy. Look, *Little Bear* is starting."

Sophie, who had no desire to persuade her mother out of her unexpected generosity with the TV, twirled around on the sofa, sat down with a thump and once again tucked herself behind a comforting barricade of pillows. She was apparently feeling quite secure today, since Bobby Bunny had been left in her room, lying on a pink cushion with one of Chloe's designer scarves draped on his overstuffed tummy.

She'd bought herself fifteen more minutes, Chloe thought with relief. She tried calling Liam, but wasn't surprised when there was no reply. His plane was still in the air, and his cell phone would be turned off according to regulations. Since Liam was out of reach, she tried calling her lawyer. Robyn, however, was with a client, awaiting a verdict, and wouldn't be available until the following morning. She could have talked to one of Robyn's assistants, but she decided against it, almost relieved that Robyn wasn't available. If Robyn had picked up the phone, what would she have said? Was she sufficiently convinced that Fred Mitchell had been Jason's lover to pass on the information? More to the point, did she believe that Fred had…been in the house the night Jason was killed?

Chloe made an impatient sound, irritated by her wimpy refusal to put her suspicions into words. Good grief, was she afraid to accuse Fred of being a murderer even in the privacy of her own thoughts? That was crazy. On the other hand, did she have any concrete evidence for suspecting him? Gut feelings weren't going to go over well with her lawyer, or with the cops.

Unable to sit still, she paced to the kitchen, opened the fridge and stared inside. She needed to meet with Fred, she realized. She wanted to look at him with clear eyes and ask herself whether this man she had known for her entire married life could actually be a killer. He had always been kind to her and Sophie and she owed him the courtesy of a face-to-face meeting before she started spreading her accusations around, even to Robyn Johnson, who was the soul of discretion.

She'd lost any desire for a soda. She shut the fridge door and tried to think of how she could meet Fred with zero risk to herself and Sophie. Obviously, the number one requirement would be to meet him where there were plenty of other people around. The second requirement was to make an excuse for the meeting that wouldn't alert him in any way to her suspicions.

Both requirements were easy to achieve. That was one of the advantages of having known Fred for years, Chloe thought wryly. He wouldn't think twice about receiving a phone call from her.

She dialed Fred's office number, which she knew by heart. It was his direct line, and she held her breath waiting to see if she would be switched through to voice mail, or if he would actually pick up the call.

He picked up. "Chloe," he said, his voice somber. "It's good to hear from you. How are you doing?"

"As well as can be expected in the circumstances."

"And Sophie? How's my favorite little girl doing?"

"She had a terrible couple of days right after…right after it happened. Now she has good moments and bad. She's young, which is good because it means she's resilient. But the sad truth is she'll probably have almost no memories of Jason by the time she's an adult, and that's a real loss for her. He loved her so much."

"Yes, he did. There's just no way to express how sad I am for you and for all of us. Jason was a good man and a great mayor. He will be missed every day by the people who knew him."

"Nobody should have their life cut short the way Jason's

was, especially a man who contributed so much to the public good. I appreciated the note you sent, Fred, and the flowers."

"I wish there were something more useful I could do than send flowers."

"There is, I think. I'm hoping to get some advice from you."

"You know I'll be happy to help in any way I can."

"It's about the memorial service for Jason tomorrow morning…"

"Yes? Is there some special arrangement or speaker you want to incorporate? I'm sorry if you feel you've been excluded from the planning. The governor wanted this to be more of a civic event as opposed to a family memorial, and it seemed best to let the professionals do the planning."

"No, I'm not worried about the actual arrangements, I'm sure they're fine. The governor's staff is very competent." She drew in an audible breath. "Fred, could Sophie and I stop by your office for a few minutes this afternoon? There's something personal I want to ask your advice about."

"Well, of course, Chloe. I'll be here for at least another two hours."

"Could we come right away? I'm not interrupting an important meeting?"

His voice warmed. "Even if you were, I'd still be delighted to see you."

"I'm indicted on a charge of felony murder, Fred. I'm not good company for an elected official."

"But I'm not elected. I'm appointed."

She noticed that he didn't make any protestations about believing her to be innocent, but perhaps she was being oversensitive and expecting ringing endorsements from everyone who'd ever met her.

"Besides, I've had enough of Colorado politics," Fred continued. "I'm thinking about moving to D.C., where I could be right at the heart of the political action. But that's a story for another day. I'll look forward to seeing you and Sophie soon."

"We'll be there within forty-five minutes. Thanks, Fred."

Twenty-Four

Chloe's question for Fred Mitchell was more than just an excuse to confront him in person; she genuinely wanted his advice. Tomorrow had been declared an official day of mourning for the mayor. The governor had announced that a wake would be held at the Convention Center—the only space large enough to accommodate the expected number of mourners. The actual memorial service would be held before the wake in the State Capitol building, with the eulogy delivered jointly by Cardinal Alvarez and the governor. Every politician who could squeeze an invitation would be in attendance, along with many of the civic and business leaders of Denver. In normal circumstances, Chloe would have been expected to attend the service as the mourner in chief. Since she'd been charged with murdering her husband, however, the circumstances were clearly far from normal.

The governor, having called to offer condolences before she was indicted, had been conspicuously silent since her arrest, as had his wife, and Chloe knew that her presence would be a protocol nightmare. She alternated between feeling that she owed it to Jason to attend and fearing that her presence might be enough to ruin what should be a dignified occasion. Jason's parents, she had learned via a TV news report, were already in Denver, staying at the governor's mansion. For their sakes, she didn't want the event turned into a media circus, even if they had so little faith in her innocence that they hadn't spoken to her since she called to tell them the tragic news of their son's death.

Her arrival at the mayor's office revealed just how acute the dilemma was. Jason's former staff greeted Sophie with all their usual affection, but it was clear that most of them would as soon have offered condolences to the devil as they would to Chloe. These people had worked closely with Jason, so she understood his death was a deeply felt loss. His staff were also civil servants, of course, so perhaps it wasn't altogether surprising that they trusted the D.A.'s office—a government agency—to have indicted the right person. Still, these were people who knew her fairly well, and she would have expected them to be more willing to withhold judgment. If this was the sort of hostility she could expect to face tomorrow, she would need a suit of Kevlar armor to deflect the hatred beaming in her direction.

It was almost a relief to be ushered into Fred Mitchell's office and to be greeted with a warm handshake and a brief hug. "Chloe, I'm so sorry. This has been a terrible week for you and for all of us."

"Yes, it has." She sat down, lifting Sophie onto her lap. Fred did his usual magic trick, pretending to pull a lollipop out of Sophie's ear and presenting it to her with a flourish. She rewarded him with a hug and lots of giggles before unwrapping the cellophane and getting down to the serious business of licking.

"I'll get right to the point," Chloe said. "As I mentioned on the phone, it's about the memorial service for Jason tomorrow. I was already worried, but my experience coming through the reception area of this office proves I'm facing a major problem. I want to attend…not to sound too old-fashioned, I feel it's my duty, as well as my chance to say a final goodbye to Jason."

"Well, of course you should attend."

"Freddy, please don't just say what you think I want to hear. You must be aware of the level of hostility there is toward me, especially among Jason's friends and co-workers. The service is to honor Jason and his service to the community. I don't want it turned into a debate over whether or not I'm guilty of committing murder." Chloe glanced down as she spoke, but Sophie seemed happily absorbed in her lollipop and she was paying no attention to the adults talking literally over her head.

"Then let me be honest, since you're asking for my advice. I think you should attend the service. You're Jason's widow and you need to be there. But I also think you need to pick the right escort." Fred cleared his throat. "To be blunt, attending the service with Liam Raven at your side would cause a lot of gossip, none of it pleasant."

"Liam barely knew Jason and wouldn't dream of attend-ing the service even if he was going to be in Denver," Chloe said coolly. "But as it happens, Liam is in Chicago at the moment, and he won't be back in Denver until tomorrow afternoon, so the question of his attendance is irrelevant."

"In that case, if you would like me to act as your escort,

I'd be honored to accompany you." Fred inclined his head in Sophie's direction. "I know that Trudi is no longer with you. Do you have a babysitter arranged?"

"Yes, thank you. There are a couple of sitters I've used almost since Sophie was born and they're apparently still willing to come into my house. Maybe they think they're saving Sophie from her wicked—"

"Don't say it. Don't torment yourself like this, Chloe." Fred got up and walked around the desk so that he could put his hand over hers. Chloe wondered if she was being comforted by her husband's murderer and then felt guilty for suspecting something so vile. When she was in Fred's presence it was a lot harder to see him as anything other than the indispensable political aide he had always been.

Father Hannity had warned her not to leap to conclusions. Was that what she'd done in suspecting her husband's chief of staff? She hadn't even considered arranging a meeting to vet Bob Attenheim and yet the evidence against him was exactly the same as the evidence against Fred: she'd seen his name on a list of fraternity brothers. She'd then constructed an entire murder plot out of that one fact. It was instinct more than anything else that made her so willing to suspect Fred. Unfortunately, she'd spent the past week in such a state of emotional turmoil that her instincts were likely to be less than reliable.

"You look sad, Chloe. It hurts me to see you this way." Fred let go of her hand and walked back behind his desk. He didn't sit down, but stood with half his attention directed to the scene outside his window, almost as if he wanted to avoid focusing on her too completely. He looked sad himself, she thought, registering the shadows under his eyes and the slight gauntness of his cheeks, as if he hadn't eaten or slept much for the past several days.

She didn't know what she was going to say until the words were out of her mouth, incapable of being called back. "Fred, did you know that Jason was gay?"

The question hung unanswered in the space between them for a shimmering instant. Then he turned fully toward her, his slender body silhouetted against the afternoon sun streaming through the window. His expression, she noticed, was concerned rather than shocked or surprised.

"Chloe...my dear....you must surely be mistaken. Jason's death was a tragic loss and I realize how much stress you're under, but is this the right moment for you to indulge in flights of fancy? Why would you choose to compromise everything he worked for by destroying his image? He loved you very much. Isn't that what you should focus on at such a difficult time?"

Fred was oozing sympathy and yet Chloe's suspicions ratcheted up to a new level. His reaction was flat wrong for somebody who had genuinely been unaware of Jason's sexual orientation: too little surprise and too much condescension. Father Hannity, for example, had been so shocked to hear her assert Jason was gay that he'd shot out of his chair, completely unable to conceal his emotions. Fred, by contrast, showed no surprise at all. He'd simply tried to convince her she was mistaken and that she owed it to Jason to keep quiet. The politician at work, Chloe thought cynically. Always worrying about negative PR, even when the subject of the PR was dead and about to be buried.

If Fred Mitchell had been Jason's lover, Chloe knew there was a distinct possibility he had also killed Jason. But she couldn't voice her accusations, not before she'd told

Liam and her lawyer just how she thought Jason might have been killed. In fact, it was vital for her to avoid alerting Fred to the true direction of her thoughts. The last thing she wanted was to warn him he was under suspicion, even if only by her and not yet by the police.

She'd been silent for too long, but she wasn't sure what to say next. She could pretend to agree that she'd been mistaken about Jason's sexual orientation, but she was so tired of the years of lies that the thought of agreeing to yet another one made her head pound. Besides, Fred was an acute observer and he was likely to wonder why she was so easily persuaded to backtrack. She would stick to her guns about Jason's sexuality, she decided, but make no reference at all to the possibility that Fred had been his lover. It seemed a reasonable compromise between honesty and safety.

"I'm not mistaken," she said quietly. "Jason was gay. He told me himself more than four years ago and I'm tired of pretending something different. Above all, I don't understand why it *destroys his image* to tell the truth about the person he was. Does the fact that he was gay destroy the fact that he single-handedly fought and won the battle to get more police officers on the streets? Does the fact that he was gay destroy the fact that he opened five new youth centers in the past two years? Does it destroy the fact that he cut the budget for snow removal and still did a more efficient job of clearing the streets than any of his predecessors? Tell me, Freddy, how does the fact that my husband was gay destroy a single atom of what he achieved?"

"Because there's a significant minority of people in this country who believe that to be gay is an intolerable sin." Fred sounded weary. "For heaven's sake, Chloe, you're about to ruin your husband's legacy. For a lot of people, everything Jason achieved would be tainted by the knowledge that he was gay. If you want to destroy your husband's work, and his relationship with his family, all you need to do is tell the world that your husband was homosexual."

Chloe shook her head. "I kept quiet for years because of just the sort of argument you're making. I've decided I don't agree with the premise. In the end, lies and secrets are always more destructive than truth."

Fred gave a bitter laugh. "I didn't realize you were so naive, Chloe."

"Is it naive to believe people in Colorado need to know that they gave the highest approval ratings in history to a politician who happened to be gay?"

Fred spread his hands, the gesture pleading. "Don't do it, Chloe. Don't open up that can of worms. There's still something to be salvaged from the wreckage of Jason's death, but only if the public never learns that he was gay."

"You knew, didn't you? You lied to me a moment ago. You knew the truth about Jason's sexual orientation long before I came here today."

He was silent for a long moment. "Let's not go there," he said.

Without warning, Sophie burst into tears. "I want my daddy. I want him to be here."

"We all do, princess." Fred's voice was husky and Chloe saw the gleam of tears in his eyes. Whether or not she agreed with Fred's desire to continue hiding the truth, he was genuinely grieving for Jason. Could a murderer grieve for the person he killed? Chloe wasn't sure. She wasn't sure of anything anymore.

She rose to her feet, holding Sophie tightly, with her

daughter's head nestled against her chest. "I'd better leave," she said. "We're not going to agree on the best course of action, so there's no point in hammering at the same points over and over again. Thank you for meeting with me, Fred. I appreciate the time and your advice."

"You know how much I admire you, Chloe. At least take my advice this far—promise me that you won't make any public statements about Jason's sex life until after the memorial service is over."

She didn't hesitate. "I can promise you that much, Fred." Liam wouldn't be back in town until hours after the memorial service was over, so it was an easy promise to make.

"Thanks, Chloe. And speaking of the memorial service, I have a limo and driver already arranged for tomorrow morning. Should we stop by your house around nine-fifteen? That gives us forty-five minutes to get to the capitol. I could even arrange for a police escort if you want."

Chloe briefly contemplated the irony of planning to attend her husband's memorial service in the company of the man she believed might well have murdered him. Then she decided she didn't have the stamina for resolving paradoxes right at this point. Unfortunately, to refuse Fred's escort would activate all the suspicions she'd been at pains not to arouse. She would just have to chalk up accepting as part of the dishonesty that had been the essence of her marriage.

She gave a tired smile. "No to the police escort, if you don't mind. I think I've seen more than enough of the Denver Police Department over the past few days. I'll risk the traffic jams and trust the limo driver to get us there on his own steam."

"Then I'll see you tomorrow morning." Fred ruffled Sophie's hair which was once again flying free of its ponytail. "Goodbye, princess. Take care of your mommy for me."

Sophie raised a tear-ravaged face and said goodbye to Fred before burying her face once again in her mother's silk blouse, no doubt depositing sticky lollipop residue in the process. Chloe found it astonishing to think that only a week ago she would actually have cared about something as trivial as lollipop stains on her blouse. Holding tight to Sophie's skinny body, she braced herself to face the renewed barrage of stares and whispers likely to confront her as she made her way out of the office.

It was a good thing that silent hatred couldn't kill, she reflected grimly, or she would have been dead before she reached the elevator.

Twenty-Five

Chloe finally heard from Liam shortly after ten o'clock. He was riding the shuttle bus from the car rental return to O'Hare's departure concourse and he was pressured for time. The last flight for Denver left within the hour and he was hoping to catch it, he told her. If the gate had already closed by the time he arrived, or if the flight was full, he planned to book into an airport hotel and would catch the first flight home in the morning. Either way, he said, he would come straight to her house as opposed to stopping off first at his own condo. In the meantime, he wanted her to know that he'd met with Paul Fairfax. Paul, he told her, had been reluctant to talk, but he eventually was persuaded to identify Fred Mitchell as the source of his information about Sophie.

Chloe managed to find that news simultaneously a big shock and not at all surprising. Part of her still saw Fred as the low-key, self-effacing political operative, a friendly shadow to Jason's bright public star. At another level, she'd already accepted that the façade Fred held up to the world was every bit as false as the one Jason had presented. Jason hadn't been a confident shining star, and Fred obviously was something a lot more complex than a quiet shadow.

Liam's shuttle arrived at its destination while she was still explaining to him that Father Hannity had faxed the list of Delta Kappa Omega members as promised and that Fred Mitchell had been enrolled both in the fraternity and at the University of Virginia at the same time as Jason.

"We've definitely found our man," Liam said. "Chloe, honey, I have to run. If you don't hear from me again, it means I've caught the plane. We'll talk about how we should handle all this new information tomorrow. Robyn needs to know that Fred Mitchell hasn't told the truth about his relationship with Jason—"

"And the police, too, surely?"

"Maybe. That's Robyn's decision. She might prefer to put a team of private investigators onto it if she thinks the police won't pursue the lead aggressively enough. Unfortunately, the police are likely to say that concealing an extramarital affair isn't proof that Fred had anything to do with Jason's murder. But we're getting there, Chloe. We're getting there."

She hung up the phone, her mood several degrees lighter. She mocked herself for allowing a single phone conversation with Liam to have so much impact on her state of mind, but she wasn't being entirely irrational. Many facts about Jason's life that had been unknown just a few days ago were now established. While it was true that she and Liam had learned nothing that proved Fred Mitchell guilty of murder, they'd certainly learned sufficient to construct a convincing alternative theory of the crime.

More cheerful than she would have believed possible an hour earlier, Chloe went to check on her daughter. Sophie was sleeping peacefully, Bobby Bunny stuffed under her cheek. Chloe pulled him out and sat him against the wall where he could be reached easily but his whiskers weren't digging into her daughter's delicate baby skin. She gave Sophie one last kiss before leaving the room, pulling the door almost closed behind her.

She ran a deep, hot bath, adding scented bubbles, and sank beneath the water, soaking away the tensions of the day. The house felt empty without Liam and she wished that the distance between Chicago and Denver could miraculously compress so that his flight would already be over and he would walk through the door right now. When the water chilled, she reluctantly got out of the bath and wrapped herself in a toweling robe. She was exhausted and yet she put off the moment of going to bed, afraid that she wouldn't be able to sleep.

She switched on the TV but flipped channels as soon as she caught film clips of herself standing on the podium to receive her Olympic gold. Flipping didn't help. All the local channels were running specials prior to Jason's memorial service the next day, and it seemed as if half the cable networks were doing the same thing. If she wasn't looking at herself skiing down a mountain, she was looking at herself being led, handcuffed, into Denver Police headquarters, or else pushing her way into her own house with Liam and Sophie trapped at her side.

She switched off the TV and picked up a book, a biography of Thomas Jefferson that she'd been reading the week before Jason died. Unfortunately, Jefferson's attempts to unite the colonists behind a Declaration of Independence failed to capture her attention. She realized that part of the reason she was having such a hard time concentrating was that this was the first night since Jason's murder that she had spent without Liam. It bothered her that she was so dependent on him after such a short time, and she gave herself a stern lecture about not forging dependency bonds when she was emotionally overwrought. She'd been in a sexless, uncomfortable marriage for the past four years and Liam was Sophie's father. It was probably inevitable that she would imagine herself in love with him the moment they were thrown together. That didn't mean she had to act as though her imagination were fact.

It was time to stop moping around and go to bed. She had the rest of her life to work out her relationship with Liam. In the meantime, Jason's memorial service was tomorrow. The babysitter was arriving at eight-thirty and Fred would be here soon after. She needed to get ready.

She selected an outfit—a black suit she had worn for the funeral of a former governor—and found new black pantyhose. She set the alarm for six-thirty so that she would have plenty of time to dress and put on makeup. Her hair was just long enough to be slicked back into a dignified twist. If she was going to be paraded in front of millions of television viewers as Chloe Devarr Hamilton, Olympic gold medalist, widow of the late mayor and indicted murderer, pride demanded that she should at least look adequately put together while enduring the onslaught.

She stared into the mirror and pulled a face at her washed-out appearance. She hesitated for a moment and then decided to take a mild sleeping pill. Whatever she had to endure tomorrow would be better if she wasn't a walking zombie.

Despite the sleeping pill, she tossed and turned for a long time. She was too hot, so she cranked up the air-conditioning. Then she was too cold and had to burrow under the comforter. The good news, she told herself, was that Liam hadn't called. That almost certainly meant he'd caught his plane and would be home some time during the night. She started a series of drowsy calculations. The plane left O'Hare at eleven or so and the flight should last no more than two and a half hours. There weren't likely to be delays from bad weather or air-traffic congestion. There was an hour's time difference between Denver and Chicago. That meant the plane would be wheels-down at DIA around twelve-thirty, give or take. Then Liam had to pick up his car and drive from the airport. No traffic at that hour of night. Liam might be here by one-thirty, she decided. She would know the moment he came into the room…maybe they would make love… She drifted off to sleep.

Chloe woke with a start. She had been dreaming, she realized. In her dream, Jason had been calling her, just as he had on the night he died, urging her to wake up and get out of bed. She shivered. The sound of his voice had been so real and so insistent she hadn't been able to stay asleep. Now she was awake the parallels to the horrors of Monday night were strong enough to envelop her in a sense of dread.

She pulled herself up on the pillow, deliberately shaking off the remnants of her dream and sensed the presence of another person in the room. Liam was home! Her spirits lifted. Her head was pounding, but she was accustomed to headaches these days and she ignored the pain. The grog-

giness she felt was unexpected—she felt almost drugged—
but the dream already suggested she'd been sleeping more
deeply than she realized.

Liam was kneeling down in front of the gas fireplace,
fiddling with one of the knobs. "Hey, Liam, what are you
doing?" But the words came out in a single, long slur.
"Heliamwadyadoin'?"

The man in front of the fireplace turned and straightened. It wasn't Liam. It wasn't even a man. Her stomach
hollowed with fear. It was a hideous monster with huge
black eyes and a mouth and chin that hung down low on
his chest, a mini Darth Vadar without the helmet and black
cape. Chloe screamed and the monster spoke, his voice
deep and echoing.

"Don't scream. You'll wake Sophie and neither of us
want that."

His voice sounded as if he were speaking under water,
the final Darth Vadar touch. It was instinctive to try to
escape from the room—although a fuzzy part of her brain
screamed a warning that running from the monster might
simply enrage him.

She soon discovered that both wisdom and folly were
irrelevant because escape was impossible; her legs were
incapable of supporting her. She collapsed on the floor by
her bed, dizzy, afraid that if she tried to sit up she would
be hideously and humiliatingly sick.

"I'm sorry you woke up. I'm very surprised you did."
The monster bent down and scooped her into his arms,
laying her back in the bed. "I imagined you would die
without ever knowing what happened."

"What did happen?"

She knew that her words were slurred almost beyond

recognition but apparently he understood her question, because he answered. "You committed suicide. I'm sorry, Chloe. You were distraught over killing Jason and you decided it was the only way out."

He spoke in the past tense. She was so sick and dizzy that for a moment she wondered if he was being factual and she was already dead. She closed her eyes, breathing deeply, but that just increased the chills and made her chest hurt. She opened her eyes again and in a moment of clarity realized that the monster's face was simply a mask. It wasn't a real monster. Of course not. Just a man wearing a gas mask.

Just Fred Mitchell wearing a mask.

She must have mumbled something because he shook his head and walked back to check again on the fireplace valve. He straightened, apparently satisfied. "Go to sleep, Chloe, it's better that way. Truly, I never planned for you to suffer. You can't escape, so don't fight it. The carbon monoxide is already combining with the hemoglobin in your blood. Did you know it has two hundred and forty times the affinity for hemoglobin that oxygen does? I'll stay here for a few more minutes until you're unconscious, and then I'll leave. I'd knock you out, to shorten your suffering, but of course that would leave a bruise and raise suspicions. You won't feel any pain if you'll just relax and go back to sleep. We did a lot of research on carbon monoxide poisoning for the city. It's known as the silent killer because people die in their sleep all the time from faulty gas valves, or defective appliances. Do you know you're more likely to die from carbon monoxide leaking from the exhaust of an internal combustion engine than you are to die in an actual automobile accident? Isn't that amazing? In fact, there's greater mortality and morbidity from carbon monoxide than from all other poisons combined. That's part of why we initiated our campaign to encourage every family in the city to install a carbon monoxide detector."

She remembered the campaign, and the death of a healthy young college student that had precipitated Jason's campaign. Fred had obviously remembered, too. He had extinguished the pilot light and opened the valve supplying gas to the bedroom fire and she was already sick with the early stages of carbon monoxide poisoning. Even in her woozy state, Chloe understood his motives. Most people already believed she was guilty of killing her husband and her suicide would confirm their beliefs. What better way to insure that the investigation into Jason's death came to a screeching halt before it could implicate Fred Mitchell?

Fear unlike anything she'd ever experienced swept over Chloe in a crushing wave. Not only fear that she would die, but also that Sophie would be the one to discover her. Sophie usually woke quite early, no later than seven. She would come in search of her mother—and find her lifeless body.

The thought of Sophie losing both her father and mother within the space of a week gave Chloe a strength and determination that nothing else on earth could have provided. She threw herself out of bed and avoided falling straight to the ground by dint of clutching onto the nightstand. She had no realistic hope of escaping, but Sophie's needs trumped reason. She launched herself toward the door, hitting the wall and grabbing the door handle in one jerky, uncoordinated move. She managed to tug it open before the monster caught up with her. Not a literal monster, perhaps, but a monster all the same.

She gulped in the fresher air outside her bedroom door and just had time to hook her arms around a pair of stair banisters before Fred grabbed her around the waist, presumably with the intention of carrying her back to the bed. She was normally strong, with muscles powerfully developed by years of intensive athletic training, but the carbon monoxide had reduced her limbs to flailing noodles.

Fred could have knocked her out with a single blow, but he didn't. Instead he struggled to hold her with one hand while his other hand pried her fingers loose from her death grip on the banisters. As soon as he released one hand, she grabbed on with the other. Why didn't he just drag her back into the bedroom by the hair? Knock her unconscious?

He didn't want to hit her. That's what Fred had said. He didn't want her body to be bruised or show signs of trauma. Chloe clung to those thoughts, although they kept slipping away, dissolving into incoherence.

She dug deep and found the thought again. She hugged it to her. Fred had said he didn't want her to be bruised. If she was bruised, the police wouldn't believe she'd committed suicide. And he needed to have her commit suicide to confirm that she was, indeed, Jason's murderer.

Maybe there was hope after all, at least a tiny thread to sustain her. Fred couldn't knock her out or even hold on too tightly or there would be the imprint of his fingers on her arms. There *was* hope in that.

She struggled silently, determination counteracting both nausea and exhaustion. The air outside the bedroom was barely tainted and she found she was able to concentrate again, at least in a limited way. She focused on the single, simple fact of keeping her arms hooked through the banisters and her hands clinging to the posts. She was terrified that the noise of their struggle would wake Sophie. If Sophie came out of her room, Fred would kill her, too. Monsters didn't care about the guilt or innocence of their victims.

She heard the sound of a door opening and she was sure her heart stopped beating. "Sophie, go back to your room! Don't come out!" She knew her words were slurred, although not as badly as before. She wasn't even sure how loud she'd managed to make the command.

"Mommy?" She heard Sophie cry. "Mommy! I scared!" *Please God, don't let him kill my baby. Not Sophie. Please God, not Sophie.*

"Go back into your room!" She wouldn't allow herself to turn toward the sound of Sophie's voice. She couldn't afford the distraction.

"Chloe! What the hell is going on?"

Liam's voice. Surely that was Liam's voice? She had never, ever heard anything more beautiful.

"Help me! Fred is trying to kill me!"

The hollow monster voice spoke in her ear, its tones angry. "I thought you said he was in Chicago!"

"Not any more, apparently."

Fred cursed Liam's arrival with vicious, obscene fluency. Suddenly he released his hold on her waist. In the second or two it took Chloe to register that she was free, he had snatched Sophie and run with her back into the master bedroom. He slammed the door and she heard the sound of it locking.

"No!" The scream ripped not just from her throat but from the depths of her soul.

Liam tore up the stairs two at a time. "What's happened?" He hauled her up into his arms, panting as much from fear as from exertion. "God, Chloe, where are you hurt?"

"Not me." She pointed to the bedroom. "Sophie." She summoned every last dreg of her control and managed to speak with reasonable clarity. "Fred has Sophie in there. He's locked the door. He's flooded the room with carbon monoxide."

Liam, thank God, understood the urgency of what she was telling him. He released her, and she collapsed against the wall as he banged with both fists on the bedroom door. "Fred, open up! You can't save yourself by hurting Sophie."

"I can ruin Chloe's life the way she ruined mine! Jason was supposed to love me, but everything was always *let's see what Chloe thinks about that, let's see what Chloe wants, let's see if Chloe agrees with that.* Fucking damn Chloe. I worked for ten years to get Jason positioned to run for the United States Senate and in one night she talked him out of it! For Christ's sake, Jason told me he was going to throw away his talents by working on a campaign for gay rights! As if this country is ever going to give gays the right to be considered human beings!"

"Open up the door and we'll talk about it. Fred, be reasonable. Sophie's not even four! You can't blame her for what her mother might have done."

"News flash, lover boy. I can blame whoever I damn well please. And I sure as hell don't care what happens to your kid. Besides, maybe I'm doing Sophie a favor if she never has to grow up and discover what a shit hole of a place the world is."

Chloe could hear Sophie crying. In a moment of dreadful clarity she knew that if she didn't manage to rescue her daughter, life would truly never be worth living again.

"He has the gas valve open," she told Liam. "Carbon monoxide damages a child's neurological system in minutes." She didn't quite manage to spit out *neurological system* correctly, but Liam got the point.

He nodded a curt acknowledgment, his focus like hers on what was happening behind the locked door. Then he stepped back and ran at the door, crashing into it with his shoulder. The door shuddered in its frame but didn't budge. He kicked the lock with contained violence, then stepped a few feet further back and ran even faster than the first time, hurling his full weight against the door. It shuddered again. He kicked hard on the edge and the lock burst. He shoved the door open.

"Liam!" Sophie was in Fred's arms, but she leaned toward him, crying. He walked straight up to Fred, driving his fists into the man's belly with the full force of his rage behind the blows. Fred's hold on Sophie loosened for a crucial moment. Liam grabbed her and carried her out of the bedroom, leaving Fred Mitchell doubled over next to the gas fire, retching.

"Hi, Liam. I'm going to be sick," Sophie announced.

"Please don't, sugar plum." He turned to Chloe. "We need to get outside right away. You can kiss and hug her as soon as we're in the fresh air." He shifted Sophie into his left arm and flipped open his cell phone with his spare hand. He punched in 9-1-1 while they were still going downstairs and asked for police and ambulance service.

"We have two people with early stage carbon monoxide poisoning," he said. "One of them is a four-year-old girl."

"I'm not four, I'm free," Sophie said.

Liam spared a moment to smile. "Yes, you are, sugar plum. A very smart three-year-old."

"Tell them we need nonrebreather oxygen masks." Chloe remembered that flooding the system with oxygen as quickly as possible was crucial in preventing long-term neurological consequences from carbon monoxide poisoning.

Liam nodded and spoke into the phone again. "Make sure you have nonrebreather oxygen masks on board the ambulance. And somebody on the rescue squad is going to need a gas mask to get into the bedroom and shut off the gas valve."

He opened the front door and dragged Chloe through. "Sit," he said, throwing his jacket onto a patch of grass next to the driveway. He put Sophie into her lap and then sat down beside them, wrapping his arm tightly around Chloe's shoulders. "Make sure she doesn't snuggle too closely against you. She needs all the fresh air she can get."

Chloe was too overwhelmed with joy to speak. She drew in a lungful of blissfully fresh air and kissed her daughter, cherishing every wriggling movement that confirmed the wonderful, fantastic fact that Sophie was alive.

When a couple of ecstatic minutes had passed, she finally allowed herself to believe that her daughter was safe. She relaxed, her head dropping onto Liam's shoulder. She heard the quick intake of his breath and remembered that he'd hurled himself against the door with every ounce of force he could muster. She lifted her head and saw that his shirt was wet with blood.

She touched him gently, just below the wound. "Thank you, Liam. Thank you for saving our daughter."

His face was somber in the moonlight. "I'm sitting here literally thanking God that I caught the plane back from Chicago tonight."

She shivered. "I think Fred wanted me dead almost as

much as he wanted to be sure Jason's murder was laid irretrievably in my lap. How could he have hidden the fact that he hated me so much?"

"He and Jason both learned to hide what they were feeling at a very young age. I guess deception eventually gets to be a dangerous habit."

Belatedly, Chloe noticed that Fred hadn't come out of the house. "Do you think he escaped by climbing out of the window?" She realized that the question didn't make much sense, but Liam understood anyway.

"I don't care what he did, so long as he isn't bothering us. He's not going to get very far, that's for sure."

The sound of emergency sirens grew louder. An ambulance and a rescue truck drew up in the driveway, lights flashing. Despite the hour, a small crowd of onlookers began to gather. It would only be a few minutes before the first TV news crew turned up, Liam thought wryly.

Paramedics jumped down from the ambulance, unloading two stretchers with swift efficiency. "Where are the carbon monoxide victims?" one of the men asked.

Liam rose to his feet and pointed to Chloe. "Here they are. Sophie, the little girl, was barely exposed. Mrs. Hamilton was sleeping when the gas valve in her bedroom was opened, and she may be more severely affected."

"What about you? You're bleeding," the paramedic said.

"It's nothing." Liam had no desire to find himself designated as a patient. He quickly walked over to the rescue squad, leaving the paramedics to check Chloe and Sophie's vital signs and to affix the tight-fitting oxygen masks that would rid their systems of any poisonous gas residue.

"I left Fred Mitchell, the late mayor's chief of staff, upstairs in the master bedroom," he told the guy who seemed to be in charge of the rescue squad. "Mitchell was wearing a hazmat mask, which should have protected him from the carbon monoxide, but he hasn't come downstairs and he could be in trouble. Your team needs to wear protective gear because the house is full of gas. By the way, I didn't see any sign that Mitchell was armed, but he sure as hell is dangerous."

Chloe and Sophie were already strapped onto stretchers, unable to speak behind their oxygen masks. "We're taking them to Denver General," the paramedic said. "You're not allowed to ride in the ambulance, but you can meet up with them in the E.R."

Liam managed to give Sophie a kiss as she was loaded into the ambulance. Out of deference to the roving TV camera van which, sure enough, was already rolling into position opposite the house, he refrained from kissing Chloe. He squeezed her hand instead. "I love you," he said softly. "Try to stay out of trouble until I get to the E.R., okay?"

Her eyes smiled above the mask. "I'll try," she mouthed.

A TV reporter ran up to him. She was a young thing, who probably couldn't believe her luck in having pulled the graveyard shift on a night when major news developed.

"Mr. Raven! Mr. Raven, would you give us a statement about what happened here tonight?"

Liam shook his head, about to refuse. Just then he noticed two members of the rescue squad coming out of the house, Fred Mitchell supported between them. He changed his mind and turned back to face the camera.

"Talk to those guys over there," he said. "I think you'll find the man they're attempting to revive is the person who killed the late mayor of Denver."

Epilogue

Liam leaned against the barn wall and watched his mother teach his daughter how to ride a pony around the pasture. He couldn't decide who was enjoying herself more, Ellie or Sophie. His daughter's face was the picture of solemn concentration, but he could read her well enough by now to know that when the lesson was over, she would be a bubbling chatterbox of enthusiasm.

Chloe was also mounted and riding around the pasture while Harry Ford offered encouragement and instruction. She wasn't enjoying the lessons nearly as much as Sophie, Liam thought with silent amusement. Chloe, apparently, saw nothing in the least scary about hurtling down a mountain at seventy miles an hour, but sitting on horseback, four feet from the ground, had her looking distinctly nervous.

Megan and Adam, her new husband, strolled out of the house to join them. Adam watched the riders for a minute or two and then laughed. "Now I know I'm a really smart guy," he said. "This is my fifth trip to the ranch, and so far I've managed to invent the world's best excuses for never getting on the back of a horse."

"You married my sister," Liam said. "I already knew you were a really smart guy."

Adam put his arm around Megan. He was as tall as Liam, which meant that he was a foot taller than his wife. He gazed down at her and his cool gray eyes were suddenly warm with love. "Yeah, I guess I am."

Harry called to him with a question about their fishing plans for the following morning, and he joined the sheriff, leaving Liam alone with his sister. "You look happy, Meg," he said quietly.

"So do you."

"Yeah, well, I guess I've discovered fatherhood suits me."

"So Mom points out," his sister said dryly. "Although probably not more than four or five times in a typical day."

Liam laughed. "You know she's not going to stop prodding until she has an entire clutch of grandkids to fuss over. Now I've set the ball rolling, she expects you to step up to the plate."

"I know. Adam and I want to have children soon, but not for another few months. The beginning of our relationship was so bumpy, we want to have a little while just to find out what sort of people we are when nobody has a gun aimed at our heads."

"I know the feeling," Liam said. "But I've discovered the perfect way to divert Mom when she starts one of her inquisitions—just ask her something about Harry."

Megan smiled. "Thanks for the tip, I'll keep it in mind." She paused. "Chloe is a really nice person, Liam."

He pushed his sunglasses down his nose and looked at her over the top. "And that, my dear sister, was about as subtle as a sledgehammer."

"Okay, so I'll bag the attempt at subtlety. Can I expect to have Chloe as a sister-in-law any time soon?"

Liam was silent for a moment, choosing his words. "Chloe endured a lot when her husband died, and it hasn't been easy since then, even though the D.A. dropped the charges against her pretty quickly in the wake of Fred Mitchell's attempt to kill her. It took an entire month to get an indictment handed down against Mitchell, and his attorney is now claiming that he suffered brain damage from the carbon monoxide and isn't competent to stand trial. That's a lot to deal with. I want to allow Chloe some breathing room before I start nagging her to marry me."

"I'm not sure that she'd need a whole lot of nagging. She looks like a woman in love to me."

"You think?" Liam realized he was staring at Chloe with what he feared was a distinctly besotted expression. He turned back to his sister and grinned. "Maybe I can negotiate a deal," he said. "All she has to do is marry me, and I'll promise she never has to ride another horse."

Megan laughed. "Now there's a deal she'd be a fool to refuse. Go for it, Liam. I'm rooting for you."

* * * * *

Turn the page to read an excerpt from
PAYBACK
the exciting conclusion to the Ravens trilogy

One

Herndon, Virginia
October 3, 2007

Luke Savarini took a second bite of the lobster ravioli just to be sure he hadn't judged too hastily. He'd been right the first time, he decided, letting the flavors dissolve on his tongue. There was too much oregano, and the sauce splashed over everything was weighted down with excess cream.

Anna, his sister, watched his reaction and then gave a crooked smile. "Not up to scratch, huh? My veal is okay, but not spectacular. Want to taste?"

"I'll take your word for it." Luke put down his fork, pushing away his heaped plate. With all the food there was in his life, he avoided eating anything he didn't completely enjoy. His waistline and his taste buds both thanked him.

"Why did you insist on bringing me here, Annie? You're not usually a fan of second-rate Italian."

"The restaurant is owned by Bruno Savarini. He's a

cousin of ours. Sort of. His grandfather and our great-grandfather were brothers."

Luke rolled his eyes. The most remote and fragile twigs of the family tree all made perfect sense to his sister, whereas he had his work cut out simply keeping track of the names and birthdays of his six nieces and nephews.

He mentally reviewed the vast clan of Savarini cousins. "Okay, I'm working hard, but I can't place a cousin Bruno."

"He's great uncle Joe's grandson. You must have run into each other at a wedding."

Luke grinned. "Yeah, but that's almost the same as saying I've never met him. Can you ever recall a Savarini wedding with less than two hundred relatives milling around—at least half of the men singing 'O Sole Mio' at the top of their lungs?"

Anna returned his grin, tacitly acknowledging the cheerful mob scenes that passed for family gatherings in the Savarini clan. "Bruno had his sixty-fifth birthday last month. He's short and stocky. He has brown eyes and an olive complexion—"

Luke laughed. "Well now, that narrows it right down. Short, stocky, brown eyes. I guess only ninety percent of Savarini men fit that description."

Anna tried to look severe. "Just because you're a six-foot genetic freak with gray eyes, there's no need to get snooty. Anyway, I brought you here because Bruno plans to retire as soon as he can find a buyer for his restaurant. He has crippling arthritis and he only comes into the restaurant occasionally nowadays. You'd be astonished at how much better the food tastes on the days when he's here."

"I wouldn't be astonished," Luke protested. "I'm a chef, remember? I know just how much difference it makes when you have somebody talented in charge of the kitchen."

"The restaurant is in a fabulous location," Anna continued, as if he hadn't spoken. "The decor is attractive and the kitchen is state of the art. And Bruno has plenty of loyal customers. Look around you. The place is full. That's pretty good on a Wednesday, especially since we're eating late."

Far from looking around the restaurant, Luke fixed his gaze on his sister with suddenly narrowed focus. "Wait. I must be slow on the uptake tonight, because I've only just realized why we're here. You want me to buy this place, don't you?"

Anna had the grace to blush. "Well, you're a chef. You own restaurants. Bruno wants to retire and he's our cousin. It seems a natural fit."

Luke felt a surge of affectionate exasperation. It was a familiar sensation in Anna's vicinity. She was a brilliant physicist, working for a government agency that she claimed was part of the Department of Education, although he'd believe crayfish grew on trees before he believed that. He loved her more than any of his four other siblings, which was saying a lot. But whereas she found quantum mechanics and string theory simple concepts, the economics of running a family business had always dangled far beyond her ability to grasp.

He took a sip of Chianti and then toasted his sister with the glass. "I appreciate your good intentions, Annie, but I can't just randomly acquire restaurants all over the country. I live in Chicago, remember?"

"News flash. Have you noticed there must be thirty flights a day between Chicago and Washington, D.C.? A thousand miles isn't so far."

Luke laughed, genuinely amused. "From your perspective, maybe. That's what comes of working all day with astronomers who consider Alpha Centauri practically banging on the back door because it's only a billion miles away—"

"You're missing several zeroes," Anna said. "And it *is* banging on the back door as stars go."

"Yeah, well, that's my point, Annie. A billion or a gazillion, it's all in a day's work for you. However, when you're running a restaurant, a thousand miles is a long way. You need to be on the spot so you can keep an iron grip on quality control, not to mention you have to be on hand to step in whenever there's a crisis."

His sister wasn't ready to give up. "But you have three restaurants in the Chicago area already, and you can only be in one of them at a time. And they're doing so well...."

Luke mentally crossed his fingers; he was superstitious where his restaurants were concerned. "You're right— Luciano's is succeeding beyond my wildest hopes. And part of the reason the restaurants are doing well is because they're all three in the Chicago area. Where I live." *And where he was already working minimum of sixty hours a week.*

She sighed. "I hoped that the lure of opening a restaurant in the D.C. area might be enough to tempt you to visit more often. I miss you, Luke, much as I hate to admit it, seeing as how when we were growing up you were a totally annoying snot."

He raised his eyebrow. "Me? A snot? You must have me confused with one of your other brothers. Tom, maybe. He has major league snot potential."

She shook her head. "Uh-uh. No confusion. I'm talking about you."

"How quickly good deeds are forgotten." Luke gave an exaggerated sigh. "What about the time I saved you from being discovered with the captain of the baseball team in Mom and Dad's whirlpool tub? When you were both naked, no less. I figure that ought to have earned me at least a decade or two of gratitude."

"My God, Robert O'Toole and the Jacuzzi." Anna's expression was suddenly arrested. "I'd forgotten about that."

"If Dad had found the two of you, trust me, it would be one of your more vivid teenage memories."

She chuckled in wry acknowledgment. "Love is weird, isn't it? For two whole months I was convinced my life would be over if Rob didn't ask me to the senior prom. And I haven't given him a single thought since the day I left for college."

"He would be devastated to hear that," Luke said dryly. "Rob definitely fancied himself."

She gave a nostalgic grin and her gaze became wistful. "Damn, I miss you, Luke. Are you sure you don't want to reconsider buying Bruno out?"

Luke quelled a moment of temptation. "I wish, Annie, but I'm already stretched way too thin, timewise. I'm sorry."

She gave a resigned shrug that didn't quite conceal her disappointment. "Oh, well. It was worth a try."

He leaned across the table and briefly rested his hand on his sister's. The movement shifted his perspective and his gaze happened to land on a couple seated at the table closest to the entrance, with the man facing the door. That meant the man's back was turned toward their table, but as Luke watched, the man laughed and reached out to put his arm around the woman's shoulder so that Luke glimpsed him in profile. The man listened to his companion for a moment, and then laughed again at whatever she had said. A sudden lull in the noise allowed Luke to hear the man's laugh. It was teasing and low, a throaty chuckle. It was also eerily familiar.

Shock momentarily froze Luke in his seat. Then he jumped to his feet, grabbing his chair just in time to prevent it toppling over. "Be right back," he told his sister, moving swiftly toward the couple.

"Luke, what's wrong? Where are you going?"

He didn't answer, partly because he was having a hard time catching his breath, partly because he was focused with hypnotic intensity on the couple by the door. The man must have sensed that he was being observed. He glanced up and his head jerked in visible shock. He immediately rose to his feet, putting his hand in the small of his companion's back and hustling her toward the exit. She followed without a word of protest, oddly compliant.

A waiter carrying a heavy tray crossed Luke's path, obscuring his view. He wished he could push the waiter violently aside, the way they did in the movies, and to hell with the food arrayed on the tray. But the habit of deferring to a server carrying dishes was ingrained and Luke skirted the waiter, losing another crucial few seconds in his journey toward the exit. He had to excuse himself twice to an oblivious woman whose chair stuck far out from the table, forming an impromptu barricade. When he'd negotiated that obstacle, he squeezed past the two final tables separating him from the hostess station and reached empty floor space. The man and his companion were nowhere in sight.

Luke ran outside, cursing himself for having wasted too

much time being polite. Why the hell hadn't he just elbowed and shoved his way across the dining room and to hell with flying dishes? Unfortunately, the parking lot was crowded and he couldn't immediately spot the couple. Dammit, surely there hadn't been time for them to drive off?

The lot served several specialty stores in addition to Bruno's restaurant, and there were at least a dozen people strolling around, as well as a van pulled up to the curb, collecting trash. The lot was rimmed by lights, but the humidity was high and there was a slight mist hanging in the night air, making it frustratingly hard to see. Luke finally picked out his quarry simply because the man was running, his companion jogging awkwardly in his wake, hampered by her high heels.

"Stop!" Luke yelled, ignoring the interested stares of passersby. "Stop, for God's sake! Ron Raven, is that you? Ron, stop!"

The man didn't answer. If anything his pace got faster. The woman, indifferent to the damp pavement, tugged off her shoes and ran barefoot across the lot.

Luke tore down the aisle of parked cars, catching up as the man clicked the car locks with his remote and slid behind the wheel of a silver-gray Mercedes. Ron, or his look-alike, didn't even wait for his female companion to get into the car before turning on the ignition. He was already backing out of his parking space before she closed her door, and long before she could have latched her seat belt.

Luke gave a final burst of speed and caught up with the couple. He stood behind the car, waving his arms. It was impossible for the driver not to have seen him, but the car continued to back up.

Jesus! The guy was going to run him over if he didn't

move, Luke realized with a flash of total incredulity. At the last minute he had no choice other than to jump to one side. Without a backward glance, the driver swung around on squealing tires and dashed for the exit.

"That man sure was in a hurry." A middle-aged woman stared at the disappearing Mercedes, her frown disapproving. "Crazy drivers. He could've killed you. If he keeps driving like that he's going to cause an accident for sure. You okay?"

"Yes, thanks." Luke realized just in time that if he could get the license plate number, the police would have a way to track down the owner. "Excuse me. Really, I'm fine."

He squeezed between two parked cars and dashed into the next aisle, where he had a better view of the Mercedes racing toward the exit. It was a Virginia plate, he saw, with the license number AB7 4K3. Or maybe it was 4K8. He squinted, trying to confirm one number or the other, but the plate was dirty, the night dark, and the car was rapidly receding. The Mercedes sped down the block and made a sharp left turn at the first corner. Luke was a fast runner, but he knew he didn't have a chance in hell of catching up with it. He reached into his jacket and pulled out his Palm-Pilot, jotting down the license numbers before he could forget them.

When he realized he'd been staring at the empty road for a full minute, he walked back into the restaurant and wove his way around servers and crowded tables, returning to his sister. His legs felt surprisingly shaky and he slumped into his seat, breathing hard. Anna started to lecture him, but changed her mind when she got a good look at him.

"What is it?" she asked. "For heaven's sake, what happened just now? Are you okay?"

"I'm not sure." He reached for his wineglass and then pushed it aside and took a gulp of water instead. He put the incredible truth into words. "I think I just saw Ron Raven."